· Age of Iron ·

J.M. COETZEE

Secker & Warburg
London

Age of Iron
first published in Great Britain in 1990
by Martin Secker & Warburg Limited
Michelin House, 81 Fulham Road, London SW3 6RB

Copyright © 1990 J. M. Coetzee

Life & Times of Michael K
first published in Great Britain in 1983
by Martin Secker & Warburg Limited
Michelin House, 81 Fulham Road, London SW3 6RB

Copyright © J. M. Coetzee 1983

The epigraph on p. v is from G. S. Kirk's translation of
Heraclitus' *The Cosmic Fragments* and is quoted by permission of
Cambridge University Press

Printed in England by Clays Ltd, St Ives plc

For

V.H.M.C. (1904–1985)
Z.C. (1912–1988)
N.G.C. (1966–1989)

· I ·

There is an alley down the side of the garage, you may remember it, you and your friends would sometimes play there. Now it is a dead place, waste, without use, where windblown leaves pile up and rot.

Yesterday, at the end of this alley, I came upon a house of carton boxes and plastic sheeting and a man curled up inside, a man I recognized from the streets: tall, thin, with a weathered skin and long, carious fangs, wearing a baggy grey suit and a hat with a sagging brim. He had the hat on now, sleeping with the brim folded under his ear. A derelict, one of the derelicts who hang around the parking lots on Mill Street, cadging money from shoppers, drinking under the flyover, eating out of refuse cans. One of the homeless for whom August, month of rains, is the worst month. Asleep in his box, his legs stretched out like a marionette's, his jaw agape. An unsavoury smell about him: urine, sweet wine, mouldy clothing, and something else too. Unclean.

For a while I stood staring down on him, staring and smelling. A visitor, visiting himself on me on this of all days.

This was the day when I had the news from Dr Syfret. The news was not good, but it was mine, for me, mine only, not to be refused. It was for me to take in my arms and fold to my chest and take home, without headshaking, without tears.

'Thank you, doctor,' I said: 'thank you for being frank.' 'We will do everything we can,' he said, 'we will tackle this together.' But already, behind the comradely front, I could see he was withdrawing. *Sauve qui peut.* His allegiance to the living, not the dying.

The trembling began only when I got out of the car. By the time I had closed the garage door I was shaking all over: to still it I had to clench my teeth, grip my handbag. It was then that I saw the boxes, saw him.

'What are you doing here?' I demanded, hearing the irritation in my voice, not checking it. 'You can't stay, you must go.'

He did not stir, lying in his shelter, looking up, inspecting the winter stockings, the blue coat, the skirt with whose hang there has always been something wrong, the grey hair cut by a strip of scalp, old woman's scalp, pink, babyish.

Then he drew in his legs and leisurely got up. Without a word he turned his back on me, shook out the black plastic, folded it in half, in quarters, in eighths. He produced a bag (Air Canada, it said) and zipped it shut. I stood aside. Leaving behind the boxes, an empty bottle and a smell of urine, he passed me. His trousers sagged; he hitched them up. I waited to be sure he had gone, and heard him stow the plastic in the hedge from the other side.

Two things, then, in the space of an hour: the news, long dreaded, and this reconnaissance, this other annunciation. The first of the carrion-birds, prompt, unerring. How long can I fend them off? The scavengers of Cape Town, whose number never dwindles. Who go bare and feel no cold. Who sleep outdoors and do not sicken. Who starve and do not waste. Warmed from within by alcohol. The contagions and infections in their blood consumed in liquid flame. Cleaners-up after the feast. Flies, dry-winged, glazen-eyed, pitiless. My heirs.

With what slow steps did I enter this empty house, from

which every echo has faded, where the very tread of footsole on board is flat and dull! How I longed for you to be here, to hold me, comfort me! I begin to understand the true meaning of the embrace. We embrace to be embraced. We embrace our children to be folded in the arms of the future, to pass ourselves on beyond death, to be transported. That is how it was when I embraced you, always. We bear children in order to be mothered by them. Home truths, a mother's truth: from now to the end that is all you will hear from me. So: how I longed for you! How I longed to be able to go upstairs to you, to sit on your bed, run my fingers through your hair, whisper in your ear as I did on school mornings, 'Time to get up!' And then, when you turned over, your body blood-warm, your breath milky, to take you in my arms in what we called 'giving Mommy a big hug,' the secret meaning of which, the meaning never spoken, was that Mommy should not be sad, for she would not die but live on in you.

To live! You are my life; I love you as I love life itself. In the mornings I come out of the house and wet my finger and hold it up to the wind. When the chill is from the north-west, from your quarter, I stand a long time sniffing, concentrating my attention in the hope that across ten thousand miles of land and sea some breath will reach me of the milkiness you still carry with you behind your ears, in the fold of your neck.

The first task laid on me, from today: to resist the craving to share my death. Loving you, loving life, to forgive the living and take my leave without bitterness. To embrace death as my own, mine alone.

To whom this writing then? The answer: to you but not to you; to me; to you in me.

All afternoon I tried to keep myself busy, cleaning out drawers, sorting and discarding papers. At dusk I came out again. Behind the garage the shelter was set up as before with the black plastic neatly spanned over it. Inside lay the man, his legs curled up, and a dog beside him that cocked its ears and wagged its tail. A collie, young, little more than a pup, black, with white points.

'No fires,' I said. 'Do you understand? I want no fires, I want no mess.'

He sat up, rubbing his bare ankles, staring around as if not knowing where he was. A horsy, weatherbeaten face with the puffiness around the eyes of an alcoholic. Strange green eyes: unhealthy.

'Do you want something to eat?' I said.

He followed me to the kitchen, the dog at his heels, and waited while I cut him a sandwich. He took a bite but then seemed to forget to chew, standing against the door-jamb with his mouth full, the light shining into his vacant green eyes, while the dog whined softly. 'I have to clean up,' I said impatiently, and made to close the door on him. He went off without a murmur; but before he turned the corner I was sure I saw him toss the sandwich away, and the dog dive after it.

There were not so many of these homeless people in your time. But now they are part of life here. Do they frighten me? On the whole, no. A little begging, a little thieving; dirt, noise, drunkenness; no worse. It is the roaming gangs I fear, the sullen-mouthed boys, rapacious as sharks, on whom the first shade of the prison-house is already beginning to close. Children scorning childhood, the time of wonder, the growing-time of the soul. Their souls, their organs of wonder, stunted, petrified. And on the other side of the great divide their white cousins soul-stunted too, spinning themselves tighter and tighter into their sleepy cocoons. Swimming lessons, riding lessons, ballet lessons; cricket on the lawn; lives passed within walled gardens guarded by bulldogs; children of paradise, blond, innocent, shining with angelic light, soft as *putti*. Their residence the limbo of the unborn, their innocence the innocence of bee-grubs, plump and white, drenched in honey, absorbing sweetness through their soft skins. Slumbrous their souls, bliss-filled, abstracted.

Why do I give this man food? For the same reason I would feed his dog (stolen, I am sure) if it came begging. For the same reason I gave you my breast. To be full enough to give and to give from one's fullness: what deeper urge is there? Out of their withered bodies even the old try to squeeze one last drop. A stubborn will to give, to nourish. Shrewd was death's aim when he chose my breast for his first shaft.

This morning, bringing him coffee, I found him urinating into the drain, which he did without any appearance of shame.

'Do you want a job of work?' I said. 'There are plenty of jobs I can give you.'

He said nothing, but drank the coffee, holding the mug in both hands.

'You are wasting your life,' I said. 'You are not a child any more. How can you live like this? How can you lie around and do nothing all day? I don't understand it.'

It is true: I do not understand it. Something in me revolts at the lassitude, the letting go, the welcoming of dissolution.

He did something that shocked me. With a straight look, the first direct look he has given me, he spat a gob of spit, thick, yellow, streaked with brown from the coffee, on to the concrete beside my foot. Then he thrust the mug at me and sauntered off.

The thing itself, I thought, shaken: the thing itself brought out between us. Spat not upon me but before me where I could see it, inspect it, think about it. His word, his kind of word, from his own mouth, warm at the instant when it left him. A word, undeniable, from a language before language. First the look and then the spitting. What kind of look? A look without respect, from a man to a woman old enough to be his mother. Here: take your coffee.

· 7 ·

He did not sleep in the alley last night. The boxes are gone too. But, poking around, I came upon the Air Canada bag in the woodshed, and a place that he must have scratched for himself amid the jumble of lumber and faggots. So I know he means to come back.

Six pages already, and all about a man you have never met and never will. Why do I write about him? Because he is and is not I. Because in the look he gives me I see myself in a way that can be written. Otherwise what would this writing be but a kind of moaning, now high, now low? When I write about him I write about myself. When I write about his dog I write about myself; when I write about the house I write about myself. Man, house, dog: no matter what the word, through it I stretch out a hand to you. In another world I would not need words. I would appear on your doorstep. 'I have come for a visit,' I would say, and that would be the end of words: I would embrace you and be embraced. But in this world, in this time, I must reach out to you in words. So day by day I render myself into words and pack the words into the page like sweets: like sweets for my daughter, for her birthday, for the day of her birth. Words out of my body, drops of myself, for her to unpack in her own time, to take in, to suck, to absorb. As they say on the bottle: old-fashioned drops, drops fashioned by the old, fashioned and packed with love, the love we have no alternative but to feel toward those to whom we give ourselves to devour or discard.

Though it rained steadily all afternoon, it was not till dark that I heard the creak of the gate and, a minute later, the click of the dog's claws on the veranda.

I was watching television. One of the tribe of *Ministers* and *Onderministers* was making an announcement to the nation. I was standing, as I always do when they speak, as a way of keeping what I can of my self-respect (who would choose to face a firing-squad sitting down?). *Ons buig nie voor dreigemente nie*, he was saying: we do not bow to threats: one of those speeches.

The curtains behind me were open. At a certain moment I became aware of him, the man whose name I do not know, watching over my shoulder through the glass. So I turned up the sound, enough for, if not the words, then the cadences to reach him, the slow, truculent Afrikaans rhythms with their deadening closes, like a hammer beating a post into the ground. Together, blow after blow, we listened. The disgrace of the life one lives under them: to open a newspaper, to switch on the television, like kneeling and being urinated on. Under them: under their meaty bellies, their full bladders. 'Your days are numbered,' I used to whisper once upon a time, to them who will now outlast me.

I was on my way out to the shops, in the act of opening the garage door, when I had a sudden attack. An attack: it was just that: the pain hurling itself upon me like a dog, sinking its teeth into my back. I cried out, unable to stir. Then he, this man, appeared from somewhere and helped me into the house.

I lay down on the sofa, on my left side, in the only comfortable posture left to me. He waited. 'Sit down,' I said. He sat. The pain began to subside. 'I have cancer,' I said. 'It has made its way into the bone. That is what hurts.'

I was not at all sure he understood.

A long silence. Then: 'This is a big house,' he said. 'You could turn it into a boarding-house.'

I made a tired gesture.

'You could let rooms to students,' he went on relent-lessly.

I yawned, and, feeling my teeth sag, covered my mouth. Once upon a time I would have blushed. But no longer.

'I have a woman who helps with the housework,' I said. 'She is away till the end of the month, visiting her people. Do you have people?'

A curious expression: to have people. Do I have people? Are you my people? I think not. Perhaps only Florence qualifies to have people.

He made no reply. There is an air of childlessness about him. Of having no children in the world but also of having no childhood in his past. His face all bone and weathered skin. As one cannot imagine a snake's head that does not look old, so one cannot see behind his face the face of a child. Green eyes, animal eyes: can one picture an infant with eyes like that?

'My husband and I parted a long time ago,' I said. 'He is dead now. I have a daughter in America. She left in 1976 and hasn't come back. She is married to an American. They have two children of their own.'

A daughter. Flesh of my flesh. You.

He took out a packet of cigarettes. 'Don't smoke in the house, please,' I said.

'What is your disability?' I said. 'You say you get a disability pension.'

He held out his right hand. Thumb and forefinger stood out; the other three fingers curled into the palm. 'I can't move them,' he said.

We gazed at his hand, at the three crooked fingers with their dirty nails. Not what I would call a work-calloused hand.

'Was it an accident?'

He nodded; the kind of nod that committed him to nothing.

'I'll pay you to cut the lawn,' I said.

For an hour, using the hedge clippers, he hacked listlessly at the grass, knee-high by now in places. In the end he had cleared a patch a few yards square. Then he quit. 'It's not my kind of work,' he said. I paid him for the hour. As he left he bumped against the cat-tray, spilling litter all over the veranda.

All in all, more trouble than he is worth. But I did not choose him. He chose me. Or perhaps he merely chose the one house without a dog. A house of cats.

The cats are unsettled by these newcomers. When they show their noses outside the dog makes playful dashes at them, so they skulk indoors, peevish. Today they would not eat. Thinking they spurned the food because it had been in the refrigerator, I stirred a little hot water into the smelly mess (what is it? seal-flesh? whale-flesh?). Still they disdained it, circling the dish, flicking the tips of their tails. 'Eat!' I said, pushing the dish at them. The big one lifted a finicky paw to avoid being touched. At which I lost control. 'Go to hell, then!' I screamed, and flung the fork wildly in their direction – 'I am sick to death of feeding you!' In my voice there was a new, mad edge; and, hearing it, I exulted. Enough of being nice to people, enough of being nice to cats! 'Go to hell!' I screamed again, at the top of my voice. Their claws scrabbled on the linoleum as they fled.

Who cares? When I am in a mood like this I am capable of putting a hand on the bread-board and chopping it off without a second thought. What do I care for this body that has betrayed me? I look at my hand and see only a tool, a hook, a thing for gripping other things. And these legs, these clumsy, ugly stilts: why should I have to carry them with me everywhere? Why should I take them to bed with me night after night and pack them in under the sheets, and pack the arms in too, higher up near the face, and lie there sleepless amid the clutter? The abdomen too, with its dead gurglings, and the heart beating, beating: why? What have they to do with me?

We sicken before we die so that we will be weaned from our body. The milk that nourished us grows thin and sour; turning away from the breast, we begin to be restless for a separate life. Yet this first life, this life on earth, on the body

· II ·

of earth – will there, can there ever be a better? Despite all the glooms and despairs and rages, I have not let go of my love of it.

In pain, I took two of Dr Syfret's pills and lay down on the sofa. Hours later I woke befuddled and cold, fumbled my way upstairs, got into bed without undressing.

In the middle of the night I became aware of a presence in the room that could only have been his. A presence or a smell. It was there, then it went away.

From the landing came a creak. Now he is entering the study, I thought; now he is switching on the light. I tried to recall whether, among the papers on the desk, any were private, but there was too much confusion in my head. Now he sees the books, shelf upon shelf, I thought, trying to bring back order, and the piles of old journals. Now he looks at the pictures on the wall: Sophie Schliemann decked out in Agamemnon's treasure hoard; the robed Demeter from the British Museum. Now, quietly, he slides out the drawers of the desk. The top drawer, full of letters, accounts, torn-off stamps, photographs, does not interest him. But in the bottom drawer there is a cigar-box full of coins: pennies, drachmas, centimes, schillings. The hand with the curled fingers dips into it, takes out two five-peseta pieces big enough to pass for rands, pockets them.

Not an angel, certainly. An insect, rather, emerging from behind the skirting-boards when the house is in darkness to forage for crumbs.

I heard him at the far end of the landing, trying the two locked doors. Only rubbish, I wanted to whisper to him – rubbish and dead memories; but the fog in my head closed in again.

Spent the day in bed. No energy, no appetite. Read Tolstoy – not the famous cancer story, which I know all too well, but the story of the angel who takes up residence with the shoemaker. What chance is there, if I take a walk down to Mill Street, of finding my own angel to bring home and succour? None, I think. Perhaps in the countryside there are still one or two sitting against milestones in the heat of the sun, dozing, waiting for what chance will bring. Perhaps in the squatter camps. But not in Mill Street, not in the suburbs. The suburbs, deserted by the angels. When a ragged stranger comes knocking at the door he is never anything but a derelict, an alcoholic, a lost soul. Yet how, in our hearts, we long for these sedate homes of ours to tremble, as in the story, with angelic chanting!

This house is tired of waiting for the day, tired of holding itself together. The floorboards have lost their spring. The insulation of the wiring is dry, friable, the pipes clogged with grit. The gutters sag where screws have rusted away or pulled loose from the rotten wood. The rooftiles are heavy with moss. A house built solidly but without love, cold, inert now, ready to die. Whose walls the sun, even the African sun, has never succeeded in warming, as though the very bricks, made by the hands of convicts, radiate an intractable sullenness.

Last summer, when the workmen were re-laying the drains, I watched them dig out the old pipes. Two metres down into the earth they went, bringing up mouldering brick, rusty iron, even a solitary horseshoe. But no bones. A site without a human past; to spirits, as to angels, of no interest.

This letter is not a baring of my heart. It is a baring of something, but not of my heart.

Since the car would not start this morning, I had to ask him, this man, this lodger to push. He pushed me down the driveway. 'Now!' he shouted, slapping the roof. The engine caught. I swung into the road, drove a few yards, then, on an impulse, stopped. 'I have to go to Fish Hoek,' I called from a cloud of smoke: 'Do you want to come along?'

So we set off, the dog on the back seat, in the green Hillman of your childhood. For a long while no word passed between us. Past the hospital, past the University, past Bishopscourt we drove, the dog leaning over my shoulder to feel the wind on its face. Up Wynberg Hill we toiled. On the long downhill swoop on the other side I switched off the engine and coasted. Faster and faster we went, till the wheel shuddered in my hands and the dog whined with excitement. I was smiling, I believe; my eyes may even have been shut.

At the foot of the hill, as we began to slow down, I cast him a glance. He sat relaxed, imperturbable. Good man! I thought.

'When I was a child,' I said, 'I used to do downhills on a bicycle with no brakes to speak of. It belonged to my elder brother. He would dare me. I was completely without fear. Children cannot conceive of what it is to die. It never crosses their minds that they may not be immortal.

'I would ride my brother's bicycle down hills even steeper than this one. The faster I went, the more alive I would feel. I would quiver with life as if I were about to burst through my skin. As a butterfly must feel when it is being born, or bearing itself.

'In an old car like this you still have the freedom to coast. With a modern car, when you switch off the engine the steering wheel locks. I am sure you know that. But people sometimes make a mistake or forget, and then can't keep the car on the road. Sometimes they go over the side and into the sea.'

Into the sea. Tussling with a locked wheel while you soar in a bubble of glass over the sun-glinting sea. Does it really happen? Do many do it? If I stood on Chapman's Peak on a Saturday afternoon, would I see them, men and women, thick in the air as midges taking off on their last flight?

'There is a story I want to tell you,' I said. 'When my mother was still a child, in the early years of the century, the family used to go to the seaside for Christmas. This was still in the age of ox-wagons. They would travel by ox-wagon all the way from Uniondale in the Eastern Cape to Plettenberg Bay at the mouth of the Piesangs River, a journey of a hundred miles taking I don't know how many days. Along the way they would camp at the roadside.

'One of their stopping-places was at the top of a mountain pass. My grandparents would spend the nights in the wagon itself while my mother and the other children had their bed underneath it. So – here the story begins – my mother lay at the top of the pass in the stillness of the night, snug in her blankets with her brothers and sisters sleeping beside her, watching the stars through the spokes of the wheels. As she watched it began to seem that the stars were moving: the stars were moving or else the wheels were moving, slowly, very slowly. She thought: What shall I do? What if the wagon is beginning to roll? Shall I call out a warning? What if I lie silent and the wagon gathers speed and rolls all the way down the mountainside with my parents inside? But what if I am imagining it all?

'Choking with fear, her heart pounding, she lay there watching the stars, watching them move, thinking, "Shall I? Shall I?," listening for the creak, the first creak. At last she fell asleep, and her sleep was full of dreams of death. But in the morning, when she re-emerged, it was into light and peace. And the wagon re-emerged with her, and her parents re-emerged, and all was well, as it had been before.'

It was time for him to say something now, about hills or cars or bicycles or about himself or his childhood. But he was stubbornly silent.

'She told no one what went on in the night,' I resumed. 'Perhaps she was waiting for me to come. I heard the story many times from her, in many forms. Always they were on their way to the Piesangs River. Such a lovely golden name! I was sure it must be the most beautiful place on earth. Years after my mother's death I visited Plettenberg Bay and saw the Piesangs River for the first time. Not a river at all, just a trickle of water choked with reeds, and mosquitoes in the evenings, and a caravan park full of screaming children and fat barefoot men in shorts braaiing sausages over gas cookers. Not Paradise at all. Not a place one would mount a journey to year after year through valleys and over mountains.'

Up Boyes Drive the car was labouring now, willing but old, like Rocinante. I gripped the wheel tighter, urging her on.

Above Muizenberg, overlooking the sweep of False Bay, I parked and switched off the engine. The dog began to whine. We let it out. It sniffed the curbstones, sniffed the bushes, relieved itself, while we watched in awkward silence.

He spoke. 'You are pointing the wrong way,' he said. 'You should be pointing downhill.'

I hid my chagrin. I have always wished to be thought a capable person. Now more than ever, with incapability looming.

'Are you from the Cape?' I said.

'Yes.'

'And have you lived here all your life?'

He shifted restlessly. Two questions: one too many.

A breaker, perfectly straight, hundreds of yards long, rolled inshore, a single crouched figure on a surfboard gliding ahead of it. Across the bay the mountains of Hottentots Holland stood out clear and blue. Hunger, I thought: it is a hunger of the eyes that I feel, such hunger that I am loth even to blink. These seas, these mountains: I want to burn them upon my sight so deeply that, no matter where I go, they will always be before me. I am hungry with love of this world.

A flock of sparrows settled on the bushes around us,

preened themselves, took off again. The surfer reached shore and began to trudge up the beach. Suddenly there were tears in my eyes. From not blinking, I told myself. But the truth was, I was crying. Hunched over the wheel, I abandoned myself, first to a quiet, decent sobbing, then to long wails without articulation, emptyings of the lungs, emptyings of the heart. 'I am so sorry,' I gasped; and then, when I was calmer: 'I am sorry, I don't know what has come over me.'

I should not have bothered to apologize. He gave no sign of having noticed anything.

I dried my eyes, blew my nose. 'Shall we go?' I said.

He opened the door, gave a long whistle. The dog bounded in. An obedient dog, no doubt stolen from a good family.

The car was indeed pointing the wrong way.

'Start in reverse,' he said.

I released the handbrake, rolled back down the hill a little way, let out the clutch. The car shuddered and stopped. 'It has never started in reverse,' I said.

'Swing over to the other side of the road,' he directed, like a husband giving a driving lesson.

I let the car roll further downhill, then swung across the road. With blaring horn a great white Mercedes shot past on the inside. 'I didn't see it!' I gasped.

'Go!' he shouted.

I stared in astonishment at this stranger shouting at me. 'Go!' he shouted again, straight into my face.

The engine caught. I drove back in stiff silence. At the corner of Mill Street he asked to be let off.

The worst of the smell comes from his shoes and feet. He needs socks. He needs new shoes. He needs a bath. He needs a bath every day; he needs clean underwear; he needs a bed, he needs a roof over his head, he needs three meals a day, he needs money in the bank. Too much to give: too much for someone who longs, if the truth be told, to creep into her own mother's lap and be comforted.

Late in the afternoon he returned. Making an effort to forget what had passed, I took him around the garden, pointing out tasks that need to be done. 'Pruning, for instance,' I said. 'Do you know how to prune?'

He shook his head. No, he didn't know how to prune. Or didn't want to.

In the bottom corner, the most heavily overgrown, thick creepers covered the old oak bench and the rabbit-hutch. 'This should all be cleared,' I said.

He lifted one edge of the mat of creepers. On the floor of the hutch was a jumble of parched bones, including the perfect skeleton of a young rabbit, its neck arched back in a last contortion.

'Rabbits,' I said. 'They used to belong to my domestic's son. I let him keep them here as pets. Then there was some commotion or other in his life. He forgot about them and they starved to death. I was in hospital and didn't know about it. I was terribly upset when I came back and found out what agony had been going on unheeded at the bottom of the garden. Creatures that can't talk, that can't even cry.'

Guavas were dropping, worm-riddled, making a malodorous pulpy carpet under the tree. 'I wish the trees would stop bearing,' I said. 'But they never do.'

The dog, following behind, sniffed perfunctorily at the hutch. The dead long dead, their smells all gone.

'Anyhow, do what you can to bring it back under control,' I said. 'So that it doesn't become a complete wilderness.'

'Why?' he said.

'Because that is how I am,' I said. 'Because I don't mean to leave a mess behind.'

He shrugged, smiling to himself.

'If you want to be paid you will have to earn it,' I said. 'I am not giving you money for nothing.'

For the rest of the afternoon he worked, hacking away at the creepers and grass, pausing now and again to stare into

the distance, pretending not to be aware that I was keeping
an eye on him from upstairs. At five o'clock I paid him. 'I
know you are not a gardener,' I said, 'and I don't want to
turn you into what you are not. But we can't proceed on a
basis of charity.'

Taking the notes, folding them, putting them in his pocket,
looking off to one side so as not to look at me, he said softly,
'Why?'

'Because you don't deserve it.'

And he, smiling, keeping his smile to himself: 'Deserve . . .
Who deserves anything?'

Who deserves anything? In a quick fury I thrust the purse
at him. 'What do you believe in, then? Taking? Taking what
you want? Go on: take!'

Calmly he took the purse, emptied it of thirty rand and
some coins, and handed it back. Then off he went, the dog
jauntily at his heels. In half an hour he was back; I heard the
clink of bottles.

Somewhere he has found himself a mattress, one of those
folding mattresses people take to the beach. In his little nest
amid the dust and mess of the woodshed, with a candle at his
head and the dog at his feet, he lay smoking.

'I want that money back,' I said.

He reached into his pocket and held out some notes. I took
them. Not all the money, but that did not matter.

'If you are in need, you can ask,' I said. 'I am not a stingy
person. And be careful with that candle. I don't want a fire.'

I turned and went. But in a minute was back.

'You told me,' I said, 'that I should turn this house into a
boarding-house for students. Well, there are better things I
could do with it. I could turn it into a haven for beggars. I
could run a soup-kitchen and a dormitory. But I don't. Why
not? Because the spirit of charity has perished in this country.
Because those who accept charity despise it, while those who
give give with a despairing heart. What is the point of charity

when it does not go from heart to heart? What do you think charity is? Soup? Money? Charity: from the Latin word for the heart. It is as hard to receive as to give. It takes as much effort. I wish you would learn that. I wish you would learn something instead of just lying around.'

A lie: charity, *caritas*, has nothing to do with the heart. But what does it matter if my sermons rest on false etymologies? He barely listens when I speak to him. Perhaps, despite those keen bird-eyes, he is more befuddled with drink than I know. Or perhaps, finally, he does not care. Care: the true root of charity. I look for him to care, and he does not. Because he is beyond caring. Beyond caring and beyond care.

Since life in this country is so much like life aboard a sinking ship, one of those old-time liners with a lugubrious, drunken captain and a surly crew and leaky lifeboats, I keep the shortwave radio at my bedside. Most of the time there is only talk to be heard; but if one persists into the unlikely hours of the night there are stations that relent and play music. Fading in, fading out, I heard last night – from where? Helsinki? the Cook Islands? – anthems of all the nations, celestial music, music that left us years ago and now comes back from the stars transfigured, gentle, as evidence that all that is given forth will at length return. A closed universe, curved like an egg, enclosing us.

There I lay in the dark, listening to the music of the stars and the crackling and humming that accompanied it like the dust of meteors, smiling, my heart filled with gratitude for this good news from afar. The one border they cannot close, I thought: the border upwards, between the Republic of South Africa and the empire of the sky. Where I am due to travel. Where no passport is called for.

Still under the spell of the music (it was, I think, Stockhausen), I sat down at the piano this afternoon and played

· 20 ·

some of the old pieces: preludes from the Well-Tempered Clavier, Chopin preludes, Brahms waltzes, from Novello and Augener editions tattered, mottled, dry as dust. I played as badly as ever, misreading the same chords as half a century ago, repeating fingering mistakes grown by now into the bone, never to be corrected. (The bones prized above all by archaeologists, I remember, are those gnarled with disease or splintered by an arrowhead: bones marked with a history from a time before history.)

After I had tired of the sweetness of Brahms I closed my eyes and played chords, searching with my fingers for the one chord I would recognize, when I came upon it, as my chord, as what in the old days we used to call the lost chord, the heart's-chord. (I speak of a time before your time, when, passing down the street on a hot Saturday afternoon, you might hear, faint but dogged from a front parlour, the maiden of the household groping among the keys for that yearned-for, elusive resonance. Days of charm and sorrow and mystery too! Days of innocence!)

'*Jerusalem!*' I sang softly, playing chords I last heard at my grandmother's knee: '*And was Jerusalem y-builded here?*'

Then at last I went back to Bach, and played clumsily, over and over again, the first fugue from Book One. The sound was muddy, the lines blurred, but every now and again, for a few bars, the real thing emerged, the real music, the music that does not die, confident, serene.

I was playing for myself. But at some point a board creaked or a shadow passed across the curtain and I knew he was outside listening.

So I played Bach for him, as well as I could. When the last bar was played I closed the music and sat with my hands in my lap contemplating the oval portrait on the cover with its heavy jowls, its sleek smile, its puffy eyes. Pure spirit, I thought, yet in how unlikely a temple! Where does that spirit find itself now? In the echoes of my fumbling performance receding through the ether? In my heart, where the music still dances? Has it made its way into the heart too of the man in the sagging trousers eavesdropping at the window? Have our two hearts, our organs of love, been tied for this brief while by a cord of sound?

The telephone rang: a woman from the flats across the road warning me of a vagrant she had spied on my property. 'He is not a vagrant,' I said. 'He is a man who works for me.'

I am going to stop answering the telephone. There is no one I am ready to speak to except you and the fat man in the picture, the fat man in heaven; and neither of you will, I think, call.

Heaven. I imagine heaven as a hotel lobby with a high ceiling and the Art of Fugue coming softly over the public address system. Where one can sit in a deep leather armchair and be without pain. A hotel lobby full of old people dozing, listening to the music, while souls pass and re-pass before them like vapours, the souls of all. A place dense with souls. Clothed? Yes, clothed, I suppose; but with empty hands. A place to which you bring nothing but an abstract kind of clothing and the memories inside you, the memories that make you. A place without incident. A railway station after the abolition of trains. Listening to the heavenly unending music, waiting for nothing, paging idly through the store of memories.

Will it be possible to sit in that armchair listening to the music without fretting about the house closed up and dark, the cats prowling in the garden, unfed, cross? It must be possible, or what is heaven for? Yet dying without succession is – forgive me for saying this – so unnatural. For peace of mind, for peace of soul, we need to know who comes after us, whose presence fills the rooms we were once at home in.

I think of those abandoned farmhouses I drove past in the Karoo and on the west coast, whose owners decamped to the cities years ago leaving fronts boarded up, gates locked. Now washing flaps on the line, smoke comes from the chimney, children play outside the back door, waving to passing cars. A land in the process of being repossessed, its heirs quietly announcing themselves. A land taken by force, used, despoiled, spoiled, abandoned in its barren late years. Loved too, perhaps, by its ravishers, but loved only in the bloomtime of its youth and therefore, in the verdict of history, not loved enough.

They open your fingers after the event to make sure you are not trying to take something with you. A pebble. A feather. A mustard seed under your fingernail.

It is like a sum, a labyrinthine sum, pages long, subtraction upon subtraction, division upon division, till the head reels. Every day I attempt it anew, in my heart the flicker of a hope that in this one case, my case, there may have been a mistake. And every day I stop before the same blank wall: death, oblivion. Dr Syfret in his rooms: 'We must face the truth.' That is to say: we must face the wall. But not he: I.

I think of prisoners standing on the brink of the trench into which their bodies will tumble. They plead with the firing-squad, they weep, they joke, they offer bribes, they offer everything they possess: the rings off their fingers, the clothes off their backs. The soldiers laugh. For they will take it all anyway, and the gold from their teeth too.

There is no truth but the shock of pain that goes through me when, in an unguarded moment, a vision overtakes me of this house, empty, with sunlight pouring through the windows on to an empty bed, or of False Bay under blue skies, pristine, deserted – when the world I have passed my life in manifests itself to me and I am not of it. My existence from day to day has become a matter of averting my eyes, of cringing. Death is the only truth left. Death is what I cannot bear to think. At every moment when I am thinking of something else, I am not thinking death, am not thinking the truth.

· 23 ·

I try to sleep. I empty my mind; calm begins to steal over me. I am falling, I think, I am falling: welcome, sweet sleep. Then at the very edge of oblivion something looms up and pulls me back, something whose name can only be *dread*. I shake myself free. I am awake in my room in my bed, all is well. A fly settles on my cheek. It cleans itself. It begins to explore. It walks across my eye, my open eye. I want to blink, I want to wave it away, but I cannot. Through an eye that is and is not mine I stare at it. It licks itself, if that is the word. There is nothing in those bulging organs that I can recognize as a face. But it is upon me, it is here: it struts across me, a creature from another world.

Or: It is two in the afternoon. I am lying on the sofa or in bed, trying to keep the weight off my hip, where the pain is worst. I have a vision of Esther Williams, of plump girls in flowered bathing costumes swimming in effortless backstroke formation through sky-blue, rippling waters, smiling and singing. Invisible guitars strum; the mouths of the girls, bows of vivid scarlet lipstick, form words. What are they singing? Sunset . . . Farewell . . . Tahiti. Longing sweeps through me for the old Savoy bioscope, for tickets at one and fourpence in a currency gone forever, melted down save for a few last farthings in my desk drawer, on one side George VI, the good king, the stammerer, on the other a pair of nightingales. Nightingales. I have never heard nightingale-song and never will. I embrace the longing, embrace the regret, embrace the king, the swimming girls, embrace whatever will occupy me.

Or I get up and switch on the television. On one channel football. On the other a black man clasping his hands over the Bible, preaching to me in a language I cannot even put a name to. This is the door I open to let the world flood in, and this is the world that comes to me. It is like peering down a pipe.

Three years ago I had a burglary (you may remember, I wrote about it). The burglars took no more than they could carry, but before they left they tipped out every drawer, slashed every mattress, smashed crockery, broke bottles, swept all the food in the pantry on to the floor.

'Why do they behave like this?' I asked the detective in bewilderment – 'What good does it do them?'

'It's the way they are,' he replied. 'Animals.'

After that I had bars installed on all the windows. They were fitted by a plump Indian man. After he had screwed the bars into the frames he filled in the head of each screw with glue. 'So that they can't be unscrewed,' he explained. When he left he said, 'Now you are safe,' and patted my hand.

'Now you are safe.' The words of a zookeeper as he locks the door for the night on some wingless, ineffectual bird. A dodo: the last of the dodos, old, past egg-laying. 'Now you are safe.' Locked up while hungry predators prowl outside. A dodo quaking in her nest, sleeping with one eye open, greeting the dawn haggard. But safe, safe in her cage, the bars intact, the wires intact: the telephone wire, down which she may cry for help in a last extremity, the television wire, down which comes the light of the world, the aerial wire, which calls in music from the stars.

Television. Why do I watch it? The parade of politicians every evening: I have only to see the heavy, blank faces so familiar since childhood to feel gloom and nausea. The bullies in the last row of school-desks, raw-boned, lumpish boys, grown up now and promoted to rule the land. They with their fathers and mothers, their aunts and uncles, their brothers and sisters: a locust horde, a plague of black locusts infesting the country, munching without cease, devouring lives. Why, in a spirit of horror and loathing, do I watch them? Why do I let them into the house? Because the reign of the locust family is the truth of South Africa, and the truth is what makes me sick? Legitimacy they no longer trouble to claim. Reason they have shrugged off. What absorbs them is power and the stupor of power. Eating and talking, munching lives, belching. Slow, heavy-bellied talk. Sitting in a circle, debating ponderously, issuing decrees like hammer-blows: death, death, death. Untroubled by the stench. Heavy eyelids, piggish eyes, shrewd with the shrewdness of generations of peasants. Plotting against each other too: slow peasant plots that take decades to mature. The new Africans, pot-bellied, heavy-jowled men on their stools of office: Cetshwayo, Dingane in white skins. Pressing downward: their power in their weight. Huge bull-testicles pressing down on their wives, their children, pressing the spark out of them. In their own hearts no spark of fire left. Sluggish hearts, heavy as blood-pudding.

And their message stupidly unchanging, stupidly forever the same. Their feat, after years of etymological meditation on the word, to have raised stupidity to a virtue. To stupefy: to deprive of feeling; to benumb, deaden; to stun with amazement. Stupor: insensibility, apathy, torpor of mind. Stupid: dulled in the faculties, indifferent, destitute of thought or feeling. From *stupere* to be stunned, astounded. A gradient from *stupid* to *stunned* to *astonished*, to be turned to stone. The message: that the message never changes. A message that turns people to stone.

We watch as birds watch snakes, fascinated by what is about to devour us. Fascination: the homage we pay to our death. Between the hours of eight and nine we assemble and they show themselves to us. A ritual manifestation, like the processions of hooded bishops during Franco's war. A thanatophany: showing us our death. *Viva la muerte!* their cry, their threat. Death to the young. Death to life. Boars that devour their offspring. The Boar War.

I say to myself that I am watching not the lie but the space behind the lie where the truth ought to be. But is it true?

I dozed (it is still yesterday I am writing about), read, dozed again. I made tea, put on a record. Bar by bar the Goldberg Variations erected themselves in the air. I crossed to the window. It was nearly dark. Against the garage wall the man was squatting, smoking, the point of his cigarette glowing. Perhaps he saw me, perhaps not. Together we listened.

At this moment, I thought, I know how he feels as surely as if he and I were making love.

Though it came unbidden, though it filled me with distaste, I considered the thought without flinching. He and I pressed breast to breast, eyes closed, going down the old road together. Unlikely companions! Like travelling in a bus in Sicily, pressed face to face, body to body against a strange man. Perhaps that is what the afterlife will be like: not a lobby with armchairs and music but a great crowded bus on its way from nowhere to nowhere. Standing room only: on one's feet forever, crushed against strangers. The air thick, stale, full of sighs and murmurs: *Sorry, sorry.* Promiscuous contact. Forever under the gaze of others. An end to private life.

Across the courtyard he squatted, smoking, listening. Two souls, his and mine, twined together, ravished. Like insects mating tail to tail, facing away from each other, still except for a pulsing of the thorax that might be mistaken for mere breathing. Stillness and ecstasy.

He flicked his cigarette away. A burst of sparks as it hit the ground, then darkness.

This house, I thought. This world. This house, this music. This.

'This is my daughter,' I said. 'The one I told you about, who lives in America.' And through his eyes regarded you in the photograph: a pleasant-faced, smiling woman in her thirties, against a field of green, raising a hand to her hair, which is blowing in the wind. Confident. That is what you have now: the look of a woman who has found herself.

'These are their children.'

Two little boys in caps and coats and boots and gloves

standing to attention beside a snowman, waiting for the shutter to click.

A pause. We were sitting at the kitchen table. I had set tea before him, and Marie biscuits. Marie biscuits: food for old people, for the toothless.

'There is something I would like you to do for me if I die. There are some papers I want to send to my daughter. But after the event. That is the important part. That is why I cannot send them myself. I will do everything else. I will make them up into a parcel with the right stamps on it. All you will have to do will be to hand the parcel over the counter at the post office. Will you do that for me?'

He shifted uncomfortably.

'It is not a favour I would ask if I could help it. But there is no other way. I will not be here.'

'Can't you ask someone else?' he said.

'Yes, I can. But I am asking you. These are private papers, private letters. They are my daughter's inheritance. They are all I can give her, all she will accept, coming from this country. I don't want them opened and read by anyone else.'

Private papers. These papers, these words that either you read *now* or else will never read. Will they reach you? Have they reached you? Two ways of asking the same question, a question to which I will never know the answer, never. To me this letter will forever be words committed to the waves: a message in a bottle with the stamps of the Republic of South Africa on it, and your name.

'I don't know,' said the man, the messenger, playing with his spoon.

He will make no promise. And even if he promises, he will do, finally, what he likes. Last instructions, never enforceable. For the dead are not persons. That is the law: all contracts lapse. The dead cannot be cheated, cannot be betrayed, unless you carry them with you in your heart and do the crime there.

'Never mind,' I said. 'I had thought of asking you to come in and feed the cats as well. But I will make another arrangement.'

What other arrangement? In Egypt they bricked in cats with their dead masters. Is that what I want: yellow eyes padding back and forth, searching for a way out of the dark cave?

'I will have to have them put down,' I said. 'They are too old to take to a new home.'

Like water against a rock my words thudded against his silence.

'I have to do something about them,' I said. 'I can't do nothing. You would feel the same, in my position.'

He shook his head. Not true. Indeed, not true. One winter's night, sooner or later, when the artificial fire in his veins is no longer hot enough to preserve him, he will perish. He will die in a doorway or an alley with his arms hugged across his chest; they will find him with this dog or some other dog by his side, whimpering, licking his face. They will cart him off and the dog will be left behind in the street and that will be the end of that. No arrangements, no bequests, no mausoleum.

'I'll post your parcel for you,' he said.

· II ·

Florence is back, bringing not only the two little girls but her fifteen-year-old son Bheki.

'Is he going to be staying long, Florence?' I asked. 'Is there going to be room for him?'

'If he is not with me he will get into trouble,' Florence replied. 'My sister cannot look after him any more. It is very bad in Guguletu, very bad.'

So now I have five people in the back yard. Five people, a dog and two cats. The old woman who lived in a shoe. And didn't know what to do.

When Florence went off at the beginning of the month I assured her I could cope with the housework. But of course I let everything slide, and soon a sour, clammy odour pervaded the upstairs, an odour of cold cream, dirty sheets, talcum powder. Now I had to follow shamefacedly after her as she took stock. Hands on hips, nostrils flaring, spectacles gleaming, she surveyed the evidence of my incompetence. Then she set to work. By the end of the afternoon the kitchen and bathroom were shining, the bedroom was crisp and neat, there was a smell of furniture polish in the air. 'Wonderful, Florence,' I said, producing the ritual phrases: 'I don't know what I would do without you.' But of course I do know. I would sink into the indifferent squalor of old age.

Having done my work, Florence turned to her own. She put supper on the stove and took the two little girls up to the bathroom. Watching her wash them, wiping hard behind the ears, between the legs, deft, decisive, impervious to their whines, I thought: What an admirable woman, but how glad I am she is not my mother!

I came upon the boy mooning about in the courtyard. Once I knew him as Digby, now he is Bheki. Tall for his age, with Florence's severe good looks. 'I can't believe how you have grown,' I said. He gave no answer. No longer the open-faced little boy who, when he came visiting, used to run first of all to the rabbit-hutch, haul out the fat white doe, and hug her to his chest. Dissatisfied, no doubt, with being separated from his friends and hidden away with baby sisters in someone's back yard.

'Since when have the schools been closed?' I asked Florence.

'Since last week. All the schools in Guguletu, Langa, Nyanga. The children have got nothing to do. All they do is run around the streets and get into trouble. It is better that he is here where I can see him.'

'He will be restless without any friends.'

She shrugged, unsmiling. I do not believe I have ever seen her smile. But perhaps she smiles on her children when she is alone with them.

'Who is this man?' asked Florence.

'His name is Mr Vercueil,' I said. 'Vercueil, Verkuil, Verskuil. That's what he says. I have never come across such a name before. I am letting him stay here for a while. He has a dog. Tell the children, if they play with it, not to get it too excited. It is a young dog, it may snap.'

Florence shook her head.

'If he gives us trouble I will ask him to leave,' I said. 'But I can't send him away for things he hasn't done.'

★

· 34 ·

A cool, windy day. I sat on the balcony in my dressing-gown. Below me in the lawn Vercueil was taking the old mower apart, with the little girls watching him. The elder, whose name, says Florence, is Hope (she does not entrust me with the real name), squatted a few yards away, out of his line of vision, her hands clasped between her knees. She was wearing new red sandals. The baby, Beauty, also wearing red sandals, staggered about the lawn, kicking out her feet, sometimes sitting down suddenly.

As I watched, the baby advanced upon Vercueil, her arms held out wide, her fists clenched. As she was about to stumble over the lawnmower he caught her and led her by the chubby little arm to a safe distance. Again, on unsteady feet, she bore down on him. Again he caught her and led her away. It was on the verge of becoming a game. But would dour Vercueil play?

Once more Beauty lunged towards him; once more he saved her. Then, wonder of wonders, he wheeled the half-dismantled lawnmower to one side and, offering one hand to the baby, one hand to Hope, began to turn in circles, first slowly, then faster. Hope, in her red sandals, had to run to keep her footing; as for the baby, she spun in the air, giving shrieks of pleasure; while the dog, closed off behind the gate, leapt and barked. Such noise! Such excitement!

At that point Florence must have come on the scene, for the spinning slowed and stopped. A few soft words, and Hope let go of Vercueil's hand, coaxed her sister away, disappeared from my sight. I heard a door shut. The dog, full of regret, whined. Vercueil returned to the lawnmower. Half an hour later it began to rain.

The boy, Bheki, spends his time sitting on Florence's bed paging through old magazines, while from a corner of the room Hope watches and worships. Sometimes when he has had enough of reading he stands in the driveway bouncing a tennis ball off the garage door. I find the noise maddening.

Though I clutch a pillow over my head the remorseless thudding still reaches me. 'When are the schools going to open again?' I ask peevishly. 'I will tell him to stop,' says Florence. A minute later the thudding stops.

Last year, when the troubles in the schools began, I spoke my mind to Florence. 'In my day we considered education a privilege,' I said. 'Parents would scrimp and save to keep their children in school. We would have thought it madness to burn a school down.

'It is different today,' replied Florence.

'Do you approve of children burning down their schools?'

'I cannot tell these children what to do,' said Florence. 'It is all changed today. There are no more mothers and fathers.'

'That is nonsense,' I said. 'There are always mothers and fathers.' On that note our exchange ended.

Of trouble in the schools the radio says nothing, the television says nothing, the newspapers say nothing. In the world they project all the children of the land are sitting happily at their desks learning about the square on the hypotenuse and the parrots of the Amazonian jungle. What I know about events in Guguletu depends solely on what Florence tells me and on what I can learn by standing on the balcony and peering north-east: namely, that Guguletu is not burning today, or, if it is burning, is burning with a low flame.

The country smoulders, yet with the best will in the world I can only half-attend. My true attention is all inward, upon the thing, the word, the word for the thing inching through my body. An ignominious occupation, and in times like these ridiculous too, as a banker with his clothes on fire is a joke while a burning beggar is not. Yet I cannot help myself. 'Look at me!' I want to cry to Florence – 'I too am burning!'

Most of the time I am careful to hold the letters of the word apart like the jaws of a trap. When I read I read warily, jumping over lines or even whole paragraphs when from the corner of an eye I catch the shadow of the word waiting in ambush.

But in the dark, in bed, alone, the temptation to look at it grows too strong. I feel myself almost pushed toward it. I think of myself as a child in a long white dress and straw hat on a great empty beach. Sand flies all around me. I hold my hat tight, I plant my feet, I brace myself against the wind. But after a while, in this lonely place where no one is watching, the effort becomes too great. I relax. Like a hand in the small of my back, the wind gives me a push. It is a relief to stop resisting. First walking, then racing, I allow the wind to take me.

It takes me, night after night, to *The Merchant of Venice*. 'Do I not eat, sleep, breathe like you?' cries Shylock the Jew: 'Do I not bleed like you?,' brandishing a dagger with a pound of bleeding flesh impaled on its point. 'Do I not bleed like you?' come the words of the Jew with the long beard and skullcap dancing in rage and anguish on the stage.

I would cry my cry to you if you were here. But you are not. Therefore it must be to Florence. Florence must be the one to suffer these moments when a veritable blast of fear goes out from me scorching the leaf on the bough. 'It will be all right': those are the words I want to hear uttered. I want to be held to someone's bosom, to Florence's, to yours, to anyone's, and told that it will be all right.

Lying in bed last night with a pillow under my hip, my arms pressed to my chest to keep the pain from moving, the clock showing 3.45, I thought with envy and yearning of Florence in her room, asleep, surrounded by her sleeping children, the four of them breathing in their four different measures, every breath strong and clean.

Once I had everything, I thought. Now you have everything and I have nothing.

The four breathings went on, without falter, and the soft ticking of the clock.

Folding a sheet of paper in two, I wrote Florence a note: 'Am having a bad night. Will try to sleep late. Please keep the children quiet. Thank you. EC.' I went downstairs and propped it in the middle of the kitchen table. Then, shivering, I returned to bed, took the four o'clock pills, closed my eyes, folded my arms, and waited for sleep that did not come.

What I want from Florence I cannot have. Nothing of what I want can I have.

Last year, when the little one was still a babe in arms, I gave Florence a ride out to Brackenfell, to the place where her husband works.

No doubt she expected me to drop her there and drive off. But out of curiosity, wanting to see the man, to see them together, I came in with her.

It was late on a Saturday afternoon. From the parking lot we followed a dusty track past two long, low sheds to a third shed where a man in blue overalls stood in a wire enclosure with chickens – pullets really – milling around his legs. The girl, Hope, tugged herself free, dashed ahead and gripped the mesh. Between the man and Florence something passed: a glance, a question, a recognition.

But there was no time for greetings. He, William, Florence's husband, had a job and the job could not be interrupted. His job was to pounce on a chicken, swing it upside down, grip the struggling body between his knees, twist a wire band around its legs, and pass it on to a second, younger man, who would hang it, squawking and flapping, on a hook on a clattering overhead conveyor that took it deeper into the shed where a third man in oilskins splashed with blood gripped its head, drew its neck taut, and cut it through with a knife so small it seemed part of his hand, tossing the head in the same movement into a bin full of other dead heads.

· 38 ·

This was William's work, and this I saw before I had the time or the presence of mind to ask whether I wanted to see it. For six days of the week this was what he did. He bound the legs of chickens. Or perhaps he took turns with the other men and hung chickens from hooks or cut off heads. For three hundred rand a month plus rations. A work he had been doing for fifteen years. So that it was not inconceivable that some of the bodies I had stuffed with breadcrumbs and egg-yolk and sage and rubbed with oil and garlic had been held, at the last, between the legs of this man, the father of Florence's children. Who got up at five in the morning, while I was still asleep, to hose out the pans under the cages, fill the feed-troughs, sweep the sheds, and then, after breakfast, begin the slaughtering, the plucking and cleaning, the freezing of thousands of carcases, the packing of thousands of heads and feet, miles of intestines, mountains of feathers.

I should have left at once, when I saw what was going on. I should have driven off and done my best to forget all about it. But instead I stood at the wire enclosure, fascinated, as the three men dealt out death to the flightless birds. And beside me the child, her fingers gripping the mesh, drank in the sight too.

So hard and yet so easy, killing, dying.

Five o'clock came, the end of the day, and I said goodbye. While I was driving back to this empty house, William took Florence and the children to the living-quarters. He washed; she cooked a supper of chicken and rice on the paraffin stove, then fed the baby. It was Saturday. Some of the other farm-workers were out visiting, recreating themselves. So Florence and William were able to put the children to bed in an empty bunk and go for a walk, just the two of them, in the warm dusk.

They walked along the side of the road. They spoke about the past week, about how it had been; they spoke about their lives.

When they came back the children were fast asleep. For the sake of privacy they hung a blanket in front of their bunk. Then they had the night to themselves, all save the half-hour when Florence slipped out and, in the dark, fed the baby.

On Sunday morning William – not his true name but the name by which he is known in the world of his work – put on his suit and hat and good shoes. He and Florence walked to the bus stop, she with the baby on her back, he holding Hope's hand. They took a bus to Kuilsrivier, then a taxi to the home in Guguletu of the sister with whom their son lodged.

It was after ten o'clock and beginning to grow hot. Church was over; the living-room was crowded with visitors, full of talk. After a while the men went off; it was time for Florence to help her sister with the cooking. Hope fell asleep on the floor. A dog came in, licked her face, was chased away; she was lifted, still sleeping, on to the sofa. In a private moment Florence gave her sister the money for Bheki's rent, for his food, his shoes, his schoolbooks; her sister put it away in her bodice. Then Bheki made his appearance and greeted his mother. The men came back from wherever they had been and they all had lunch: chicken from the farm or factory or plant or whatever it is, rice, cabbage, gravy. From outside Bheki's friends began to call: hurriedly he finished his food and left the table.

All of this happened. All of this must have happened. It was an ordinary afternoon in Africa: lazy weather, a lazy day. Almost it is possible to say: This is how life should be.

The time came for them to leave. They walked to the bus stop, Hope riding now on her father's shoulders. The bus arrived; they said goodbye. The bus bore Florence and her daughters off. It bore them to Mowbray, from where they took another bus to St George's Street, and then a third up Kloof Street. From Kloof Street they walked. By the time they reached Schoonder Street the shadows were lengthening.

It was time to give Hope, fretful and tired, her supper, to bath the baby, to finish yesterday's ironing.

At least it is not cattle he is slaughtering, I told myself; at least it is only chickens, with their crazy chicken-eyes and their delusions of grandeur. But my mind would not leave the farm, the factory, the *enterprise* where the husband of the woman who lived side by side with me worked, where day after day he bestrode his pen, left and right, back and forth, around and around, in a smell of blood and feathers, in an uproar of outraged squawking, reaching down, scooping up, gripping, binding, hanging. I thought of all the men across the breadth of South Africa who, while I sat gazing out of the window, were killing chickens, moving earth, barrowful upon barrowful; of all the women sorting oranges, sewing buttonholes. Who would ever count them, the spadefuls, the oranges, the buttonholes, the chickens? A universe of labour, a universe of counting: like sitting in front of a clock all day, killing the seconds as they emerged, counting one's life away.

Ever since Vercueil took my money he has been drinking steadily, drinking not only wine but brandy. Some days he does not drink till noon, using the hours of abstinence to make surrender more voluptuous. More often he is intoxicated by the time he leaves the house in mid-morning.

The sun was shining bleakly today when he returned from his outing. I was upstairs on the balcony; he did not see me as he sat down in the yard with his back to the wall, the dog beside him. Florence's son was already there, with a friend I had not seen before, and Hope, devouring their every move with her eyes. They had a radio on; the scraping and thudding of the music was even worse than the tennis ball.

'Water,' Vercueil called to the boys – 'Bring me some water.'

The new boy, the friend, crossed the yard and squatted

beside him. What passed between them I did not hear. The boy stretched out a hand. 'Give,' he said.

Lazily Vercueil beat down his hand.

'Give it to me,' the boy said, and on his knees began to tug the bottle from Vercueil's pocket.

Vercueil resisted, but only lackadaisically.

The boy unscrewed the cap and poured the brandy out on to the ground. Then he tossed the bottle aside. It shattered. A stupid thing to do: I almost called out.

'They are making you into a dog!' said the boy. 'Do you want to be a dog?'

The dog, Vercueil's dog, whined eagerly.

'Go to hell,' replied Vercueil with a thick tongue.

'Dog!' said the boy. 'Drunkard!'

He turned his back on Vercueil and went back to Bheki, a swagger in his walk. What a self-important child, I thought. If this is how the new guardians of the people conduct themselves, Lord spare us from them.

The little girl sniffed at the brandy and wrinkled her nose.

'You go to hell too,' said Vercueil, waving her away. She did not stir. Then at once she turned and ran to her mother's room.

The music ground on. Vercueil fell asleep, slumped sideways against the wall with the dog's head on his knee. I returned to my book. After a while the sun went behind the clouds and it grew chilly. A light drizzle began to fall. The dog shook itself and went into the shed. Vercueil got to his feet and followed. I gathered my things.

Inside the shed there was a commotion. First the dog scuttled out, faced around, and stood barking; then Vercueil emerged backwards; then the two boys followed. As the second boy, the friend, neared him, Vercueil struck out and hit him on the neck with the flat of his hand. The boy drew in his breath with a hiss of surprise: even from the balcony I heard it. He struck back at Vercueil, who stumbled and nearly fell. The dog danced around, yapping. The boy struck Vercueil again, and now Bheki joined in. 'Stop it!' I shouted down at them. They paid me no heed. Vercueil was on the ground; they were kicking him; Bheki took out the belt from his trousers and began to lash him. 'Florence!' I shouted – 'Stop them!' Vercueil put his hands over his face to protect himself. The dog made a leap at Bheki; Bheki knocked it backwards and went on flailing Vercueil with his belt. 'Stop it, you two!' I shouted, gripping the rail. 'Stop it at once or I'll call the police!'

Then Florence appeared. She spoke sharply, and the boys backed off. Vercueil struggled to his feet. I came downstairs as fast as I could.

'Who is this boy?' I asked Florence.

The boy stopped speaking to Bheki and regarded me. I did not like that look: arrogant, combative.

'He is a friend from school,' said Florence.

'He must go home,' I said. 'This is getting too much for me. I can't have brawling in my back yard. I can't have strangers walking in and out.'

There was blood coming from Vercueil's lip. Strange to see blood on that leathery face. Like honey on ashes.

'He is not a stranger, he is visiting,' said Florence.

'Must we have a pass to come in here?' said Bheki. He and his friend exchanged glances. 'Must we have a pass?' They waited for my answer, challenging me. The radio was still playing: an inhuman noise, wearying: I wanted to clasp my hands over my ears.

'I did not say anything about passes,' I said. 'But what right does he have to come here and assault this man? This man lives here. It is his home.'

Florence's nostrils flared.

'Yes,' I said, turning to her, 'he lives here too, it is his home.'

'He lives here,' said Florence, 'but he is rubbish. He is good for nothing.'

'*Jou moer!*' said Vercueil. He had taken off his hat and was punching out the crown; now he raised the hand with the hat as if to strike her. '*Jou moer!*'

Bheki snatched the hat from him and tossed it up on to the garage roof. The dog barked furiously. Slowly the hat tumbled down the slope of the roof.

'He is not a rubbish person,' I said, lowering my voice, speaking to Florence alone. 'There are no rubbish people. We are all people together.'

But Florence had no desire to be preached to. 'Good for nothing but drinking,' she said. 'Drink, drink, drink all day. I do not like him here.'

A good-for-nothing: was that what he was? Yes, perhaps: good-for-nothing: a good old English word, heard too seldom nowadays.

'He is my messenger,' I said.

Florence regarded me suspiciously.

'He is going to carry messages for me,' I said.

She shrugged. Vercueil shambled off with his hat and his dog. I heard the gate-latch click. 'Tell the boys to leave him alone,' I said. 'He is doing no harm.'

Like an old tom chased off by the rising males, Vercueil has gone into hiding to lick his wounds. I foresee myself searching the parks, calling softly, 'Mr Vercueil! Mr Vercueil!' An old woman in search of her cat.

Florence is openly proud of how Bheki got rid of the good-for-nothing, but predicts that he will be back as soon as it starts raining. As for me, I doubt we will see him as long as the boys are here. I said so to Florence. 'You are showing Bheki and his friends that they can raise their hands against their elders with impunity. That is a mistake. Yes, whatever you may think of him, Vercueil is their elder!

'The more you give in, Florence, the more outrageously the children will behave. You told me you admire your son's generation because they are afraid of nothing. Be careful: they may start by being careless of their own lives and end by being careless of everyone else's. What you admire in them is not necessarily what is best.

'I keep thinking of what you said the other day: that there are no more mothers and fathers. I can't believe you mean it. Children cannot grow up without mothers or fathers. The burnings and killings one hears of, the shocking callousness, even this matter of beating Mr Vercueil – whose fault is it in the end? Surely the blame must fall on parents who say, "Go, do as you wish, you are your own master now, I give up authority over you." What child in his heart truly wants to be told that? Surely he will turn away in confusion, thinking to himself, "I have no mother now, I have no father: then let my mother be death, let my father be death." You wash your hands of them and they turn into the children of death.'

Florence shook her head. 'No,' she said firmly.

'But do you remember what you told me last year, Florence, when those unspeakable things were happening in the townships? You said to me, "I saw a woman on fire, burning, and when she screamed for help, the children laughed and threw more petrol on her." You said, "I did not think I would live to see such a thing."'

'Yes, I did say that, and it is true. But who made them so cruel? It is the whites who made them so cruel! Yes!' She breathed deeply, passionately. We were in the kitchen. She was doing the ironing. The hand that held the iron pressed down hard. She glared at me. Lightly I touched her hand. She raised the iron. On the sheet was the beginning of a brown scorch-mark.

· 45 ·

No mercy, I thought: a war without mercy, without limits. A good war to miss.

'And when they grow up one day,' I said softly, 'do you think the cruelty will leave them? What kind of parents will they become who were taught that the time of parents is over? Can parents be recreated once the idea of parents has been destroyed within us? They kick and beat a man because he drinks. They set people on fire and laugh while they burn to death. How will they treat their own children? What love will they be capable of? Their hearts are turning to stone before our eyes, and what do you say? You say, "This is not my child, this is the white man's child, this is the monster made by the white man." Is that all you can say? Are you going to blame them on the whites and turn your back?'

'No,' said Florence. 'That is not true. I do not turn my back on my children.' She folded the sheet crosswise and lengthwise, crosswise and lengthwise, the corners falling together neatly, decisively. 'These are good children, they are like iron, we are proud of them.' On the board she spread the first of the pillowslips. I waited for her to say more. But there was no more. She was not interested in debating with me.

Children of iron, I thought. Florence herself, too, not unlike iron. The age of iron. After which comes the age of bronze. How long, how long before the softer ages return in their cycle, the age of clay, the age of earth? A Spartan matron, iron-hearted, bearing warrior-sons for the nation. 'We are proud of them.' We. Come home either with your shield or on your shield.

And I? Where is my heart in all of this? My only child is thousands of miles away, safe; soon I will be smoke and ash; so what is it to me that a time has come when childhood is despised, when children school each other never to smile, never to cry, to raise fists in the air like hammers? Is it truly a time out of time, heaved up out of the earth, misbegotten, monstrous? What, after all, gave birth to the age of iron but the age of granite? Did we not have Voortrekkers, generation after generation of Voortrekkers, grim-faced, tight-lipped Afrikaner children, marching, singing their patriotic hymns, saluting their flag, vowing to die for their fatherland? *Ons sal lewe, ons sal sterwe.* Are there not still white zealots preaching the old regime of discipline, work, obedience, self-sacrifice, a regime of death, to children some too young to tie their own shoelaces? What a nightmare from beginning to end! The spirit of Geneva triumphant in Africa. Calvin, black-robed, thin-blooded, forever cold, rubbing his hands in the after-world, smiling his wintry smile. Calvin victorious, reborn in the dogmatists and witch-hunters of both armies. How fortunate you are to have put all this behind you!

The other boy, Bheki's friend, arrived on a red bicycle with fat sky-blue tyres. When I went to bed last night the bicycle was in the courtyard, glistening wet in the moonlight. At seven this morning, when I looked out of the window, it was still there. I took the morning pills and had another hour's sleep. I dreamed I was trapped in a crowd. Shapes pushed at me, hit at me, swore in words I could not make out, filthy, full of menace. I hit back, but my arms were a child's arms: *foo, foo* went my blows, like puffs of air.

I awoke to the sound of raised voices, Florence's and someone else's. I rang the bell once, twice, three times, four times. At last Florence came.

'Is there someone at the door, Florence?'

Florence picked up the quilt from the floor and folded it over the foot of the bed. 'It is nobody,' she said.

'Did your son's friend stay here last night?'

'Yes. He cannot ride a bicycle in the dark, it is too danger-ous.'

'And where did he sleep?'

Florence drew herself up. 'In the garage. Bheki and he slept in the garage.'

'But how did they get into the garage?'

'They opened the window.'

'Can't they ask me before they do something like that?'

A silence. Florence picked up the tray.

'Is this boy going to be living here too, in the garage? Are they sleeping in my car, Florence?'

Florence shook her head. 'I do not know. You must ask them yourself.'

Midday, and the bicycle was still here. Of the boys themselves no sign. But when I went out to the mailbox there was a yellow police van parked across the street with two uniformed men in it, the one on the near side asleep, his cheek against the glass.

I beckoned to the man behind the wheel. The engine came to life, the sleeper sat up, the van climbed the sidewalk, made a brisk U-turn, and pulled up beside me.

I expected them to get out. But no, there they sat without a word, waiting for me to speak. A cold north-wester was blowing. I held my dressing-gown closed at my throat. The radio in the van crackled. '*Vier-drie-agt*,' said a woman's voice. They ignored it. Two young men in blue.

'Can I help you?' I said. 'Are you waiting for someone?'

'Can you help us? I don't know, lady. You tell us, can you help us.'

In my day, I thought, policemen spoke respectfully to ladies. In my day children did not set fire to schools. *In my day*: a phrase one came across in this day only in Letters to the Editor. Old men and women, trembling with just fury, taking up the pen, weapon of last resort. In my day, now over; in my life, now past.

'If you are looking for those boys, I want you to know they have my permission to be here.'

'Which boys, lady?'

· 48 ·

'The boys who are visiting here. The boys from Guguletu. The schoolboys.'

There was a burst of noise from the radio.

'No, lady, I don't know anything about boys from Guguletu. Do you want us to look out for them?'

A glance passed between the two of them, a glance of merriment. I gripped the bar of the gate. The dressing-gown gaped, I felt the cold wind on my throat, my chest. 'In my day,' I said, enunciating clearly each old, discredited, comical word, 'a policeman did not speak to a lady like that.' And I turned my back on them.

The radio squawked like a parrot behind me; or perhaps they made the sound come from it, I would not put it past them. An hour later the yellow van was still outside the gate.

'I really think you should send this other boy home,' I told Florence. 'He is going to get your son into trouble.'

'I cannot send him home,' said Florence. 'If he goes Bheki will go with him. They are like this.' She held up a hand, two fingers intertwined. 'It is safer for them here. In Guguletu there is trouble all the time, and then the police come in and shoot.'

Shooting in Guguletu: whatever Florence knows about it, whatever you know ten thousand miles away, I do not know. In the news that reaches me there is no mention of trouble, of shooting. The land that is presented to me is a land of smiling neighbours.

'If they are here to get away from the fighting then why are the police after them?'

Florence drew a deep breath. Since the birth of the baby there has been an air of barely contained outrage about her. 'You must not ask *me*, madam,' she declared, 'why the police are coming after the children and chasing them and shooting them and putting them in jail. You must not ask *me*.'

'Very well,' I said, 'I will not make that mistake again. But I cannot turn my home into a haven for all the children running away from the townships.'

· 49 ·

'But why not?' asked Florence, leaning forward: 'Why not?'

I ran a hot bath, undressed, and painfully lowered myself into the water. *Why not?* I hung my head; the ends of my hair, falling over my face, touched the water; my legs, mottled, blue-veined, stuck out like sticks before me. An old woman, sick and ugly, clawing on to what she has left. The living, impatient of long dyings; the dying, envious of the living. An unsavoury spectacle: may it be over soon.

No bell in the bathroom. I cleared my throat and called: 'Florence!' Bare pipes and white walls gave back a hollow sound. Absurd to imagine that Florence would hear me. And if she heard, why should she come?

Dear mother, I thought, look down on me, stretch forth your hand!

Shivers began to run through me from head to toe. Behind closed eyes I saw my mother as she is when she appears to me, in her drab old person's clothes, her face hidden.

'Come to me!' I whispered.

But she would not. Stretching out her arms as a coasting hawk does, my mother began to ascend into the sky. Higher and higher she rose above me. She reached the layer of the clouds, pierced it, soared on. With each mile she ascended she became younger. Her hair grew dark again, her skin fresh. The old clothes fell from her like dry leaves, revealing the blue dress with the feather in the buttonhole that she wears in my earliest memory of her, from the time when the world was young and all things were possible.

On she soared, in the eternal perfection of youth, changeless, smiling, rapt, forgetful, to the rim of the heavenly sphere itself. 'Mother, look down on me!' I whispered into the bare bathroom.

The rains began early this year. This is the fourth month of rain. Where one touches the walls, streaks of damp form. There are patches where the plaster is blistering and bursting. My clothes have a bitter, mouldy smell. How I long, just once more, to put on crisp underwear smelling of the sun! Let me be granted just one more summer-afternoon walk down the Avenue amid the nut-brown bodies of children on their way home from school, laughing, giggling, smelling of clean young sweat, the girls every year more beautiful, *plus belles*. And if that is not to be, let there still be, to the last, gratitude, unbounded, heartfelt gratitude, for having been granted a spell in this world of wonders.

I write these words sitting in bed, my knees pressed together against the August cold. *Gratitude*: I write down the word and read it back. What does it mean? Before my eyes it grows dense, dark, mysterious. Then something happens. Slowly, like a pomegranate, my heart bursts with gratitude; like a fruit splitting open to reveal the seeds of love. *Gratitude, pomegranate*: sister words.

At five this morning I was woken by heavy rain. It came down in sheets, streaming over the edges of the clogged gutters, dripping through cracked rooftiles. I went downstairs, made myself tea, and, wrapped in a blanket, settled down with the month's accounts.

The gate clicked and steps came up the driveway. A figure crouched under a black plastic sack scurried past the window.

I went out on to the veranda. 'Mr Vercueil!' I called into the teeming rain. There was no answer. Hunching my shoulders, clutching the dressing-gown about me, I stepped out. At once my slippers with their silly lambswool collars were soaked through. Through runnels of water I slopped across the yard. In the dark entrance to the shed I collided with someone: Vercueil, standing with his back to me. He swore.

'Come inside!' I shouted above the rain. 'Come into the house! You can't sleep there!'

Still holding the bag like a hood over his head, he followed me into the kitchen and into the light. 'Leave that wet thing outside,' I said. Then with a shock I saw that someone had followed him in. It was a woman, small, no higher than my shoulder, but old, or at least not young, with a leering, bloated face and livid skin.

'Who is this?' I said.

Vercueil stared back at me, yellow-eyed, defiant. Dog-man! I thought.

'You can wait indoors till the rain stops, then I want you out,' I said coldly, and turned my back on the pair of them.

I changed my clothes, locked myself in my bedroom, and tried to read. But the words rustled past me like leaves. With mild surprise I felt my eyelids droop, heard the book slide through my hands.

When I awoke the one thought in my mind was to get them out of the house.

Of the woman there was no sign; but Vercueil was asleep in the living-room, curled up on the sofa, his hands between his knees, the hat still somehow on his head. I shook him. He stirred, wet his lips, made a reluctant, mumbling, sleepy sound. It was the same sound – it came back to me at once – that you used to make when I woke you for school. 'Time to get up!' I would call as I drew open the curtains; and, turning away from the light, you would mumble just like that. 'Come, my darling, it's time to get up!' I would whisper in your ear, not urging you too hard yet, giving myself time to sit beside you and stroke your hair, stroke after stroke, my fingertips alive with love, while you clung to the last to the body of sleep. Let it be like this forever! I would think, my

· 52 ·

hand on your head, the current of love coursing through it.

And now your sleepy, comfortable murmur reborn in the throat of this man! Should I sit beside him too, lift off his hat, stroke his greasy hair? A shudder of distaste went through me. How easy it is to love a child, how hard to love what a child turns into! Once upon a time, with his fists to his ears and his eyes pinched shut in ecstasy, this creature too floated in a woman's womb, drank of her blood, belly to belly. He too passed through the gates of bone into the radiance outside, was allowed to know mother-love, *amor matris*. Then in the course of time was weaned away from it, made to stand alone, and began to grow dry, stunted, crooked. A life apart, deprived, like all lives; but in this case, surely, more undernourished than most. A man in his middle years still sucking on bottles, yearning for the original bliss, reaching for it in his stupors.

While I stood regarding him, his woman entered the room. Ignoring me, she stumbled back into a nest of cushions on the floor. She reeked of cologne water: mine. Behind her came Florence, bristling.

'Don't ask me to explain, Florence,' I said. 'Just leave them alone, they are sleeping something off.'

Florence's glasses flashed, she had something to say, but I cut her short. 'Please! They are not going to stay.'

Though I flushed the toilet several times, a smell lingered, both sickly sweet and foul. I tossed the floor-mat out in the rain.

Later, when the children were in the kitchen with Florence having breakfast, I came downstairs again. Without preamble I addressed Bheki.

'I hear you and your friend have been sleeping in my car. Why didn't you ask my permission?'

Silence fell. Bheki did not look up. Florence went on cutting bread.

· 53 ·

'Why didn't you ask my permission? Answer me!'

The little girl stopped chewing, stared at me.

Why was I behaving in this ridiculous fashion? Because I was irritated. Because I was tired of being used. Because it was my car they were sleeping in. My car, my house: mine: I was not yet gone.

Then, fortunately, Vercueil made his appearance and the tension was broken. He passed through the kitchen, glancing neither left nor right, and out on to the veranda. I followed. The dog was leaping up at him, bounding, frisking, full of joy. It leapt at me too, streaking my skirt with its wet paws. How silly one looks fending off a dog!

'Will you get your friend out of the house, please,' I said to him.

Staring up into an overcast sky, he made no reply.

'Get her out at once or I will get her out!' I shouted in a fury.

He ignored me.

'Help me,' I ordered Florence.

The woman lay face down on her bed of cushions, a patch of wetness at the corner of her mouth. Florence tugged her by the arm. Groggily she stood up. Half guiding, half pushing, Florence propelled her out of the house. On the pathway Vercueil caught up with us. 'This is too much!' I snapped at him.

The two boys were already out on the street with their bicycle. Pretending not to notice our squabble, they set off up Schoonder Street, Bheki hunched on the crossbar, his friend pedalling.

In a hoarse voice, in a rambling stream of obscenity, the woman began to curse Florence. Florence gave me a malicious look. 'Rubbish person,' she said, and stamped off.

'I don't ever want to see this woman again,' I said to Vercueil.

The bicycle with the two boys on it reappeared over the

crest of Schoonder Street and raced towards us, Bheki's friend pedalling hard. On their heels followed the yellow police van from yesterday.

A light truck stood parked at the curbside, with pipes and rods in the back, plumbing materials. There was room enough for the bicycle to pass. But as the yellow van drew level with the boys, the near-side door swung open and slapped them sideways. The bicycle wobbled and went out of control. I had a glimpse of Bheki sliding down, his arms above his head, of the other boy standing on the pedals, averting his face, stretching out a hand in a warding gesture. Above the sound of the traffic from Mill Street I heard quite clearly the thud of a body stopped in mid-flight, a deep, surprised 'Ah!' of exhaled breath, the crash of the bicycle colliding with the plumber's truck. 'God!' I screamed in a shrill voice that, hanging in the air, I did not recognize as my own. Time seemed to stop and then resume, leaving a gap: in one instant the boy put out a hand to save himself, in the next he was part of a tangle in the gutter. Then the echo of my scream dwindled and the scene reassembled itself in all its familiarity: Schoonder Street on a quiet weekday morning, with a canary-yellow van just turning the corner.

A dog, a retriever, came trotting up to investigate. Vercueil's dog sniffed the retriever, while the retriever, ignoring him, sniffed at the pavement, then began to lick it. I wanted to move but could not. There was a coldness in me, my limbs felt distant, the word *fainting* occurred to me, though I have never fainted in my life. *This country!*, I thought. And then: *Thank God she is out!*

A gate opened and a man in blue work-clothes appeared. He kicked at the retriever, which sprang away in hurt surprise. 'Jesus!' said the man. He bent down and began to thread limbs through the frame of the bicycle.

I approached, shaking. 'Florence!' I called. But there was no sign of Florence.

· 55 ·

Straddling the bodies, the man lifted the bicycle aside. Bheki lay under the other boy. There was a deep frown on his face; he wet his lips with his tongue over and over; his eyes were closed. Vercueil's dog tried to lick him. 'Go away!' I whispered, and gave it a push with my foot. It wagged its tail.

A woman appeared at my elbow, drying her hands on a towel. 'Are they newspaper boys?' she said. 'Are they newspaper boys, do you know?' I shook my head.

With an uncertain air, the man in blue straddled the bodies again. What he should have done was to lift the dead weight of the other boy, who lay face down across Bheki. But he did not want to, nor did I want him to. There was something wrong, something unnatural in the way the boy lay.

'I'll go and phone for an ambulance,' said the woman.

I bent and raised the boy's limp arm. 'Wait!' said the man. 'Let's be careful.'

Coming erect, I was overtaken with such dizziness that I had to close my eyes.

Clasping him under the shoulders, he dragged the boy off Bheki and laid him out on the pavement. Bheki opened his eyes.

'Bheki,' I said. Bheki gave me a calm, incurious look. 'Everything is all right,' I said. From entirely peaceful eyes he continued to regard me, accepting the lie, letting it pass. 'The ambulance is on its way,' I said.

Then Florence was there, kneeling beside her son, speaking to him urgently, stroking his head. He began to reply: slow, mumbled words. Her hand paused as she listened. 'They crashed into the back of this truck,' I explained. 'It's my truck,' said the man in blue. 'The police pushed them,' I said: 'it's appalling, quite appalling. It was those same two policemen who were here yesterday, I am sure.'

Florence slid a hand under Bheki's head. Slowly he sat up. One shoe was off; a trouser-leg was torn open and wet with

· 56 ·

blood. Gingerly he held aside the torn material and peered at the wound. His palms were raw, the skin hung in strips. 'The ambulance is on its way,' I said. 'We do not need the ambulance,' said Florence.

She was wrong. The other boy lay sprawled on his back now. With his jacket the plumber was trying to staunch the blood that streamed down his face. But the flow would not stop. He lifted the wadded jacket and for an instant, before it darkened with blood again, I saw that the flesh across the forehead hung open in a loose flap as if sliced with a butcher's knife. Blood flowed in a sheet into the boy's eyes and made his hair glisten; it dripped on to the pavement; it was everywhere. I did not know blood could be so dark, so thick, so heavy. What a heart he must have, I thought, to pump that blood and go on pumping!

'Is the ambulance coming?' said the plumber. 'Because I don't know how to stop this.' He was sweating; he changed position and his shoe, soggy with blood, squelched.

You were eleven, I remember, when you sliced your thumb in the bread machine. I rushed you to the emergency section at Groote Schuur. We sat on a bench waiting our turn, you with your thumb wrapped in lint, pressing it to stop the bleeding. 'What's going to happen to me?' you whispered. 'They will give you an injection and put in stitches,' I whispered back. 'Just a few stitches, just a few pricks.'

It was early on a Saturday evening, but already the casualties were trickling in. A man in white shoes and a rumpled black suit spat blood steadily into a dish. A youth on a stretcher, naked to the waist, his belt open, held a wad of sodden cloth to his belly. Blood on the floor, blood on the benches. What did our timid thimbleful count for beside this torrent of black blood? Child Snowdrop lost in the cavern of blood, and her mother lost too. A country prodigal of blood. Florence's husband in yellow oilskins and boots, wading through blood. Oxen keeling over, their throats slit, hurling last jets into the

air like whales. The dry earth soaking up the blood of its
creatures. A land that drinks rivers of blood and is never
sated.

'Let me,' I said to the plumber. He made way. Kneeling,
I lifted aside the sodden blue jacket. Blood ran down the
boy's face in a steady, even sheet. Between thumbs and
forefingers I pinched together as much as I could of the open
flap. Vercueil's dog came pushing in again. 'Get that dog
away,' I snapped. The plumber gave it a kick. It yelped and
sidled away. Where was Vercueil? Was it true, was he truly
good for nothing? 'Go and phone again,' I ordered the
plumber.

As long as I pinched tight I could hold in most of the flow.
But when I relaxed blood poured again steadily. It was blood,
nothing more, blood like yours and mine. Yet never before
had I seen anything so scarlet and so black. Perhaps it was an
effect of the skin, youthful, supple, velvet dark, over which
it ran; but even on my hands it seemed both darker and more
glaring than blood ought to be. I stared at it, fascinated,
afraid, drawn into a veritable stupor of staring. Yet it was
impossible, in my deepest being impossible, to give myself
up to that stupor, to relax and do nothing to stop the flow.
Why, I ask myself now? And I answer: Because blood is
precious, more precious than gold and diamonds. Because
blood is one: a pool of life dispersed among us in separate
existences, but belonging by nature together: lent, not given:
held in common, in trust, to be preserved: seeming to live in
us, but only seeming, for in truth we live in it.

A sea of blood, come back together: is that how it will be
at the end of days? The blood of all: a Baikal Sea scarlet-black
under a wintry blue Siberian sky, ice-cliffs around it, its
snow-white shores lapped by blood, viscous, sluggish. The
blood of mankind, restored to itself. A body of blood. Of all
mankind? No: in a place apart, in a mud-walled dam in the
Karoo with barbed wire around it and the sun blazing down,

the blood of the Afrikaners and their tribute-bearers, still, stagnant.

Blood, sacred, abominated. And you, flesh of my flesh, blood of my blood, bleeding every month into foreign soil.

For twenty years I have not bled. The sickness that now eats at me is dry, bloodless, slow and cold, sent by Saturn. There is something about it that does not bear thinking of. To have fallen pregnant with these growths, these cold, obscene swellings; to have carried and carried this brood beyond any natural term, unable to bear them, unable to sate their hunger: children inside me eating more every day, not growing but bloating, toothed, clawed, forever cold and ravenous. Dry, dry: to feel them turning at night in my dry body, not stretching and kicking as a human child does but changing their angle, finding a new place to gnaw. Like insect-eggs laid in the body of a host, now grown to grubs and implacably eating their host away. My eggs, grown within me. *Me, mine*: words I shudder to write, yet true. My daughters death, sisters to you, my daughter life. How terrible when motherhood reaches a point of parodying itself! A crone crouched over a boy, her hands sticky with his blood: a vile image, as it comes up in me now. I have lived too long. Death by fire the only decent death left. To walk into the fire, to blaze like tow, to feel these secret sharers cringe and cry out too, at the last instant, in their harsh unused little voices; to burn and be gone, to be rid of, to leave the world clean. Monstrous growths, misbirths: a sign that one is beyond one's term. This country too: time for fire, time for an end, time for what grows out of ash to grow.

When the ambulance came I was so stiff that I had to be lifted to my feet. In detaching my sticky fingers from the gash I opened it again. 'He has lost a lot of blood,' I said. 'It's not serious,' said the ambulance-man curtly. He held the boy's eyelid open. 'Concussed,' he said. 'How did it happen?'

★

· 59 ·

Bheki sat on the bed, his trousers off, his hands in a basin of water; Florence knelt before him bandaging his leg.

'Why did you leave me alone to look after him? Why didn't you stay and help?'

I sounded querulous, certainly, but for once was I not in the right?

'I do not want to be involved with the police,' said Florence.

'That is not the question. You leave me alone to take care of your son's friend. Why must I be the one to take care of him? He is nothing to me.'

'Where is he?' said Bheki.

'They took him to Woodstock Hospital. He is concussed.'

'What does it mean, concussed?'

'He is unconscious. He hit his head. Do you know why you crashed?'

'They pushed us,' he said.

'Yes, they pushed you. I saw it. You are lucky to be alive, both of you. I am going to lay a complaint.'

A glance passed between Bheki and his mother. 'We do not want to be involved with the police,' Florence repeated. 'There is nothing you can do against the police.' Again a glance, as though checking she had her son's approval.

'If you don't complain they will go on behaving as they like. Even if it gets you nowhere, you must stand up to them. I am not talking about the police only. I am talking about men in power. They must see you are not afraid. This is a serious matter. They could have killed you, Bheki. What have they got against you anyway? What have you and that friend of yours been up to?'

Florence knotted the bandage around his leg and murmured something to him. He took his hands out of the basin. There was a smell of antiseptic.

'Is it bad?' I said.

He held out his hands, palms upward. Blood continued to ooze from the raw flesh. Honourable wounds? Would these count on the roll as honourable wounds, wounds of war? Together we regarded the bleeding hands. I had the impression he was holding back tears. A child, no more than a child, playing on a bicycle.

'Your friend,' I said – 'Don't you think his parents should know?'

'I can phone,' said Florence.

Florence telephoned. A long, loud conversation. 'Woodstock Hospital,' I heard.

Hours later there was a call from a public telephone, a woman wanting Florence.

'He is not in the hospital,' Florence reported.

'Was that his mother?' I asked.

'His grannie.'

I telephoned Woodstock Hospital. 'You won't have his name, he was unconscious when they took him,' I said.

'No record of such a patient,' said the man.

'He had a terrible gash across the forehead.'

'No record,' he repeated. I gave up.

'They work with the police,' said Bheki. 'They are all the same, the ambulances, the doctors, the police.'

'That is nonsense,' I said.

'Nobody trusts the ambulance any more. They are always talking to the police on their radios.'

'Nonsense.'

He smiled a smile not without charm, relishing this chance to lecture me, to tell me about real life. I, the old woman who lived in a shoe, who had no children and didn't know what to do. 'It is true,' he said – 'listen and you will hear.'

'Why are the police after you?'

'They are not after me. They are after everybody. I have done nothing. But anybody they see they think should be in school, they try to get them. We do nothing, we just say we are not going to school. Now they are waging this terror against us. They are terrorists.'

'Why won't you go to school?'

'What is school for? It is to make us fit into the apartheid system.'

Shaking my head, I turned to Florence. There was a tight little smile on her lips which she did not bother to hide. Her son was winning hands down. Well, let him. 'I am too old for this,' I said to her. 'I can't believe you want your son out on the streets killing time till apartheid comes to an end. Apartheid is not going to die tomorrow or the next day. He is ruining his future.'

'What is more important, that apartheid must be destroyed or that I must go to school?' asked Bheki, challenging me, smelling victory.

'That is not the choice,' I answered wearily. But was I right? If that was not the choice, what was the choice? 'I will take you to Woodstock,' I offered. 'But then we must leave at once.'

When Florence saw Vercueil waiting, she bridled. But I insisted. 'He must come along in case I have trouble with the car,' I said.

So I drove them to Woodstock, Vercueil beside me smelling worse than ever, somehow smelling miserable too, Florence and Bheki silent in the back. The car struggled up the gentle slope to the hospital; for once I had the presence of mind to park pointing downhill.

'I tell you, there is no such person here,' said the man at the desk. 'If you don't believe me, go and look in the wards.'

Tired though I was, I trailed through the male wards behind Florence and Bheki. It was the hour of the siesta; doves were calling softly from the trees outside. We saw no black boys with bandaged heads, only old white men in pyjamas staring emptily at the ceiling while the radio played soothing music. My secret brothers, I thought: this is where I belong.

'If they didn't bring him here, where would they have taken him?' I asked at the desk.

'Try Groote Schuur.'

The parking lot at Groote Schuur was full. For half an hour we sat at the gate with the engine idling, Florence and her son talking softly together, Vercueil blank-eyed, I yawning. Like a sleepy weekend in South Africa, I thought; like taking the family for a drive. We could have played a word-game to pass the time, but what chance was there of enlisting those three? Word-games, from a past that I alone could look back to with nostalgia, when we of the middle classes, the comfortable classes, passed our Sundays roaming the country-side from beauty-spot to beauty-spot, bringing the afternoon to a close with tea and scones and strawberry jam and cream in a tea-room with a nice view, preferably westward over the sea.

A car came out, we went in. 'I'll stay here,' said Vercueil.

'Where would someone with concussion be taken?' I asked the clerk.

Down long, crowded corridors we passed looking for ward C–5. We crammed ourselves into a lift with four Moslem women wearing veils, carrying dishes of food. Bheki, self-conscious about his bandaged hands, held them behind his back. Through C–5, through C–6, and no sign of the boy. Florence stopped a nurse. 'Try the new wing,' she suggested. Exhausted, I shook my head. 'I can't walk any further,' I said. 'You and Bheki go on; I will meet you at the car.'

It was true, I was tired, my hip ached, my heart was thumping, there was an unpleasant taste in my mouth. But there was more to it than that. I was seeing too many sick old people, and too suddenly. They oppressed me, oppressed and intimidated me. Black and white, men and women, they shuffled about the corridors, watching each other covetously, eyeing me as I approached, catching unerringly on me the smell of death. 'Impostor!' they seemed to whisper, ready to grasp my arm, draw me back: 'Do you think you can come and go here as you please? Don't you know the rule? This is

· 63 ·

the house of shadow and suffering through which you must pass on the way to death. That is the sentence passed upon all: a term in prison before the execution.' Old hounds patrolling the corridors, seeing that none of the condemned flee back to the air, the light, the bounteous world above. Hades this place, and I a fugitive shade. I shuddered as I passed through the doorway.

In silence we waited in the car, Vercueil and I, like a couple married too long, talked out, grumpy. I am even getting used to the smell, I thought. Is this how I feel toward South Africa: not loving it but habituated to its bad smell? Marriage is fate. What we marry we become. We who marry South Africa become South Africans: ugly, sullen, torpid, the only sign of life in us a quick flash of fangs when we are crossed. South Africa: a bad-tempered old hound snoozing in the doorway, taking its time to die. And what an uninspired name for a country! Let us hope they change it when they make their fresh start.

A group of nurses passed, laughing, gay, their shift over. It is their ministrations I have been evading, I thought. What a relief it would be to give myself up to them now! Clean sheets, brisk hands on my body, a release from pain, a release into helplessness – what is it that keeps me from yielding? I felt a constriction in my throat, a welling up of tears, and turned my face away. A passing shower, I told myself – English weather. But the truth is, I cry more and more easily, with less and less shame. I knew a woman once (do you mind if your mother talks of these things?) to whom pleasure, orgasm came very easily. Orgasms would pass through her, she said, like little shudders, one after another, rippling her body like water. How would it be, I used to wonder, to live in a body like that? To be turned to water: is that what bliss is? Now I have an answer of a kind in these flurries of tears, these deliquescences of mine. Tears not of sorrow but of sadness. A light, fickle sadness: the blues, but not the dark blues: the pale blues, rather, of far skies, clear winter days. A private matter, a disturbance of the pool of the soul, which I take less and less trouble to hide.

I dried my eyes, blew my nose. 'You needn't be embarrassed,' I said to Vercueil. 'I cry without reason. Thank you for coming along.'

'I don't see what you need me for,' he said.

'It is hard to be alone all the time. That's all. I didn't choose you, but you are the one who is here, and that will have to do. You arrived. It's like having a child. You can't choose the child. It just arrives.'

Looking away, he gave a slow, crafty smile.

'Besides,' I said, 'you push the car. If I couldn't use the car I would be trapped at home.'

'All you need is a new battery.'

'I don't want a new battery. You don't understand that, do you? Do I have to explain? This car is old, it belongs to a world that barely exists any more, but it works. What is left of that world, what still works, I am trying to hold on to. Whether I love it or hate it does not matter. The fact is, I belong to it as I do not belong, thank God, to what it has become. It is a world in which cars cannot be depended on to start whenever you want them to. In my world you try the self-starter. If that does not work you try the crank-handle. If that does not work you get someone to push. And if the car still does not start you get on your bicycle or walk or stay at home. That is how things are in the world where I belong. I am comfortable there, it is a world I understand. I don't see why I should change.'

Vercueil said nothing.

'And if you think I am a fossil from the past,' I added, 'it is time you took a look at yourself. You have seen what the children of today think of drinking and lying around and *leeglopery*. Be warned. In the South Africa of the future everyone will have to work, including you. You may not

· 65 ·

like the prospect, but you had better prepare yourself for it.'

Darkness was falling over the parking lot. Where was Florence? The pain in my back was wearing me down. It was past the time for my pills.

I thought of the empty house, the long night yawning before me. Tears came again, easy tears.

I spoke: 'I told you about my daughter in America. My daughter is everything to me. I have not told her the truth, the whole truth about my condition. She knows I was sick, she knows I had an operation; she thinks it was successful and I am getting better. When I lie in bed at night and stare into the black hole into which I am falling, all that keeps me sane is the thought of her. I say to myself: I have brought a child into the world, I have seen her to womanhood, I have seen her safely to a new life: that I have done, that can never be taken from me. That thought is the pillar I cling to when the storms hit me.

'There is a little ritual I go through sometimes, that helps me to stay calm. I say to myself: It is two in the morning here, on this side of the world, therefore it is six in the evening there, on her side. Imagine it: six in the evening. Now imagine the rest. Imagine everything. She has just come in from work. She hangs up her coat. She opens the refrigerator and takes out a packet of frozen peas. She empties the peas into a bowl. She takes two onions and begins to peel them. Imagine the peas, imagine the onions. Imagine the world in which she is doing these things, a world with its own smells and sounds. Imagine a summer evening in North America, with gnats at the screen door, children calling from down the street. Imagine my daughter in her house, in her life, with an onion in one hand, in a land where she will live and die in peace. The hours pass, in that land and this one and all the rest of the world, at the same pace. Imagine them passing. They pass: here it grows light, there it grows dark. She goes to bed; drowsily she lies beside the body of her husband in their bed of marriage in their peaceful country. I think of her body, still, solid, alive, at peace, escaped. I ache to embrace her. "I am so thankful," I want to say, from a full heart. I also want to say, but never do: "Save me!"

'Do you understand? Do you understand?'

The car door was open. Vercueil leaned away from me, his head against the doorpost, one foot on the ground. He sighed a heavy sigh; I heard it. Wishing for Florence to return and rescue him, no doubt. How tedious these confessions, these pleas, these demands!

'Because that is something one should never ask of a child,' I went on: 'to enfold one, comfort one, save one. The comfort, the love should flow forward, not backward. That is a rule, another of the iron rules. When an old person begins to plead for love everything turns squalid. Like a parent trying to creep into bed with a child: unnatural.

'Yet how hard it is to sever oneself from that living touch, from all the touches that unite us with the living! Like a steamer pulling away from the quay, the ribbons tightening, snapping, falling away. Setting off on a last voyage. The dear departed. It is all so sad, so sad! When those nurses passed us a little while ago I was on the point of getting out of the car and giving up, surrendering to the hospital again, letting myself be undressed and put to bed and ministered to by their hands. It is their hands above all that I find myself craving. The touch of hands. Why else do we hire them, these girls, these children, if not to touch, to stroke, in that brisk way of theirs, flesh that has grown old and unlovable? Why do we give them lamps and call them angels? Because they come in the dead of night to tell us it is time to go? Perhaps. But also because they put out a hand to renew a touch that has been broken.'

'Tell this to your daughter,' said Vercueil quietly. 'She will come.'

'No.'

'Tell her right now. Phone her in America. Tell her you need her here.'

'No.'

'Then don't tell her afterwards, when it is too late. She won't forgive you.'

The rebuke was like a slap in the face.

'There are things you don't understand,' I said. 'I have no intention of summoning my daughter back. I may long for her but I don't want her here. That is why it is called longing. It has to go a long way. To the ends of the earth.'

To his credit, he was not deflected by this nonsense. 'You have to choose,' he said. 'Tell her or don't tell her.'

'I won't tell her, you can be sure,' I said (what a liar I am!). Something was rising in my voice, a tone I could not control. 'Let me remind you, this is not a normal country. People can't just come and go as they wish.'

He did nothing to help me.

'My daughter will not come back till things have changed here. She has made a vow. She will not come back to South Africa as you and she and I know it. She will certainly not apply to – what can I call them? – *those people* for permission to come. She will come back when they are hanging by their heels from the lamp-posts, she says. She will come back then to throw stones at their bodies and dance in the streets.'

Vercueil showed his teeth in a broad grin. Yellow horse-teeth. An old horse.

'You don't believe me,' I said, 'but perhaps one day you will meet her, and then you will see. She is like iron. I am not going to ask her to go back on her vows.'

'You are like iron too,' he said, to me.

A silence fell between us. Inside me something broke.

'Something broke inside me when you said that,' I said, the words just coming. I did not know how to go on. 'If I were made of iron, surely I would not break so easily,' I said.

The four women we had met in the lift crossed the lot,

escorted by a little man in a blue suit and white skullcap. He ushered them into a car and drove them off.

'Did your daughter do something, that she had to leave?' said Vercueil.

'No, she didn't do anything. She had simply had enough. She went away; she didn't come back. She made another life for herself. She got married and started a family. It was the best thing to do, the sensible thing.'

'But she hasn't forgotten.'

'No, she hasn't forgotten. Though who am I to say? Perhaps one does forget, slowly. I can't imagine it, but perhaps it does happen. She says, "I was born in Africa, in South Africa." I have heard her use that phrase in conversation. It sounds to me like the first half of a sentence. There ought to be a second half, but it never comes. So it hangs in the air like a lost twin. "I was born in South Africa and will never see it again." "I was born in South Africa and will one day return." Which is the lost twin?'

'So she is an exile?'

'No, she is not an exile. I am the exile.'

He was learning to talk to me. He was learning to lead me on. I felt an urge to interrupt: 'It is such a pleasure!' I wanted to say. After long silence it is such a pleasure: tears come to the eyes.

'I don't know whether you have children. I don't even know whether it is the same for a man. But when you bear a child from your own body you give your life to that child. Above all to the first child, the firstborn. Your life is no longer with you, it is no longer yours, it is with the child. That is why we do not really die: we simply pass on our life, the life that was for a while in us, and are left behind. I am just a shell, as you can see, the shell my child has left behind. It doesn't matter what happens to me. It doesn't matter what happens to old people. Still – I say the words, I cannot expect you to understand, but never mind – it is frightening to be on the edge of leaving. Even if it is only the touch of fingertip to fingertip: one does not want to let go.'

Florence and her son were crossing the car-park now, walking swiftly towards us.

'You should have gone to stay with her,' said Vercueil.

I smiled. 'I can't afford to die in America,' I said. 'No one can, except Americans.'

Florence got vehemently into the back seat; the car rocked as she settled down.

'Did you find him?' I asked.

'Yes,' she replied. Her face was like thunder. Bheki got in beside her.

'And?' I said.

'Yes, we found him, he is in this hospital,' said Florence.

'And he is well?'

'Yes, he is well.'

'Good,' I snapped. 'Thank you for telling me.'

We drove off in silence. Only when we got home did Florence have her say. 'They have put him with the old men in the hospital. It is too terrible. There is one who is mad, who is shouting and swearing all the time, the nurses are afraid to go near him. They should not put a child in a room like that. It is not a hospital where he is, it is a waiting-room for the funeral.'

A waiting-room for the funeral: I could not get the words out of my mind. I tried to eat but had no appetite.

I found Vercueil in the woodshed doing something to a shoe by candlelight. 'I am going back to the hospital,' I said: 'Will you come with me?'

The ward Florence had described was at the far end of the old building, reached by going down to the basement, past the kitchens, then up again.

It was true. A man with a shaven skull, thin as a rake, was sitting up in bed, beating his palms on his thighs and chanting in a loud voice. A broad black strap passed around his middle and under the bed. What was he singing? The words belonged to no tongue I knew of. I stood in the doorway unable to enter, fearing that at any moment he would fix me with his gaze, stop singing, raise one of those skeletal black arms and point.

'DTs,' said Vercueil. 'He's got the DTs.'

'No, it's worse than that,' I whispered.

Vercueil took my elbow. I let him lead me in.

There was a long table down the middle of the ward with a jumble of trays on it. Someone was coughing soggily as though his lungs were full of milk. 'In the corner,' said Vercueil.

He did not know who we were, nor did I easily recognize the boy whose blood had stuck my fingers together. His head was bandaged, his face puffy, his left arm strapped against his chest. He wore pale blue hospital pyjamas.

'Don't talk,' I said. 'We have just come to make sure you are all right.'

He opened the swollen lips and closed them again.

'Do you remember me? I am the woman Bheki's mother works for. I was watching this morning: I saw everything that happened. You must get well quickly. I have brought you some fruit.' On the cabinet I placed the fruit: an apple, a pear.

His expression did not change.

I did not like him. I do not like him. I look into my heart and nowhere do I find any trace of feeling for him. As there are people to whom one spontaneously warms, so there are people to whom one is, from the first, cold. That is all. This boy is not like Bheki. He has no charm. There is something stupid about him, something deliberately stupid, obstructive, intractable. He is one of those boys whose voices deepen too early, who by the age of twelve have left childhood behind and turned brutal, knowing. A simplified person, simplified in every way: swifter, nimbler, more tireless than real people,

without doubts or scruples, without humour, ruthless, inno-
cent. While he lay in the street, while I thought he was dying,
I did what I could for him. But, to be candid, I would rather
I had spent myself on someone else.

I remember a cat I once nursed, an old ginger tom whose
jaw was locked shut by an abscess. I took him in when he
was too weak to resist, fed him milk through a tube, dosed
him with antibiotics. When he got back his strength I set him
free, but continued to put out food for him. For a year, on
and off, I saw him in the neighbourhood; for a year the food
was taken. Then he vanished for good. In all this time he
treated me without compromise as one of the enemy. Even
when he was at his weakest his body was hard, tense, resistant
under my hand. Around this boy I now felt the same wall of
resistance. Though his eyes were open, he did not see; what
I said he did not hear.

I turned to Vercueil. 'Shall we go?' I said. And on an
impulse – no, more than that, with a conscious effort not to
block the stirring of the impulse – I touched the boy's free
hand.

It was not a clasp, not a long touch; it was the merest brush,
the merest lingering of my fingertips on the back of his hand.
But I felt him stiffen, felt an angry electric recoil.

For your mother, who is not here, I said within myself.
Aloud I said: 'Be slow to judge.'

Be slow to judge: what did I mean? If I did not know, who
else could be expected to? Certainly not he. Yet in his case, I
was sure, the incomprehension ran deeper. My words fell off
him like dead leaves the moment they were uttered. The
words of a woman, therefore negligible; of an old woman,
therefore doubly negligible; but above all of a white.

I, a white. When I think of the whites, what do I see? I see
a herd of sheep (not a flock: a herd) milling around on a dusty
plain under the baking sun. I hear a drumming of hooves, a
confusion of sound which resolves itself, when the ear grows

attuned, into the same bleating call in a thousand different inflections: 'I!' 'I!' 'I!' And, cruising among them, bumping them aside with their bristling flanks, lumbering, saw-toothed, red-eyed, the savage, unreconstructed old boars grunting 'Death!' 'Death!' Though it does me no good, I flinch from the white touch as much as he does; would even flinch from the old white woman who pats his hand if she were not I.

I tried again.

'Before I retired,' I said, 'I was a teacher. I taught at the university.'

Vercueil eyed me keenly from the other side of the bed. But I was not talking to him.

'If you had been in my Thucydides class,' I went on, 'you might have learned something about what can happen to our humanity in time of war. Our humanity, that we are born with, that we are born into.'

There was something smoky about the boy's eyes: the whites without lustre, the pupils flat, dark, like printer's ink. Though he may have been sedated, he knew I was there, knew who I was, knew I was talking to him. He knew and he did not listen, as he had never listened to any of his teachers, but had sat like a stone in the classroom, impervious to words, waiting for the bell to ring, biding his time.

'Thucydides wrote of people who made rules and followed them. Going by rule they killed entire classes of enemies without exception. Most of those who died felt, I am sure, that a terrible mistake was being made, that, whatever the rule was, it could not be meant for them. "I! –": that was their last word as their throats were cut. A word of protest: I, the exception.

'Were they exceptions? The truth is, given time to speak, we would all claim to be exceptions. For each of us there is a case to be made. We all deserve the benefit of the doubt.

'But there are times when there is no time for all that close listening, all those exceptions, all that mercy. There is no time, so we fall back on the rule. And that is a great pity, the greatest pity. That is what you could have learned from Thucydides. It is a great pity when we find ourselves entering upon times like those. We should enter upon them with a sinking heart. They are by no means to be welcomed.'

Quite deliberately he put his good hand under the sheet, in case I should touch it again.

'Good night,' I said. 'I hope you sleep well and feel better in the morning.'

The old man had stopped chanting. His hands flapped loosely on his thighs like dying fish. His eyes were rolled back, there were streaks of spittle on his chin.

The car would not start, and Vercueil had to push.

'That boy is different from Bheki, quite different,' I said, talking too much now, a little out of control. 'I try not to show it, but he makes me nervous. I am sorry Bheki has fallen under his influence. But there are hundreds of thousands like him, I suppose. More than there are like Bheki. The rising generation.'

We got home. Uninvited, he followed me in.

'I have to sleep, I am exhausted,' I said; and then, when he made no move to leave: 'Do you want something to eat?'

I put food in front of him, took my pills, waited.

Holding the loaf of bread with his bad hand, he cut a slice, buttered it thickly, cut cheese. His fingernails filthy. Who knows what else he had been touching. And this is the one to whom I speak my heart, whom I trust with last things. Why this crooked path to you?

My mind like a pool, which his finger enters and stirs. Without that finger stillness, stagnation.

A way of indirection. By indirection I find direction out. A crab's-walk.

His dirty fingernail entering me.

'You look grey,' he said.

· 74 ·

'I am tired.'

He chewed, showing long teeth.

He watches but does not judge. Always a faint haze of alcohol about him. Alcohol, that softens, preserves. *Mollificans*. That helps us to forgive. He drinks and makes allowances. His life all allowances. He, Mr V, to whom I speak. Speak and then write. Speak in order to write. While to the rising generation, who do not drink, I cannot speak, can only lecture. Their hands clean, their fingernails clean. The new puritans, holding to the rule, holding up the rule. Abhorring alcohol, that softens the rule, dissolves iron. Suspicious of all that is idle, yielding, roundabout. Suspicious of devious discourse, like this.

'And I am sick too,' I said. 'Sick and tired, tired and sick. I have a child inside that I cannot give birth to. Cannot because it will not be born. Because it cannot live outside me. So it is my prisoner or I am its prisoner. It beats on the gate but it cannot leave. That is what is going on all the time. The child inside is beating at the gate. My daughter is my first child. She is my life. This is the second one, the afterbirth, the unwanted. Would you like to watch television?'

'I thought you wanted to sleep.'

'No, I would rather not be alone now. The one inside isn't beating so hard, anyway. He has had his pill, he is getting drowsy. The dose is always two pills, you notice, one for me, one for him.'

We sat down side by side on the sofa. A ruddy-faced man was being interviewed. He owned a game farm, it appeared, and rented out lions and elephants to film companies.

'Tell us about some of the overseas personalities you have met,' said the interviewer.

'I'm going to make some tea,' I said, getting up.

'Is there anything else in the house?' said Vercueil.

'Sherry.'

When I returned with the sherry bottle he was standing at

the bookshelf. I switched off the television. 'What are you looking at?' I asked.

He held up one of the heavy quartos.

'You will find that book interesting,' I said. 'The woman who wrote it travelled through Palestine and Syria disguised as a man. In the last century. One of those intrepid English-women. But she didn't do the pictures. They were done by a professional illustrator.'

Together we paged through the book. By some trick of perspective the illustrator had given to moonlit encampments, desert crags, ruined temples an air of looming mystery. No one has done that for South Africa: made it into a land of mystery. Too late now. Fixed in the mind as a place of flat, hard light, without shadows, without depth.

'Read whatever you like,' I said. 'There are many more books upstairs. Do you like reading?'

Vercueil put down the book. 'I'll go to bed now,' he said.

Again a flicker of embarrassment passed across me. Why? Because, to be candid, I do not like the way he smells. Because Vercueil in his underwear I prefer not to think of. The feet worst of all: the horny, caked toenails.

'Can I ask you a question?' I said. 'Where did you live before? Why did you start wandering?'

'I was at sea,' said Vercueil. 'I told you that.'

'But one doesn't live at sea. One isn't born at sea. You haven't been at sea all your life.'

'I was on trawlers.'

'And?'

He shook his head.

'I am just asking,' I said. 'We like to know a little about the people near to us. It's quite natural.'

He gave that crooked smile of his in which one canine suddenly reveals itself, long and yellow. You are hiding something, I thought, but what? A tragic love? A prison sentence? And I broke into a smile myself.

So we stood smiling, the two of us, each with our private cause to smile.

'If you prefer,' I said, 'you can sleep on the sofa again.'

He looked dubious. 'The dog is used to sleeping with me.'

'You didn't have the dog with you last night.'

'He will carry on if I don't come.'

I heard no carrying on by the dog last night. As long as he feeds it, does the dog really care where he sleeps? I suspect he uses the fiction of the anxious dog as other men use the fiction of the anxious wife. On the other hand, perhaps it is because of the dog that I trust him. Dogs, that sniff out what is good, what evil: patrollers of boundaries: sentries.

The dog has not warmed to me. Too much cat-smell. Cat-woman: Circe. And he, after roaming the seas in trawlers, making landfall here.

'As you please,' I said, and let him out, pretending not to notice he still had the sherry-bottle.

A pity, I thought (my last thought before the pills took me away): we could set up house, the two of us, after a fashion, I upstairs, he downstairs, for this last little while. So that there will be someone at hand in the nights. For that is, after all, what one wants in the end: someone to be there, to call to in the dark. Mother, or whoever is prepared to stand in for mother.

Since I had declared to Florence I would do so, I visited Caledon Square and tried to lay a charge against the two policemen. But laying a charge, it appears, is permitted only to 'parties directly affected.'

'Give us the particulars and we will investigate,' said the desk officer. 'What are the names of the two boys?'

'I can't give you their names without their permission.'

He put down his pen. A young man, very neat and correct, one of the new breed of policeman. Whose training is rounded off with a stint in Cape Town to strengthen their self-control in the face of liberal-humanist posturing.

'I don't know whether you take any pride in that uniform,' I said, 'but your colleagues on the street are disgracing it. They are also disgracing me. I am ashamed. Not for them: for myself. You won't let me lay a charge because you say I am not affected. But I am affected, very directly affected. Do you understand what I am saying?'

He did not reply, but stood stiffly erect, wary, ready for whatever might come next. The man behind him bent over his papers, pretending not to listen. But there was nothing to fear. I had no more to say, or at least not the presence of mind to think of more.

Vercueil sat in the car in Buitenkant Street. 'I made such a fool of myself,' I said, suddenly on the edge of tears again. ' "You make me feel ashamed," I told them. They are probably still laughing among themselves. *Die ou kruppel dame met die kaffertjies.* Yet how else can one feel? Perhaps I should simply accept that that is how one must live from now on: in a state of shame. Perhaps shame is nothing more than the name for the way I feel all the time. The name for the way in which people live who would prefer to be dead.'

Shame. Mortification. Death in life.

There was a long silence.

'Can I borrow ten rand?' said Vercueil. 'My disability comes through on Thursday. I'll pay you back then.'

· III ·

In the small hours of last
night there was a telephone call. A woman, breathless,
with the breathlessness of fat people. 'I want to speak to
Florence.'

'She is sleeping. Everyone is sleeping.'

'Yes, you can call her.'

It was raining, though not hard. I knocked at Florence's
door. At once it opened, as if she had been standing there
waiting for the summons. From behind her came the sleepy
groan of a child. 'Telephone,' I said.

Five minutes later she came up to my room. Without her
glasses, bareheaded, in a long white nightdress, she seemed
much younger.

'There is trouble,' she said.

'Is it Bheki?'

'Yes, I must go.'

'Where is he?'

'First I must go to Guguletu, then after that, I think, to
Site C.'

'I have no idea where Site C is.'

She gave me a puzzled look.

'I mean, if you can show me the way I will take you by
car,' I said.

'Yes,' she said, but still hesitated. 'But I cannot leave the children alone.'

'Then they must come along.'

'Yes,' she said. I could not remember ever seeing her so indecisive.

'And Mr Vercueil,' I said: 'he must come to help with the car.'

She shook her head.

'Yes,' I insisted: 'he must come.'

The dog lay at Vercueil's side. It tapped its tail on the floor when I came in but did not get up.

'Mr Vercueil!' I said loudly. He opened his eyes; I held the light away. He broke wind. 'I have to take Florence to Guguletu. It is urgent, we have to leave at once. Will you come along?'

He made no reply, but curled up on his side. The dog rearranged itself.

'Mr Vercueil!' I said, pointing the light at him.

'Fuck off,' he mumbled.

'I can't wake him,' I reported to Florence. 'I have to have someone along to push the car.'

'I will push,' she said.

With the two children on the back seat warmly covered, Florence pushed. We set off. Peering through glass misted over with our breathing, I crawled over De Waal Drive, got lost for a while in the streets of Claremont, then found Lansdowne Road. The first buses of the day were abroad, brightly lit and empty. It was not yet five o'clock.

We passed the last houses, the last streetlights. Into a steady rain from the north-west we drove, following the faint yellow glow of our headlights.

'If people wave to you to stop, or if you see things in the road, you must not stop, you must drive on,' said Florence.

'I will certainly not,' I said. 'You should have warned me

earlier. Let me make myself clear, Florence: at the first sign of trouble I am turning back.'

'I do not say it will happen, I am just telling you.'

Full of misgiving I drove on into the darkness. But no one barred the way, no one waved, there was nothing across the road. Trouble, it seemed, was still in bed; trouble was recuperating for the next engagement. The roadside, along which, at this hour, thousands of men would ordinarily have been plodding to work, was empty. Swirls of mist floated toward us, embraced the car, floated away. Wraiths, spirits. Aornos this place: birdless. I shivered, met Florence's gaze. 'How much further?' I asked.

'Not far.'

'What did they say on the telephone?'

'They were shooting again yesterday. They were giving guns to the *witdoeke* and the *witdoeke* were shooting.'

'Are they shooting in Guguletu?'

'No, they are shooting out in the bush.'

'At the first hint of trouble, Florence, I am turning back. We are fetching Bheki, that is all we are going to do, then we are going home. You should never have let him leave.'

'Yes, but you must turn here, you must turn left.'

I turned. A hundred metres further there was a barrier across the road with flashing lights, cars parked along the verges, police with guns. I stopped; a policeman came up.

'What is your business here?' he asked.

'I am taking my domestic home,' I said, surprised at how calmly I lied.

He peered at the children sleeping on the back seat. 'Where does she live?'

'Fifty-seven,' said Florence.

'You can drop her here, she can walk, it is not far.'

'It is raining, she has small children, I am not letting her walk alone,' I said firmly.

He hesitated, then with his flashlight waved me through.

· 83 ·

On the roof of one of the cars stood a young man in battle-dress, his gun at the ready, staring out into the darkness.

Now there was a smell of burning in the air, of wet ash, burning rubber. Slowly we drove down a broad unpaved street lined with matchbox-houses. A police van armoured in wire mesh cruised past us. 'Turn right here,' said Florence. 'Turn right again. Stop here.'

With the baby on her arm and the little girl, only half awake, stumbling behind, she splashed up the path to No. 219, knocked, was admitted. Hope and Beauty. It was like living in an allegory. Keeping the engine running, I waited.

The police van that had passed us drew up alongside. A light shone in my face. I held up a hand to shield my eyes. The van pulled away.

Florence re-emerged holding a plastic raincoat over herself and the baby, and got into the back seat. Dashing through the rain behind her came not Bheki but a man in his thirties or forties, slight, dapper, with a moustache. He got in beside me. 'This is Mr Thabane my cousin,' said Florence. 'He will show us the way.'

'Where is Hope?' I asked.

'I have left her with my sister.'

'And where is Bheki?'

There was silence.

'I am not sure,' said the man. His voice was surprisingly soft. 'He came in yesterday morning and put his things down and went out. After that we did not see him at all. He did not come home to sleep. But I know where his friends live. We can start looking there.'

'Is this what you want, Florence?' I asked.

'We must look for him,' said Florence: 'there is nothing else we can do.'

'If you would prefer me to drive I can drive,' said the man. 'It is anyhow better, you know.'

I got out and sat beside Florence in the back. The rain was

· 84 ·

coming down more heavily now; the car splashed through pools on the uneven road. Left and right we turned under the sick orange of the streetlights, then stopped. 'Careful, don't switch off,' I said to Mr Thabane the cousin.

He got out and knocked at a window. A long conversation followed with someone I could not see. By the time he came back he was soaked and cold. With clumsy fingers he took out a pack of cigarettes and tried to light one. 'Please, not in the car,' I said. A look of exasperation passed between him and Florence.

We sat in silence. 'What are we waiting for?' I asked.

'They are sending someone to show us the way.'

A little boy wearing a balaclava cap too large for him came trotting out of the house. With entire self-assurance, greeting us all with a smile, he got into the car and began to give directions. Ten years old at most. A child of the times, at home in this landscape of violence. When I think back to my own childhood I remember only long sun-struck afternoons, the smell of dust under avenues of eucalyptus, the quiet rustle of water in roadside furrows, the lulling of doves. A childhood of sleep, prelude to what was meant to be a life without trouble and a smooth passage to Nirvana. Will we at least be allowed our Nirvana, we children of that bygone age? I doubt it. If justice reigns at all, we will find ourselves barred at the first threshold of the underworld. White as grubs in our swaddling bands, we will be dispatched to join those infant souls whose eternal whining Aeneas mistook for weeping. White our colour, the colour of limbo: white sands, white rocks, a white light pouring down from all sides. Like an eternity of lying on the beach, an endless Sunday among thousands of our own kind, sluggish, half asleep, in earshot of the comfortable lap of the waves. *In limine primo*: on the threshold of death, the threshold of life. Creatures thrown up by the sea, stalled on the sands, undecided, indecisive, neither hot nor cold, neither fish nor fowl.

We had passed the last of the houses and were driving in grey early-morning light through a landscape of scorched earth, blackened trees. A pickup truck passed us with three men in the back sheltering under a tarpaulin. At the next road-block we caught up with them again. They gazed expressionlessly at us, eye to eye, as we waited to be inspected. A policeman waved them through, waved us through too.

We turned north, away from the mountain, then off the highway on to a dirt road that soon became sand. Mr Thabane stopped. 'We can't drive further, it is too dangerous,' he said. 'There is something wrong with your alternator,' he added, pointing to the red light glowing on the dashboard.

'I am letting things run down,' I said. I did not feel like explaining.

He switched off the engine. For a while we sat listening to the rain drumming on the roof. Then Florence got out, and the boy. Tied on her back, the baby slept peacefully.

'It is best if you keep the doors locked,' said Mr Thabane to me.

'How long will you be?'

'I cannot say, but we will hurry.'

I shook my head. 'I am not staying here,' I said.

I had no hat, no umbrella. The rain beat against my face, pasted my hair to my scalp, ran down my neck. From this sort of outing, I thought, one catches one's death of cold. The boy, our guide, had already dashed ahead.

'Put this over your head,' said Mr Thabane, offering the plastic raincoat.

'Nonsense,' I said, 'I don't mind a little rain.'

'Still, hold it over you,' he insisted. I understood. 'Come,' he said. I followed.

Around us was a wilderness of grey dune-sand and Port Jackson willow, and a stench of garbage and ash. Shreds of plastic, old iron, glass, animal bones littered both sides of the path. I was already shivering with cold, but when I tried to walk faster my heart pounded unpleasantly. I was falling behind. Would Florence pause? No: *amor matris*, a force that stopped for nothing.

At a fork in the path Mr Thabane was waiting. 'Thank you,' I gasped, 'you are kind. I am sorry to be holding you up. I have a bad hip.'

'Take my arm,' he said.

Men passed us, dark, bearded, stern, armed with sticks, walking swiftly in single file. Mr Thabane stepped off the path. I held tighter to him.

The path widened, then came to an end in a wide, flat pond. On the far side of the pond the shanties started, the lowest-lying cluster surrounded by water, flooded. Some built sturdily of wood and iron, others no more than skins of plastic sheeting over frames of branches, they straggled north over the dunes as far as I could see.

At the brink of the pond I hesitated. 'Come,' said Mr Thabane. Holding on to him I stepped in, and we waded across, in water up to our ankles. One of my shoes was sucked off. 'Watch out for broken glass,' he warned. I retrieved the shoe.

Save for an old woman with a sagging mouth standing in a doorway, there was no one in sight. But as we walked further the noise we had heard, which at first might have been taken for wind and rain, began to break up into shouts, cries, calls, over a ground-bass which I can only call a sigh: a deep sigh, repeated over and over, as if the wide world itself were sighing.

Then the little boy, our guide, was with us again, tugging Mr Thabane's sleeve, talking excitedly. The two of them broke away; I struggled behind them up the duneside.

We were at the rear of a crowd hundreds strong looking down upon a scene of devastation: shanties burnt and smouldering, shanties still burning, pouring forth black smoke. Jumbles of furniture, bedding, household objects stood in the pouring rain. Gangs of men were at work trying to rescue the contents of the burning shacks, going from one to another, putting out the fires; or so I thought till with a shock it came to me that these were no rescuers but incendiaries, that the battle I saw them waging was not with the flames but with the rain.

It was from the people gathered on the rim of this amphitheatre in the dunes that the sighing came. Like mourners at a funeral they stood in the downpour, men, women and children, sodden, hardly bothering to protect themselves, watching the destruction.

A man in a black overcoat swung an axe. With a crash a window burst. He attacked the door, which caved in at the third blow. As if released from a cage, a woman with a baby in her arms flew out of the house, followed by three barefoot children. He let them pass. Then he began to hack at the door-frame. The whole structure creaked.

One of his fellows stepped inside carrying a jerry-can. The woman dashed in after him, emerged with her arms full of bedclothes. But when she tried to make a second foray she was hurled out bodily.

A new sigh rose from the crowd. Wisps of smoke began to blow from inside the shack. The woman got to her feet, dashed indoors, was again hurled out.

A stone came sailing out of the crowd and fell with a clatter on the roof of the burning shack. Another hit the wall, another landed at the feet of the man with the axe. He gave a menacing shout. He and half a dozen of his fellows stopped what they were doing and, brandishing sticks and bars, advanced on the crowd. Screaming, people turned to flee, I among them. But in the clinging sand I could barely lift my feet. My heart pounded, pains shot through my chest. I stopped, bent over, gasping. *Can this really be happening to me?* I thought. *What am I doing here?* I had a vision of the little green car waiting quietly at the roadside. There was nothing

I longed for more than to get into my car, slam the door behind me, close out this looming world of rage and violence.

A girl, an enormously fat teenager, shouldered me out of her way. 'Damn you!' I gasped as I fell. 'Damn you!' she gasped back, glaring with naked animosity: 'Get out! Get out!' And she toiled up the duneside, her huge backside quaking.

One more such blow, I thought, face down in the sand, and I am gone. These people can take many blows, but I, I am fragile as a butterfly.

Feet crunched past me. I caught a glimpse of a brown boot, the tongue flapping, the sole tied on with string. The blow I shrank from did not fall.

I got up. There was a fight of some kind going on to my left; all the people who a minute ago had been fleeing into the bush were just as suddenly pouring back. A woman screamed, high and loud. How could I get away from this terrible place? Where was the pond I had waded across, where was the path to the car? There were ponds everywhere, pools, lakes, sheets of water; there were paths everywhere, but where did they lead?

Distinctly I heard the pop of gunfire, one, two, three shots, not nearby, but not far away either.

'Come,' said a voice, and Mr Thabane strode past. 'Yes!' I gasped, and gratefully struggled after him. But I could not catch up. 'Slower, please,' I called. He waited; together he and I recrossed the pool and reached the path.

A young man came up beside us, his eyes bloodshot. 'Where are you going?' he demanded. A hard question, a hard voice.

'I am going away, I am getting away, I am out of place here,' I answered.

'We are going to fetch the car,' said Mr Thabane.

'We want to use that car,' said the young man.

'I am not letting anyone have my car,' I said.

'This is a friend of Bheki,' said Mr Thabane.

'I don't care, I am not letting him have my car.'

The young man – not a man at all, in fact, but a boy dressed like a man, bearing himself like a man – made a strange gesture: holding one hand at head-height, he struck it with the other, palm against palm, a glancing blow. What did it mean? Did it mean anything?

My back was in agony from the walking. I slowed down and stopped. 'I must get home soon,' I said. It was an appeal; I could hear the unsteadiness in my voice.

'You have seen enough?' said Mr Thabane, sounding more distant than before.

'Yes, I have seen enough. I didn't come here to see sights. I came to fetch Bheki.'

'And you want to go home?'

'Yes, I want to go home. I am in pain, I am exhausted.'

He turned and walked on. I hobbled behind. Then he stopped again. 'You want to go home,' he said. 'But what of the people who live here? When they want to go home, this is where they must go. What do you think of that?'

We stood in the rain, in the middle of the path, face to face. Passers-by stopped too, regarding me curiously, my business their business, everyone's business.

'I have no answer,' I said. 'It is terrible.'

'It is not just terrible,' he said, 'it is a crime. When you see a crime being committed in front of your eyes, what do you say? Do you say, "I have seen enough, I didn't come to see sights, I want to go home"?'

I shook my head in distress.

'No, you don't,' he said. 'Correct. Then what do you say? What sort of crime is it that you see? What is its name?'

He is a teacher, I thought: that is why he speaks so well. What he is doing to me he has practised in the classroom. It is the trick one uses to make one's own answer seem to come from the child. Ventriloquism, the legacy of Socrates, as oppressive in Africa as it was in Athens.

I glanced around the ring of spectators. Were they hostile? There was no hostility I could detect. They were merely waiting for me to say my part.

'There are many things I am sure I could say, Mr Thabane,' I said. 'But then they must truly come from me. When one speaks under duress – you should know this – one rarely speaks the truth.'

He was going to respond, but I stopped him.

'Wait. Give me a minute. I am not evading your question. There are terrible things going on here. But what I think of them I must say in my own way.'

'Then let us hear what you have to say! We are listening! We are waiting!' He raised his hands for silence. The crowd murmured approval.

'These are terrible sights,' I repeated, faltering. 'They are to be condemned. But I cannot denounce them in other people's words. I must find my own words, from myself. Otherwise it is not the truth. That is all I can say now.'

'This woman talks shit,' said a man in the crowd. He looked around. 'Shit,' he said. No one contradicted him. Already some were drifting away.

'Yes,' I said, speaking directly to him – 'you are right, what you say is true.'

He gave me a look as if I were mad.

'But what do you expect?' I went on. 'To speak of this' – I waved a hand over the bush, the smoke, the filth littering the path – 'you would need the tongue of a god.'

'Shit,' he said again, challenging me.

Mr Thabane turned and walked off. I trailed behind him. The crowd parted. In a minute the boy passed me, hurrying. Then the car came in sight.

'It is a Hillman, your car, isn't it,' said Mr Thabane. 'There can't be many left on the roads.'

I was surprised. After what had passed I thought there was a line drawn between us. But he seemed to bear no grudge.

'From the time when British was Best,' I replied. 'I am sorry if I do not make sense.'

He ignored the apology, if that is what it was. 'Was British ever best?' he asked.

'No, of course not. It was just a slogan for a while after the War. You won't remember, you were too young.'

'I was born in 1943,' he said. 'I'm forty-three. Don't you believe me?' He turned, offering me his neat good looks. Vain; but an appealing vanity.

I pulled the starter. The battery was dead. Mr Thabane and the boy got out and pushed, struggling for a footing in the sand. At last the engine caught. 'Go straight,' said the boy. I obeyed.

'Are you a teacher?' I asked Mr Thabane.

'I was a teacher. But I have left the profession temporarily. Till better times arrive. At present I sell shoes.'

'And you?' I asked the boy.

He mumbled something I did not hear.

'He is an unemployed youth,' said Mr Thabane. 'Are you not?'

The boy smiled selfconsciously. 'Turn here, just after the shops,' he said.

Alone in the wilderness stood a row of three little shops, gutted, scorched. BHAWOODIEN CASH STORE, said the one sign still legible.

'From long ago,' said Mr Thabane. 'From last year.'

We had come out on a broad dirt road. To our left stood a cluster of houses, proper houses, with brick walls and asbestos roofs and chimneys. Among them, around them, stretching into the distance across the flats, were squatter shacks.

'That building,' said the boy, pointing ahead.

It was a long, low building, a hall or school perhaps,

surrounded by a mesh fence. But great lengths of the fence
had been trampled down, and of the building itself only the
smoke-blackened walls were still standing. In front of it a
crowd had gathered. Faces turned to watch the Hillman's
approach.

'Shall I switch off?' I said.

'You can switch off, there is nothing to be afraid of,' said
Mr Thabane.

'I am not afraid,' I said. Was it true? In a sense, yes; or at
least, after the episode in the bush, I cared less what happened
to me.

'There is no need to be afraid anyway,' he continued
smoothly: 'your boys are here to protect you.' And he
pointed.

I saw them then, further down the road: three khaki-brown
troop-carriers almost merging into the trees, and, outlined
against the sky, helmeted heads.

'In case you were thinking,' he concluded, 'that this was
just a quarrel among blacks, a spot of faction-fighting. Look:
there is my sister.'

My sister he called her, not *Florence*. Perhaps I alone in all
the world called her Florence. Called her by an alias. Now I
was on ground where people were revealed in their true
names.

She stood with her back to the wall, sheltering from the
rain: a sober, respectable woman in a burgundy coat and
white knitted cap. We threaded our way toward her. Though
she gave no sign, I was sure she saw me. 'Florence!' I called.
She looked up dully. 'Have you found him?'

She nodded toward the gutted interior, then turned away,
not greeting me. Mr Thabane began to push past the throng
in the entranceway. Embarrassed, I waited. People milled
past, skirting me as though I were bad luck.

A girl in an apple-green school tunic advanced on me, her
hand raised as if to give me a slap. I flinched, but it was only

in play. Or perhaps I should say: she forbore from actually striking.

'I think you should look too,' said Mr Thabane, re-emerging, breathing fast. He went over to Florence and took her in his arms. Lifting her glasses aside, she put her head on his shoulder and burst into tears.

The inside of the hall was a mess of rubble and charred beams. Against the far wall, shielded from the worst of the rain, were five bodies neatly laid out. The body in the middle was that of Florence's Bheki. He still wore the grey flannel trousers, white shirt and maroon pullover of his school, but his feet were bare. His eyes were open and staring, his mouth open too. The rain had been beating on him for hours, on him and his comrades, not only here but wherever they had been when they met their deaths; their clothes, their very hair, had a flattened, dead look. In the corners of his eyes there were grains of sand. There was sand in his mouth.

Someone was tugging my arm. Dazed, I looked down at a little girl with wide, solemn eyes. 'Sister,' she said, 'sister . . . ,' but then did not know how to go on.

'She is asking, are you one of the sisters?' explained a woman, smiling benignly.

I did not want to be drawn away, not now. I shook my head.

'She means, are you one of the sisters from the Catholic Church,' said the woman. 'No,' she went on, speaking to the child in English, 'she is not one of the sisters.' Gently she unlocked the child's fingers from my sleeve.

Florence was surrounded by a press of people.

'Must they lie there in the rain?' I asked Mr Thabane.

'Yes, they must lie there. So that everyone can see.'

'But who did it?'

I was shaking: shivers ran up and down my body, my hands trembled. I thought of the boy's open eyes. I thought:

What did he see as his last sight on earth? I thought: This is
the worst thing I have witnessed in my life. And I thought:
Now my eyes are open and I can never close them again.

'Who did it?' said Mr Thabane. 'If you want to dig the
bullets out of their bodies, you are welcome. But I will tell
you in advance what you will find. "Made in South Africa.
SABS Approved." That is what you will find.'

'Please listen to me,' I said. 'I am not indifferent to this . . .
this war. How can I be? No bars are thick enough to keep
it out.' I felt like crying; but here, beside Florence, what
right had I? 'It lives inside me and I live inside it,' I
whispered.

Mr Thabane shrugged impatiently. His look had grown
uglier. No doubt I grow uglier too by the day. Metamorphosis, that thickens our speech, dulls our feelings, turns us
into beasts. Where on these shores does the herb grow that
will preserve us from it?

I tell you the story of this morning mindful that the story-
teller, from her office, claims the place of right. It is through
my eyes that you see; the voice that speaks in your head is
mine. Through me alone do you find yourself here on these
desolate flats, smell the smoke in the air, see the bodies of the
dead, hear the weeping, shiver in the rain. It is my thoughts
that you think, my despair that you feel, and also the first
stirrings of welcome for whatever will put an end to thought:
sleep, death. To me your sympathies flow; your heart beats
with mine.

Now, my child, flesh of my flesh, my best self, I ask you
to draw back. I tell you this story not so that you will feel
for me but so that you will learn how things are. It would be
easier for you, I know, if the story came from someone else,
if it were a stranger's voice sounding in your ear. But the fact
is, there is no one else. I am the only one. I am the one
writing: I, I. So I ask you: attend to the writing, not to me.
If lies and pleas and excuses weave among the words, listen

for them. Do not pass them over, do not forgive them easily. Read all, even this adjuration, with a cold eye.

Someone had thrown a rock through the windscreen. Big as a child's head, mute, it lay on the seat amid a scattering of glass as if it now owned the car. My first thought was: Where will I get a windscreen for a Hillman? And then: How fortunate that everything is coming to an end at the same time!

I tumbled the rock from the seat and began to pick out the loose shards from the windscreen. Now that I had something to do I felt calmer. But I was calmer too because I no longer cared if I lived. What might happen to me no longer mattered. I thought: My life may as well be waste. We shoot these people as if they are waste, but in the end it is we whose lives are not worth living.

I thought of the five bodies, of their massive, solid presence in the burned-down hall. Their ghosts have not departed, I thought, and will not depart. Their ghosts are sitting tight, in possession.

If someone had dug a grave for me there and then in the sand, and pointed, I would without a word have climbed in and lain down and folded my hands on my breast. And when the sand fell in my mouth and in the corners of my eyes I would not have lifted a finger to brush it away.

Do not read in sympathy with me. Let your heart not beat with mine.

I held out a coin through the window. There was a rush of takers. The children pushed, the engine started. Into thrust-out hands I emptied my purse.

Drawn up among the bushes where the road dwindled to a track stood the military vehicles I had seen, not three, as I had thought, but five. Under the eye of a boy in an olive rain-cape I got out of the car, so cold in my wet clothes that I might as well have been naked.

I had hoped the words I needed would just come, but they

did not. I held out my hands, palms upward. I am bereft, my hands said, bereft of speech. I come to speak but have nothing to say.

'*Wag in die motor, ek sal die polisie skakel,*' he called down to me. A boy with pimples playing this self-important, murderous game. Wait in the car, I will call the police. I shook my head, went on shaking my head. He was talking to someone beside him, someone I could not see. He was smiling. No doubt they had been watching from the beginning, had their own opinion of me. A mad old do-gooder caught in the rain, bedraggled as a hen. Were they right? Am I a do-gooder? No, I have done no good that I can think of. Am I mad? Yes, I am mad. But they are mad too. All of us running mad, possessed by devils. When madness climbs the throne, who in the land escapes contagion?

'Don't call the police, I can take care of myself,' I called. But the murmuring, the sideways looks continued. Perhaps they were already on the radio.

'What do you think you are doing?' I called up to the boy. The smile stiffened on his lips. '*What do you think you are doing?*' I shouted, my voice beginning to crack. Shocked, he stared down. Shocked to be screamed at by a white woman, and one old enough to be his grandmother.

A man in battledress came over from the next vehicle in the line. Levelly he regarded me. '*Wat is die moeilikheid?*' he asked the boy in the troop-carrier. '*Nee, niks moeilikheid nie.*' No problem. '*Net hierdie dame wat wil weet wat aangaan.*'

'This is a dangerous place to be, lady,' he said, turning to me. An officer, evidently. 'Anything can happen here. I am going to send for an escort to take you back to the road.'

I shook my head. I was in command of myself, I was not even tearful, though I did not put it past myself to break down at any moment.

What did I want? What did the old lady want? What she wanted was to bare something to them, whatever there was that might be bared at this time, in this place. What she wanted, before they got rid of her, was to bring out a scar, a hurt, to force it upon them, to make them see it with their own eyes: a scar, any scar, the scar of all this suffering, but in the end my scar, since our own scars are the only scars we can carry with us. I even brought a hand up to the buttons of my dress. But my fingers were blue, frozen.

'Have you seen inside that hall?' I asked in my cracked voice. Now the tears were beginning to come.

The officer dropped his cigarette, ground it into the wet sand.

'This unit hasn't fired a shot in twenty-four hours,' he said softly. 'Let me suggest to you: don't get upset before you know what you are talking about. Those people in there are not the only ones who have died. The killings are going on all the time. Those are just the bodies they picked up from yesterday. The fighting has subsided for the time being, but as soon as the rain stops it will flare up again. I don't know how you got here – they should have closed the road – but this is a bad place, you shouldn't be here. We'll radio the police, they can escort you out.'

'*Ek het reeds geskakel,*' said the boy in the troop-carrier.

'Why don't you just put down your guns and go home, all of you?' I said. 'Because surely nothing can be worse than what you are doing here. Worse for your souls, I mean.'

'No,' he said. I had expected incomprehension, but no, he understood exactly what I meant. 'We will see it through now.'

I was shivering from head to foot. My fingers, curled into the palms of my hands, would not straighten. The wind drove the sodden clothing against my skin.

'I knew one of those dead boys,' I said. 'I have known him since he was five. His mother works for me. You are all too young for this. It sickens me. That is all.'

I drove back to the hall and, sitting in the car, waited. They were bringing the bodies out now. From the gathering crowd I felt a wave of something come out at me: resentment, animosity. Worse than that: hatred. Would it have been different if I had not been seen speaking to the soldiers? No.

Mr Thabane came over to see what I wanted. 'I am sorry, but I am not sure of the way back,' I said.

'Get on to the tar road, turn right, follow the signs,' he said curtly.

'Yes, but which signs?'

'The signs to civilization.' And he turned on his heel.

I drove slowly, in part because of the wind beating into my face, in part because I was numb in body and soul. I strayed into a suburb I had never heard of and spent twenty minutes driving around indistinguishable streets looking for a way out. At last I found myself in Voortrekker Road. Here, for the first time, people began to stare at the car with the shattered windscreen. Stares followed me all the way home.

The house felt cold and alien. I told myself: Have a hot bath, rest. But an icy lethargy possessed me. It took an effort to drag myself upstairs, peel off the wet clothes, wrap myself in a robe, get into bed. Sand, the grey sand of the Cape Flats, had crusted between my toes. I will never be warm again, I thought. Vercueil has a dog to lie against. Vercueil knows how to live in this climate. But as for me, and for that cold boy soon to be put into the earth, no dog will help us any more. Sand already in his mouth, creeping in, claiming him.

Sixteen years since I shared a bed with man or boy. Sixteen years alone. Does that surprise you?

I wrote. I write. I follow the pen, going where it takes me. What else have I now?

I woke up haggard. It was night again. Where had the day gone?

The light in the toilet was on. Sitting on the seat, his

trousers around his knees, his hat on his head, fast asleep, was Vercueil. I stared in astonishment.

He did not wake; on the contrary, though his head lolled and his jaw hung open, he slept as sweetly as a babe. His long lean thigh was quite hairless.

The kitchen door stood open and garbage from the over-turned bucket was strewn over the floor. Worrying at an old wrapping-paper was the dog. When it saw me it hung its ears guiltily and thumped its tail. 'Too much!' I murmured: 'Too much!' The dog slunk out.

I sat down at the table and gave myself up to tears. I cried not for the confusion in my head, not for the mess in the house, but for the boy, for Bheki. Wherever I turned he was before me, his eyes open in the look of childish puzzlement with which he had met his death. Head on arms I sobbed, grieving for him, for what had been taken from him, for what had been taken from me. Such a good thing, life! Such a wonderful idea for God to have had! The best idea there had ever been. A gift, the most generous of all gifts, renewing itself endlessly through the generations. And now Bheki, robbed of it, gone, torn away!

'I want to go home!' So I had whinged, to my shame, to Mr Thabane the shoe salesman. From an old person's throat a child's voice. Home to my safe house, to my bed of childhood slumber. Have I ever been fully awake? I might as well ask: Do the dead know they are dead? No: to the dead it is not given to know anything. But in our dead sleep we may at least be visited by intimations. I have intimations older than any memory, unshakeable, that once upon a time I was alive. Was alive and then was stolen from life. From the cradle a theft took place: a child was taken and a doll left in its place to be nursed and reared, and that doll is what I call I.

A doll? A doll's life? Is that what I have lived? Is it given to a doll to conceive such a thought? Or does the thought come and go as another intimation, a flash of lightning, a piercing of the fog by the lance of an angel's intelligence? Can a doll recognize a doll? Can a doll know death? No: dolls grow, they acquire speech and gait, they perambulate the world; they age, they wither, they perish; they are wheeled into the fire or buried in the earth; but they do not die. They exist forever in that moment of petrified surprise prior to all recollection when a life was taken away, a life not theirs but in whose place they are left behind as a token. Their knowing a knowledge without substance, without worldly weight, like a doll's head itself, empty, airy. As they themselves are not babies but the ideas of babies, more round, more pink, more blank and blue-eyed than a baby could ever be, living not life but an idea of life, immortal, undying, like all ideas.

Hades, Hell: the domain of ideas. Why has it ever been necessary that hell be a place on its own in the ice of Antarctica or down the pit of a volcano? Why can hell not be at the foot of Africa, and why can the creatures of hell not walk among the living?

'Father, can't you see I'm burning?' implored the child, standing at his father's bedside. But his father, sleeping on, dreaming, did not see.

That is the reason – I bring it forward now for you to see – why I cling so tightly to the memory of my mother. For if she did not give me life, no one did. I cling not just to the memory of her but to her herself, to her body, to my birth from her body into the world. In blood and milk I drank her body and came to life. And then was stolen, and have been lost ever since.

There is a photograph of me you have seen but will probably not remember. It was taken in 1918, when I was not yet two. I am on my feet; I appear to be reaching towards the camera; my mother, kneeling behind me, restrains me by some kind of rein that passes over my shoulders. Standing to one side, ignoring me, is my brother Paul, his cap at a jaunty angle.

My brow is furrowed, my eyes are fixed intensely on the

camera. Am I merely squinting into the sun or, like the savages of Borneo, do I have a shadowy sense that the camera will rob me of my soul? Worse: does my mother hold me back from striking the camera to the ground because I, in my doll's way, know that it will see what the eye cannot: that I am not there? And does my mother know this because she too is not there?

Paul, dead, to whom the pen has led me. I held his hand when he was going. I whispered to him, 'You will see Mama, you will both be so happy.' He was pale, even his eyes had the blanched hue of far-off sky. He gave me a tired, empty look as if to say: How little you understand! Did Paul ever really live? My sister life, he called me once in a letter, in borrowed words. Did it come to him at the end that he had made a mistake? Did those translucent eyes see through me?

We were photographed, that day, in a garden. There are flowers behind us that look like hollyhocks; to our left is a bed of melons. I recognize the place. It is Uniondale, the house in Church Street bought by my grandfather when ostrich-feathers were booming. Year after year fruit and flowers and vegetables burgeoned in that garden, pouring forth their seed, dying, resurrecting themselves, blessing us with their profuse presence. But by whose love tended? Who clipped the hollyhocks? Who laid the melon-seeds in their warm, moist bed? Was it my grandfather who got up at four in the icy morning to open the sluice and lead water into the garden? If not he, then whose was the garden rightfully? Who are the ghosts and who the presences? Who, outside the picture, leaning on their rakes, leaning on their spades, waiting to get back to work, lean also against the edge of the rectangle, bending it, bursting it in?

Dies irae, dies illa when the absent shall be present and the present absent. No longer does the picture show who were in the garden frame that day, but who were not there. Lying all these years in places of safekeeping across the country, in albums, in desk drawers, this picture and thousands like it have subtly matured, metamorphosed. The fixing did not hold or the developing went further than one would ever have dreamed – who can know how it happened? – but they have become negatives again, a new kind of negative in which we begin to see what used to lie outside the frame, occulted.

Is that why my brow is furrowed, is that why I struggle to reach the camera: do I obscurely know that the camera is the enemy, that the camera will not lie about us but uncover what we truly are: doll-folk? Am I struggling against the reins in order to strike the camera out of the hands of whoever holds it before it is too late? And who holds the camera? Whose formless shadow leans toward my mother and her two offspring across the tilled bed?

Grief past weeping. I am hollow, I am a shell. To each of us fate sends the right disease. Mine a disease that eats me out from inside. Were I to be opened up they would find me hollow as a doll, a doll with a crab sitting inside licking its lips, dazed by the flood of light.

Was it the crab I saw so presciently when I was two, peeping out of the black box? Was I trying to save us all from the crab? But they held me back, they pressed the button, and the crab sprang out and entered me.

Gnawing at my bones now that there is no flesh left. Gnawing the socket of my hip, gnawing my backbone, beginning to gnaw at my knees. The cats, if the truth be told, have never really loved me. Only this creature is faithful to the end. My pet, my pain.

I went upstairs and opened the toilet door. Vercueil was still there, slumped in his deep sleep. I shook him. 'Mr Vercueil!' I said. One eye opened. 'Come and lie down.'

But he did not. First I heard him on the stairs, taking one step at a time like an old man. Then I heard the back door close.

A beautiful day, one of those still winter days when light seems to stream evenly from all quarters of the sky. Vercueil drove me down Breda Street and into Orange Street. Across from Government Avenue I told him to park.

'I thought of driving the car all the way down the Avenue,' I said. 'Once I am past the chain, I don't see how anyone can stop me. But do you think there is room to get past?'

(You may remember, there are two cast-iron bollards at the head of the avenue with a chain stretched between them.)

'Yes, you can get past at the side,' he said.

'After that it would just be a matter of keeping the car straight.'

'Are you really going to do this?' he asked. His chicken-eyes glinted cruelly.

'If I can find the courage.'

'But why? What for?'

Hard to make grand responses in the teeth of that look. I closed my eyes and tried to hold on to my vision of the car, moving fast enough for the flames to fan out backwards, rolling down the paved avenue past the tourists and tramps and lovers, past the museum, the art gallery, the botanical gardens, till it slowed down and came to rest before the house of shame, burning and melting.

'We can go back now,' I said. 'I just wanted to make sure it could be done.'

He came indoors and I gave him tea. The dog sat at his feet, cocking its ears at us in turn as we spoke. A nice dog: a bright presence, star-born, as some people are.

'To answer your question *What for?*' I said: 'it has to do with my life. To do with a life that isn't worth much any more. I am trying to work out what I can get for it.'

His hand moved restfully over the dog's fur, back and forth. The dog blinked, closed its eyes. Love, I thought: however unlikely, it is love I witness here.

I tried again. 'There is a famous novel in which a woman

is convicted of adultery – adultery was a crime in the old days – and condemned to go in public with the letter A stitched on her dress. She wears the A for so many years that people forget what it stands for. They forget that it stands for anything. It simply becomes something she wears, like a ring or a brooch. It may even be that she was the one to start the fashion of wearing writing on one's clothing. But that isn't in the book.

'These public shows, these manifestations – this is the point of the story – how can one ever be sure what they stand for? An old woman sets herself on fire, for instance. Why? Because she has been driven mad? Because she is in despair? Because she has cancer? I thought of painting a letter on the car to explain. But what? A? B? C? What is the right letter for my case? And why explain anyway? Whose business is it but my own?'

I might have said more, but at that moment the gate-latch clicked and the dog began to growl. Two women, one of whom I recognized as Florence's sister, came up the path carrying suitcases.

'Good afternoon,' said the sister. She held up a key. 'We have come to fetch my sister's things. Florence.'

'Yes,' I said.

They let themselves into Florence's room. After a while I followed. 'Is Florence all right?' I asked.

The sister, who had been unpacking a drawer, stood up straight, breathing heavily. Clearly she relished this foolish question.

'No, I cannot say she is all right,' she said. 'Not *all right*. How can she be *all right*?'

The other woman, pretending not to hear, continued to fold baby-clothes. There was far more in the room than they could carry in two suitcases.

'I didn't mean that,' I said; 'but never mind. Can I ask you to take something to Florence from me?'

'Yes, I can take it if it is not big.'

I wrote out a cheque.

'Tell Florence I am sorry. Tell her I am more sorry than I can say. I think of Bheki all the time.'

'You are sorry.'

'Yes.'

Another day of clear skies. Vercueil in a strangely excited state. 'So today is the day?' he asked. 'Yes,' I replied, stiffening against his indecent eagerness, on the point of adding: 'But what business is it of yours?'

Yes, I said: today is the day. Yet today has passed and I have not gone through with what I promised. For as long as the trail of words continues, you know with certainty that I have not gone through with it: a rule, another rule. Death may indeed be the last great foe of writing, but writing is also the foe of death. Therefore, writing, holding death at arm's length, let me tell you that I meant to go through with it, began to go through with it, did not go through with it. Let me tell you more. Let me tell you that I bathed. Let me tell you that I dressed. Let me tell you that, as I prepared my body, some faint glow of pride began to return to it. Between waiting in bed for the breathing to stop and going out to make one's own end, what a difference!

I meant to go through with it: is that the truth? Yes. No. Yes-no. There is such a word, but it has never been allowed into the dictionaries. Yes-no: every woman knows what it means as it defeats every man. 'Are you going to do it?' asked Vercueil, his man-eyes gleaming. 'Yes-no,' I should have answered.

I wore white and blue: a light blue suit, a white blouse with a bow at the throat. I did my face carefully, and my hair. All the while I sat in front of the mirror I was trembling lightly. I felt no pain at all. The crab had stopped gnawing.

· 106 ·

Luminous with curiosity, Vercueil followed me into the kitchen and prowled about while I was having breakfast. At last, irritated, unsettled, I burst out: 'Would you please leave me alone!' At which he turned away with a look of such childish hurt that I gave his sleeve a tug. 'I didn't mean that,' I said. 'But please sit down: you make me nervous when I need calm. I veer back and forth so much! At one moment I think: Let me hurry to put an end to it, to this worthless life. At the next I think: But why should I bear the blame? Why should I be expected to rise above my times? Is it my doing that my times have been so shameful? Why should it be left to me, old and sick and full of pain, to lift myself unaided out of this pit of disgrace?

'I want to rage against the men who have created these times. I want to accuse them of spoiling my life in the way that a rat or a cockroach spoils food without even eating it, simply by walking over it and sniffing it and performing its bodily functions on it. It is childish, I know, to point fingers and blame others. But why should I accept that my life would have been worthless no matter who held power in this land? Power is power, after all. It invades. That is its nature. It invades one's life.

'You want to know what is going on with me and I am trying to tell you. I want to sell myself, redeem myself, but am full of confusion about how to do it. That, if you like, is the craziness that has got into me. You need not be surprised. You know this country. There is madness in the air here.'

Throughout this speech Vercueil had worn the same tight, secretive little look. Now he said a strange thing: 'Would you like to go for a drive?'

'We can't go for a drive, Mr Vercueil. There are a thousand reasons why we can't.'

'We can see some sights, be back by twelve o'clock.'

'We can't go sightseeing in a car with a hole in the windscreen. It is ridiculous.'

'I'll take out the windscreen. It's just glass, you don't need it.'

Why did I give in? Perhaps what won me in the end was the new attention he was paying me. He was like a boy in a state of excitement, sexual excitement, and I was his object. I was flattered; in a distant way, despite all, I was even amused. Obscurely I may have felt something unsavoury in it, as in the excitement of a dog digging for carrion not buried deep enough. But I was in no condition to draw lines. What did I want, after all? I wanted a suspension. To be suspended without thought, without pain, without doubt, without apprehension, till noon came. Till the noonday gun boomed on Signal Hill and, with a bottle of petrol on the seat beside me, I either drove or did not drive past the chain and down the Avenue. But to be thoughtless till then; to hear birds sing, to feel the air on my skin, to see the sky. To live.

So I yielded. Vercueil wrapped a towel around his hand and broke out more of the glass till the hole was big enough for a child to climb through. I gave him the key. A push, and we were away.

Like lovers revisiting the scenes of their first declarations, we took the mountainside drive above Muizenberg. (Lovers! What had I ever declared to Vercueil? That he should stop drinking. What had he declared to me? Nothing: perhaps not even his true name.) We parked at the same spot as before. Now: feast a last time on these sights, I told myself, digging my nails into my palms, staring out over False Bay, bay of false hope, and southward over the bleak winter-waters of the most neglected of oceans.

'If we had a boat you could take me out to sea,' I murmured.

Southward: Vercueil and I alone, sailing till we reached the latitudes where albatrosses fly. Where he could lash me to a barrel or a plank, it did not matter which, and leave me bobbing on the waves under the great white wings.

· 108 ·

Vercueil reversed on to the road. Was I wrong, or did the engine throb more sweetly in his hands than in mine?

'I am sorry if I am not making sense,' I said. 'I am trying my best not to lose direction. I am trying to keep up a sense of urgency. A sense of urgency is what keeps deserting me. Sitting here among all this beauty, or even sitting at home among my own things, it seems hardly possible to believe there is a zone of killing and degradation all around me. It seems like a bad dream. Something presses, nudges inside me. I try to take no notice, but it insists. I yield an inch; it presses harder. With relief I give in, and life is suddenly ordinary again. With relief I give myself back to the ordinary. I wallow in it. I lose my sense of shame, become shameless as a child. The shamefulness of that shamelessness: that is what I cannot forget, that is what I cannot bear afterwards. That is why I must take hold of myself, point myself down the path. Otherwise I am lost. Do you understand?'

Vercueil crouched over the wheel like someone with poor eyesight. He of the hawk's-eye. Did it matter if he did not understand?

'It is like trying to give up alcohol,' I persisted. 'Trying and trying, always trying, but knowing in your bones from the beginning that you are going to slide back. There is a shame to that private knowledge, a shame so warm, so intimate, so comforting that it brings more shame flooding with it. There seems to be no limit to the shame a human being can feel.

'But how hard it is to kill oneself! One clings so tight to life! It seems to me that something other than the will must come into play at the last instant, something foreign, something thoughtless, to sweep you over the brink. You have to become someone other than yourself. But who? Who is it that waits for me to step into his shadow? Where do I find him?'

My watch said 10.20. 'We have to go back,' I said.

Vercueil slowed down. 'If that is what you want, I'll take you back,' he said. 'Or, if you like, we can go on driving. We can drive all the way round the Peninsula. It's a nice day.'

I should have answered: No, take me back at once. But I hesitated, and in that moment of hesitation the words died within me.

'Stop here,' I said.

Vercueil drew off the road and parked.

'I have a favour to ask of you,' I said. 'Please don't make fun of me.'

'Is that the favour?'

'Yes. Now or in the future.'

He shrugged.

On the far side of the road a man in tattered clothes sat beside a pyramid of firewood for sale. He looked us over, looked away.

Time passed.

'I told you a story once about my mother,' I said at last, trying to speak more softly. 'About how when she was a little girl she lay in the dark not knowing what was rolling over her, the wagon-wheels or the stars.

'I have held on to that story all my life. If each of us has a story we tell to ourself about who we are and where we come from, then that is my story. That is the story I choose, or the story that has chosen me. It is there that I come from, it is there that I begin.

'You ask whether I want to go on driving. If it were practically possible, I would suggest that we drive to the Eastern Cape, to the Outeniqua Mountains, to that stopping-place at the top of Prince Alfred's Pass. I would even say, Leave maps behind, drive north and east by the sun, I will recognize it when we come to it: the stopping-place, the starting-place, the place of the navel, the place where I join the world. Drop me off there, at the top of the pass, and drive away, leaving me to wait for the night and the stars and the ghostly wagon to come rolling over.

'But the truth is, with or without maps, I can no longer find the place. Why? Because a certain desire has gone from me. A year ago or a month ago it would have been different. A desire, perhaps the deepest desire I am capable of, would have flowed from me toward that one spot of earth, guiding me. *This is my mother*, I would have said, kneeling there: *this is what gives life to me*. Holy ground, not as a grave but as a place of resurrection is holy: resurrection eternal out of the earth.

'Now that desire, which one may as well call love, is gone from me. I do not love this land any more. It is as simple as that. I am like a man who has been castrated. Castrated in maturity. I try to imagine how life is for a man to whom that has been done. I imagine him seeing things he has loved before, knowing from memory that he ought still to love them, but able no longer to summon up the love itself. Love: what was that? he would say to himself, groping in memory for the old feeling. But about everything there would now be a flatness, a stillness, a calmness. Something I once had has been betrayed, he would think, and concentrate, trying to feel that betrayal in all its keenness. But there would be no keenness. Keenness would be what would be gone from everything. Instead he would feel a tug, light but continual, toward stupor, detachment. *Detached*, he would say to himself, pronouncing the sharp word, and he would reach out to test its sharpness. But there too a blurring, a blunting would have intervened. All is receding, he would think; in a week, in a month I will have forgotten everything, I will be among the lotus-eaters, separated, drifting. For a last time he would try to feel the pain of that separation, but all that would come to him would be a fleeting sadness.

'I don't know whether I am being plain enough, Mr Vercueil. I am talking about resolve, about trying to hold on to

· 111 ·

my resolve and failing. I confess, I am drowning. I am sitting here next to you and drowning.'

Vercueil slouched against the door. The dog whined softly. Standing with its paws on the front seat, it peered ahead, eager to get moving again. A minute passed.

Then from his jacket pocket he drew a box of matches and held it out to me. 'Do it now,' he said.

'Do what?'

'It.'

'Is that what you want?'

'Do it now. I'll get out of the car. Do it, here, now.'

At the corner of his mouth a ball of spittle danced up and down. Let him be mad, I thought. Let it be possible to say that about him: that he is cruel, mad, a mad dog.

He shook the box of matches at me. 'Are you worried about him?' He gestured at the man with the firewood. 'He won't interfere.'

'Not here,' I said.

'We can go to Chapman's Peak. You can drive over the edge if that's what you want.'

It was like being trapped in a car with a man trying to seduce you and getting cross when you did not give in. It was like being transported back to the worst days of girlhood.

'Can we go home?' I said.

'I thought you wanted to do it.'

'You don't understand.'

'I thought you wanted a push down the path. I'm giving you a push.'

Outside the hotel in Hout Bay he stopped the car again. 'Have you got some money for me?' he said.

I gave him a ten-rand note.

He went into the off-licence, returned with a bottle in a brown paper packet. 'Have a drink,' he said, and twisted off the cap.

'No, thank you. I don't like brandy.'

'It's not brandy, it's medicine.'

I took a sip, tried to swallow, choked and coughed; my teeth came loose.

'Hold it in your mouth,' he said.

I took another sip and held it in my mouth. My gums and palate burned, then grew dead. I swallowed and closed my eyes. Something began to lift inside me: a curtain, a cloud. Is this it, then, I thought? Is this all? Is this how Vercueil points the way?

He turned the car, drove back up the hill, and parked in a picnic area high above the bay. He drank and offered me the bottle. Cautiously I drank. The veil of greyness that had covered everything grew visibly lighter. Dubious, marvelling, I thought: Is it really so simple – not a matter of life and death at all?

'Let me tell you finally,' I said: 'What set me off was not my own condition, my sickness, but something quite different.'

The dog complained softly. Vercueil reached out a languid hand; it licked his fingers.

'Florence's boy was shot on Tuesday.'

He nodded.

'I saw the body,' I went on, taking another sip, thinking: Shall I now grow loquacious? Lord preserve me! And as I grow loquacious will Vercueil grow loquacious too? He and I, under the influence, loquacious together in the little car?

'I was shaken,' I said. 'I won't say *grieved* because I have no right to the word, it belongs to his own people. But I am still – what? – disturbed. It has something to do with his deadness, his dead weight. It is as though in death he became very heavy, like lead or like that thick, airless mud you get at the bottoms of dams. As though in the act of dying he gave a last sigh and all the lightness went out of him. Now he is lying on top of me with all that weight. Not pressing, just lying.

· 113 ·

'It was the same when that friend of his was bleeding in the street. There was the same heaviness. Heavy blood. I was trying to stop it from flowing down the gutters. So much blood! If I had caught it all I would not have been able to lift the bucket. Like trying to lift a bucket of lead.

'I have not seen black people in their death before, Mr Vercueil. They are dying all the time, I know, but always somewhere else. The people I have seen die have been white and have died in bed, growing rather dry and light there, rather papery, rather airy. They burned well, I am sure, leaving a minimum of ash to sweep up afterwards. Do you want to know why I set my mind on burning myself? Because I thought I would burn well.

'Whereas these people will not burn, Bheki and the other dead. It would be like trying to burn figures of pig-iron or lead. They might lose their sharpness of contour, but when the flames subsided they would still be there, heavy as ever. Leave them long enough and they may sink, millimetre by millimetre, till the earth closes over them. But then they would sink no further. They would stay there, bobbing just under the surface. If you so much as scuffled with your shoe you would uncover them: the faces, the dead eyes, open, full of sand.'

'Drink,' said Vercueil, holding out the bottle. His face was changing, the lips filling out, gorged, wet, the eyes growing vague. Like the woman he had brought home. I took the bottle and wiped it on my sleeve.

'You must understand, it is not just a personal thing, this disturbance I am telling you about,' I pursued. 'In fact it is not personal at all. I was fond of Bheki, certainly, when he was still a child, but I was not happy with the way he turned out. I had hoped for something else. He and his comrades say they have put childhood behind them. Well, they may have ceased being children, but what have they become? Dour little puritans, despising laughter, despising play.

'So why should I grieve for him? The answer is, I saw his face. When he died he was a child again. The mask must have dropped in sheer childish surprise when it broke upon him in that last instant that the stone-throwing and shooting was not a game after all; that the giant who came shambling towards him with a paw full of sand to stop into his mouth would not be turned away by chants or slogans; that at the end of the long passageway where he choked and gagged and could not breathe there was no light.

'Now that child is buried and we walk upon him. Let me tell you, when I walk upon this land, this South Africa, I have a gathering feeling of walking upon black faces. They are dead but their spirit has not left them. They lie there heavy and obdurate, waiting for my feet to pass, waiting for me to go, waiting to be raised up again. Millions of figures of pig-iron floating under the skin of the earth. The age of iron waiting to return.

'You think I am upset but will get over it. Cheap tears, you think, tears of sentiment, here today, gone tomorrow. Well, it is true, I have been upset in the past, I have imagined there could be no worse, and then the worse has arrived, as it does without fail, and I have got over it, or seemed to. But that is the trouble! In order not to be paralyzed with shame I have had to live a life of getting over the worse. What I cannot get over any more is that *getting over*. If I get over it this time I will never have another chance *not* to get over it. For the sake of my own resurrection I cannot get over it this time.'

Vercueil held out the bottle. A full four inches were gone. I pushed his hand away. 'I don't want to drink any more,' I said.

'Go on,' he said: 'get drunk for a change.'

'No!' I exclaimed. A tipsy anger flared up in me against his crudity, his indifference. What was I doing here? In the exhausted car the two of us must have looked like nothing so much as belated refugees from the *platteland* of the Great

Depression. All we lacked was a coir mattress and a chicken-coop tied on the roof. I snatched the bottle from his hand; but while I was still rolling down the window to throw it out, he wrested it back.

'Get out of my car!' I snapped.

Taking the key from the ignition lock, he got out. The dog bounded after him. In full sight of me he tossed the key into the bushes, turned, and, bottle in hand, stalked down the hill towards Hout Bay.

Burning with rage I waited, but he did not turn.

Minutes passed. A car pulled off the road and drew up beside me. Music blared from it, loud and metallic. In that welter of noise a couple sat gazing over the sea. South Africa at its recreations. I got out and tapped at their window. The man turned a vacant look on me, chewing. 'Can you turn down the music?' I said. He fiddled or pretended to fiddle with something, but the volume did not change. I tapped again. Through the glass he mouthed words at me, then in a flurry of dust reversed the car and parked on the other side of the area.

I searched in the bushes where Vercueil had thrown the key, with no success.

As the other car drove off at last, the woman turned to glare at me. Her face not unattractive yet ugly: closed, bunched, as if afraid that light, air, life itself were going to gather and strike her. Not a face but an expression, yet an expression worn so long as to be hers, her. A thickening of the membrane between the world and the self inside, a thickening become thickness. Evolution, but evolution backwards. Fish from the primitive depths (I am sure you know this) grew patches of skin sensitive to the fingerings of light, patches that in time became eyes. Now, in South Africa, I see eyes clouding over again, scales thickening on them, as the land-explorers, the colonists, prepare to return to the deep.

Should I have come when you invited me? In my weaker

moments I have often longed to cast myself on your mercy. How lucky, for both our sakes, that I have held out! You do not need an albatross from the old world around your neck; and as for me, would I truly escape South Africa by running to you? How do I know the scales are not already thickening over my own eyes? That woman in the car: perhaps, as they drove off, she was saying to her companion: 'What a sour old creature! What a closed-off face!'

And then, what honour is there in slipping off in these times when the worm-riddled ship is so clearly sinking, in the company of tennis players and crooked brokers and generals with pocketfuls of diamonds departing to set up retreats in the quieter backwaters of the world? General G, Minister M on their holdings in Paraguay, grilling beefsteaks over coals under southern skies, drinking beer with their cronies, singing songs of the old country, looking to pass away in their sleep at a great old age with grandchildren and peons hat in hand at the foot of the bed: the Afrikaners of Paraguay joining the Afrikaners of Patagonia in their sullen diaspora: ruddy men with paunches and fat wives and gun collections on their living-room walls and safety-deposit boxes in Rosario, exchanging Sunday-afternoon visits with the sons and daughters of Barbie, Eichmann: bullies, thugs, torturers, killers – what company!

Besides, I am too tired. Tired beyond cause, tired as an armour against the times, yearning to close my eyes, to sleep. What is death, after all, but an ascent into the final reaches of tiredness?

I remember your last telephone call. 'How are you feeling?' you asked. 'Tired but otherwise well,' I replied. 'I am taking things slowly. Florence is a pillar of strength, as ever, and I have a new man to help in the garden.' 'I'm so glad,' you said in your brisk American voice – 'You must rest a lot and concentrate on getting your strength back.'

Mother and daughter on the telephone. Midday there,

evening here. Summer there, winter here. Yet the line as clear as if you were next door. Our words taken apart, hurled through the skies, put together again whole, flawless. No longer the old undersea cable linking you to me but an efficient, abstract, skyborne connection: the idea of you connected to the idea of me; not words, not living breath passing between us, but the ideas of words, the idea of breath, coded, transmitted, decoded. At the end you said, 'Good night, mother,' and I, 'Goodbye, my dear, thank you for phoning,' on the word *dear* allowing my voice to rest (what self-indulgence!) with the full weight of my love, praying that the ghost of that love would survive the cold trails of space and come home to you.

On the telephone, love but not truth. In this letter from elsewhere (so long a letter!) truth and love together at last. In every *you* that I pen love flickers and trembles like St Elmo's fire; you are with me not as you are today in America, not as you were when you left, but as you are in some deeper and unchanging form: as the beloved, as that which does not die. It is the soul of you that I address, as it is the soul of me that will be left with you when this letter is over. Like a moth from its case emerging, fanning its wings: that is what, reading, I hope you will glimpse: my soul readying itself for further flight. A white moth, a ghost emerging from the mouth of the figure on the deathbed. This struggling with sickness, the gloom and self-loathing of these days, the vacillation, the rambling too (there is little more to tell about the Hout Bay episode – Vercueil returned drunk and bad-tempered, found the key, and drove me home, and that was that; perhaps, if the truth be known, his dog led him back) – all part of the metamorphosis, part of shaking myself loose from the dying envelope.

And after that, after the dying? Never fear, I will not haunt you. There will be no need to close the windows and seal the chimney to keep the white moth from flapping in during the night and settling on your brow or on the brow of one of the children. The moth is simply what will brush your cheek ever so lightly as you put down the last page of this letter, before it flutters off on its next journey. It is not my soul that will remain with you but the spirit of my soul, the breath, the stirring of the air about these words, the faintest of turbulence traced in the air by the ghostly passage of my pen over the paper your fingers now hold.

Letting go of myself, letting go of you, letting go of a house still alive with memories: a hard task, but I am learning. The music too. But the music I will take with me, that at least, for it is wound into my soul. The ariosos from the Matthew Passion, wound in and knotted a thousand times, so that no one, nothing can undo them.

If Vercueil does not send these writings on, you will never read them. You will never even know they existed. A certain body of truth will never take on flesh: my truth: how I lived in these times, in this place.

What is the wager, then, that I am making with Vercueil, on Vercueil?

It is a wager on trust. So little to ask, to take a package to the post office and pass it over the counter. So little that it is almost nothing. Between taking the package and not taking it the difference is as light as a feather. If there is the slightest breath of trust, obligation, piety left behind when I am gone, he will surely take it.

And if not?

If not, there is no trust and we deserve no better, all of us, than to fall into a hole and vanish.

Because I cannot trust Vercueil I must trust him.

I am trying to keep a soul alive in times not hospitable to the soul.

Easy to give alms to the orphaned, the destitute, the hungry. Harder to give alms to the bitter-hearted (I think of Florence). But the alms I give Vercueil are hardest of all.

What I give he does not forgive me for giving. No charity in him, no forgiveness. (*Charity?* says Vercueil. *Forgiveness?*) Without his forgiveness I give without charity, serve without love. Rain falling on barren soil.

When I was younger I might have given myself to him bodily. That is the sort of thing one does, one did, however mistakenly. Now I put my life in his hands instead. This is my life, these words, these tracings of the movements of crabbed digits over the page. These words, as you read them, if you read them, enter you and draw breath again. They are, if you like, my way of living on. Once upon a time you lived in me as once upon a time I lived in my mother; as she still lives in me, as I grow towards her, may I live in you.

I give my life to Vercueil to carry over. I trust Vercueil because I do not trust Vercueil. I love him because I do not love him. Because he is the weak reed I lean upon him.

I may seem to understand what I say, but, believe me, I do not. From the beginning, when I found him behind the garage in his cardboard house, sleeping, waiting, I have understood nothing. I am feeling my way along a passage that grows darker all the time. I am feeling my way toward you; with each word I feel my way.

Days ago I caught a cold, which has now settled on my chest and turned into a dry, hammering cough that goes on for minutes at a stretch and leaves me panting, exhausted.

As long as the burden is a burden of pain alone I bear it by holding it at a distance. It is not I who am in pain, I say to myself: the one in pain is someone else, some body else who shares this bed with me. So, by a trick, I hold it off, keep it elsewhere. And when the trick will not work, when the pain insists on owning me, I bear it anyhow.

(As the waves rise I have no doubt my tricks will be swept away like the dikes of Zeeland.)

But now, during these spasms of coughing, I cannot keep any distance from myself. There is no mind, there is no body, there is just I, a creature thrashing about, struggling for air, drowning. Terror, and the ignominy of terror! Another vale to be passed through on the way to death. *How can this be happening to me?* I think at the height of the coughing: *Is it fair?* The ignominy of naîveté. Even a dog with a broken back breathing its last at the roadside would not think, *But is this fair?*

Living, said Marcus Aurelius, calls for the art of the wrestler, not the dancer. Staying on your feet is all; there is no need for pretty steps.

Yesterday, with the pantry bare, I had to go shopping. Trudging home with my bags, I had a bad spell. Three passing schoolboys stopped to stare at the old woman leaning against a lamp-post with her groceries spilled around her feet. In between the coughing I tried to wave them away. What I looked like I cannot imagine. A woman in a car slowed down. 'Are you all right?' she called. 'I have been shopping,' I panted. 'What?' she said, frowning, straining to hear. 'Nothing!' I gasped. She drove off.

How ugly we are growing, from being unable to think well of ourselves! Even the beauty queens look irritable. Ugliness: what is it but the soul showing through the flesh?

Then last night the worst happened. Into the confusion of my drugged, unsavoury slumber penetrated the sound of barking. On and on it went, steady, relentless, mechanical. Why did Vercueil not put a stop to it?

I did not trust myself on the stairs. In bathrobe and slippers I went out on to the balcony. It was cold, a light rain was falling. 'Mr Vercueil!' I croaked – 'What is the dog barking about? Mr Vercueil!'

The barking stopped, then started again. Vercueil did not appear.

I went back to bed and lay there unable to sleep, the barking like hammering in my ears.

This is how old women fall and break their hips, I warned myself: this is how the trap is laid, and this is how they are caught.

Holding to the banister with both hands I crept downstairs.

There was someone in the kitchen and it was not Vercueil. Whoever it was did not try to hide. My God, I thought: Bheki! A chill ran through me.

In the eerie light cast by the open refrigerator he confronted me, his forehead with the bullet wound covered by a white bandage.

'What do you want?' I whispered. 'Do you want food?'

He spoke: 'Where is Bheki?'

The voice was lower, thicker than Bheki's. Who could it be then? Befuddled, I searched for a name.

He closed the refrigerator door. Now we were in darkness. 'Mr Vercueil!' I croaked. The dog barked without let-up. 'The neighbours will come,' I whispered.

As he passed me his shoulder brushed mine. Flinching, I smelled him and knew who he was.

He reached the door. The barking grew frantic.

'Florence isn't here any more,' I said. I turned on the light.

He was not wearing his own clothes. Or perhaps it is a fashion. The jacket seemed to belong to a full-grown man and the trousers were too long. One arm of the jacket was empty.

'How is your arm?' I asked.

'I must not move the arm,' he said.

'Come away from the door,' I said.

I opened the door a crack. The dog leapt excitedly. I tapped it on the nose. 'Stop it at once!' I commanded. It whined softly. 'Where is your master?' It cocked its ears. I closed the door.

'What do you want here?' I asked the boy.

'Where is Bheki?'

'Bheki is dead. He was killed last week while you were in hospital. He was shot. He died at once. The day after that affair with the bicycle.'

He licked his lips. There was a cornered, uncertain look about him.

'Do you want something to eat?'

He shook his head. 'Money. I have no money,' he said. 'For the bus.'

'I will give you money. But where do you intend to go?'

'I must go home.'

'Don't do that, I urge you. I know what I am talking about, I have seen what is happening on the Flats. Stay away till things have gone back to normal.'

'Things will never be normal –'

'Please! I know the argument, I haven't the time or interest to go through it again. Stay here till things are quieter. Stay till you are better. Why did you leave the hospital? Are you discharged?'

'Yes. I am discharged.'

'Whose clothes are you wearing?'

'They are mine.'

'They are not your clothes. Where did you get them?'

'They are mine. A friend brought them to me.'

He was lying. He lied no better than any other fifteen-year-old.

'Sit down. I will give you something to eat, then you can get some sleep. Wait till morning before you make up your mind what to do next.'

I made tea. He sat down, paying me no attention at all. It did not embarrass him that I did not believe his story. What I believed was of no account. What did he think of me? Did he give me any thought? Was he a thinking person? No: compared with Bheki he was unthinking, inarticulate, unimaginative. But he was alive and Bheki was dead. The lively

· 123 ·

ones are picked off, the stolid ones survive. Bheki too quick for his own good. I was never afraid of Bheki; as for this one, I am not so sure.

I put a sandwich and a cup of tea in front of him. 'Eat, drink,' I said. He did not stir. With his head on his arm, his eyes rolled back, he was fast asleep. I patted his cheek. 'Wake up!' I said. He gave a start, sat straight, took a bite, and chewed rapidly. Then the chewing slowed. His mouth full, he sat in a stupor of exhaustion. I took the sandwich out of his hand, thinking: When they are in trouble they come to a woman. To Florence he comes, except that there is no Florence. Has he no mother of his own?

In Florence's room he recovered briefly. 'The bicycle,' he mumbled.

'It is safe, I have kept it. It must be fixed, that is all. I will ask Mr Vercueil to look at it.'

So this house that was once my home and yours becomes a house of refuge, a house of transit.

My dearest child, I am in a fog of error. The hour is late and I do not know how to save myself. As far as I can confess, to you I confess. What is my error, you ask? If I could put it in a bottle, like a spider, and send it to you to examine, I would do so. But it is like a fog, everywhere and nowhere. I cannot touch it, trap it, put a name to it. Slowly, reluctantly, however, let me say the first word. I do not love this child, the child sleeping in Florence's bed. I love you but I do not love him. There is no ache in me towards him, not the slightest.

Yes, you reply, he is not lovable. But did you not have a part in making him unlovable?

I do not deny that. But at the same time I do not believe it. My heart does not accept him as mine: it is as simple as that. In my heart I want him to go away and leave me alone.

That is my first word, my first confession. I do not want to die in the state I am in, in a state of ugliness. I want to be saved. How shall I be saved? By doing what I do not want to do. That is the first step: that I know. I must love, first of all, the unlovable. I must love, for instance, this child. Not bright little Bheki, but this one. He is here for a reason. He is part of my salvation. I must love him. But I do not love him. Nor do I want to love him enough to love him despite myself.

It is because I do not with a full enough heart want to be otherwise that I am still wandering in a fog.

I cannot find it in my heart to love, to want to love, to want to want to love.

I am dying because in my heart I do not want to live. I am dying because I want to die.

Therefore let me utter my second, dubious word. Not wanting to love him, how true can I say my love is for you? For love is not like hunger. Love is never sated, stilled. When one loves, one loves more. The more I love you, the more I ought to love him. The less I love him, the less, perhaps, I love you.

Cruciform logic, that takes me where I do not want to go! But would I let myself be nailed upon it if I truly were not willing?

I thought, when I began this long letter, that its pull would be as strong as the tide's, that beneath the waves beating this way and that on its surface there would be a tug as constant as the moon's drawing you to me and me to you: the blood-tug of daughter to mother, woman to woman. But with every day I add to it the letter seems to grow more abstract, more abstracted, the kind of letter one writes from the stars, from the farther void, disembodied, crystalline, bloodless. Is that to be the fate of my love?

I remember, when the boy was hurt, how abundantly he bled, how rudely. How thin, by comparison, my bleeding on to the paper here. The issue of a shrunken heart.

I have written about blood before, I know. I have written

about everything, I am written out, bled dry, and still I go on. This letter has become a maze, and I a dog in the maze, scurrying up and down the branches and tunnels, scratching and whining at the same old places, tiring, tired. Why do I not call for help, call to God? Because God cannot help me. God is looking for me but he cannot reach me. God is another dog in another maze. I smell God and God smells me. I am the bitch in her time, God the male. God smells me, he can think of nothing else but finding me and taking me. Up and down the branches he bounds, scratching at the mesh. But he is lost as I am lost.

I dream, but I doubt that it is God I dream of. When I fall asleep there commences a restless movement of shapes behind my eyelids, shapes without body or form, covered in a haze, grey or brown, sulphurous. *Borodino* is the word that comes to me in my sleep: a hot summer afternoon on the Russian plain, smoke everywhere, the grass dry and burning, two hosts that have lost all cohesion plodding about, parched, in terror of their lives. Hundreds of thousands of men, faceless, voiceless, dry as bones, trapped on a field of slaughter, repeating night after night their back-and-forth march across that scorched plain in the stench of sulphur and blood: a hell into which I plummet when I close my eyes.

I am more than half convinced it is the red pills, Diconal, that call up these armies inside me. But without the red pills I can no longer sleep.

Borodino, Diconal: I stare at the words. Are they anagrams? They look like anagrams. But for what, and in what language?

When I wake out of the Borodino sleep I am calling or crying or coughing with sounds that come from deep in my chest. Then I quieten down and lie staring about me. My room, my house, my life: too close a rendering to be an imitation: the real thing: I am back: again and again I am back, from the belly of the whale disgorged. A miracle each time, unacknowledged, uncelebrated, unwelcome. Morning after morning I am disgorged, cast up on the shore, given another chance. And what do I do with it? Lie without motion on the sands waiting for the night tide to return, to encircle me, to bear me back into the belly of darkness. Not properly born: a liminal creature, unable to breathe in water, that lacks the courage to leave the sea behind and become a dweller on land.

At the airport, the day you left, you gripped me and stared into my eyes. 'Do not call me back, Mother,' you said, 'because I will not come.' Then you shook the dust of this country from your feet. You were right. Nevertheless, there is part of me that is always on the alert, always turned to the north-west, longing to welcome you, embrace you, should you relent and, in whatever form, come visiting. There is something as terrible as it is admirable in that will of yours, in the letters you write in which – let me be candid – there is not enough love, or at least not enough of the loving-yielding that brings love to life. Affectionate, kind, confiding even, full of concern for me, they are nonetheless the letters of someone grown strange, estranged.

Is this an accusation? No, but it is a reproach, a heartfelt reproach. And this long letter – I say it now – is a call into the night, into the north-west, for you to come back to me. Come and bury your head in my lap as a child does, as you used to, your nose burrowing like a mole's for the place you came from. Come, says this letter: do not cut yourself off from me. My third word.

If you would say you came from me, I would not have to say I came from the belly of the whale.

I cannot live without a child. I cannot die without a child.

What I bear, in your absence, is pain. I produce pain. You are my pain.

Is this an accusation? Yes. *J'accuse*. I accuse you of abandoning me. I fling this accusation at you, into the north-west, into the teeth of the wind. I fling my pain at you.

Borodino: an anagram for *Come back* in some language or other. Diconal: *I call*.

Words vomited up from the belly of the whale, misshapen, mysterious. Daughter.

In the middle of the night I telephoned Lifeline. 'Home deliveries?' said the woman – 'I don't know of anyone who does home deliveries any more except Stuttafords. Would you like to try Meals on Wheels?'

'It is not a question of cooking,' I said. 'I can do my own cooking. I just want the groceries delivered. I am having difficulty carrying things.'

'Give me your number and I'll get a social worker to phone you in the morning,' she said.

I put down the receiver.

The end comes galloping. I had not reckoned that as one goes downhill one goes faster and faster. I thought the whole road could be taken at an amble. Wrong, quite wrong.

There is something degrading about the way it all ends – degrading not only to us but to the idea we have of ourselves, of humankind. People lying in dark bedrooms, in their own mess, helpless. People lying in hedges in the rain. You will not understand this, yet. Vercueil will.

Vercueil has disappeared again, leaving the dog behind. A pity about Vercueil. No Odysseus, no Hermes, perhaps not even a messenger. A circler-around. A ditherer, despite the weatherworn front.

And I? If Vercueil has failed his test, what was mine? Was my test whether I had the courage to incinerate myself in front of the House of Lies? I have gone over that moment a thousand times in my mind, the moment of striking the match when my ears are softly buffeted and I sit astonished and even pleased in the midst of the flames, untouched, my clothes burning without singeing, the flames a cool blue. *How easy to give meaning to one's life*, I think with surprise, thinking very fast in the last instant before the eyelashes catch, and the eyebrows, and one no longer sees. Then after that no thought any more, only pain (for nothing comes without its price).

Would the pain be worse than toothache? Than childbirth? Than this hip? Than childbirth multiplied by two? How many Diconal to mute it? Would it be playing the game to swallow all the Diconal before turning the car down Government Avenue, edging past the chain? Must one die in full knowledge, fully oneself? Must one give birth to one's death without anaesthetic?

The truth is, there was always something false about that impulse, deeply false, no matter to what rage or despair it answered. If dying in bed over weeks and months, in a purgatory of pain and shame, will not save my soul, why should I be saved by dying in two minutes in a pillar of flames? Will the lies stop because a sick old woman kills herself? Whose life will be changed, and how? I go back to Florence, as so often. If Florence were passing by, with Hope at her side and Beauty on her back, would she be impressed by the spectacle? Would she even spare it a glance? A juggler, a clown, an entertainer, Florence would think: not a serious person. And stride on.

What would count in Florence's eyes as a serious death? What would win her approval? Answer: a death that crowns a life of honourable labour; or else that comes of itself, irresistible, unannounced, like a clap of thunder, like a bullet between the eyes.

Florence is the judge. Behind the glasses her eyes are still, measuring all. A stillness she has already passed on to her daughters. The court belongs to Florence; it is I who pass under review. If the life I live is an examined life, it is because for ten years I have been under examination in the court of Florence.

'Have you got Dettol?'

His voice startled me as I sat in the kitchen writing. His, the boy's.

'Go upstairs. Look in the bathroom, the door on the right. Look in the cupboard under the basin.'

There were splashing noises, then he came down again. The bandage was off; with surprise I noticed that the stitches were still in.

'Didn't they take out the stitches?'

He shook his head.

'But when did you leave the hospital?'

'Yesterday. The day before yesterday.'

Why the need to lie?

'Why didn't you stay and let them take care of you?'

No response.

'You must keep that cut covered, otherwise it will get infected and leave you with a scar.' With a mark like a whiplash across his forehead for the rest of his life. A memento.

Who is he to me that I should nag him? Yet I held closed his open flesh, staunched the flow of his blood. How persistent the impulse to mother! As a hen that loses its chicks will take in a duckling, oblivious of the yellow fur, the flat beak, and teach it to take sand-baths, peck at worms.

I shook out the red tablecloth and began to cut it. 'I don't have any bandage in the house,' I said, 'but this is quite clean, if you don't mind red.' Around his head I wound a strip twice and knotted it behind. 'You must go to a doctor soon, or a clinic, to have the stitches taken out. You can't leave them in.'

His neck stiff as a poker. A smell coming from him, the smell that must have set the dog off: nervousness, fear.

'My head is not sore,' he said, clearing his throat, 'but my arm' – he moved his shoulder gingerly – 'I must rest my arm.'

'Tell me, are you running away from someone?'

He was silent.

'I want to speak to you seriously,' I said. 'You are too young for this kind of thing. I told Bheki so and I tell you again. You must listen to me. I am an old person, I know what I am talking about. You are still children. You are throwing away your lives before you know what life can be. What are you – fifteen years old? Fifteen is too young to die. Eighteen is too young. Twenty-one is too young.'

He got up, brushing the red band with his fingertips. A favour. In the age of chivalry men hacked other men to death with women's favours fluttering on their helmets. A waste of breath to preach prudence to this boy. The instinct for battle too strong in him, driving him on. Battle: nature's way of liquidating the weak and providing mates for the strong. Return covered in glory and you shall have your desire. Gore and glory, death and sex. And I, an old woman, crone of death, tying a favour around his head!

'Where is Bheki?' he said.

I searched his face. Had he not understood what I told him? Had he forgotten? 'Sit down,' I said.

He sat.

I leaned across the table. 'Bheki is in the ground,' I said. 'He is in a box in a hole with earth heaped on top of him. He is never going to leave that hole. Never, never, never. Understand: this is not a game like football, where after you fall down you get up and go on playing. The men you are playing against don't say to each other, "That one is just a child, let us shoot a child's bullet at him, a play bullet." They don't think of you as a child at all. They think of you as the enemy and they hate you quite as much as you hate them. They will have no qualms about shooting you: on the contrary, they will smile with pleasure when you fall and make another notch on their gunstocks.'

He stared back at me as if I were striking him in the face,

· 131 ·

blow after blow. But, jaw set, lips clenched, he refused to wince. Over his eyes that smoky film.

'You think their discipline is poor,' I said. 'You are wrong. Their discipline is very good. What holds them back from exterminating every male child, every last one of you, is not compassion or fellow-feeling. It is discipline, nothing else: orders from above, that can change any day. Compassion is flown out of the window. This is war. Listen to what I am saying! I know what I am talking about. You think I am trying to lure you out of the struggle. Well, that is true. That is what I am doing. I say: Wait, you are too young.'

He shifted restlessly. Talk, talk! Talk had weighed down the generation of his grandparents and the generation of his parents. Lies, promises, blandishments, threats: they had walked stooped under the weight of all the talk. Not he. He threw off talk. Death to talk!

'You say it is time to fight,' I said. 'You say it is time to win or lose. Let me tell you something about that *win or lose*. Let me tell you something about that *or*. Listen to me.

'You know I am sick. Do you know what is wrong with me? I have cancer. I have cancer from the accumulation of shame I have endured in my life. That is how cancer comes about: from self-loathing the body turns malignant and begins to eat away at itself.

'You say, "What is the point of consuming yourself in shame and loathing? I don't want to listen to the story of how you feel, it is just another story, why don't you *do* something?" And when you say that, I say, "Yes." I say, "Yes." I say, "Yes."

'There is nothing I can reply but "Yes" when you put that question to me. But let me tell you what it is like to utter that "Yes." It is like being on trial for your life and being allowed only two words, Yes and No. Whenever you take a breath to speak out, you are warned by the judges: "Yes or

No: no speeches." "Yes," you say. Yet all the time you feel other words stirring inside you like life in the womb. Not like a child kicking, not yet, but like the very beginnings, like the deep-down stirring of knowledge a woman has when she is pregnant.

'There is not only death inside me. There is life too. The death is strong, the life is weak. But my duty is to the life. I must keep it alive. I must.

'You do not believe in words. You think only blows are real, blows and bullets. But listen to me: can't you hear that the words I speak are real? Listen! They may only be air but they come from my heart, from my womb. They are not Yes, they are not No. What is living inside me is something else, another word. And I am fighting for it, in my manner, fighting for it not to be stifled. I am like one of those Chinese mothers who know that their child will be taken away from them, if it is a daughter, and done away with, because the need, the family's need, the village's need, is for sons with strong arms. They know that after the birth someone will come into the room, someone whose face will be hidden, who will take the child from the midwife's arms and, if the sex is wrong, turn his back on them, out of delicacy, and stifle it just like that, pinching the little nose to, holding the jaw shut. A minute and all is done.

'Grieve if you like, the mother is told afterwards: grief is only natural. But do not ask: What is this thing called a son? What is this thing called a daughter, that it must die?

'Do not misunderstand me. You are a son, somebody's son. I am not against sons. But have you ever seen a newborn baby? Let me tell you, you would find it hard to tell the difference between boy and girl. Every baby has the same puffy-looking fold between the legs. The spout, the tendril that is said to mark out the boy is no great thing, really. Very little to make the difference between life and death. Yet everything else, everything indefinite, everything that gives when you press it, is condemned unheard. I am arguing for that unheard.

'You are tired of listening to old people, I can see. You are itching to be a man and do a man's things. You are tired of getting ready for life. It is time for life itself, you think. What an error you are making! Life is not following a stick, a pole, a flagstaff, a gun, and seeing where it will take you. Life is not around the corner. You are already in the midst of life.'

The telephone rang.

'It's all right, I am not going to answer it,' I said.

In silence we waited for the ringing to stop.

'I don't know your name,' I said.

'John.'

John: a *nom de guerre* if ever I heard one.

'What are your plans?'

He looked uncomprehending.

'What do you plan to do? Do you want to stay here?'

'I must go home.'

'Where is home?'

He stared back at me doggedly, too tired to think up another lie. 'Poor child,' I whispered.

I did not mean to spy. But I was wearing slippers, the door to Florence's room was open, his back was to me. He was sitting on the bed, intent on some object he had in his hand. When he heard me he gave a start and thrust it beneath the bedclothes.

'What is it you have there?' I asked.

'It is nothing,' he said, giving me one of his forced stares.

I would not have pressed him had I not noticed that a length of skirting-board had been prised from the wall and lay on the floor, revealing unplastered brickwork.

'What are you up to?' I said. 'Why are you pulling the room to pieces?'

He was silent.

'Show me what you are hiding.'

He shook his head.

I peered at the wall. There was a gap in the brickwork where a ventilator had been let in; through the gap one could reach under the floorboards.

'Are you putting things under the floor?'

'I am not doing anything.'

I dialled the number Florence had left. A child answered. 'Can I speak to Mrs Mkubukeli,' I said. Silence. 'Mrs Mkubukeli. Florence.'

Murmurs, then a woman's voice: 'Who do you want to speak to?'

'Mrs Mkubukeli. Florence.'

'She is not here.'

'This is Mrs Curren,' I said. 'Mrs Mkubukeli used to work for me. I am phoning about her son's friend, the boy who calls himself John, I don't know his real name. It is important. If Florence is not there, can I speak to Mr Thabane?'

Again a long silence. Then a man's voice: 'Yes, this is Thabane.'

'This is Mrs Curren. You remember, we met. I am phoning about Bheki's friend, from his school. Perhaps you don't know, but he has been in hospital.'

'I know.'

'Now he has left the hospital, or run away, and come here. I have reason to believe he has a weapon of some kind, I don't know what exactly, which he and Bheki must have hidden in Florence's room. I think that is why he has come back.'

'Yes,' he said flatly.

'Mr Thabane, I am not asking you to assert authority over the boy. But he is not well. He was quite badly injured. And I think he is in an emotionally disturbed state. I don't know how to get in touch with his family, I don't even know whether he has family in Cape Town. He won't tell me. All

I am asking is that someone should come and talk to him, someone he trusts, and take him away before something happens to him.'

'He is in an emotionally disturbed state. What do you mean?'

'I mean he needs help. I mean he may not be responsible for his actions. I mean he has had a blow to the head. I mean I cannot take care of him, it is beyond me. Someone must come.'

'I will see.'

'No, that is not good enough. I want an undertaking.'

'I will ask someone to fetch him. But I cannot tell you when.'

'Today?'

'I cannot say today. Perhaps today, perhaps tomorrow. I will see.'

'Mr Thabane, let me make one thing clear to you. I am not trying to prescribe to this boy or to anyone else what he should do with his life. He is old enough and self-willed enough to do what he will do. But as for this killing, this bloodletting in the name of *comradeship*, I detest it with all my heart and soul. I think it is barbarous. That is what I want to say.'

'This is not a good line, Mrs Curren. Your voice is very tiny, very tiny and very far away. I hope you can hear me.'

'I can hear you.'

'Good. Then let me say, Mrs Curren, I don't think you understand very much about comradeship.'

'I understand enough, thank you.'

'No, you don't,' he said, quite certain of himself. 'When you are body and soul in the struggle as these young people are, when you are prepared to lay down your lives for each other without question, then a bond grows up that is stronger than any bond you will know again. That is comradeship. I see it every day with my own eyes. My generation has nothing that can compare. That is why we must stand back for them, for the youth. We stand back but we stand behind them. That is what you cannot understand, because you are too far away.'

'I am far away, certainly,' I said, 'far away and tiny. Nevertheless, I fear I know comradeship all too well. The Germans had comradeship, and the Japanese, and the Spartans. Shaka's impis too, I am sure. Comradeship is nothing but a mystique of death, of killing and dying, masquerading as what you call a bond (a bond of what? Love? I doubt it.). I have no sympathy with this comradeship. You are wrong, you and Florence and everyone else, to be taken in by it and, worse, to encourage it in children. It is just another of those icy, exclusive, death-driven male constructions. That is my opinion.'

More passed between us, but I won't repeat it. We exchanged opinions. We agreed to differ.

The afternoon dragged on. No one came to fetch the boy. I lay in bed, groggy with drugs, a cushion under my back, trying with one small adjustment after another to ease the pain, longing for sleep, dreading the dream of Borodino.

The air thickened, it began to rain. From the blocked gutter came a steady drip. The smell of cat urine wafted in from the carpet on the landing. A tomb, I thought: a late bourgeois tomb. My head turned this way and that. Grey hair on the pillow, unwashed, lank. And in Florence's room, in the growing dark, the boy, lying on his back with the bomb or whatever it is in his hand, his eyes wide open, not veiled now but clear: thinking, more than thinking, envisioning. Envisioning the moment of glory when he will arise, fully himself at last, erect, powerful, transfigured. When the fiery flower will unfold, when the pillar of smoke will rise. The bomb on his chest like a talisman: as Christopher Columbus lay in the dark of his cabin, holding the compass to his chest, the mystic instrument that would guide him to the Indies, the Isles of the Blest. Troops of maidens with bared breasts singing to him, opening their arms, as he wades to them through the shallows holding before him the needle that never wavers, that points forever in one direction, to the future.

Poor child! Poor child! From somewhere tears sprang and blurred my sight. Poor John, who in the old days would have been destined to be a garden boy and eat bread and jam for lunch at the back door and drink out of a tin, battling now for all the insulted and injured, the trampled, the ridiculed, for all the garden boys of South Africa!

In the cold early morning I heard the gate to the courtyard being tried. Vercueil, I thought: Vercueil is back. Then the doorbell rang, once, twice, long rings, peremptory, impatient, and I knew it was not Vercueil.

It takes me minutes nowadays to get downstairs, particularly if I am befuddled by the pills. While I crept down in the half-dark they went on ringing the bell, rapping at the door. 'I am coming!' I called as loudly as I could. But I was too slow. I heard the courtyard gate swing open. There was a burst of knocking at the kitchen door, and voices speaking Afrikaans. Then, as flat and unremarkable as one stone striking another, came the sound of a shot.

A silence fell in which I clearly heard the tinkle of breaking glass. 'Wait!' I called, and ran, truly ran – I did not know I had it in me – to the kitchen door. 'Wait!' I called, slapping at the pane, fumbling with the bolts and chains – 'Don't do anything!'

There was someone in a blue overcoat standing on the veranda with his back to me. Though he must have heard me, he did not turn.

I drew the last bolt, flung the door open, appeared among them. I had forgotten my gown, my feet were bare, I stood there in my white nightdress like, for all I know, a body risen from the dead. 'Wait!' I said. 'Don't do anything yet, he is just a child!'

There were three of them. Two were in uniform. The third, wearing a pullover with reindeer running in a band across his chest, held a pistol pointing downward. 'Give me a chance to talk to him,' I said, splashing through the night's puddles. They stared in astonishment but did not try to stop me.

The window of Florence's room was shattered. The room itself was in darkness; but, peering through the hole, I could make out a figure crouched beside the bed at the far end.

'Open the door, my boy,' I said. 'I won't let them hurt you, I promise.'

It was a lie. He was lost, I had no power to save him. Yet something went out from me to him. I ached to embrace him, to protect him.

One of the policemen appeared beside me, pressed against the wall. 'Tell him to come out,' he said. I turned on him in a fury. 'Go away!' I screamed, and fell into a fit of coughing.

The sun was coming up, rosy, in a sky full of drifting cloud.

'John!' I called through the coughing. 'Come out! I will not let them do anything to you.'

Now the man in the pullover was at my side. 'Tell him to pass out his weapons,' he said in a low voice.

'What weapons?'

'He has a pistol, I don't know what else. Tell him to pass everything out.'

'First promise you will not hurt him.'

His fingers closed on my arm. I resisted, but he was too strong. 'You are going to catch pneumonia out here,' he said. Something descended on me from behind: a coat, an overcoat, one of the policemen's overcoats. '*Neem haar binne,*' he murmured. They guided me back to the kitchen and closed the door on me.

I sat down, stood up again. The coat stank of cigarette smoke. I dropped it on the floor and opened the door. My feet were blue with cold. 'John!' I called. The three men were huddled over a radio. The one who had given me his coat turned with an exasperated air. 'Lady, it is dangerous out here,' he said. He bundled me indoors again, then could not find the key to lock the door.

'He is just a child,' I said.

'Let us do our work, lady,' he replied.

'I am watching you,' I said: 'I am watching everything you do. I tell you, he is just a child!'

He drew a breath as though about to respond, then let it out in a sigh and waited for me to talk myself out. A young man, solid, raw-boned. Son to someone, cousin to many. Many cousins, many aunts and uncles, great-aunts and great-uncles, standing about him, behind him, above him like a chorus, guiding, admonishing.

What could I say? What did we have in common to make intercourse possible, except that he was here to defend me, to defend my interests, in the wider sense?

'*Ek staan nie aan jou kant nie,*' I said. '*Ek staan aan die teenkant.*' I stand on the other side. But on the other bank too, the other bank of the river. On the far bank, looking back.

He turned, inspecting the stove, the sink, the racks, occupying *die ou dame* while his friends did their business outside. All in a day's work.

'That's all,' I said. 'I'm finished. I wasn't talking to you anyway.'

To whom then? To you: always to you. How I live, how I lived: my story.

The doorbell rang. More men, men in boots and caps and camouflage uniforms, tramping through the house. They clustered at the kitchen window. '*Hy sit daar in die buitekamer,*' explained the policeman, pointing to Florence's room. '*Daar's net die een deur en die een venster.*'

'*Nee, dan het ons hom,*' said one of the newcomers.

'I warn you, I'm watching everything you do,' I said.

He turned to me. 'Do you know this boy?' he said.

'Yes, I know him.'

'Did you know he had arms?'

I shrugged. 'God save the unarmed in these days.'

Someone else came in, a young woman in uniform with a crisp, clean air about her. '*Is dit die dame dié?*' she said; and then, to me: 'We are going to clear the house for a little while, till this business is over. Is there anywhere you would like to go, friends or relatives?'

'I am not leaving. This is my house.'

Her friendliness, her concern did not waver. 'I know,' she said, 'but it's too dangerous to stay. For just a little while we must ask you to leave.'

The men at the window had stopped talking now: they were impatient for me to be gone. '*Bel die ambulans,*' said one of them. '*Ag, sy kan sommer by die stasie wag,*' said the woman. She turned to me. 'Come now, Mrs . . .' She waited for me to supply the name. I did not. 'A nice warm cup of tea,' she offered.

'I am not going.'

They paid my words no more attention than they would a child's. '*Gaan haal 'n kombers,*' said the man – '*sy's amper blou van die koue.*'

The woman went upstairs and came back with the quilt from my bed. She wrapped it around me, gave me a hug, then helped me into my slippers. No sign of disgust at my legs, my feet. A good girl, reared to make someone a good wife.

'Are there are any pills or medicines or anything else you want to take along?' she asked.

'I'm not leaving,' I repeated, gripping my chair.

Murmured words passed between her and the men. Without warning I was lifted from behind, under the arms. The woman took my legs. Like a carpet they carried me to the front door. Pain racked my back. 'Put me down!' I cried.

'In a minute,' said the woman soothingly.

'*I have cancer!*' I screamed – '*Put me down!*'

Cancer! What a pleasure to fling the word at them! It stopped them in their tracks like a knife. '*Sit haar neer, dalk kom haar iets oor,*' said the man holding me – '*Ek het mos gesê jy moet die ambulans bel.*' Gingerly they laid me down on the sofa.

'Where is the pain?' asked the woman, frowning.

'In my heart,' I said. She looked puzzled. 'I have cancer of the heart.' Then she understood; she shook her head as if shaking off flies.

'Does it pain you to be carried?'

'It pains me all the time,' I said.

She caught the eye of the man behind me; something passed between them so amusing that she could not keep back a smile.

'I caught it by drinking from the cup of bitterness,' I plunged on. What did it matter if they thought me dotty? 'You will probably catch it too one day. It is hard to escape.'

There was a crash of breaking glass. Both of them rushed from the room; I got up and limped behind.

Nothing had changed except that a second windowpane was gone. The courtyard itself was empty; the policemen, half a dozen of them now, were crouching on the veranda, guns at the ready.

'*Weg!*' shouted one of them furiously. '*Kry haar weg!*'

The woman bundled me indoors. As she closed the door there was a curt explosion, a fusillade of shots, then a long stunned silence, then low talk and, from somewhere, the sound of Vercueil's dog yapping.

I tried to pull open the door, but the woman held me tight.

'If you have hurt him I will never forgive you,' I said.

'It's all right, we'll phone again for the ambulance,' she said, trying to soothe me.

But the ambulance was already there, drawn up on the sidewalk. Scores of people were gathering excitedly from all directions, neighbours, passers-by, young and old, black and white; from the balconies of the flats people stared down. By the time the policewoman and I emerged from the front door they were wheeling the body, covered in a blanket, down the driveway, and loading it aboard.

I made to climb into the ambulance after it; one of the attendants even took my arm to help me in, but a policeman intervened. 'Wait, we'll send another ambulance for her,' he said.

'I don't want another ambulance,' I said. He put on a kindly, nonplussed look. 'I want to go with him,' I said, and made another attempt to climb in. The quilt fell to my feet.

He shook his head. 'No,' he said. He gestured and the attendant closed the doors.

'God forgive us!' I breathed. With the quilt clasped around me I began to walk down Schoonder Street, away from the crowd. I had almost reached the corner when the police-woman came trotting after me. 'You must come home now!' she ordered. 'It's not my home any more,' I replied in a fury, and kept walking. She took my arm; I shook myself free. 'Sy's van haar kop af,' she remarked to no one in particular, and gave up.

In Buitenkant Street, under the flyover, I sat down to rest. A steady stream of cars flowed past heading for the city. No one spared me a glance. With my wild hair and pink quilt I might be a spectacle on Schoonder Street; here, amid the rubble and filth, I was just part of the urban shadowland.

A man and woman passed on foot on the other side of the street. Did I recognise the woman? Was it the one Vercueil had brought to the house, or did all the women who hung around the Avalon Hotel and Solly Kramer's Liquor Store have those wasted, spidery legs? The man, carrying a knotted plastic bag over his shoulder, was not Vercueil.

I wrapped myself tighter in the quilt and lay down. Through my bones I could feel the rumble of traffic on the flyover. The pills were in the house, the house in other hands. Could I survive without the pills? No. But did I want to survive? I was beginning to feel the indifferent peace of an old animal that, sensing its time is near, creeps, cold and sluggish, into the hole in the ground where everything will contract to the slow thudding of a heart. Behind a concrete pillar, in a place where the sun had not shone for thirty years, I curled up on my good side, listening to the beat of the pain that might as well have been the beat of my pulse.

I must have slept. Time must have passed. When I opened my eyes there was a child kneeling beside me, feeling inside the folds of the quilt. His hand crept over my body. 'There is nothing for you,' I tried to say, but my teeth were loose. Ten years old at most, with a shaven skull and bare feet and a hard look. Behind him two companions, even younger. I slipped out the teeth. 'Leave me alone,' I said: 'I am sick, you will get sick from me.'

Slowly they withdrew and, like crows, stood waiting.

I had to empty my bladder. Yielding, I urinated where I lay. Thank God for the cold, I thought, thank God for the numbness: all things work together toward an easy birth.

The boys came closer again. I awaited the prying of their hands, not caring. The roar of wheels lulled me; like a grub in a hive, I was absorbed into the hum of the spinning world. The air dense with noise. Thousands of wings passing and repassing without touching. How was there space for them all? How is there space in the skies for the souls of all the departed? Because, says Marcus Aurelius, they fuse one with another: they burn and fuse and so are returned to the great cycle.

Death after death. Bee-ash.

The flap of the quilt was drawn back. I felt light on my eyelids, coldness too on my cheeks where the tears had run.

Something pressed between my lips, was forced between my gums. I gagged and pulled away. All three children were clustered over me now in the gloom; there may have been others too, behind them. What were they doing? I tried to push the hand away but it pressed all the harder. An ugly noise came from my throat, a dry rasp like wood splitting. The hand withdrew. 'Don't –' I said; but my palate was sore, it was hard to form words.

What did I want to say? *Don't do that!? Don't you see I have nothing?? Don't you have any mercy??* What nonsense. Why should there be mercy in the world? I thought of beetles, those big black beetles with the humped backs, dying, waving their legs feebly, and ants pouring over them, gnawing at the soft places, the joints, the eyes, tearing away the beetle-flesh.

It was a stick, nothing more, a stick a few inches long that he had forced into my mouth. I could taste the grains of dirt it left behind.

With the tip of the stick he lifted my upper lip. I pulled back and tried to spit. Impassively he stood up. With a bare foot he kicked, and a little rain of dust and pebbles struck my face.

A car passed, outlining the children in its headlights. They began to move off down Buitenkant Street. Darkness returned.

Did these things really happen? Yes, these things happened. There is no more to be said about it. They happened a stone's throw from Breda Street and Schoonder Street and Vrede Street, where a century ago the patricians of Cape Town gave orders that there be erected spacious homes for themselves and their descendants in perpetuity, foreseeing nothing of the day when, in their shadows, the chickens would come home to roost.

There was a fog in my head, a grey confusion. I shivered; paroxysms of yawning passed over me. For a while I was nowhere.

Then something was sniffing at my face: a dog. I tried to ward it off but it found a way past my fingers. So I yielded, thinking, there are worse things than a dog's wet nose, its eager breath. I let it lick my face, lick my lips, lick up the salt of my tears. Kisses, if one wanted to look at them that way.

Someone was with the dog. Did I recognize the smell? Was it Vercueil, or did all street-wanderers smell of mouldering leaves, of underwear rotting in the ash-heap? 'Mr Vercueil?' I croaked, and the dog whined with excitement, giving a great sneeze straight into my face.

A match flared. Yes, it was Vercueil, hat and all. 'Who put you here?' he asked. 'Myself,' I said, past the raw place on my palate. The match died. Tears came again, which the dog eagerly consumed.

With his high shoulderblades and his chest narrow as a gull's, I would not have guessed that Vercueil could be so strong. But he lifted me, wet patch and all, and carried me. I thought: forty years since I was last carried by a man. The misfortune of a tall woman. Will this be how the story ends: with being carried in strong arms across the sands, through the shallows, past the breakers, into the darker depths?

We were away from the flyover, in blessed stillness. How much more bearable everything was suddenly becoming! Where was the pain? Was the pain in a better humour too? 'Don't go back to Schoonder Street,' I ordered.

We passed under a streetlight. I saw the strain in the muscles of his neck, heard his breath coming fast. 'Put me down for a minute,' I said. He put me down and rested. When would the time come when the jacket fell away and great wings sprouted from his shoulders?

Up Buitenkant Street he bore me, across Vrede Street, street of peace, and, treading more slowly, groping before each step, into a dark wooded space. Through branches I glimpsed the stars.

He set me down.

'I am so happy to see you,' I said, the words coming from my heart, heartfelt. And then: 'I was attacked by some children before you came. Attacked or violated or explored, I don't know which. That is why I talk so strangely. They pushed a stick into my mouth, I still don't understand why. What pleasure could it have given them?'

'They wanted your gold teeth,' he said. 'They get money for gold from the pawnshops.'

'Gold teeth? How strange. I haven't any gold teeth. I took my teeth out anyway. Here they are.'

From somewhere in the dark he fetched cardboard, a carton box folded flat. He spread it and helped me to lie down. Then without haste, without ceremony, he lay down too with his back to me. The dog settled between our legs.

'Do you want some of the quilt?' I said.

'I'm OK.'

Time passed.

'I'm sorry, but I'm terribly thirsty,' I whispered. 'Is there no water here?'

He got up and came back with a bottle. I smelled it: sweet wine, the bottle half full. 'It's all I've got,' he said. I drank it down. It did nothing for my thirst, but in the sky the stars began to swim. Everything grew remote: the smell of damp earth, the cold, the man beside me, my own body. Like a crab after a long day, tired, folding its claws, even the pain went to sleep. I swooped back into darkness.

When I awoke he had turned and flung an arm across my neck. I could have freed myself, but preferred not to disturb him. So while by slow degrees the new day broke, I lay face to face with him, not stirring. His eyes opened once, alert, like an animal's. 'I am not gone,' I murmured. The eyes closed.

The thought came: Whom, of all beings on earth, do I know best at this hour? Him. Every hair of his beard, every crease of his forehead known to me. Him, not you. Because he is here, beside me, now.

· 147 ·

Forgive me. Time is short, I must trust my heart and tell the truth. Sightless, ignorant, I follow where the truth takes me.

'Are you awake?' I murmured.

'Yes.'

'Both those boys are dead now,' I said. 'They have killed them both. Did you know?'

'I know.'

'You know what happened at the house?'

'Yes.'

'Do you mind if I talk?'

'Talk.'

'Let me tell you: I met Florence's brother the day Bheki died – brother or cousin or whatever. An educated man. I told him how I wished Bheki had never got involved in – what shall I call it? – the struggle. "He is just a child," I said: "He isn't ready. But for that friend of his, he would never have been drawn in."

'Later I spoke to him again on the telephone. I told him frankly what I thought of the comradeship for which both those children have now died. A mystique of death, I called it. I blamed people like Florence and him for doing nothing to discourage it.

'He heard me out civilly. I was entitled to my opinions, he said. I did not change his mind.

'But now I ask myself: What right have I to opinions about comradeship or anything else? What right have I to wish Bheki and his friend had kept out of trouble? To have opinions in a vacuum, opinions that touch no one, is, it seems to me, nothing. Opinions must be heard by others, heard and weighed, not merely listened to out of politeness. And to be weighed they must have weight. Mr Thabane does not weigh what I say. It has no weight to him. Florence does not even hear me. To Florence what goes on in my head is a matter of complete indifference, I know that.'

Vercueil got up, went behind a tree, urinated. Then, to my surprise, he came and lay down again. The dog snuggled against him, its nose in his crotch. With my tongue I probed the sore place in my mouth, tasting the blood.

'I have not changed my mind,' I said. 'I still detest these calls for sacrifice that end with young men bleeding to death in the mud. War is never what it pretends to be. Scratch the surface and you find, invariably, old men sending young men to their death in the name of some abstraction or other. Despite what Mr Thabane says (I do not blame him, the future comes disguised, if it came naked we would be petrified by what we saw), it remains a war of the old upon the young. *Freedom or death!* shout Bheki and his friends. Whose words? Not their own. *Freedom or death!*, I have no doubt, those two little girls are rehearsing in their sleep. *No!* I want to say: *Save yourselves!*

'Whose is the true voice of wisdom, Mr Vercueil? Mine, I believe. Yet who am I, *who am I* to have a voice at all? How can I honourably urge them to turn their back on that call? What am I entitled to do but sit in a corner with my mouth shut? I have no voice; I lost it long ago; perhaps I have never had one. I have no voice, and that is that. The rest should be silence. But with this – whatever it is – this voice that is no voice, I go on. On and on.'

Was Vercueil smiling? His face was hidden. In a toothless whisper sticky with sibilants I went on.

'A crime was committed long ago. How long ago? I do not know. But longer ago than 1916, certainly. So long ago that I was born into it. It is part of my inheritance. It is part of me, I am part of it.

'Like every crime it had its price. That price, I used to think, would have to be paid in shame: in a life of shame and a shameful death, unlamented, in an obscure corner. I accepted that. I did not try to set myself apart. Though it was not a crime I asked to be committed, it was committed in my name.

· 149 ·

I raged at times against the men who did the dirty work – you have seen it, a shameful raging as *stupid* as what it raged against – but I accepted too that, in a sense, they lived inside me. So that when in my rages I wished them dead, I wished death on myself too. In the name of honour. Of an honourable notion of honour. *Honesta mors*.

'I have no idea what freedom is, Mr Vercueil. I am sure Bheki and his friend had no idea either. Perhaps freedom is always and only what is unimaginable. Nevertheless, we know unfreedom when we see it – don't we? Bheki was not free, and knew it. You are not free, at least not on this earth, nor am I. I was born a slave and I will most certainly die a slave. A life in fetters, a death in fetters: that is part of the price, not to be quibbled at, not to be whined about.

'What I did not know, *what I did not know* – listen to me now! – was that the price was even higher. I had miscalculated. Where did the mistake come in? It had something to do with honour, with the notion I clung to through thick and thin, from my education, from my reading, that in his soul the honourable man can suffer no harm. I strove always for honour, for a private honour, using shame as my guide. As long as I was ashamed I knew I had not wandered into dishonour. That was the use of shame: as a touchstone, something that would always be there, something you could come back to like a blind person, to touch, to tell you where you were. For the rest I kept a decent distance from my shame. I did not wallow in it. Shame never became a shameful pleasure; it never ceased to gnaw me. I was not proud of it, I was ashamed of it. My shame, my own. Ashes in my mouth day after day after day, which never ceased to taste like ashes.

'It is a confession I am making here, this morning, Mr Vercueil,' I said, 'as full a confession as I know how. I withhold no secrets. I have been a good person, I freely confess to it. I am a good person still. What times these are when to be a good person is not enough!

'What I had not calculated on was that more might be called for than to be good. For there are plenty of good people in this country. We are two a penny, we good and nearly-good. What the times call for is quite different from goodness. The times call for heroism. A word that, as I speak it, sounds foreign to my lips. I doubt that I have ever used it before, even in a lecture. Why not? Perhaps out of respect. Perhaps out of shame. As one drops one's gaze before a naked man. I would have used the words *heroic status* instead, I think, in a lecture. The hero with his heroic status. The hero, that antique naked figure.'

A deep groan came from Vercueil's throat. I craned over, but all I could see was the stubble on his cheek and a hairy ear. 'Mr Vercueil!' I whispered. He did not stir. Asleep? Pretending to sleep? How much had passed him by unheard? Had he heard about goodness and heroism? About honour and shame? Is a true confession still true if it is not heard? Do you hear me, or have I put you to sleep too?

I went behind a bush. Birds were singing all around. Who would have thought there was such birdlife in the suburbs! It was like Arcady. No wonder Vercueil and his friends lived out of doors. What is a roof good for but to keep off the rain? Vercueil and his comrades.

I lay down beside him again, my feet cold and muddy. It was quite light now. On our flattened-out box in the vacant lot we must have been visible to every passer-by. That is how we must be in the eyes of the angels: people living in houses of glass, our every act naked. Our hearts naked too, beating in chests of glass. Birdsong poured down like rain.

'I feel so much better this morning,' I said. 'But perhaps we should go back now. Feeling better is usually a warning that I am going to feel worse.'

Vercueil sat up, took off his hat, scratched his scalp with long, dirty nails. The dog came trotting up from somewhere and fussed around us. Vercueil folded the cardboard and hid it in the bushes.

'Do you know I have had a breast removed?' I said out of the blue.

He fidgeted, looked uncomfortable.

'I regret it now, of course. Regret that I am marked. It becomes like trying to sell a piece of furniture with a scratch or a burn mark. It's still a perfectly good chair, you say, but people aren't interested. People don't like marked objects. I am talking about my life. It may not be perfectly good, but it is still a life, not a half-life. I thought I would sell it or spend it to save my honour. But who will accept it in its present state? It is like trying to spend a drachma. A perfectly good coin somewhere else, but not here. Suspiciously marked.

'But I haven't quite given up yet. I am still casting around for something to do with it. Do you have any suggestions?'

Vercueil put on his hat, tugging it down firmly fore and aft.

'I would love to buy you a new hat,' I said.

He smiled. I took his arm; slowly we set off along Vrede Street.

'Let me tell you the dream I had,' I said. 'The man in my dream didn't have a hat, but I think it was you. He had long oily hair brushed straight back from his forehead.' Long and oily; dirty too, hanging down at the back in ugly rat's-tails; but I did not mention that.

'We were at the seaside. He was teaching me to swim. He held me by the hands and drew me out while I lay flat and kicked. I was wearing a knitted costume, the kind we had in the old days, navy blue. I was a child. But then in dreams we are always children.

'He was drawing me out, backing into the sea, fixing me with his eyes. He had eyes like yours. There were no waves, just a ripple of water coming in, glinting with light. In fact the water was oily too. Where his body broke the surface the oil clung to him with the heavy sheen oil has. I thought to myself: sardine oil: I am the little sardine: he is taking me out into the oil. I wanted to say *Turn back*, but dared not open my mouth for fear the oil would flood in and fill my lungs. Drowning in oil: I had not the courage for that.'

I paused to let him speak, but he was silent. We turned the corner into Schoonder Street.

'Of course I am not telling you this dream innocently,' I said. 'Retailing a dream is always meant to achieve something. The question is, what?

'The day I first saw you behind the garage was the day I had the bad news about myself, about my case. It was too much of a coincidence. I wondered whether you were not, if you will excuse the word, an angel come to show me the way. Of course you were not, are not, cannot be – I see that. But that is only half the story, isn't it? We half perceive but we also half create.

'So I have continued to tell myself stories in which you lead, I follow. And if you say not a word, that is, I tell myself, because the angel is wordless. The angel goes before, the woman follows. His eyes are open, he sees; hers are shut, she is still sunk in the sleep of worldliness. That is why I keep turning to you for guidance, for help.'

The front door was locked but the gate to the courtyard swung open. The broken glass had not been swept up, the door to Florence's room hung askew. I cast my gaze down, treading carefully, not ready yet to look into the room, not strong enough.

The kitchen door was unlocked. They had not found the key.

'Come in,' I said to Vercueil.

The house was and was not as it had been. Things in the kitchen were out of place. My umbrella hung where it had never hung before. The sofa had been shifted, exposing an old stain on the carpet. And over all a strange smell: not only cigarette smoke and sweat but something sharp and penetrating that I could not place. They have left their mark on everything, I thought: thorough workers. Then I remembered the file on my desk, the letter, all the pages thus far. That too! I thought: they will have been through that too! Soiled fingers turning the pages, eyes without love going over the naked words. 'Help me upstairs,' I said to Vercueil.

The file, left open when I last wrote, was closed. The lock of the filing-cabinet was broken. There were gaps in the bookshelves.

The two unused rooms had had their locks forced.

They had been through the cupboard, the chest of drawers.

Nothing left untouched. Like the last visit the burglars paid. The search a mere pretext. The true purpose the touching, the fingering. The spirit malevolent. Like rape: a way of filthying a woman.

I turned to Vercueil, wordless, sick to the stomach.

'There's someone downstairs,' he said.

From the landing we could hear someone talking on the telephone.

The voice stopped. A young man in uniform emerged into the hallway and nodded to us.

'What are you doing in my house?' I called down.

'Just checking,' he replied quite cheerfully. 'We didn't want strangers coming in.' He gathered up a cap, a coat, a rifle. Was it the rifle I had smelled? 'The detectives will be here at eight,' he said. 'I'll wait outside.' He smiled; he seemed to think he had done me a service; he seemed to be expecting thanks.

'I must have a bath,' I said to Vercueil.

But I did not have a bath. I closed the bedroom door, took two of the red pills and lay down trembling all over. The trembling got worse till I was shaking like a leaf in a storm. I was cold but the trembling was not from the cold.

A minute at a time, I told myself: do not fall to pieces now: think only of the next minute.

The trembling began to subside.

Man, I thought: the only creature with a part of his existence in the unknown, in the future, like a shadow cast before him. Trying continually to catch up with that moving shadow, to inhabit the image of his hope. But I, I cannot afford to be man. Must be something smaller, blinder, closer to the ground.

There was a knock and Vercueil came in, followed by the policeman who yesterday had worn the reindeer jersey and now wore a jacket and tie. The trembling began again. He motioned for Vercueil to leave the room. I sat up. 'Don't go, Mr Vercueil,' I said; and to him: 'What right have you to come into my house?'

'We have been worried about you.' He did not seem worried at all. 'Where were you last night?' And then, when I did not reply: 'Are you sure you are all right by yourself, Mrs Curren?'

Though I clenched my fists, the trembling grew worse till it convulsed me. 'I am not by myself!' I screamed at him: 'You are the one who is by himself!'

He was not taken aback. On the contrary, he seemed to be encouraging me to go on.

Hold yourself together, I thought! They will commit you, they will call you mad and take you away!

'What do you want here?' I asked more quietly.

'I just want to ask a few questions. How did you come across this boy Johannes?'

Johannes: was that his true name? Surely not.

'He was a friend of my domestic's son. A school-friend.'

Out of his pocket he brought a little cassette recorder and set it on the bed beside me.

'And where is your domestic's son?'

'He is dead and buried. Surely you know these things.'

· 155 ·

'What happened to him?'

'He was shot out on the Flats.'

'And are there any more of them that you know of?'

'More of whom?'

'More friends.'

'Thousands. Millions. More than you can count.'

'I mean, more from that cell. Are there any others who have used your premises?'

'No.'

'And do you know how these arms came into their hands?'

'What arms?'

'A pistol. Three detonators.'

'I know nothing about detonators. I don't know what a detonator is. The pistol was mine.'

'Did they take it from you?'

'I lent it to them. Not to them. To the boy, John.'

'You lent him the pistol? Was the pistol yours?'

'Yes.'

'Why did you lend him the pistol?'

'To defend himself.'

'To defend himself against who, Mrs Curren?'

'To defend himself against attack.'

'And what kind of pistol was it, Mrs Curren? Can you show me the licence for it?'

'I know nothing about kinds of pistol. I have had it for a long time, from before all this fuss about licences.'

'Are you sure you gave it to him? You know this is a chargeable offence we are talking about.'

The pills were beginning to take effect. The pain in my back grew more distant, my limbs relaxed, the horizon began to expand again.

'Do you really want to go on with this nonsense?' I said. I lay back on the pillow and closed my eyes. My head was spinning. 'These are dead people we are talking about. There is nothing more you can do to them. They are safe. You have had the execution. Why bother with a trial? Why not just close the case?'

He picked up the recorder, fiddled with it, put it back on the pillow. 'Just checking,' he said.

With a languorous arm I brushed the recorder away. He caught it before it hit the floor.

'You have been through my private papers,' I said. 'You have taken books that belong to me. I want them back I want everything back. All my things. They are no business of yours.'

'We are not going to eat your books, Mrs Curren. You will get everything back in the end.'

'I don't want things back in the end. I want them back now. They are mine. They are private.'

He shook his head. 'This is not private, Mrs Curren. You know that. Nothing is private any more.'

The languor was getting to my tongue now. 'Leave me,' I said thickly.

'Just a few more questions. Where were you last night?'

'With Mr Vercueil.'

'Is this Mr Vercueil?'

It took too much of an effort to open my eyes. 'Yes,' I murmured.

'Who is Mr Vercueil?' And then, in quite a different tone: '*Wie is jy?*'

'Mr Vercueil takes care of me. Mr Vercueil is my right-hand man. Come here, Mr Vercueil.'

I reached out and found Vercueil's trouser-leg, then his hand, the bad hand with the curled fingers. With the numb, clawlike grip of the old I clung to it.

'*In Godsnaam,*' said the detective somewhere far away. In God's name: mere fulmination, or a curse on the pair of us? My grip broke, I began to slide away.

A word appeared before me: Thabanchu, Thaba Nchu. I

tried to concentrate. Nine letters, anagram for what? With a great effort I placed the *b* first. Then I was gone.

I awoke thirsty, groggy, full of pain. The clockface stared at me but I could make no sense of the hands. The house was silent with the silence of deserted houses.

Thabanchu: *banch*? *bath*? With stupid hands I unwrapped the sheet from around me. Must I have a bath?

But my feet did not take me to the bathroom. Holding to the rail, bent over, groaning, I went downstairs and dialled the Guguletu number. On and on the phone rang. Then at last someone answered, a child, a girl. 'Is Mr Thabane there?' I asked. 'No.' 'Then can I speak to Mrs Mkubuleki – no, not Mrs Mkubuleki, Mrs Mkubukeli?' 'Mrs Mkubukeli does not live here.' 'But do you know Mrs Mkubukeli?' 'Yes, I know him.' 'Mrs Mkubukeli?' 'Yes.' 'Who are you?' 'I am Lily.' Lee-lee. 'Are you the only one at home?' 'There is my sister too.' 'How old is your sister?' 'She is six.' 'And you – how old are you?' 'Ten.' 'Can you take a message to Mrs Mkubukeli, Lily?' 'Yes.' 'It is about her brother Mr Thabane. She must tell Mr Thabane to be careful. Say it is very important. Mr Thabane must be careful. My name is Mrs Curren. Can you write that down? And this is my number.' I read out the number, spelled my name. Mrs Curren: nine letters, anagram for what?

Vercueil knocked and came in. 'Do you want something to eat?' he said.

'I am not hungry. But help yourself to anything you can find.'

I wanted to be left alone. But he lingered, eyeing me curiously. I was sitting up in bed, gloves on my hands, the writing-pad on my knees. For half an hour I had sat with the page blank before me.

'I am just waiting for my hands to warm up,' I said.

But it was not cold fingers that kept me from writing. It was the pills, which I take more of now, and more often. They are like smoke-flares. I swallow them and they release a fog inside me, a fog of extinction. I cannot take the pills and go on with the writing. So without pain no writing: a new and terrible rule. Except that, when I have taken the pills, nothing is terrible any more, everything is indifferent, everything is the same.

Nevertheless I do write. In the dead of night, with Vercueil asleep downstairs, I take up this letter to tell you one more thing about that 'John,' that sullen boy I never took to. I want to tell you that, despite my dislike of him, he is with me more clearly, more piercingly than Bheki has ever been. He is with me or I am with him: him or the trace of him. It is the middle of the night but it is the grey of his last morning too. I am here in my bed but I am there in Florence's room too, with its one window and one door and no other way out. Outside the door men are waiting, crouched like hunters, to present the boy with his death. In his lap he holds the pistol that, for this interval, keeps the hunters at bay, that was his and Bheki's great secret, that was going to make men of them; and beside him I stand or hover. The barrel of the pistol is between his knees; he strokes it up and down. He is listening to the murmur of voices outside, and I listen with him. He is readying himself for the smoke that will choke his lungs, the kick that will burst the door open, the torrent of fire that will sweep him away. He is readying himself to raise the pistol in that instant and fire the one shot he will have time to fire into the heart of the light.

His eyes are unblinking, fixed on the door through which he is going to leave the world. His mouth is dry but he is not afraid. His heart beats steadily like a fist in his chest clenching and unclenching.

His eyes are open and mine, though I write, are shut. My eyes are shut in order to see.

Within this interval there is no time, though his heart beats time. I am here in my room in the night but I am also with him, all the time, as I am with you across the seas, hovering.

A hovering time, but not eternity. A *time being*, a suspension, before the return of the time in which the door bursts open and we face, first he, then I, the great white glare.

· IV ·

I have had a dream of Florence, a dream or vision. In the dream I see her striding again down Government Avenue holding Hope by the hand and carrying Beauty on her back. All three of them wear masks. I am there too, with a crowd of people of all kinds and conditions gathered around me. The air is festive. I am to provide a show.

But Florence does not stop to watch. Gaze fixed ahead, she passes as if through a congregation of wraiths.

The eyes of her mask are like eyes in pictures from the ancient Mediterranean: large, oval, with the pupil in the centre: the almond eyes of a goddess.

I stand in the middle of the avenue opposite the Parliament buildings, circled by people, doing my tricks with fire. Over me tower great oaks. But my mind is not on my tricks. I am intent on Florence. Her dark coat, her dull dress have fallen away. In a white slip ruffled by the wind, her feet bare, her head bare, her right breast bare, she strides past, the one child, masked, naked, trotting quickly beside her, the other stretching an arm out over her shoulder, pointing.

Who is this goddess who comes in a vision with uncovered breast cutting the air? It is Aphrodite, but not smile-loving Aphrodite, patroness of pleasures: an older figure, a figure of urgency, of cries in the dark, short and sharp, of blood and earth, emerging for an instant, showing herself, passing.

From the goddess comes no call, no signal. Her eye is open and is blank. She sees and does not see.

Burning, doing my show, I stand transfixed. The flames flowing from me are blue as ice. I feel no pain.

It is a vision from last night's dream-time but also from outside time. Forever the goddess is passing, forever, caught in a posture of surprise and regret, I do not follow. Though I peer and peer into the vortex from which visions come, the wake of the goddess and her god-children remains empty, the woman who should follow behind not there, the woman with serpents of flame in her hair who beats her arms and cries and dances.

I related the dream to Vercueil.

'Is it real?' he asked.

'Real? Of course not. It isn't even authentic. Florence has nothing to do with Greece. Figures in dreams have another kind of import. They are signs, signs of other things.'

'Were they real? Was she real?' he repeated, bringing me up short, refusing to be deflected. 'What else did you see?'

'What else? Is there more? Do you know?' I said more softly, feeling my way after him now.

He shook his head, baffled.

'All the days you have known me,' I said, 'I have been standing on the river-bank awaiting my turn. I am waiting for someone to show me the way across. Every minute of every day I am here, waiting. That is what else I see. Do you see it too?'

He said nothing.

'The reason I fight against going back to hospital is that in hospital they will put me to sleep. That is the expression they use for animals, as a kindness, but they may as well use it for people. They will put me into a sleep without dreams. They will feed me mandragora till I grow drowsy and fall into the

· 164 ·

river and am drowned and washed away. That way I will never cross. I cannot allow it to happen. I have come too far. I cannot have my eyes closed.'

'What do you want to see?' said Vercueil.

'I want to see you as you really are.'

Diffidently he shrugged. 'Who am I?'

'Just a man. A man who came without being invited. More I can't say yet. Can you?'

He shook his head. 'No.'

'If you want to do something for me,' I said, 'you can fix the aerial for the radio.'

'Don't you want me to bring the television up instead?'

'I haven't the stomach to watch television. It will make me sick.'

'Television can't make you sick. It's just pictures.'

'There is no such thing as just pictures. There are men behind the pictures. They send out their pictures to make people sick. You know what I am talking about.'

'Pictures can't make you sick.'

Sometimes he does this: contradicts me, provokes me, chips away at me, watching for signs of irritation. It is his way of teasing, so clumsy, so unappealing that my heart quite goes out to him.

'Fix the aerial, please, that's all I ask.'

He went downstairs. Minutes later he came stamping up with the television set in his arms. He plugged it in facing the bed, switched it on, fiddled with the aerial, stood aside. It was mid-afternoon. Against blue sky a flag waved. A brass band played the anthem of the Republic.

'Switch it off,' I said.

He turned the sound louder.

'*Switch it off!*' I screamed.

He wheeled, took in my angry glare. Then, to my surprise,

he began to do a little shuffle. Swaying his hips, holding his hands out, clicking his fingers, he danced, unmistakably danced, to music I never thought could be danced to. He was mouthing words too. What were they? Not, certainly, the words I knew.

'*Off!*' I screamed again.

An old woman, toothless, in a rage: I must have looked a sight. He turned the sound down.

'*Off!*'

He switched it off. 'Don't get so upset,' he murmured.

'Then don't be silly, Vercueil. And don't make fun of me. Don't trivialize me.'

'Still, why get in a state?'

'Because I am afraid of going to hell and having to listen to *Die stem* for all eternity.'

He shook his head. 'Don't worry,' he said: 'it's all going to end. Have patience.'

'I haven't got time for patience. You may have time but I haven't got time.'

Again he shook his head. 'Maybe you've also got time,' he whispered, and gave me his toothed leer.

For an instant it was as if the heavens opened and light blazed down. Hungry for good news after a lifetime of bad news, unable to help myself, I smiled back. 'Really?' I said. He nodded. Like two fools we grinned each at the other. He clicked his fingers suggestively; awkward as a gannet, all feathers and bone, he repeated a step of his dance. Then he went out, climbed the ladder and joined the broken wire, and I had the radio again.

But what was there to listen to? The airwaves so bulge nowadays with the nations peddling their wares that music is all but squeezed out. I fell asleep to *An American in Paris* and awoke to a steady patter of morse. Where did it come from? From a ship at sea? From some old-fashioned steamship plying the waves between Walvis Bay and Ascension Island?

The dots and dashes followed on without haste, without falter, in a stream that promised to flow till the cows came home. What was their message? Did it matter? Their patter, like rain, a rain of meaning, comforted me, made the night bearable as I lay waiting for the hour to roll round for the next pill.

I say I do not want to be put to sleep. The truth is, without sleep I cannot endure. Whatever else it brings, the Diconal at least brings sleep or a simulacrum of sleep. As the pain recedes, as time quickens. as the horizon lifts, my attention, concentrated like a burning-glass on the pain, can slacken for a while; I can draw breath, unclench my balled hands, straighten my legs. Give thanks for this mercy, I say to myself: for the sick body stunned, for the soul drowsy, half out of its casing, beginning to float.

But the respite is never long. Clouds come over, thoughts begin to bunch, to take on the dense, angry life of a swarm of flies. I shake my head, trying to clear them away. This is my hand, I say, opening my eyes wide, staring at the veins on the back of my hand; this is the bedspread. Then as quick as lightning something strikes. In an instant I am gone and in another instant I am back, still staring at my hand. Between these instants an hour may have passed or the blink of an eye, during which I have been absent, gone, struggling with something thick and rubbery that invades the mouth and grips the tongue at its root, something that comes from the depths of the sea. I surface, shaking my head like a swimmer. In my throat is a taste of bile, of sulphur. Madness! I say to myself: this is what it tastes like to be mad!

Once I came to myself facing the wall. In my hand was a pencil, its point broken. All over the wall were sprawling, sliding characters, meaningless, coming from me or someone inside me.

I telephoned Dr Syfret. 'My reaction to the Diconal seems to be getting worse,' I said, and tried to describe it. 'I wonder, is there no alternative you can prescribe?'

'I was not aware that you still regarded yourself as under my care,' replied Dr Syfret. 'You should be in hospital getting proper attention. I can't conduct a surgery over the telephone.'

'I am asking for very little,' I said. 'The Diconal is giving me hallucinations. Is there nothing else I can take?'

'And I say, I can't treat you without seeing you. That is not how I work, that is not how any of my colleagues work.'

I was silent so long he must have thought he had lost me. The truth was, I was wavering. Don't you understand? I wanted to say: I am tired, tired unto death. *In manus tuas*: take me into your hands, care for me, or, if you cannot, do whatever is next best.

'Let me ask one last question,' I said. 'The reactions I am having – do other people have them too?'

'Patients react in many different ways. Yes, it is possible your reactions are due to the Diconal.'

'Then if by some chance you have a change of heart,' I said, 'could you telephone a new prescription through to the Avalon Pharmacy in Mill Street? I have no illusions about my condition, doctor. It is not care I need, just help with the pain.'

'And if you change your mind and want to see me at any time, Mrs Curren, day or night, you have only to pick up the telephone.'

An hour later the doorbell rang. It was the delivery man from the pharmacy bringing a new prescription in a fourteen-day supply.

I telephoned the pharmacist. 'Tylox,' I asked: 'is that the strongest?'

'What do you mean?'

'I mean, is it the last one prescribed?'

'That is not the way it works, Mrs Curren. There is no first and no last.'

I took two of the new pills. Again the miraculous draining away of pain, the euphoria, the feeling of being restored to life. I had a bath, got back into bed, tried to read, fell into a confused sleep. In an hour I was awake again. The pain was creeping back, bringing with it nausea and the first edge of the familiar shadow of depression.

The drug over the pain: a shaft of light but then darkness redoubled.

Vercueil came in.

'I have taken the new pills,' I said. 'They are no improvement. Slightly stronger, perhaps; that's all.'

'Take more,' said Vercueil. 'You don't have to wait four hours.'

A drunkard's advice.

'I'm sure I will,' I said. 'But if I am free to take them whenever I like, why not take them all together?'

There was silence between us.

'Why did you choose me?' I said.

'I didn't choose you.'

'Why did you come here, to this house?'

'You didn't have a dog.'

'Why else?'

'I thought you wouldn't make trouble.'

'And have I made trouble?'

He came toward me. His face was puffy, I could smell liquor on his breath. 'If you want me to help you I'll help you,' he said. He leaned over and took me by the throat, his thumbs resting lightly on my larynx, the three bad fingers bunched under my ear. 'Don't,' I whispered, and pushed his hands away. My eyes swam with tears. I took his hands in mine and beat them on my chest in a gesture of lamentation quite foreign to me.

After a while I was still. He continued to lean over me,

allowing me to use him. The dog put its nose over the edge of the bed, sniffing at us.

'Will you let the dog sleep with me?' I said.

'Why?'

'For the warmth.'

'He won't stay. He sleeps where I sleep.'

'Then sleep here too.'

There was a long wait while he went downstairs. I had another pill. Then the light on the landing went off. I heard him take off his shoes. 'Take off the hat too, for a change,' I said.

He lay down at my back, on top of the bedclothes. The smell of his dirty feet reached me. He whistled softly; the dog leapt up, did its circle dance, settled between his legs and mine. Like Tristan's sword, keeping us honest.

The pill worked its wonders. For half an hour, while he and the dog slept, I lay still, free of pain, my soul alert, darting. A vision passed before my eyes of the child Beauty riding towards me on her mother's back, bobbing, staring imperiously ahead. Then the vision faded and clouds of dust, the dust of Borodino, came rolling over my sight like the wheels of the carriage of death.

I switched on the lamp. It was midnight.

I will draw a veil soon. This was never meant to be the story of a body, but of the soul it houses. I will not show to you what you will not be able to bear: a woman in a burning house running from window to window, calling through the bars for help.

Vercueil and his dog, sleeping so calmly beside these torrents of grief. Fulfilling their charge, waiting for the soul to emerge. The soul, neophyte, wet, blind, ignorant.

I have the story now of how he lost the use of his fingers. It was in an accident at sea. They had to abandon ship. In the

scramble his hand was caught in a pulley and crushed. All
night he floated on a raft with seven other men and a boy, in
agony. The next day they were picked up by a Russian trawler
and his hand was given attention. But by then it was too late.

'Did you learn any Russian?' I asked.

All he remembered, he said, was *xorosho*.

'No one mentioned Borodino?'

'I don't remember Borodino.'

'You didn't think of staying with the Russians?'

He looked at me strangely.

He has never been to sea since then.

'Don't you miss the sea?' I asked.

'I'll never set foot in a boat again,' he replied decidedly.

'Why?'

'Because next time I won't be so lucky.'

'How do you know? If you had faith in yourself you could
walk on water. Don't you believe in the doings of faith?'

He was silent.

'Or a whirlwind would arrive and pluck you out of the
water and set you down on dry land. And there are always
dolphins. Dolphins rescue drowning sailors, don't they? Why
did you become a sailor anyway?'

'You don't always think ahead. You don't always know.'

I pinched his ring finger lightly. 'Can't you feel anything?'

'No. The nerves are dead.'

I always knew he had a story to tell, and now he begins to
tell it, starting with the fingers of one hand. A mariner's
story. Do I believe it? Verily, I do not care. There is no lie
that does not have at its core some truth. One must only
know how to listen.

He has worked at the docks too, lifting things, loading
things. One day, he said, unloading a crate, they smelled
something bad and opened it and found the body of a man,
a stowaway who had starved to death in his hiding-place.

'Where did he come from?' I asked.

· 171 ·

'China. A long way away.'

He has also worked for the SPCA, at their kennels.

'Was that where you got to like dogs?'

'I always got on with dogs.'

'Did you have a dog as a child?'

'Mm,' he said, meaning nothing. Early on he decided he could get away with choosing which of my questions to hear, which not to hear.

Nevertheless, piece by piece I put together the story of a life as obscure as any on earth. What is in store for him next, I wonder, when the episode of the old woman in the big house is over with? One hand crippled, unable to do all its offices. His sailor's skill with knots lost. Not dextrous any more, nor fully decent. In the middle years of his course, and at his side no wife. Alone: *stoksielalleen*: a stick in an empty field, a soul alone, sole. Who will watch over him?

'What will you do with yourself when I am gone?'

'I will go on.'

'I am sure you will; but who will there be in your life?'

Cautiously he smiled. 'Do I need somebody in my life?'

Not a riposte. A real question. He does not know. He is asking me, this rudimentary man.

'Yes. I would say you need a wife, if the idea does not strike you as eccentric. Even that woman you brought here, as long as there is feeling for her in your heart.'

He shook his head.

'Never mind. It is not marriage I am talking about but something else. I would promise to watch over you, except that I have no firm idea of what is possible after death. Perhaps there will be no watching over allowed, or very little. All these places have their rules, and, whatever one may wish, it may not be possible to get around them. There may not even be secrets allowed, secret watching. There may be no way of keeping a space in the heart private for you or anyone else. All may be erased. All. It is a terrible thought. Enough to make one rebel, to make one say: If that is how things are to be, I withdraw: here is my ticket, I am handing it back. But I doubt very much that the handing back of tickets will be allowed, for whatever reason.

'That is why you should not be so alone. Because I may have to go away entirely.'

He sat on the bed with his back to me, bent over, gripping the dog's head between his knees, stroking it.

'Do you understand me?'

'Mm.' The *mm* that could mean yes but in fact means nothing.

'No, you don't. You don't understand at all. It is not the prospect of your solitude that appals me. It is the prospect of my own.'

Every day he goes off to do the shopping. In the evenings he cooks, then hovers over me, watching to see that I eat. I am never hungry but haven't the heart to tell him. 'I find it hard to eat while you watch,' I say as gently as I can, then hide the food and feed it to the dog.

His favourite concoction is white bread fried in egg with tuna on the bread and tomato sauce on the tuna. I wish I had had the foresight to give him cooking lessons.

Though he has the whole house to spread himself in, he lives, in effect, with me in my room. He drops empty packets, old wrapping papers on the floor. When there is a draught they scud around like ghosts. 'Take the rubbish away,' I plead. 'I will,' he promises, and sometimes does, but then leaves more.

We share a bed, folded one upon the other like a page folded in two, like two wings folded: old mates, bunkmates, conjoined, conjugal. *Lectus genialis, lectus adversus.* His toe-nails, when he takes off his shoes, are yellow, almost brown, like horn. Feet that he keeps out of water for fear of falling: falling into depths where he cannot breathe. A dry creature, a creature of air, like those locust-fairies in Shakespeare with their whipstock of cricket's bone, lash of spider-film. Huge swarms of them borne out to sea on the wind, out of sight of land, tiring, settling one upon another upon another, resolving to drown the Atlantic by their numbers. Swallowed, all of them, to the last. Brittle wings on the sea-floor sighing like a forest of leaves; dead eyes by the million; and the crabs moving among them, clutching, grinding.

He snores.

From the side of her shadow husband your mother writes. Forgive me if the picture offends you. One must love what is nearest. One must love what is to hand, as a dog loves.

Mrs V.

September 23, the equinox. Steady rain falling from a sky that has closed in tight against the mountain, so low that one could reach up with a broomstick and touch it. A soothing, muffling sound, like a great hand, a hand of water, folding over the house; the patter on the rooftiles, the ripple in the gutters ceasing to be noise, become a thickening, a liquefaction of the air.

'What is this?' asked Vercueil.

He had a little hinged rosewood case. Held open at a certain angle to the light, it reveals a young man with long hair in an old-fashioned suit. Change the angle, and the image decomposes into silver streaks behind a glass surface.

'It is a photograph from the olden days. From before photographs.'

'Who is it?'

'I am not sure. It may be one of my grandfather's brothers.'

'Your house is like a museum.'

(He has been poking around in the rooms the police broke into.)

'In a museum things have labels. This is a museum where

the labels have fallen off. A museum in decay. A museum that ought to be in a museum.'

'You should sell these old things if you don't want them.'

'Sell them if you like. Sell me too.'

'For what?'

'For bones. For hair. Sell my teeth too. Unless you think I am worth nothing. It's a pity we don't have one of those carts that children used to wheel the Guy around in. You could wheel me down the Avenue with a letter pinned to my front. Then you could set fire to me. Or you could take me to some more obscure place, the rubbish dump for instance, and dispose of me there.'

He used to go out on to the balcony when he wanted to smoke. Now he smokes on the landing and the smoke drifts back into my room. I cannot stand it. But it is time to begin getting used to what I cannot stand.

He came upon me washing my underwear in the basin. I was in pain from the bending: no doubt I looked terrible. 'I will do that for you,' he offered. I refused. But then I could not reach the line, so he had to hang it for me: an old woman's underwear, grey, listless.

When the pain bites deepest and I shudder and go pale and a cold sweat breaks out on me, he sometimes holds my hand. I twist in his grip like a hooked fish; I am aware of an ugly look on my face, the look people have when they are rapt in lovemaking: brutal, predatory. He does not like that look; he turns his eyes away. As for me, I think: let him see, let him learn what it is like!

He carries a knife in his pocket. Not a clasp knife but a menacing blade with a sharp point embedded in a cork. When he gets into bed he puts it on the floor beside him, with his money.

So I am well guarded. Death would think twice before trying to pass this dog, this man.

What is Latin? he asked.

· 175 ·

A dead language, I replied, a language spoken by the dead.
'Really?' he said. The idea seemed to tickle him.
'Yes, really,' I said. 'You only hear it at funerals nowadays.
Funerals and the odd wedding.'
'Can you speak it?'
I recited some Virgil, Virgil on the unquiet dead:

> *nec ripas datur horrendas et rauca fluenta*
> *transportare prius quam sedibus ossa quierunt.*
> *centum errant annos volitantque haec litora circum;*
> *tum demum admissi stagna exoptata revisunt.*

'What does it mean?' he said.
'It means that if you don't mail the letter to my daughter I
will have a hundred years of misery.'
'It doesn't.'
'Yes, it does. *Ossa*: that is the word for a diary. Something
on which the days of your life are inscribed.'
Later he came back. 'Say the Latin again,' he asked. I spoke
the lines and watched his lips move as he listened. He is
memorizing, I thought. But it was not so. It was the dactyl
beating in him, with its power to move the pulse, the throat.
'Was that what you taught? Was that your job?'
'Yes, it was my job. I made a living from it. Giving voice
to the dead.'
'And who paid you?'
'The taxpayers. The people of South Africa, both great and
small.'
'Could you teach me?'
'I could have taught you. I could have taught you most
things Roman. I am not so sure about the Greek. I could still
teach you, but there would not be time for everything.'
He was flattered, I could see.
'You would find Latin easy,' I said. 'There would be much
you remembered.'

· 176 ·

Another challenge issued, another intimation that *I know*. I am like a woman with a husband who keeps a mistress on the sly, scolding him, coaxing him to come clean. But my hints pass him by. He is not hiding anything. His ignorance is real. His ignorance, his innocence.

'There is something that won't come, isn't there?' I said. 'Why don't you just speak and see where the words take you?'

But he was at a threshold he could not cross. He stood baulked, wordless, hiding behind the cigarette smoke, narrowing his eyes so that I should not see in.

The dog circled him, came to me, drifted off again, restless. Is it possible that the dog is the one sent, and not he?

You will never get to see him, I suppose. I would have liked to send you a picture, but my camera was taken in the last burglary. In any case, he is not the kind of person who photographs well. I have seen the picture on his identity card. He looks like a prisoner torn from the darkness of a cell, thrust into a room full of blinding lights, shoved against a wall, shouted at to stand still. His image raped from him, taken by force. He is like one of those half-mythical creatures that come out in photographs only as blurs, vague forms disappearing into the undergrowth that could be man or beast or merely a bad spot on the emulsion: unproved, unattested. Or disappearing over the edge of the picture, leaving behind in the shutter-trap an arm or a leg or the back of a head.

'Would you like to go to America?' I asked him.

'Why?'

'To take my letter. Instead of mailing it, you could take it in person: fly to America and fly back. It would be an adventure. Better than sailing. My daughter would meet you and take care of you. I would buy the ticket in advance. Would you go?'

He smiled bravely. But some of my jokes touch a sore spot, I know.

'I am serious,' I said.

But the truth is, it is not a serious suggestion. Vercueil with a haircut, in shop clothes, mooning about in your guest bedroom, desperate for a drink, too shy to ask; and you in the next room, the children asleep, your husband asleep, poring over this letter, this confession, this madness – it does not bear thinking of. *I do not need this*, you say to yourself through gritted teeth: *this is what I came here to get away from, why does it have to follow me?*

With time on my hands, I have been shuffling through the pictures you have sent from America over the years, looking at the backgrounds, at all the things that fell willy-nilly within the frame at the instant you pressed the button. In the picture you sent of the two boys in their canoe, for instance, my eye wanders from their faces to the ripples on the lake and the deep green of the fir-trees and then back to the orange lifejackets they wear, like waterwings of old. The dull, bland sheen of their surfaces quite hypnotizes me. Rubber or plastic or something in between: some substance coarse to the touch, tough. Why is it that this material, foreign to me, foreign perhaps to humankind, shaped, sealed, inflated, tied to the bodies of your children, signifies so intensely for me the world you now live in, and why does it make my spirit sink? I have no idea. But since this writing has time and again taken me from where I have no idea to where I begin to have an idea, let me say, in all tentativeness, that perhaps it dispirits me that your children will never drown. All those lakes, all that water: a land of lakes and rivers: yet if by some mischance they ever tip out of their canoe, they will bob safely in the water, supported by their bright orange wings, till a motor-boat comes to pick them up and bear them off and all is well again.

A recreation area, you call it on the back of the photograph. The lake tamed, the forest tamed, renamed.

You say you will have no more children. The line runs out, then, in these two boys, seed planted in the American snows, who will never drown, whose life-expectancy is seventy-five and rising. Even I, who live on shores where the waters swallow grown men, where life-expectancy declines every year, am having a death without illumination. What can these two poor underprivileged boys paddling about in their recreation area hope for? They will die at seventy-five or eighty-five as stupid as when they were born.

Do I wish death upon my grandchildren? Are you, at this very instant, flinging the page away from you in disgust? *Mad old woman!* are you crying out?

They are not my grandchildren. They are too distant to be children of mine of whatever sort. I do not leave behind a numerous family. A daughter. A consort and his dog.

By no means do I wish death upon them. The two boys whose lives have brushed mine are in any event already dead. No, I wish your children life. But the wings you have tied on them will not guarantee them life. Life is dust between the toes. Life is dust between the teeth. Life is biting the dust.

Or: life is drowning. Falling through water, to the floor.

The time is nearly upon me when I will have to depend on help for the most intimate things. High time, then, to put an end to this sorry story. Not that I doubt Vercueil would help. When it comes to last things, I no longer doubt him in any way. There has always been in him a certain hovering if undependable solicitude for me, a solicitude he knows no way of expressing. I have fallen and he has caught me. It is not he who fell under my care when he arrived, I now understand, nor I who fell under his: we fell under each other, and have tumbled and risen since then in the flights and swoops of that mutual election.

Yet he is as far from being a nurse, a *nourrice*, a nourisher as I can imagine. He is dry. His drink is not water but fire. Perhaps that is why I cannot imagine children of his: because his semen would be dry, dry and brown, like pollen or like the dust of this country.

I need his presence, his comfort, his help, but he needs help too. He needs the help only a woman can give a man. Not a seduction but an induction. He does not know how to love. I speak not of the motions of the soul but of something simpler. He does not know how to love as a boy does not know how to love. Does not know what zips and buttons and clasps to expect. Does not know what goes where. Does not know how to do what he has to do.

The nearer the end comes, the more faithful he is. Yet still I have to guide his hand.

I remember the day when we sat in the car, when he held out the matches to me and told me to *Do it*. I was outraged. But was I fair to him? It seems to me now that he has no more conception of death than a virgin has of sex. But the same curiosity. The curiosity of a dog that sniffs at one's crotch, wagging its tail, its tongue hanging out red and stupid as a penis.

Yesterday, as he was helping me into the bath, my robe slipped open and I caught him staring. Like those children on Mill Street: no decency in him. Decency: the inexplicable: the ground of all ethics. Things we do not do. We do not stare when the soul leaves the body, but veil our eyes with tears or cover them with our hands. We do not stare at scars, which are places where the soul has struggled to leave and been forced back, closed up, sewn in.

I asked him whether he was still feeding the cats. 'Yes,' he said, lying. For the cats are gone, chased out. Do I care? No, not any more. After I have cared for you, for him, there is little space left in my heart. The rest must, as they say, go to pot.

Last night, growing terribly cold, I tried to call you up to say goodbye. But you would not come. I whispered your name. 'My daughter, my child,' I whispered into the darkness;

but all that appeared to me was a photograph: a picture of you, not you. Severed, I thought: that line severed too. Now there is nothing to hold me.

But I fell asleep, and woke up, and was still here, and this morning feel quite strong. So perhaps it is not only I who do the calling. Perhaps when I grow cold it is because I am being called out of my body across the seas, and do not know it.

As you see, I still believe in your love.

I am going to release you soon from this rope of words. There is no need to be sorry for me. But spare a thought for this man left behind who cannot swim, does not yet know how to fly.

I slept and woke up cold: my belly, my heart, my very bones cold. The door to the balcony was open, the curtains were waving in the wind.

Vercueil stood on the balcony staring out over a sea of rustling leaves. I touched his arm, his high, peaked shoulders, the bony ridge of his spine. Through chattering teeth I spoke: 'What are you looking at?'

He did not answer. I stood closer. A sea of shadows beneath us, and the screen of leaves shifting, rustling, like scales over the darkness.

'Is it time?' I said.

I got back into bed, into the tunnel between the cold sheets. The curtains parted; he came in beside me. For the first time I smelled nothing. He took me in his arms and held me with mighty force, so that the breath went out of me in a rush. From that embrace there was no warmth to be had.

1986–89

Life & Times of Michael K

War is the father of all and king of all.
Some he shows as gods, others as men.
Some he makes slaves, and others free.

I

THE FIRST THING THE MIDWIFE NOTICED ABOUT Michael K when she helped him out of his mother into the world was that he had a hare lip. The lip curled like a snail's foot, the left nostril gaped. Obscuring the child for a moment from its mother, she prodded open the tiny bud of a mouth and was thankful to find the palate whole.

To the mother she said: 'You should be happy, they bring luck to the household.' But from the first Anna K did not like the mouth that would not close and the living pink flesh it bared to her. She shivered to think of what had been growing in her all these months. The child could not suck from the breast and cried with hunger. She tried a bottle; when it could not suck from the bottle she fed it with a teaspoon, fretting with impatience when it coughed and spluttered and cried.

'It will close up as he grows older,' the midwife promised. However, the lip did not close, or did not close enough, nor did the nose come straight.

She took the child with her to work and continued to take it when it was no longer a baby. Because their smiles and whispers hurt her, she kept it away from other children. Year after year Michael K sat on a blanket watching his mother polish other people's floors, learning to be quiet.

Because of his disfigurement and because his mind was not quick, Michael was taken out of school after a short trial and committed to the protection of Huis Norenius in Faure, where at the expense of the state he spent the rest of his childhood in the company of other variously afflicted and unfortunate children learning the elements of reading, writing, counting, sweeping, scrubbing, bedmaking, dishwashing, basketweaving, woodwork and digging. At the age of fifteen he passed out of Huis Norenius and joined the Parks and Gardens division of the municipal services of the City of Cape Town as Gardener, grade 3(b). Three years later he left Parks and Gardens and, after a spell of unemployment which he spent lying on his bed looking at his hands, took a job as night attendant at the public lavatories on Greenmarket Square. On his way home from work late one Friday he was set upon in a subway by two men who beat him, took his watch, his money and his shoes,

4

and left him lying stunned with a slash across his arm, a dislocated thumb and two broken ribs. After this incident he quit night work and returned to Parks and Gardens, where he rose slowly in the service to become Gardener, grade 1.

Because of his face K did not have women friends. He was easiest when he was by himself. Both his jobs had given him a measure of solitariness, though down in the lavatories he had been oppressed by the brilliant neon light that shone off the white tiles and created a space without shadows. The parks he preferred were those with tall pine trees and dim agapanthus walks. Sometimes on Saturdays he failed to hear the boom of the noon gun and went on working by himself all through the afternoon. On Sunday mornings he slept late; on Sunday afternoons he visited his mother.

Late one morning in June, in the thirty-first year of his life, a message was brought to Michael K as he raked leaves in De Waal Park. The message, at third hand, was from his mother: she had been discharged from hospital and wanted him to come and fetch her. K put away his tools and made his way by bus to Somerset Hospital, where he found his mother seated on a bench in a patch of sunlight outside the entrance. She was fully dressed, save that her street shoes stood beside her. When she saw her son she began to weep, holding a hand before her eyes so that other patients and visitors should not see.

For months Anna K had been suffering from gross

5

swelling of the legs and arms; later her belly had begun to swell too. She had been admitted to hospital unable to walk and barely able to breathe. She had spent five days lying in a corridor among scores of victims of stabbings and beatings and gunshot wounds who kept her awake with their noise, neglected by nurses who had no time to spend cheering up an old woman when there were young men dying spectacular deaths all about. Revived with oxygen when she arrived, she was treated with injections and pills to bring down the swelling. When she wanted a bedpan, however, there was seldom anyone to bring it. She had no dressing-gown. Once, feeling her way along the wall to the lavatory, she had been stopped by an old man in grey pyjamas who spoke filth and exposed himself. The needs of her body became a source of torment. When the nurses asked about the pills she said she had taken them, but often she was lying. Then, though the breathlessness abated, her legs grew so itchy that she had to lie on her hands to control the urge to scratch. By the third day she was pleading to be sent home, though evidently not pleading with the right person. The tears she wept on the sixth day were thus largely tears of relief that she was escaping this purgatory.

At the desk Michael K asked for the use of a wheelchair and was refused it. Carrying her handbag and shoes for her, he supported his mother the fifty paces to the bus stop. There was a long queue. The timetable pasted on the pole promised a bus every fifteen minutes. They waited for an hour while the shadows lengthened and the wind grew chilly. Unable to stand, Anna K sat against a wall with her legs before her like a beggarwoman while Michael kept their place in the line. When the bus came there were no seats. Michael held on to a rail and embraced his mother to keep her from lurching. It was five o'clock before they arrived at her room in Sea Point.

For eight years Anna K had been employed as a domestic servant by a retired hosiery manufacturer and his wife living in a five-roomed flat in Sea Point overlooking the Atlantic Ocean. In terms of her contract she came in at nine in the morning and stayed till eight at night, with a three-hour break in the afternoon. She worked alternately five and six days a week. She had a fortnight's paid holiday and a room of her own in the block. The wage was fair, her employers were reasonable people, jobs were hard to come by, and Anna K was not discontented. A year ago, however, she had begun to experience dizziness and tightness of the chest when she bent down. Then the dropsy had set in. The Buhrmanns kept her on to do the cooking, cut her pay by a third, and hired a younger woman for the housework. She was allowed to stay on in her room, over which the Buhrmanns had the disposal. The dropsy grew worse. For weeks before entering hospital she had been bedridden, unable to work. She lived in dread of the end of the Buhrmanns' charity.

Her room under the stairs of the Côte d'Azur had

been intended for air-conditioning equipment which had never been installed. On the door was a sign: a skull and crossed bones painted in red, and underneath the legend DANGER – GEVAAR – INGOZI. There was no electric light and no ventilation; the air was always musty. Michael opened the door for his mother, lit a candle, and stepped outside while she prepared for bed. He spent this, the first evening of her return, and every evening for the next week, with her: he warmed soup for her on the paraffin stove, saw to her comfort as far as he was able, carried out necessary tasks, and consoled her by stroking her arms when she fell into one of her fits of tears. One evening the buses from Sea Point did not run at all and he had to spend the night in her room sleeping on the mat with his coat on. In the middle of the night he woke chilled to the bone. Unable to sleep, unable to leave because of the curfew, he sat shivering on the chair till daylight while his mother groaned and snored.

Michael K did not like the physical intimacy that the long evenings in the tiny room forced upon the two of them. He found the sight of his mother's swollen legs disturbing and turned his eyes away when he had to help her out of bed. Her thighs and arms were covered with scratch marks (for a while she even wore gloves at night). But he did not shirk any aspect of what he saw as his duty. The problem that had exercised him years ago behind the bicycle shed at Huis Norenius, namely why he had been brought into the world, had received its answer: he had been brought into the world to look after his mother.

Nothing that her son said could calm Anna K's fear of what might happen to her if she lost her room. Her nights among the dying in the corridors of Somerset Hospital had brought it home to her how indifferent the world could be to an old woman with an unsightly illness in time of war. Unable to work, she saw herself withheld from the gutter only by the unreliable goodwill of the Buhrmanns, the dutifulness of a dull son, and, in the last resort, the savings she kept in a handbag in a suitcase under her bed, the new currency in one purse, the old currency, valueless now, that she had been too suspicious to exchange, in another.

Thus when Michael arrived one evening speaking of layoffs in Parks and Gardens, she began to revolve in her mind something she had hitherto only idly dreamed of: a project of quitting a city that held little promise for her and returning to the quieter countryside of her girlhood.

Anna K had been born on a farm in the district of Prince Albert. Her father was not steady; there was a problem with drinking; and in her early years they had moved from one farm to another. Her mother had done laundry and worked in the various kitchens; Anna had helped her. Later they had moved to the town of Oudtshoorn, where for a while Anna went to school. After the birth of her own first child she had come to Cape Town. There was a second child, from another father, then a third one who died, then Michael. In Anna's memories the years before Oudtshoorn remained the happiest of her life, a time of warmth and plenty. She remembered sitting in the dust of the chicken-run while the chickens clucked and scratched; she remembered looking for eggs under bushes. Lying in bed in her airless room through the winter afternoons with rain dripping from the steps outside, she dreamed of escaping from the careless violence, the packed buses, the food queues, arrogant shopkeepers, thieves and beggars, sirens in the night, the curfew, the cold and wet, and returning to a countryside where, if she was going to die, she would at least die under blue skies.

In the plan she outlined to Michael she did not mention death or dying. She proposed that he should quit Parks and Gardens before he was laid off and accompany her by train to Prince Albert, where she would hire a room while he looked for work on a farm. If it happened that his quarters were large enough, she would stay with him and keep house; if not, he could visit her at weekends. To prove her seriousness she had him bring out the suitcase from under the bed, and before his eyes counted out the purseful of new notes, which, she said, she had been putting aside for this purpose.

She expected Michael to ask how she could believe that a small country town would take to its bosom two strangers, one of them an old woman in bad health. She had even prepared an answer. But not for an instant did Michael doubt her. Just as he had believed through all the years in Huis Norenius that his mother had left him there for a reason which, if at first dark, would in the end become clear, so now he accepted without question the wisdom of her plan for them. He saw, not the banknotes spread out on the quilt, but in his mind's eye a whitewashed cottage in the broad veld with smoke curling from its chimney, and standing at the front door his mother, smiling and well, ready to welcome him home at the end of a long day.

Michael did not report for work the next morning. With his mother's money stuffed in two wads into his socks, he made his way to the railway station and the main line booking office. Here the clerk told him that, while he would happily sell him two tickets to Prince Albert or the nearest point to it on the line ('Prince Albert or Prince Alfred?' he asked), K should not expect to board a train without both a seat reservation and a permit to leave the proclaimed Cape Peninsula police area. The earliest reservation he could give him would be for the eighteenth of August, two months away; as for the permit, that could be obtained only from the police. K pleaded for an earlier departure, but in vain: the state of his mother's health did not constitute special grounds, the clerk told him; on the contrary, he would advise him not to mention her condition at all.

From the station K went to Caledon Square and

stood for two hours in a queue behind a woman with a whimpering baby. He was given two sets of forms, one set for his mother, one for himself. 'Pin the train reservations to the blue forms, take them to room E-5,' said the policewoman at the desk.

When it rained Anna K pushed an old towel against the bottom of the door to keep water from seeping in. The room smelled of Dettol and talcum powder. 'I feel like a toad under a stone living here,' she whispered. 'I can't wait till August.' She covered her face and lay in silence. After a while K found that he could not breathe. He went to the corner shop. There was no bread. 'No bread, no milk,' said the assistant – 'come tomorrow.' He bought biscuits and condensed milk, then stood under the awning watching the rain fall. The next day he took the forms to room E-5. Permits would be mailed in due course, they told him, after the applications had been seen and approved by the police in Prince Albert.

He went back to De Waal Park and was told, as he had expected, that he was to be paid off at the end of the month. 'It doesn't matter,' he told the foreman – 'we are leaving anyhow, my mother and I.' He remembered his mother's visits to Huis Norenius. Sometimes she had brought marshmallows, sometimes chocolate biscuits. They had walked together on the playing-field, then gone to the hall for tea. On visiting days the boys wore their khaki best and their brown sandals. Some of the boys did not have parents, or had been forgotten. 'My father is dead, my mother is working,' he had said in respect of himself.

He made a nest of cushions and blankets in the corner of the room and spent the evenings sitting in the dark listening to his mother breathe. She was sleeping more and more. Sometimes he too fell asleep where he sat and missed the bus. He would wake in the morning with a headache. During the day he wandered about the streets. Everything was suspended while they waited for the permits, which did not come.

Early one Sunday morning he visited De Waal Park and broke the lock on the shed where the gardeners kept their equipment. He took hand-tools and a wheelbarrow which he trundled back to Sea Point. Working in the alley behind the flats, he broke up an old crate and knocked together a platform two feet square, with a raised back, which he lashed to the wheelbarrow with wire. Then he tried to coax his mother out for a ride. 'The air will do you good,' he said. 'No one will see, it's after five, the front is empty.' 'People can see from the flats,' she replied: 'I'm not making myself into a spectacle.' The next day she relented. Wearing her hat and coat and slippers, she shuffled out into the grey late afternoon and allowed Michael to settle her in the barrow. He wheeled her across Beach Road and on to the paved promenade along the seafront. There was no one about but an old couple walking a dog. Anna K held stiffly to the sides of the platform, breathing in the cold sea air, while her son wheeled her a hundred yards along the promenade, stopped to allow her to watch the waves breaking on the rocks, wheeled her another hundred yards, stopped again, then wheeled her back. He was disconcerted to find how heavy she was and how unstable the barrow. There was a moment when it tipped and nearly spilled her. 'It does you good to get fresh air in your lungs,' he said. The next afternoon it was raining and they stayed indoors.

He thought of building a hand-cart with a box as body mounted on a pair of bicycle wheels, but could not think where to find an axle.

Then late one afternoon in the last week of June a military jeep travelling down Beach Road at high speed struck a youth crossing the street, hurling him back among the vehicles parked at the curbside. The jeep itself swerved off and came to a halt on the overgrown lawns outside the Côte d'Azur, where its two occupants were confronted by the youth's angry companions. There was a fight, and a crowd soon gathered. Parked cars were smashed open and pushed broadside on into the street. Sirens announced the curfew and were ignored. An ambulance that arrived with a motorcycle escort turned about short of the barrier and raced off, chased by a hail of stones. Then from the balcony of a fourth-floor flat a man began to fire revolver shots. Amid screams the crowd dashed for cover, spreading into the beachfront apartment blocks, racing along the corridors, pounding upon doors, breaking windows and lights. The man with the revolver was hauled from his hiding-place, kicked into insensibility, and tossed down to the pavement. Some residents of the flats chose to cower in the dark behind locked doors, others fled into the streets. A woman, trapped at the end of a corridor, had her clothes torn from her body; someone slipped on a fire escape and broke an ankle. Doors were beaten down and flats ransacked. In the flat immediately above Anna K's room looters tore down curtains, heaped clothing on the floor, broke furniture and lit a fire which, though it did not spread, sent out dense clouds of smoke. On the lawns outside the Côte d'Azur, the Côte d'Or and the Copacabana a constantly growing mob, some with piles of stolen goods at their feet, hurled stones from the rockery gardens through the great seafront windows till not a pane was left intact.

A police van with a flashing blue light drew up on the promenade fifty yards away. There was a burst of fire from a machine pistol, and from behind the barricade of cars answering shots. The van backed precipitately away, while amid screams and shouts the crowd retreated down Beach Road. It was another twenty minutes, and darkness had fallen, before police and riot troops arrived in force. Floor by floor they occupied the affected blocks, encountering no resistance from an enemy who fled down back alleys. One looter, a woman who did not run fast enough, was shot dead. From streets all around the police picked up abandoned goods which they stacked on the lawns. There, late into the night, the folk of the flats searched by flashlight to recover their own. At midnight, when the operation was about to be declared concluded, a rioter with a bullet through his lung was discovered huddled in an unlit angle of a passageway in a block further down the road and taken away. Guards were posted for the night and the main force retired. In the early hours of the morning the wind rose and heavy rain began to fall, beating through the broken windows of the Côte d'Azur, the Côte d'Or, the Copacabana, as well as of the Egremont and the Malibu Heights, which had hitherto offered a sheltered prospect of the east-west shipping lanes around the Cape of Good Hope, whipping the curtains, soaking the carpets, and in some cases flooding the floors.

Throughout these events Anna K and her son huddled quiet as mice in their room beneath the stairs, not stirring even when they smelled the smoke, even when heavy boots stamped past and a hand rattled the locked door. They could not guess that the tumult, the screams, the shots and the sound of breaking glass were confined to a few adjoining blocks: sitting side by side on the bed, barely daring to whisper, the conviction grew in them that the real war had come to Sea Point and found them out. Till long after midnight, when his mother at last dozed off, Michael sat with his ears pricked, staring at the strip of grey light under the door, breathing very quietly. When his mother began to snore he gripped her shoulder to make her stop.

Thus, sitting upright with his back to the wall, he finally fell asleep. When he awoke the light under the door was brighter. He unlocked the door and crept out. The passage was littered with glass. At the entrance to the block two helmeted soldiers sat in deckchairs with their backs to him, gazing out at the rain and the grey sea. K slipped back into his mother's room and went to sleep on the mat.

Later that day, when the tenants of the Côte d'Azur had begun to return to clean up the mess or pack their belongings or simply stare at the damage and weep, and when the rain had stopped falling, K made a journey to Oliphant Road in Green Point, to St Joseph's Mission, where in earlier times one had been able to find a cup of soup and a bed for the night, no questions asked, and where he hoped he might lodge his mother for a while away from the devastated block. But the plaster statue of St Joseph with his beard and his staff was gone, the bronze plate had been removed from the gatepost, the windows were shuttered. He knocked next door and heard a floorboard creak, but no one came.

Crossing the city on his way to work, K rubbed shoulders every day with the army of the homeless and destitute who in the last years had taken over the streets of the central district, begging or thieving or waiting in lines at the relief agencies or simply sitting in the corridors of public buildings to keep warm, finding shelter by night in the gutted warehouses around the

17

docks or the blocks and blocks of derelict premises above Bree Street where the police never ventured afoot. During the year before the authorities had finally imposed controls on personal movement, Greater Cape Town had been flooded with people from the country-side looking for work of any kind. There was no work, no accommodation to be had. If they fell into that sea of hungry mouths, K thought, what chance would he and his mother have? How long could he push her around the streets in a wheelbarrow begging for food? He wandered aimlessly all day, and returned to the room sunk in gloom. For supper he laid out soup and rusks and canned pilchards, shielding the stove behind a blanket in case a show of light might draw attention to them.

Their hopes settled on the permit that would allow them to leave the city. But the Buhrmanns' postbox, to which the police would send the permit if they ever meant to send it, was locked; and after the night of looting the Buhrmanns themselves, in a state of shock, had been taken away by friends, leaving no word of when they would be back. So Anna K sent her son up to the flat with instructions to fetch the postbox key.

K had never been into the flat before. He found it in chaos. In a wash of water driven through the windows by high winds lay broken furniture, gutted mattresses, fragments of glass and crockery, withered pot-plants, sodden bedding and carpeting. A paste of cake flour, breakfast cereal, sugar, cat litter and earth stuck to his shoes. In the kitchen the refrigerator lay on its face, its motor still purring, a yellow scum leaking past its hinges into the half-inch of water on the tiled floor. Rows of jars had been swept off the shelves; there was a reek of wine. On the gleaming white wall someone had written in oven cleaner, TO HEL.

Michael persuaded his mother to come and see the destruction for herself. She had not been upstairs for two months. She stood on a breadboard in the doorway of the living room, tears in her eyes. 'Why did they do it?' she whispered. She did not want to go into the kitchen. 'Such nice people!' she said. 'I don't know how they are going to get over it!' Michael helped her to her room again. She would not settle down, asking again and again where the Buhrmanns were staying, who was going to clean up, when they would be back.

Leaving her, Michael returned to the devastated flat. He righted the refrigerator, emptied it, swept the broken glass into a corner, mopped up some of the water. He filled half a dozen garbage sacks and stacked them at the front door. Food that was still edible he put to one side. He did not try to clean the living room, but pinned the curtains across the gaping windowframes as best he could. I do what I do, he told himself, not for the old people's sake but for my mother's.

It was plain that until the windows were repaired and the carpets, already beginning to smell, were stripped away, the Buhrmanns could not live here. Nevertheless, the idea of annexing the apartment for

19

himself did not occur to him till he saw the bathroom for the first time.

'Just for a night or two,' he pleaded with his mother, 'so that you can have a chance to sleep by yourself. Till we know what we are going to do. I'll move a divan into the bathroom. In the morning I'll put everything back. I promise. They will never know.'

He made up the divan in the bathroom with layers of sheets and tablecloths. He wedged cardboard over the window and switched on the light. There was hot water: he had a bath. In the morning he hid his traces. The postman came. There was nothing for the Buhrmanns' box. It was raining. He went outdoors and sat in the bus shelter watching the rain fall. In the middle of the afternoon, when it was clear that again the Buhrmanns were not coming, he returned to the flat.

Day after day it rained. There was no word from the Buhrmanns. K swept the worst of the standing water out on to the balcony and unclogged the runoff pipes. Though the wind blew through the flat, the stench of mould grew worse. He cleaned the kitchen floor and took the garbage bags downstairs.

He began to spend not only the nights but the days in the flat. In a kitchen cupboard he discovered piles of magazines. He lay in bed, or lay in the bath, paging through pictures of beautiful women and luscious food. The food absorbed him more deeply. He showed his mother a picture of a gleaming flank of roast pork garnished with cherries and pineapple rings and set off with a bowl of raspberries and cream and a gooseberry tart. 'People don't eat like that any more,' his mother said. He disagreed. 'The pigs don't know there is a war on,' he said. 'The pineapples don't know there is a war on. Food keeps growing. Someone has to eat it.'

He went back to the hostel where he lived and paid the back rent. 'I've given up my job,' he told the warden. 'My mother and I are going to the country to get away from things. We are just waiting for the permit.' He took his bicycle and his suitcase. Stopping at a scrapyard he bought a metre length of steel rod. The wheelbarrow with the box seat stood where he had abandoned it in the alley behind the flats; now he returned to the project of using the wheels from his bicycle to make a cart in which to take his mother for walks. But though the wheel bearings slid smoothly over the new axlerod, he had no way of preventing the wheels from spinning off. For hours he struggled without success to make clips out of wire. Then he gave up. Something will come to me, he told himself, and left the bicycle dismantled on the Buhrmanns' kitchen floor.

Among the debris in the front room had been a transistor radio. The needle was stuck at the end of the scale, the batteries were weak, and he had soon given up fiddling with it. Exploring the kitchen drawers, however, he found a lead that enabled him to plug the radio into the mains. So now he could lie in the

21

bathroom in the dark listening to music from the other room. Sometimes it sent him to sleep. He would wake in the mornings with the music still playing; or there would be resonant talk in a language he understood not a word of, from which he picked out names of faroff places: Wakkerstroom, Pietersburg, King William's Town. Sometimes he found himself singing tonelessly along.

Exhausting the magazines, he began paging through old newspapers from under the kitchen sink, so old that he remembered none of the events they told of, though he recognized some of the football players. KHAMIESKROON KILLER TRACKED DOWN said the headline in one, over a picture of a handcuffed man in a torn white shirt standing between two stiff policemen. Though the handcuffs brought his shoulders forward and down, the Khamieskroon killer looked at the camera with what seemed to K a smile of quiet achievement. Below was a second picture: a rifle with a sling photographed against a blank background and captioned 'Killer's weapon'. K stuck the page with the story on the refrigerator door; for days afterwards, when he looked up from his intermittent work on the wheels, his eyes continued to meet those of the man from Khamieskroon, wherever that was.

At a loss for things to do, he tried to dry out the Buhrmanns' waterlogged books by hanging them over a line across the living room; but the process took too long and he lost interest. He had never liked books,

22

and he found nothing to engage him here in stories of military men or women with names like Lavinia, though he did spend some time unsticking the leaves of picture-books of the Ionian Islands, Moorish Spain, Finland Land of Lakes, Bali, and other places in the world.

Then one morning Michael K started up at the scrape of the front-door lock and found himself facing four men in overalls who pushed past him without a word and set about clearing the flat of its contents. Hastily he moved the pieces of his bicycle out of their way. His mother shuffled out in her housecoat and stopped one of the men on the stairs. 'Where's the boss? Where's Mr Buhrmann?' she asked. The man shrugged. K went out into the street and spoke to the driver of the van. 'Are you from Mr Buhrmann?' he asked. 'What does it look like, man?' said the driver.

Michael helped his mother back into bed. 'What I don't understand,' she said, 'is why they don't let me know anything. What must I do if someone knocks on the door and says I must clear out at once, he wants the room for his domestic? Where must I go?' For a long while he sat beside her stroking her arm, listening to her lament. Then he took the two bicycle wheels and the steel rod and his tools out into the alley and sat down in a patch of sunlight to confront anew the problem of how to prevent the wheels from spinning off the axle. He worked all afternoon; by evening, using a hacksaw blade, he had painstakingly incised a thread down either end of the rod, along which he could wind clumps of one-inch washers. With the wheels mounted on the rod between the washers, it was only a matter of tightening loop after loop of wire around the rod to hold the washers flush against the wheels and the problem seemed to be solved. He barely ate or slept that night, so impatient was he to get on with his work. In the morning he broke down the old barrow platform-seat and rebuilt it as a narrow three-sided box with two long handles, which he wired in place over the axle. He now had a squat rickshaw which, though hardly of sturdy build, would take his mother's weight; and the same evening, when a cold wind from the north-west had driven all but the hardiest promenaders indoors, he was again able to take his mother, wrapped in coat and blanket, for a seafront ride that brought a smile to her lips.

Now was the time. No sooner had they returned to the room than he came out with the plan he had been pondering ever since building the first barrow. They were wasting their time waiting for permits, he said. The permits would never come. And without permits they could not leave by train. Any day now they would be expelled from the room. Would she therefore not allow him to take her to Prince Albert in the cart? She had seen for herself how comfortable it was. The damp weather was not good for her, nor was the unending worry about the future. Once settled in Prince Albert she would quickly recover her health. At most they

24

would be a day or two on the road. People were decent, people would stop and give them lifts.

For hours he argued with her, surprising himself with the adroitness of his pleading. How could he expect her to sleep in the open in the middle of winter, she objected. With luck, he responded, they might even reach Prince Albert in a day -- it was after all only five hours away by car. But what would happen if it rained? she asked. He would put a canopy over the cart, he replied. What if the police stopped them? Surely the police had better things to do, he answered, than to stop two innocent people who wanted nothing more than a chance to find their own way out of an overcrowded city. 'Why should the police want us to spend nights hiding on other people's stoeps and beg in the streets and make a nuisance of ourselves?' So persuasive was he that finally Anna K yielded, though on two conditions: that he make a last visit to the police to find out about the permits that had not come, and that she ready herself for the journey without being hurried. Joyfully Michael acceded.

Next morning, instead of waiting for a bus that might never come, he jogged from Sea Point to the city along the main road, taking pleasure in the soundness of his heart, the strength of his limbs. There were already scores of people queuing under the sign HERVESTIGING -- RELOCATION; it was an hour before he found himself at the counter facing a policewoman with wary eyes.

He held out the two train tickets. 'I just want to ask if the permit has come through,' he said.

She pushed the familiar forms towards him. 'Fill in the forms and take them to E-5. Have your tickets and reservation slips with you.' She glanced over K's shoulder to the man behind him. 'Yes?'

'No,' said K, struggling to regain her attention, 'I already applied for the permit. All I want to know is, has the permit come?'

'Before you can have a permit you must have a reservation! Have you got a reservation? When is it for?'

'August eighteenth. But my mother – '

'August eighteenth is a month away! If you applied for a permit and the permit is granted, the permit will come, the permit will be sent to your address! Next!'

'But that is what I want to know! Because if the permit isn't going to come I must make other plans. My mother is sick – '

The policewoman slapped the counter to still him. 'Don't waste my time! I am telling you for the last time, *if the permit is granted the permit will come!* Don't you see all these people waiting? Don't you understand? Are you an idiot? *Next!*' She braced herself against the counter and glared pointedly over K's shoulder: '*Yes, you, next!*'

But K did not budge. He was breathing fast, his eyes stared. Reluctantly the policewoman turned back to him, to the thin moustache and the naked lip-flesh it did not hide. '*Next!*' she said.

An hour before dawn the next day K roused his mother and, while she dressed, packed the cart, padding the box with blankets and cushions and lashing the suitcase across the shafts. The cart now had a hood of black plastic sheeting that made it look like a tall perambulator. When his mother saw it she stopped and shook her head. 'I don't know, I don't know, I don't know,' she said. He had to coax her to get in; it took a long time. The cart was not really big enough, he realized: it bore her weight, but she had to sit hunched under the canopy unable to move her limbs. Over her legs he spread a blanket, then piled on that a packet of food, the paraffin stove and a bottle of fuel packed in a box, odds and ends of clothing. A light winked on in the flats next door. They could hear the waves breaking on the rocks. 'Just a day or two,' he whispered, 'then we'll be there. Don't move too much from side to side if you can help it.' She nodded but continued to hide her face in her woollen gloves. He bent towards her. 'Do you want to stay, Ma?' he said. 'If you want to stay we can stay.' She shook her head. So he put on his cap, lifted the handles, and wheeled the cart out on to the misty road.

He took the shortest route, past the devastated area around the old fuel storage tanks where the demolition of burnt-out buildings had only just begun, past the dock quarter and the blackened shells of the

27

warehouses that had in the past year been taken over by the city's street bands. They were not stopped. Indeed, few of the people they passed at this early hour spared them a glance. Stranger and stranger conveyances were emerging on the streets: shopping trolleys fitted with steering bars; tricycles with boxes over the rear axle; baskets mounted on pushcart undercarriages; crates on castors; barrows of all sizes. A donkey fetched eighty rands in new currency, a cart with tyres over a hundred.

K kept up a steady pace, stopping every half-hour to rub his cold hands and flex his aching shoulders. The moment he settled his mother in the cart in Sea Point he realized that, with all the luggage packed in the front, the axle was off centre, too far back. Now, the more his mother slid down the box trying to make herself comfortable, the greater the deadweight he found himself lifting. He kept a smiling face to hide the strain he felt. 'We just have to get on to the open road,' he panted, 'then someone is bound to stop for us.'

By noon they were passing through the ghostly industrial quarter of Paarden Eiland. A couple of workmen sitting on a wall eating their sandwiches watched them roll past in silence. CRASH-FLASH said the faded black lettering beneath their feet. K felt his arms going numb but plodded on another half mile. Where the road passed under the Black River Parkway he helped his mother out and settled her on the grass verge beneath the bridge. They ate their lunch. He was struck by the emptiness of the roads. There was such stillness that he could hear birdsong. He lay back in the thick grass and closed his eyes.

He was roused by a rumbling in the air. At first he thought it was faroff thunder. The noise grew louder, however, beating in waves off the base of the bridge above them. From their right, from the direction of the city, at deliberate speed, came two pairs of uniformed motorcyclists, rifles strapped across their backs, and behind them an armoured car with a gunner standing in the turret. Then followed a long and miscellaneous procession of heavy vehicles, most of them trucks empty of cargo. K crept up the verge to his mother; side by side they sat and watched in a roar of noise that seemed to turn the air solid. The convoy took minutes to pass. The rear was brought up by scores of automobiles, vans and light trucks, followed by an olive-green army truck with a canvas hood under which they glimpsed two rows of seated helmeted soldiers, and then another pair of motorcyclists.

One of the lead motorcyclists had turned a pointed stare on K and his mother as he went past. Now the last two motorcyclists peeled off from the convoy. One waited at the roadside, the other climbed the verge. Raising his visor he addressed them: 'No stopping along the expressway,' he said. He glanced into the barrow. 'Is this your vehicle?' K nodded. 'Where are you going?' K whispered, cleared his throat, spoke a second time: 'To Prince Albert. In the Karoo.' The motorcyclist whistled, rocked the barrow lightly,

29

called down something to his companion. He turned back to K. 'Along the road, just around the bend, there is a checkpoint. You stop at the checkpoint and show your permit. You got a permit to leave the Peninsula?'

'Yes.'

'You can't travel outside the Peninsula without a permit. Go to the checkpoint and show them your permit and your papers. And listen to me: you want to stop on the expressway, you pull fifty metres off the roadside. That's the regulation: fifty metres either side. Anything nearer, you can get shot, no warning, no questions asked. Understand?'

K nodded. The motorcyclists remounted and roared off after the convoy. K could not meet his mother's eye. 'We should have picked a quieter road,' he said.

He could have turned back at once; but at the risk of a second humiliation he helped his mother back into the barrow and pushed her as far as the old hangars where, indeed, there was a jeep parked by the roadside and three soldiers brewing tea over a camp stove. His pleas were in vain. 'Have you got a permit, yes or no?' demanded the corporal in command. 'I don't care who you are, who your mother is, if you haven't got a permit you can't leave the area, finished.' K turned to his mother. From under the black canopy she gazed out expressionlessly at the young soldier. The soldier threw up his hands. 'Don't give me a hard time!' he shouted. 'Just get the permit, then I'll let you through!' He watched while K hoisted the shafts and wheeled the cart through an arc. One of the wheels had begun to wobble.

Night had already fallen when they passed the traffic lights marking the start of Beach Road. The hulks that had blocked the road during the siege of the apartment blocks had been pushed on to the lawns. The key was still in the door under the stairway. The room was as they had left it, neatly swept for the next occupant. Anna K laid herself down in her coat and slippers on the bare mattress; Michael brought in their belongings. A shower of rain had soaked the cushions. 'We'll try again in a day or two, Ma,' he whispered. She shook her head. 'Ma, the permit isn't going to come!' he said. 'We'll try again, but next time we'll go by the back roads. They can't block every road out.' He sat down beside her on the mattress and remained there, his hand on her arm, till she fell asleep; then he went upstairs to sleep on the Buhrmanns' floor.

Two days later they set off again, leaving Sea Point a full hour before dawn. The zest of the first venture was gone. K knew now that they might have to spend many nights on the road. Furthermore, his mother had lost all appetite for travel to far places. She complained of pains in her chest and sat stiff and sullen in the box under the plastic apron K pinned across her to keep out the worst of the rain. At a steady trot, with the tyres hissing on the wet tarmac, he followed a new route through the centre of the city, along Sir Lowry Road and the suburban Main Road, over the Mowbray

31

railway bridge, and past the one-time Children's Hospital on to the old Klipfontein Road. Here, with only a trampled fence between them and the cardboard-and-iron shanties clustered on the fairways of the golf course, they made their first stop. After they had eaten, K stood at the roadside with his mother clasped to his side trying to flag down passing vehicles. There was little traffic. Three light trucks sped past nose to tail, wire mesh over their lights and windows. Later came a neat horsecart, the bay horses wearing clusters of bells on their harness, a troop of children in the back jeering and making signs at the pair of them. Then after a long empty interval a lorry stopped, the driver offering them a lift as far as the cement works, even helping K to lift the barrow aboard. Sitting safe and dry in the cab, counting off the kilometres out of the corner of an eye, K nudged his mother and met her prim answering smile.

That was the end of good luck for the day. For an hour they waited outside the cement works; but though there was a steady stream of pedestrians and cyclists, the only vehicles to pass were sewage department trucks. The sun was declining, the wind beginning to bite, when K hauled his cart on to the road and set off again. Perhaps, he thought, it was better when one did not have to rely on other people. Since the first trip he had moved the axle two inches forward; now, once he got it going, the cart was as light as a feather. At a trot he overtook a man pushing a barrow loaded with brushwood, nodding in greeting as he passed. In her dark little cabin, pinned upright between the high sides, his mother sat with her eyes closed and her head drooping forward.

A hazy moon was coming through the clouds when, half a mile short of the arterial road, K drew up, helped his mother out, and plunged into the dense Port Jackson scrub to seek out a stopping-place for the night. In this half-world of straggling roots and damp earth and subtle rotten smells no site seemed more sheltered from the elements than any other. He returned to the roadside shivering. 'It is not very nice,' he told his mother, 'but for one night we will have to put up with it.' He concealed the cart as best he could; supporting her on one arm, carrying the suitcase, he groped his way back into the bush.

They ate cold food and settled down on a bed of leaves through which the damp palpably seeped into their clothes. At midnight a gentle rain began to fall. They huddled together as close as they could under a scrub-tree while the rain dripped on the blanket they held over their heads. When the blanket became soaked Michael crept on hands and knees back to the cart and fetched the plastic apron. He cradled his mother's head on his shoulder and heard the laboured shallowness of her breathing. For the first time it occurred to him that the reason she had ceased complaining might be that she was too exhausted, or no longer cared.

His intention had been to set off so early as to reach

33

the turnoff to Stellenbosch and Paarl before it grew light. But at dawn his mother was still asleep against his side and he was loath to wake her. The air grew warmer, he found it harder not to nod himself. Thus it was mid-morning before he helped her out of the bush back to the road. Here, as they were packing their sodden bedding into the cart, they were accosted by a pair of passers-by who, coming upon a man of meagre build and an old woman in a lonely place, concluded that they might strip them of their possessions with impunity. As a sign of this intention one of the strangers displayed to K (allowing the blade to slip from his sleeve into his palm) a carving knife, while the other laid hands on the suitcase. In the instant of the flash of the blade, K saw before him the prospect of being humiliated again while his mother watched, of trudging back behind the cart to the room in Sea Point, of sitting on the floormat with his hands over his ears enduring day after day the burden of her silence. He reached into the cart and brought out his sole weapon, the fifteen-inch length he had sawn from the axlerod. Brandishing this, lifting his left arm to guard his face, he advanced on the youth with the knife, who circled away from him toward his companion while Anna K filled the air with shrieks. The strangers backed off. Wordlessly, still glaring, still menacing with the bar, K recovered the suitcase and helped his quaking mother into the cart with the robbers hovering not twenty paces away. Then he hauled the cart out backwards on to the road and slowly drew her away from them. For a while they trailed behind, the one with the knife miming obscenities and threats to K's life with elaborate play of lips and tongue. Then as suddenly as they had appeared they slipped into the bush.

There were no vehicles on the expressway, but people, many people, walking where none had walked before, in the middle of the highway, in their Sunday best. By the roadside a tangle of weeds grew as high as a man's chest; the road surface was cracked, and grass sprouted in the cracks. K caught up with three children, sisters dressed in identical pink frocks on their way to church. They peered into Mrs K's little cabin and chatted to her. For the last stretch, before Michael turned off to Stellenbosch, the eldest child walked holding Mrs K's hand. When they parted Mrs K brought out her purse and gave each little girl a coin.

The children had told them that no convoys ran on Sundays; but on the Stellenbosch road they were passed by a farmers' convoy, a train of light trucks and cars preceded by a lorry armoured in heavy mesh in whose open back stood two men with automatic rifles scanning the ground ahead. K drew off the road till they had passed. The passengers gave them curious glances, the children pointing and saying things K could not hear.

Leafless vineyards stretched before and behind. A flock of sparrows materialized out of the sky, settled for a moment on the bushes all around them, then flitted off. Across the fields they heard church bells.

35

Memories came to K of Huis Norenius, of sitting up in bed in the infirmary, slapping his pillow and watching the play of dust in a beam of sunlight.

It was dark when he plodded into Stellenbosch. The streets were empty, a cold wind gusted. He had not thought where they would sleep. His mother was coughing; after each spell she would gasp for breath. He stopped at a café and bought curried pasties. He ate three of them, she one. She had no appetite. 'Mustn't you see a doctor?' he asked. She shook her head, patted her chest. 'It's just dryness in my throat,' she said. She seemed to expect to be in Prince Albert the next day or the day after, and he did not disillusion her. 'I forget the actual name of the farm,' she said, 'but we can ask, people will know. There was a chicken-run against one wall of the wagonhouse, a long chicken-run, and a pump up on the hill. We had a house on the hillside. There was prickly pear outside the back door. That is the place you must look for.'

They slept in an alley on a bed of flattened cartons. Michael propped a long side of cardboard at a pitch over their bed, but the wind blew it over. His mother coughed throughout the night, keeping him awake. Once a patrolling police van passed slowly down the street and he had to hold his hand over her mouth.

At first light he lifted her back into the cart. Her head lolled, she did not know where she was. He stopped the first person he saw and asked the way to the hospital. Anna K could no longer sit upright; and

36

as she slumped, Michael had to struggle to keep the cart from toppling. She was feverish, she laboured to breathe. 'My throat is so dry,' she whispered; but her coughing was soggy.

In the hospital he sat supporting her till it was her turn to be taken away. When next he saw her she was lying on a trolley amid a sea of trolleys with a tube up her nose, unconscious. Not knowing what to do, he loitered in the corridor till he was sent away. He spent the afternoon in the courtyard in the thin warmth of the winter sun. Twice he sneaked back in to check whether the trolley had been moved. A third time he tiptoed up to his mother and bent over her. He could detect no sign of breathing. Fear gripping his heart, he ran to the nurse at the desk and tugged at her sleeve. 'Please come and see, quickly!' he said. The nurse shook herself free. 'Who are you?' she hissed. She followed him to the trolley and took his mother's pulse, staring into the distance. Then without a word she returned to her desk. K stood before her like a dumb dog while she wrote. She turned to him. 'Now listen to me,' she said in a tight whisper. 'Do you see all these people here?' She gestured towards the corridor and the wards. 'These are all people waiting to be attended to. We are working twenty-four hours a day to attend to them. When I come off duty – no, listen to me, don't go away!' – it was she now who tugged him back, her voice was rising, her face was near to his, he could see angry tears starting in her eyes – 'When I

37

come off duty I am so tired I can't eat, I just fall asleep with my shoes on. I am just one person. Not two, not three – one. Do you understand that, or is it too difficult to understand?' K looked away. 'Sorry,' he mumbled, not knowing what else to say, and returned to the yard.

The suitcase was with his mother. He had no money save the change from the previous evening's meal. He bought a doughnut and drank from a tap. He took a walk about the streets, kicking his feet in the sea of dry leaves on the pavement. Finding a park, he sat on a bench staring up through the bare branches at the pale blue sky. A squirrel chattered at him and he started. Suddenly anxious that the cart might have been stolen, he rushed back to the hospital. The cart was where he had left it in the parking lot. He removed the blankets and cushions and stove but then did not know where to hide them.

At six he saw the nurses from the day shift leave and felt free to sneak back. His mother was not in the corridor. At the desk he asked where to find her and was sent to a remote wing of the hospital where no one knew what he was talking about. He returned to the desk and was told to come back in the morning. He asked whether he might spend the night on one of the benches in the hall and was refused.

He slept in the alley with his head in a cardboard box. He had a dream: his mother came visiting him in Huis Norenius, bringing a parcel of food. 'The cart is too slow,' she said in the dream – 'Prince Albert is coming to fetch me.' The parcel was curiously light. He awoke so cold that he could barely straighten his legs. Far away a clock tolled three or perhaps four. Stars shone on him out of a clear sky. He was surprised that the dream had not left him upset. With a blanket wrapped around him he first paced up and down the alley, then wandered out along the street peering into the dim shop windows where behind diamond grille-work mannekins displayed spring fashions.

When at last he was allowed into the hospital he found his mother in the women's ward wearing no longer her black coat but a white hospital smock. She lay with her eyes closed and the familiar tube up her nose. Her mouth sagged, her face was pinched, even the skin of her arms seemed to have wrinkled. He squeezed her hand but met with no response. There were four rows of beds in the ward with no more than a one-foot space between them; there was nowhere to sit.

At eleven o'clock an orderly brought tea and left a cup at his mother's bedside with a biscuit in the saucer. Michael raised her head and held the cup to her lips but she would not drink. For a long while he waited as his stomach rumbled and the tea grew cold. Then, with the orderly about to return, he gulped down the tea and swallowed the biscuit.

He inspected the charts at the foot of the bed but could not make out whether they referred to his mother or someone else.

In the corridor he stopped a man in a white coat and asked for work. 'I don't want money,' he said, 'just something to do. Sweep the floor or something like that. Clean the garden.' 'Go and ask at the office downstairs,' said the man, and pushed past him. K could not find the right office.

A man in the hospital yard fell into conversation with him. 'You here for stitches?' he inquired. K shook his head. The man looked critically at his face. Then he told a long story of a tractor that had toppled over on him, crushing his leg and breaking his hip, and of the pins the doctors had inserted in his bones, silver pins that would never rust. He walked with a curiously angled aluminium stick. 'You don't know where I could get something to eat?' asked K. 'I haven't eaten since yesterday.' 'Man,' said the man, 'why don't you go and get us both a pie,' and passed K a one-rand coin. K went to the bakery and brought back two hot chicken pies. He sat beside his friend on the bench and ate. The pie was so delicious that tears came to his eyes. The man told him of his sister's uncontrollable fits of shaking. K listened to the birds in the trees and tried to remember when he had known such happiness.

He spent an hour at his mother's bedside in the afternoon and another hour in the evening. Her face was grey, her breathing barely detectable. Once her jaw moved: fascinated, K watched the string of saliva between her withered lips shorten and lengthen. She seemed to be whispering something, but he could not make out what. The nurse who asked him to leave told him she was under sedation. 'What for?' asked K. He stole his mother's tea and that of the old woman in the next bed, gulping it down like a guilty dog while the orderly's back was turned.

When he went back to his alley he found that the cardboard boxes had been cleared away. He spent the night in a doorway recessed from the street. A brass plate above his head read: LE ROUX & HATTINGH – PROKUREURS. He woke when the police cruised past but soon fell asleep again. It was not as cold as on the previous night.

His mother's bed was occupied by a strange woman whose head was wrapped in bandages. K stood at the foot of the bed and stared. Perhaps I am in the wrong ward, he thought. He stopped a nurse. 'My mother – she was here yesterday . . .' 'Ask at the desk,' said the nurse.

'Your mother passed away during the night,' the woman doctor told him. 'We did what we could to keep her, but she was very weak. We wanted to contact you but you didn't leave a number.'

He sat down on a chair in the corner.

'Do you want to make a phone call?' said the doctor.

This was evidently a code for something, he did not know what. He shook his head.

Someone brought him a cup of tea, which he drank. People hovering over him made him nervous. He clasped his hands and stared hard at his feet. Was he expected to say something? He separated his hands and clasped them, over and over.

They took him downstairs to see his mother. She lay with her arms at her sides, still wearing the smock with the legend KPA - CPA on the breast. The tube was gone. For a while he looked at her; then he no longer knew where to look.

'Are there other relatives?' asked the nurse at the desk. 'Do you want to phone them? Do you want us to phone them?' 'It doesn't matter,' said K, and went and sat again on his chair in the corner. After that he was left alone, till at midday a tray of hospital food appeared, which he ate.

He was still sitting in the corner when a man in a suit and tie came to speak to him. What had been his mother's name, age, place of abode, religious denomination? What had her business been in Stellenbosch? Did K have her travel documents? 'I was taking her home,' replied K. 'It was cold where she lived in Cape Town, it was raining all the time, it was bad for her health. I was taking her to a place where she could get better. We did not plan to stop in Stellenbosch.' Then he began to fear he was giving away too much, and would answer no more questions. The man gave up and went away. After a while he came back, squatted in front of K, and asked: 'Have you yourself ever spent time in an asylum or institution for the handicapped or place of shelter? Have you ever held paid employment?' K would not answer. 'Sign your name here,' said the man, and held out a paper, pointing to the space. When K shook his head the man signed the paper himself.

The shifts changed, and K wandered out into the parking lot. He walked about and looked up into the clear night sky. Then he returned to his chair against the wall. He was not told to leave. Later, when there was no one about, he went downstairs to look for his mother. He could not find her, or else the door that led to her was locked. He climbed into a great wire cage containing soiled linen and slept there, curled up like a cat.

The second day after his mother's death a nurse he had never seen appeared before him. 'Come, it is time to go now, Michael,' she said. He followed her to the desk in the hall. The suitcase was waiting for him, and two brown paper parcels. 'We have packed your late mother's clothes and personal possessions in her suit-case,' the strange nurse said: 'you may take it now.' She wore glasses; she sounded as if she were reading the words from a card. K noticed that the girl at the desk was watching them out of the corner of her eye. 'This parcel,' the nurse went on, 'contains your mother's ashes. Your mother was cremated this morning, Michael. If you choose, we can dispose of the ashes fittingly, or else you can take them with you.' With a fingernail she touched the parcel in question. Both parcels were neatly sealed with brown paper tape; this was the smaller. 'Would you like us to take charge of it?' she said. Her finger stroked it lightly. K shook his

43

head. 'And in this parcel,' she went on, pushing the second one firmly across to him, 'we have put a few small things for you that you may find useful, clothes and toiletries.' She looked him candidly in the eye and gave him a smile. The girl at the desk turned back to her typewriter.

So there is a place for burning, K thought. He imagined the old women from the ward fed one after another, eyes pinched against the heat, lips pinched, hands at their sides, into the fiery furnace. First the hair, in a halo of flame, then after a while everything else, to the last things, burning and crumbling. And it was happening all the time. 'How do I know?' he said. 'How do you know what?' the nurse said. Impatiently he indicated the box. 'How do I know?' he challenged. She refused to answer, or did not understand.

In the parking lot he tore open the bigger parcel. It contained a safety razor, a bar of soap, a hand towel, a white jacket with maroon flashes on the shoulders, a pair of black trousers, and a black beret with a shiny metal badge reading ST JOHN AMBULANCE.

He held out the clothes to the girl at the desk. The nurse with glasses had disappeared. 'Why do you give me this?' he asked. 'Don't ask me,' said the girl. 'Maybe someone left them behind.' She would not look him in the face.

He threw the soap and razor away and thought of throwing the clothes away too, but did not. His own clothes had begun to smell.

Though he had no more business there, he found it hard to tear himself from the hospital. By day he pushed the cart around the streets in the vicinity; by night he slept under culverts, behind hedges, in alleys. It seemed strange to him that children should be riding their bicycles home from school in the afternoons, ringing their bells, racing one another; it seemed strange that people should be eating and drinking as usual. For a while he went around asking for garden jobs, but grew to shrink from the distaste that householders, owing him no charity, showed as they opened their doors on him. When it rained he crawled under the cart. There were long periods when he sat staring at his hands, his mind blank.

He fell into the company of men and women who slept under the railway bridge and haunted the vacant lot behind the liquor shop on Andringa Street. Sometimes he lent them his cart. In a fit of largesse he gave away the stove. Then one night someone tried to pull the suitcase from under his head while he was sleeping. There was a fight, and he moved on.

Once a police van stopped beside him in the street and two policemen got out to inspect the cart. They opened the suitcase and rummaged through its contents. They stripped the wrapping paper from the second parcel. Inside was a cardboard box, and inside that a plastic bag of dark grey ash. It was the first time K had seen it. He looked away. 'What's this?' asked the policeman. 'It's my mother's ashes,' said K. The policeman tossed the packet speculatively from hand to hand and made a comment to his friend that K did not hear.

For hours at a time he stood across the street from the hospital. It was smaller than it had once seemed, merely a long low building with a red tiled roof.

He ceased to observe the curfew. He did not believe that any harm would come to him; and if it should come, it would not matter. Dressed in his new clothes, the white jacket and black pants and beret, he pushed his cart where and when he wished. Sometimes spells of airiness came over him. He felt weaker than before, but not sick. He ate once a day, buying doughnuts or pies with money from his mother's purse. There was pleasure in spending without earning: he took no heed of how fast the money went.

He tore a black strip from the lining of his mother's coat and pinned it around his arm. But he did not miss her, he found, except insofar as he had missed her all his life.

With nothing to do, he slept more and more. He discovered that he could sleep anywhere, at any time, in any position: on the sidewalk at noon, with people stepping over his body; standing against a wall, with the suitcase between his legs. Sleep settled inside his head like a benign fog; he had no will to resist it. He did not dream of anyone or anything.

One day the barrow disappeared. He shrugged off the loss.

It appeared that he had to stay in Stellenbosch for a certain length of time. There was no way of shortening the time. He stumbled through the days, losing his way often.

He was walking along the Banhoek road one day, as he sometimes did, with the suitcase. It was a subdued, misty morning. He heard the clip-clop of a horse's hoofs behind him; first there was a smell of fresh manure, then he was slowly overtaken by a cart, an old green municipal refuse cart without hatches, drawn by a Clydesdale driven by an old man in black oilskins. For a while they were moving side by side. The old man gave a little nod; and K, hesitating a moment, peering down the long straight avenue of mist, found that there was after all nothing any more to keep him. So he hoisted himself up and took his place beside the old man. 'Thank you,' he said. 'If you need help I can help.'

But the old man did not need help, nor was he in the mood for talk. He dropped K a mile past the top of the pass and turned off down a dirt track. K walked all day and slept the night in a eucalyptus grove with the wind roaring in the branches high overhead. By midday the next day he had skirted Paarl and was heading north-ward along the national road. He halted only within sight of the first checkpoint, and waited in a skulking-place till he was sure that no one on foot was being stopped.

Several times he was passed by long convoys of vehicles with armed escorts. Each time he left the road and stood well clear, not trying to hide, keeping his hands visible, as he saw other people do.

He slept at the roadside and woke wet with dew. Before him the road wound upward into the mist. Birds flitted from bush to bush, their chirping muffled. He carried the suitcase on a stick over his shoulder. He had not eaten for two days; however, there seemed no limit to his endurance.

A mile up the pass a fire winked through the mist and he heard voices. As he came closer the smell of frying bacon made his stomach churn. There were men standing around a fire keeping warm. At his approach they stopped talking and stared at him. He touched his beret but no one responded. He passed them, passed a second roadside fire, passed a column of vehicles parked head to tail with their lights on, and then came upon the reason for the stoppage. Lying on its side, blocking the road, its rearmost wheels hanging over the lip of the gorge, was an articulated truck painted a blank eggshell blue. The cab was burnt out, the van blackened with smoke. A lorry loaded with sacks had collided with the wreck, and bursts of white flour marked the road. Backed up around the bend as far as K could see was the rest of the convoy. Two radios played loudly on competing stations; from up ahead came the forlorn bleating of sheep. K thought for a moment of stopping to scoop up pocketfuls of the spilled flour, but was not sure what he would do with it. He plodded past truck after truck; he passed the

truckload of sheep, packed so tight that some stood on
their hind legs; he passed a group of soldiers around a
fire who paid no attention to him. At the rear of the
convoy two beacons stood flashing, and further on a
tarbucket burned in the middle of the road, tended by
no one.

Once the convoy was behind him K relaxed, thinking
he was free; but at the next bend in the road a soldier in
camouflage uniform stepped from behind the bushes
pointing an automatic rifle at his heart. K stopped in
his tracks. The soldier lowered his rifle, lit a cigarette,
took a puff, and raised the rifle again. Now, K judged, it
pointed at his face, or at his throat.

'So who are you?' said the soldier. 'Where do you
think you are going?'

About to reply, K was cut short. 'Show me,' said the
soldier. 'Come. Show me what's in there.'

They were out of sight of the convoy, though faint
music still came on the air. K lifted the suitcase off
his shoulder and opened it. The soldier waved him
back, pinched out his cigarette, and in a single movement overturned the case. Everything lay there in the
road: the blue felt slippers, the white bloomers, the
pink plastic bottle of calamine lotion, the brown bottle
of pills, the fawn plastic handbag, the floral scarf, the
scallop-rim scarf, the black woollen coat, the jewelry
box, the brown skirt, the green blouse, the shoes, the
other underwear, the brown paper packets, the white
plastic packet, the coffee tin that rattled, the talcum

49

powder, handkerchiefs, letters, photographs, the box of ashes. K did not stir.

'Where did you steal all this?' said the soldier. 'You're a thief, aren't you? A thief running away over the mountains.' He prodded the handbag with his boot. 'Show me,' he said. He touched the jewelry box. He touched the coffee tin. He touched the other box. 'Show me,' he said, and stepped back.

K opened the coffee tin. It contained curtain rings. He held them out in the palm of his hand, then poured them back into the tin and closed it. He opened the jewelry box and held it out. His heart thundered in his chest. The soldier stirred the contents around, picked out a brooch, and stood back. He was smiling. K closed the box. He opened the handbag and held it out. The soldier gestured. K emptied it on the road. There was a handkerchief, a comb and mirror, a powder compact, and the two purses. The soldier pointed and K handed him the purses. He slipped them into his tunic pocket.

K licked his lips. 'That's not my money,' he said thickly. 'That's my mother's money, that she worked for.' It was not true: his mother was dead, she had no need of money. Nevertheless. There was a silence. 'What do you think the war is for?' K said. 'For taking other people's money?'

'*What do you think the war is for*,' said the soldier, parodying the movements of K's mouth. 'Thief. Watch it. You could be lying in the bushes with flies all over

50

you. Don't you tell me about war.' He pointed his gun at the box of ashes. 'Show me,' he said.

K took off the lid and held out the box. The soldier peered at the plastic bag. 'What's that stuff?' he said.

'Ash,' said K. His voice was steadier now.

'Open it,' said the soldier. K opened the bag. The soldier took a pinch and smelled it cautiously. 'Jesus,' he said. His eyes met K's.

K knelt and packed his mother's things back into the suitcase. The soldier stood aside. 'So can I go now?' said K.

'Papers in order – you can go,' said the soldier. K hoisted the stick with the suitcase on to his shoulder.

'Just a minute,' said the soldier. 'You work for the ambulance or something?'

K shook his head.

'Just a minute, just a minute,' said the soldier. He took one of the purses from his pocket, peeled a brown ten-rand note from the roll, and flicked it in K's direction. 'Tip,' he said. 'Buy yourself an ice-cream.'

K came back and picked up the note. Then he set off again. In a minute or two the soldier had receded into the mist.

It did not seem to him that he had been a coward. Nevertheless, a little further on it struck him that there was no point in keeping the suitcase now. He clambered up a slope and left it in the bushes, retaining only the black coat, for the cold, and the box of ashes, leaving the lid open so that the rain could fall and the sun scorch and the insects gnaw, if they wanted to, without hindrance.

The convoys from up-country were evidently halted, for he had the road to himself. By late afternoon he was in sight of the tunnel through the mountain and the guard post at its south entrance. Quitting the road, he took to the slopes and pushed his way through dense, soggy bush till by nightfall he was high on the saddle overlooking the Elandsrivier and the road to the north. He heard baboons barking in the distance. He slept under an overhang wrapped in his mother's coat with a stick beside him. At dawn he was moving again, making a wide arc down into the valley to avoid the road bridge. The first convoy of the new day passed.

All day he walked, keeping off the road where that was possible. He spent the night in a bungalow in the corner of an overgrown field with rugby poles, separated from the road by a line of eucalyptus trees. The windows of the bungalow were shattered, the door broken off its hinges. The floor was covered in broken glass, old newspapers and drifting leaves; pale yellow grass grew in through cracks in the walls; snails clustered under the waterpipes; but the roof was intact. He swept a pile of leaves and paper into a corner to make a bed. He slept intermittently, woken by high winds and heavy rain.

It was still raining when he got up. Dizzy with hunger, he stood in the doorway staring out on the sodden grassland, the drenched trees, and the grey-misted hills beyond. For an hour he waited for the rain to abate; then he turned up his collar and ran into the downpour. At the far end of the field he clambered over a barbed wire fence and entered an apple orchard overgrown with grass and weeds. Worm-eaten fruit lay everywhere underfoot; the fruit on the branches was undersized and infested. With the beret beaten flat over his ears by the rain and the black coat clinging to his body like a pelt, he stood and ate, taking bites of good flesh here and there, chewing as quickly as a rabbit, his eyes vacant.

He moved deeper into the orchard. Everywhere was evidence of neglect. Indeed, he had begun to believe he was on abandoned land when the apple-trees gave way to a stretch of cleared ground beyond which he saw brick outhouses and the thatched roof and white-washed walls of a farmhouse. In the cleared ground were neatly tended patches of vegetables: cauliflower, carrots, potatoes. He emerged from the shelter of the trees into the downpour and on hands and knees began to pull yellow half-grown carrots out of the soft earth. It is God's earth, he thought, I am not a thief. Never-theless he imagined a shot cracking out from the back window of the farmhouse, he imagined a huge Alsatian streaking out to attack him. When his pockets were full he stood nervously erect. Instead of taking the carrot-tops with him to scatter under the trees as he had intended, he left them where they lay.

During the night the rain stopped. In the morning he was back on the road in his damp clothes, his belly bloated with raw food. When he heard the rumble of an approaching convoy he would creep away into the bushes, though he wondered whether by now, with his filthy clothes and his air of gaunt exhaustion, he would not be passed over as a mere footloose vagrant from the depths of the country, too benighted to know that one needed papers to be on the road, too sunk in apathy to be of harm. One of the convoys, with an escort of motorcycle outriders, armoured cars and trucks full of helmeted boy soldiers, took a full five minutes to pass. He peered steadily out from his hiding-place; the machine-gunner in the last car, muffled in scarf, goggles and woollen cap, seemed to look for an instant straight into his eyes before being borne away backwards into the Boland.

He slept under a culvert. By nine o'clock the next morning he was in sight of the chimneys and pylons of Worcester. He was no longer alone on the road but one of a straggling line of people. Three young men passed him walking briskly, their breath leaving them in white puffs.

On the outskirts of the town there was a roadblock, the first he had seen since Paarl, with police vehicles and people clustered densely around them. For a moment he wavered. To his left were houses, to his right a brickfield. The only way out was back: he pressed on.

'What do they want?' he whispered to the woman ahead of him in the line. She looked at him, looked away again, said nothing.

It was his turn. He held out his green card. From the head of the line, between the two police trucks, he could see those who had passed through the check; but also, to one side, a silent group of men, men only, guarded by a policeman with a dog. If I look very stupid, he thought, perhaps they will let me through.

'Where are you from?'

'From Prince Albert.' His mouth was dry. 'I am going home to Prince Albert.'

'Permit?'

'I lost it.'

'Right. Wait there.' The policeman pointed with his baton.

'I don't want to stop, I don't have time,' K whispered. Could they smell fear on him? Someone gripped his arm. He baulked, like a beast at the shambles. A hand behind him in the line was holding out a green card. No one was listening to him. The policeman with the dog made an impatient gesture. Shoved forward, K walked the last paces himself and entered captivity, his fellows shuffling aside as if to avoid contamination. He clasped the box and looked back into the yellow eyes of the dog.

In the company of fifty strangers K was driven to the railway yards, fed cold porridge and tea, and herded

55

into a lone carriage at a siding. The doors were locked and they waited, watched over by an armed guard in the brown and black uniform of the Railways Police, till another thirty prisoners arrived and were loaded aboard.

Next to K, by the window, sat an older man dressed in a suit. K touched his sleeve. 'Where are they taking us?' he asked. The stranger looked him over and shrugged. 'Why does it matter where they are taking us?' he said. 'There are only two places, up the line and down the line. That is the nature of trains.' He brought out a roll of sweets and offered one to K.

A steam locomotive was backed up to the siding and, with whistles and jerks and clashes, coupled to the carriage. 'North,' said the stranger. 'Touws River.' When K did not reply he seemed to lose interest in him.

They pulled away from the siding and began to move through the back yards of Worcester, where women hung out washing and children stood on fences to wave, the train gradually picking up speed. K watched the telegraph wires rise and fall, rise and fall. They passed mile after mile of bare and neglected vineyards circled over by crows; then the engine began to labour as they entered the mountains. K shivered. He could smell his own sweat through the musty odour of his clothes.

They came to a halt; a guard unlocked the doors; and the moment they stepped out the reason for stopping became clear. The train could go no further: the track ahead was covered in a mountain of rocks and red clay that had come pouring down the slope, tearing a wide gash in the hillside. Someone made a remark, and there was a burst of laughter.

From the top of the earthslide they could see another train far down the track on the other side: there were men struggling like ants to roll a mechanical shovel out of a truck and down a ramp.

K found himself assigned to a gang working on the track, which was dislocated for some distance short of the obstruction. All afternoon, under the eye of an overseer and a guard, he and his fellows worked at moving the buckled rails, firming the bed of the track, and laying sleepers. By evening there was enough new track for an empty truck to advance to the foot of the slide. They broke off for a supper of bread and jam and tea. Then, in the glare of the locomotive's headlight, they climbed the mound and began to shovel clay and stones. At first they were high enough to pitch a load straight into the truck; as the mound grew lower each shovelful had to be lifted over its side. When the truck was filled the locomotive hauled it back down the track, and the same men emptied it in darkness.

Revived by the suppertime break, K soon began to flag again. Every spadeful he lifted cost him an effort; when he stood erect there was a stabbing in his back and the world spun. He laboured more and more slowly, then sat down at the trackside with his head between his knees. Time passed, he had no idea how much time. Sounds grew faint in his ears.

He was tapped on the knee. 'Get up!' said a voice. He scrambled to his feet and in the faint light faced the gang overseer in his black coat and cap.

'Why have I got to work here?' K said. His head swam; the words seemed to echo from far away.

The overseer shrugged. 'Just do what you're told,' he said. He raised his stick and prodded K in the chest. K picked up his shovel.

Till midnight they toiled, moving like sleepwalkers. Herded back into the carriage at last, they slept slumped against one another on the seats or sprawled on the bare floor, the windows shut against the bitter upland cold, while outside the guards stamped up and down and shivered and cursed and took turns to sneak into the cab to warm their hands.

Tired and cold, K lay with the box of ashes in his arms. His neighbour pressed against him and embraced him in his sleep. He thinks I am his wife, thought K, the wife in whose bed he slept last night. He stared at the misty window, longing for the night to pass. Later he fell asleep; when the guards unlocked the doors in the morning his body was so stiff that he could barely stand.

Again there was porridge and tea. He found himself sitting beside the man who had spoken to him on the journey from Worcester.

'Are you feeling sick?' said the man.

K shook his head.

'You don't talk,' said the man. 'I thought you must be sick.'

'I'm not sick,' said K.

'Then don't be so miserable. This isn't jail. This isn't a life sentence. This is just a labour gang. It's peanuts.'

K could not finish the lukewarm slab of mealie-porridge. The guards and the two overseers were going among them now, clapping their hands and prodding them to stand up.

'There's nothing special about you,' said the man. 'There's nothing special about any of us.' His gesture embraced them all: prisoners, guards, foremen. K scraped the uneaten porridge out on to the earth and they stood up. The hooknosed overseer passed by, slapping the tail of his coat with his stick. 'Cheer up!' said the man, giving K a smile, punching him lightly on the shoulder. 'Soon you'll be your own man again!'

The mechanical shovel had at last been brought up on the other side of the slide and was steadily biting the earth away. By noon a passage had been cut three metres wide, and the regular repair crew from Touws River could move in to raise and re-lay the uncovered track. The train on the north side began to get up steam. In his filthy white ambulance jacket, carrying the coat and the box, in the company of other silent and exhausted men, K climbed aboard. No one stopped him. Slowly the train backed away, heading northward up the single track, with the two armed guards at the end of the carriage peering up the line.

For all of the two-hour ride K pretended to be asleep. Once the man sitting opposite him, perhaps looking for something to eat, nudged the box out from between his feet and opened it. When he saw it held ash he closed it and pushed it back. K watched through half-closed eyes but did not interfere.

They were unloaded at Touws River at five in the afternoon. K stood on the platform not knowing what was to happen next. They might discover he had boarded the wrong train and ship him back to Worcester; or they might lock him up in this strange bleak windy place for not having papers; or there might be enough emergencies along the line, enough earth-slides and washaways and explosions in the night and broken tracks, to make it necessary for a gang of fifty men to be shuttled north and south from Touws River for years to come, unpaid, fed on porridge and tea to keep their strength up. But in fact the two guards, having escorted them off the platform, turned without a word and abandoned them on the cinder expanse of the marshalling yards to resume their interrupted lives.

Without waiting, K crossed the tracks, ducked through a hole in the fence, and took the path that led away from the station towards the oasis of filling stations, roadhouses and children's playgrounds on the national road. The gay paint on the rocking-horses and roundabouts was peeling and the filling stations had long been shut down, but a small shop with a Coca-Cola sign over the doorway and a crate of withered oranges in the window still seemed to be open. K had reached the door, had even stepped into the shop, when a little old woman in black scuttled forward with outstretched arms to meet him. Before he could brace himself she had forced him back bodily over the threshold and with a rattle of bolts closed the door in his face. He peered through the glass and knocked; he held up the ten-rand note to show good faith; but the old woman, without so much as a look, disappeared behind the high counter. Two other men from the train, following behind K, had seen his repulse. One of them angrily hurled a handful of gravel at the window; then they turned and left.

K stayed on. Beyond the rack of paperback books, through the sweets in the display cases, he could still see the edge of the black dress. He shielded his eyes with his hands and waited. There was nothing to hear but the wind across the veld and the creaking of the sign overhead. After a while the old woman brought her head up over the counter and met his stare. She wore glasses with thick black rims; her silver hair was drawn back tight. On shelves behind her K could make out canned food, packets of mealie-meal and sugar, detergent powders. On the floor in front of the counter was a basket of lemons. He held the banknote flat against the glass above his head. The old woman did not budge.

He tried the water-tap beside one of the petrol pumps, but it was dry. He drank from a tap at the rear of the shop. In the veld behind the filling-station stood the hulks of scores of cars. He tried doors till he found one that opened. The back seat of the car had been removed, but he was too tired to search further. The sun was going down behind the mountains, the clouds were turning orange. He pulled the door to, lay down on the dusty concave floor with the box under his head, and was soon asleep.

In the morning the shop was open. There was a tall man in khaki behind the counter, from whom, without any trouble, K bought three cans of beans in tomato sauce, a packet of powdered milk, and matches. He retreated behind the filling-station and made a fire; while one of the cans was warming he poured milk powder into his palm and licked at it. Having eaten, he set off, trudging along the highway with the sun on his right. He walked steadily all day. In this flat landscape of scrub and stone there was nowhere one could hide. Convoys passed in both directions, but he ignored them. When dusk fell he broke from the road, crossed a fence, and found a place for the night in a dry river-course. He made a fire and ate the second can of beans. He slept close to the embers, oblivious of the night noises, the tiny scurryings across the pebbles, the rustle of feathers in the trees.

Having once crossed the fence into the veld, he found it more restful to walk across country. He walked all day. In the fading light he was lucky enough to bring down a turtle-dove with a stone as it came to roost in a thorntree. He twisted its neck, cleaned it, roasted it on a skewer of wire, and ate it with the last can of beans.

In the morning he was woken roughly by an old countryman in a tattered brown army coat. With strange vehemence the old man warned him off the land. 'I just slept here, nothing else,' K objected. 'Don't come looking for trouble!' said the old man. 'They find you in their veld, they shoot you! You just make trouble! Now go!' K asked for directions, but the old man waved him off and began to kick dirt over the ashes of the fire. So he retreated, and for an hour trudged along the highway; then, feeling safe, he recrossed the fence.

From a feeding trough beside a dam he scooped half a tinful of crushed mealies and bonemeal, boiled it in water, and ate the gritty mush. He filled his beret with more of the feed, thinking: At last I am living off the land.

Sometimes the only sound he could hear was that of his trouser-legs whipping together. From horizon to horizon the landscape was empty. He climbed a hill and lay on his back listening to the silence, feeling the warmth of the sun soak into his bones.

Three strange creatures, little dogs with big ears, started from behind a bush and raced away.

I could live here forever, he thought, or till I die.

Nothing would happen, every day would be the same as the day before, there would be nothing to say. The anxiety that belonged to the time on the road began to leave him. Sometimes, as he walked, he did not know whether he was awake or asleep. He could understand that people should have retreated here and fenced themselves in with miles and miles of silence; he could understand that they should have wanted to bequeath the privilege of so much silence to their children and grandchildren in perpetuity (though by what right he was not sure); he wondered whether there were not forgotten corners and angles and corridors between the fences, land that belonged to no one yet. Perhaps if one flew high enough, he thought, one would be able to see.

Two aircraft streaked across the sky from south to north leaving vapour trails that slowly faded, and a noise like waves.

The sun was declining as he climbed the last hills outside Laingsburg; by the time he crossed the bridge and reached the wide central avenue of the town the light was a murky violet. He passed filling stations, shops, roadhouses, all closed. A dog began barking and, having begun, went on. Other dogs joined in. There were no street lights.

He was standing before a display of children's clothing in a dim shop window when someone passed behind him, halted, and came back. 'It's curfew when the bell goes,' said a voice. 'You'd better get off the street.'

64

K turned. He saw a man younger than himself wearing a green and gold track suit and carrying a wooden tool-chest. What the stranger saw he did not know.

'Are you all right?' said the young man.

'I don't want to stop,' said K. 'I'm going to Prince Albert and it's a long way.'

But he went home with the stranger after all and slept at his house, after a meal of soup and pan-bread. There were three children. All the while K ate, the youngest, a girl, sat on her mother's lap staring, and though her mother whispered in her ear would not take her eyes off him. The two elder children kept their gaze severely on their plates. After hesitating, K spoke of his journey. 'I met a man the other day,' he said, 'who told me they shoot people they find on their land.' His friend shook his head. 'I've never heard of that,' he said. 'People must help each other, that's what I believe.'

K allowed this utterance to sink into his mind. Do I believe in helping people? he wondered. He might help people, he might not help them, he did not know beforehand, anything was possible. He did not seem to have a belief, or did not seem to have a belief regarding help. Perhaps I am the stony ground, he thought.

When the light was switched off K lay for a long time listening to the stirring of the children, whose bed he had taken and who now slept on a mattress on the floor. He woke once during the night with the feeling that he had been talking in his sleep; but no one seemed to have heard him. When he woke next there was a light on and the parents were getting their children off to school, trying to hush them for the sake of the guest. Mortified, he slipped on his trousers under the bedclothes and stepped outdoors. The stars were still shining; in the east there was a pink glow on the horizon.

The boy came to summon him to breakfast. At the table the urge again came over him to speak. He gripped the edge of the table and sat stiffly upright. His heart was full, he wanted to utter his thanks, but finally the right words would not come. The children stared at him; a silence fell; their parents looked away.

The two elder children were instructed to walk with him as far as the turnoff to Seweweekspoort. At the turnoff, before they parted, the boy spoke. 'Are those the ashes?' he said. K nodded. 'Would you like to see?' he offered. He opened the box, unknotted the plastic bag. First the boy smelled the ashes, then his sister. 'What are you going to do with them?' asked the boy. 'I am taking them back to where my mother was born long ago,' said K. 'That was what she wanted me to do.' 'Did they burn her up?' asked the boy. K saw the burning halo. 'She didn't feel anything,' he said, 'she was already spirit by then.'

It took him three days to cover the distance from Laingsburg to Prince Albert, following the direction of the dirt road, making wide circles around farmhouses, trying to live off the veld but for the main part going hungry. Once, in the heat of the day, he stripped off his clothes and submerged himself in the water of a lonely dam. Once he was called to the roadside by a farmer driving a light truck. The farmer wanted to know where he was going. 'To Prince Albert,' he said, 'to visit my family.' But his accent was strange and it was clear that the farmer was not satisfied. 'Jump in,' he said. K shook his head. 'Jump in,' repeated the farmer, 'I'll give you a ride.' 'I'm OK,' said K, and walked on. The truck drove off in a cloud of dust; and at once K left the road, cut down into a river-bed, and hid till nightfall.

Remembering the farmer afterwards, he could recall only the gaberdine hat and the stubby fingers that beckoned him. On each joint of each finger there was a little feather of bronze hair. His memories all seemed to be of parts, not of wholes.

On the morning of the fourth day he was squatting on a hill watching the sun come up over what he knew at last to be Prince Albert. Cocks crowed; light blinked on the windowpanes of houses; a child was driving two donkeys down the long main street. The air was utterly still. As he descended the hillside toward the town, he began to be aware of a man's voice rising up to meet him in an even and unending monologue without visible origin. Puzzled, he stopped to listen. Is this the voice of Prince Albert? he wondered. I thought Prince Albert was dead. He tried to make out words, but though the voice pervaded the air like a mist or an aroma, the words, if there were words, if the voice were not simply lulling or chanting tones, were too faint or too smooth to hear. Then the voice ceased, giving way to a tiny faraway brass band.

K joined the road that entered the town from the south. He passed the old millwheel; he passed fenced gardens. A pair of liver-coloured dogs galloped up and down inside a fence baying, eager to get at him. A few houses further along the street a young woman was kneeling at an outside tap washing a bowl. She glanced over her shoulder at him: he touched his beret: she looked away.

Now there were shops on both sides of the street: a baker, a café, a clothing store, a bank agency, a welding shop, a general dealer, garages. Grids of steel mesh were locked across the front of the general dealer's. K sat down on the stoep with his back to the mesh and closed his eyes against the sun. Now I am here, he thought. Finally.

An hour later K was still sitting there, asleep, his mouth agape. Children, whispering and giggling, had gathered around him. One of them delicately lifted the beret from his head, put it on, and twisted his mouth in parody. His friends snorted with laughter. He dropped the beret askew on K's head and tried to worm the box away from him; but both hands were folded over it.

The shopkeeper arrived with his keys; the children

fell back; and when he began to remove the grillework
K woke up.

The interior of the shop was dim and cluttered.
Galvanized iron bathtubs and bicycle wheels hung
from the ceiling alongside fan belts and radiator hoses;
there were bins of nails and pyramids of plastic buckets,
shelves of canned goods, patent medicines, sweets,
babywear, cold drinks.

K stepped to the counter. 'Mr Vosloo or Mr Visser,'
he said. Those were the names his mother had remembered from the past. 'I'm looking for a Mr Vosloo or a
Mr Visser who is a farmer.'

'Mrs Vosloo,' said the shopkeeper. 'Is that who you
mean? Mrs Vosloo at the hotel? There is no Mr Vosloo.'

'Mr Vosloo or Mr Visser who was a farmer long ago,
that is who I am looking for. I don't know the name for
sure, but if I find the farm I will recognize it.'

'There is no Vosloo or Visser who farms. Visagie – is
that who you mean? What do you want the Visagies
for?'

'I have to take something there.' He held up the
box.

'Then you have come a long way for nothing. There
is no one at the Visagies' place, it has been empty for
years. Are you sure the name you want is Visagie? The
Visagies left long ago.'

K asked for a packet of ginger snaps.

'Who sent you here?' asked the shopkeeper. K
looked stupid. 'They should have got someone who

69

knows what he is doing. Tell them that when you see them.' K mumbled and left.

He was walking up the street wondering where to try next when one of the children came running after him. 'Mister, I can tell you where Visagies is!' he called. K stopped. 'But it's empty, there's no one there,' the child said. He gave directions that would take K north along the road to Kruidfontein and then east by a farm road along the valley of the Moordenaarsrivier. 'How far is the farm from the big road?' asked K. 'A long way or a short way?' The boy was vague, nor did his companions know. 'You turn off at the sign of the finger pointing,' he said. 'Visagies is before the mountains, quite a long way if you are walking.' K gave them money for sweets.

It was noon before he reached the pointing finger and turned off on to a track that led into desolate grey flats; the sun was going down when he climbed a crest and came in sight of a low whitewashed farmhouse beyond which the land rose from rippling flats to foothills and then to the steep dark slopes of the mountains themselves. He approached the house and circled it. The shutters were closed and a rock-pigeon flew in at a hole where one of the gables had crumbled, leaving timbers exposed and galvanized roof-plates buckled. A loose plate flapped monotonously in the wind. Behind the house was a rockery garden in which nothing was growing. There was no old wagonhouse such as he had imagined, but a wood-and-iron shed, and against it an empty chicken-run with streamers of yellow plastic blowing in the netting-wire. On the rise behind the house stood a pump whose head was missing. Far out in the veld the vanes of a second pump glinted.

Front and back doors were locked. He yanked at a shutter and the restraining hook came loose. Cupping his eyes he peered through the window but could make out nothing.

As he entered the shed a pair of startled swallows flew out. A harrow covered in dust and cobwebs occupied most of the floor. Barely able to see in the gloom, breathing an odour of paraffin and wool and tar, he scratched along the walls among picks and spades, odds and ends of piping, loops of wire, cartons of empty bottles, till he came upon a pile of empty feed-sacks which he dragged into the open, shook clean, and laid out as a bed for himself on the stoep.

He ate the last of the biscuits he had bought. He still had half of his money left but no more use for it. The light faded. There was a flutter of bats under the eaves. He lay on his bed listening to the noises on the night air, air denser than the air of day. Now I am here, he thought. Or at least I am somewhere. He went to sleep.

The first thing he discovered in the morning was that there were goats running on the farm. A flock of twelve or fourteen appeared from behind the house and crossed the yard at an amble, led by an old male with curling horns. K stood up in his bed to look,

71

whereupon the goats started and clattered down the track to the river-bed. In a moment they had vanished from sight. He had sat down and was idly tying his shoelaces before it came home to him that these snorting long-haired beasts, or creatures like them, would have to be caught, killed, cut up and eaten if he hoped to live. Armed with nothing but his penknife he plunged off after the goats. He spent all day hunting them down. Wild at first, they later grew used to the human being trotting after them; as the sun became hotter they sometimes stopped all together and allowed him to approach to within a few paces before casually showing him their heels. At such moments, closing stealthily in on them, K felt his whole body begin to tremble. It was hard to believe that he had become this savage with the bared knife; nor could he shake off a fear that when he stabbed into the dappled brown and white neck of the ram the blade of the penknife would fold back and cut his hand. Then the goats would trot off again, and to keep up his spirits he would have to say to himself: They have many thoughts, I have only one thought, my one thought will in the end be stronger than their many. He tried to herd the goats against a fence, but always they slipped away.

They were leading him in a great circle, he found, round the pump and dam he had observed from the farmhouse the previous day. From closer by he could see that the square concrete dam was in fact full to overflowing; for yards around it there was muddy water and lush marshgrass, and as he approached he could hear the plop of frogs. Only after he had drunk did it occur to him to be puzzled at this luxuriance and to ask himself who saw to it that the dam was full. Later in the afternoon, as he pursued his dogged chase, the goats now ambling ahead of him from one patch of shade to the next, he had his answer: a light wind rose, the wheel creaked and began to turn, from the pump came a dry clanking, and an intermittent trickle of water ran from the pipe.

Famished and exhausted, too deeply committed to the hunt now to give it up, fearful of losing his quarry during the night in these miles of unknown veld, he fetched his bags, made his bed on the bare earth under the full moon as near to the goats as he dared, and fell into a fitful sleep. He was woken in the middle of the night by splashing and snorting as the goats drank. Still dizzy with exhaustion he rose and stumbled towards them. For an instant they bunched together, turning to face him, in water up to their hocks; then, as he plunged into the water after them, they scattered in all directions in an explosion of alarm. Almost under his feet one slipped and slid, kicking like a fish in the mud to regain its footing. K hurled the whole weight of his body upon it. I must be hard, the thought came to him, I must press through to the end, I must not relent. He could feel the goat's hindquarters heaving beneath him; it bleated again and again in terror; its body jerked in spasms. K straddled it, clenched his hands around its neck, and bore down with all his strength, pressing the head under the surface of the water and into the thick ooze below. The hindquarters thrashed, but his knees were gripping the body like a vice. There was a moment when the kicking began to weaken and he almost let up. But the impulse passed. Long after the last snort and tremor, he continued to press the goat's head under the mud. Only when the cold of the water had begun to numb his limbs did he rise and drag himself out.

For the rest of the night he did not sleep but stamped about in his wet clothes, his teeth chattering, while the moon traversed the sky. When dawn came and it was light enough to see, he returned to the farmhouse and without a second thought put an elbow through a windowpane. The last tinkle of the last shard died away and silence closed in as deep as ever before. He loosened the catch and opened the window wide. From room to room he wandered. But for some larger pieces of furniture – cupboards, beds, wardrobes – there was nothing. His feet left prints on the dusty floor. When he entered the kitchen there was a flurry of wings as birds flew out through the hole in the roof. Droppings lay everywhere; there was a pile of masonry against the far wall where the gable had crumbled, out of which there was even a tiny veld-plant growing.

Off the kitchen led a small pantry. K opened the window and threw back the shutters. Along one wall stood a row of wooden bins, all empty save one that contained what looked like sand and mouse droppings.

On one rack were items of kitchenware, odd members of sets, plastic cups, glass jars, all covered in dust and cobwebs. On another were half-empty bottles of oil and vinegar, jars of icing-sugar and powdered milk, and three bottles of preserves. K opened one, dug away the candlewax seal, and wolfed down what tasted like apricots. The sweetness of the fruit in his mouth mingled with the smell of old slime rising from his wet clothes and made him retch. He took the bottle outside and, standing in the sunlight, ate the rest of it more slowly.

He crossed the mile of veld back to the dam. Though the air was warm he was still shivering.

The mud-brown hump of the goat's flank stuck out of the water. He waded in and, using all his strength, hauled the corpse out by the hind legs. Its teeth were bared, its yellow eyes stood wide; a trickle of water ran out of its mouth. It was a ewe. The urgency of the hunger that had possessed him yesterday was gone. The thought of cutting up and devouring this ugly thing with its wet, matted hair repelled him. The rest of the goats stood on a rise some distance away, their ears pricked towards him. He found it hard to believe that he had spent a day chasing after them like a madman with a knife. He had a vision of himself riding the ewe to death under the mud by the light of the moon, and shuddered. He would have liked to bury the ewe somewhere and forget the episode; or else, best of all, to slap the creature on its haunch and see it scramble to its feet and trot off. It took him hours to drag it back across the veld to the house. There was no way of unlocking the doors: he had to lift it through a window to get it into the kitchen. Then it occurred to him that it would be stupid to butcher it indoors, if the kitchen with its plants and birds could be counted as part of the indoors. So he hauled it out again. He had a feeling that he was losing his grip on why he had come all these hundreds of miles, and had to pace about with his hands over his face before he felt better again.

He had never cleaned an animal before. There was nothing to use but the penknife. He slit the belly and pushed his arm into the slit; he expected blood-heat but inside the goat encountered again the clammy wetness of marsh-mud. He wrenched and the organs came tumbling out at his feet, blue and purple and pink; he had to drag the carcass a distance away before he could continue. He peeled back as much of the skin as he was able but could not cut off the feet and head until, searching in the shed, he found a bow-saw. In the end the flayed carcass that he hung from the pantry ceiling seemed diminutive by comparison with the mound of remains that he rolled in a sack and buried in the top tier of the rockery. His hands and sleeves were full of gore; there was no water nearby; he scoured himself with sand but was still followed by flies when he returned to the house.

He brushed the stove clean and made a fire. There was nothing to cook in. He cut off a haunch and held it over the open flame till it was charred on the outside and juices dripped. He ate without pleasure, thinking only: What will I do when the goat is consumed?

He was sure he had caught a cold. His skin felt hot and dry, his head ached, he swallowed with difficulty. He took glass jars to the dam to fill with water. On the way back his strength suddenly deserted him and he had to sit down. Sitting in the bare veld with his head between his knees he allowed himself to imagine lying in a clean bed between crisp white sheets. He coughed, and gave a little hoot like an owl, and heard the sound depart from him without trace of an echo. Though his throat hurt, he made the sound again. It was the first time he had heard his own voice since Prince Albert. He thought: Here I can make any sound I like.

By nightfall he was feverish. He dragged his bed of sacks into the front room and slept there. He had a dream in which he lay in pitch darkness in the dormitory of Huis Norenius. When he stretched out his hand he touched the head of the iron bedstead; from the coir mattress came the smell of old urine. Afraid to move lest he wake the boys sleeping all about him, he lay with his eyes open so that he would not lapse back into the perils of sleep. It is four o'clock, he said to himself, by six o'clock it will be light. No matter how wide he opened his eyes he could not make out the position of the window. His eyelids grew heavy. I am falling, he thought.

In the morning he felt stronger. He put on his shoes

and wandered about the house. On top of a wardrobe he found a suitcase; but it contained only broken toys and pieces of jigsaw puzzle. There was nothing in the house of use to him, nor anything that gave a clue to why the Visagies who had lived here before him had departed.

The kitchen and pantry were noisy with the buzzing of flies. Though he had no appetite, he lit a fire and boiled a little of the goat-meat in water in a jam tin. He found tealeaves in a jar in the pantry; he made tea and went back to bed. He had begun to cough.

The box of ashes waited in a corner of the living-room. He hoped that his mother, who was in some sense in the box and in some sense not, being released, a spirit released into the air, was more at peace now that she was nearer her natal earth.

There was a pleasure in abandoning himself to sick-ness. He opened all the windows and lay listening to the doves, or to the stillness. He dozed and woke through-out the day. When the afternoon sun shone straight in on him he closed the shutters.

In the evening he was delirious again. He was trying to cross an arid landscape that tilted and threatened to tip him over its edge. He lay flat, dug his fingers into the earth, and felt himself swooping through darkness.

After two days the hot and cold fits ended; after another day he began to recover. The goat in the pantry was stinking. The lesson, if there was a lesson, if there were lessons embedded in events, seemed to be not to kill such large animals. He cut himself a Y-shaped stick and, with the tongue of an old shoe and strips of rubber from an inner tube, made himself a catapult with which to knock birds out of the trees. He buried the remains of the goat.

He explored the single-roomed cottages on the hillside behind the farmhouse. They were built of brick and mortar, with cement floors and iron roofs. It was not possible that they were half a century old. But a few yards away a little rectangle of weathered mudbrick stood out from the bare earth. Was this where his mother had been born, amid a garden of prickly pear? He fetched the box of ashes from the house, set it in the middle of the rectangle, and sat down to wait. He did not know what he expected; whatever it was, it did not happen. A beetle scurried across the ground. The wind blew. There was a cardboard box standing in the sunlight on a patch of baked mud, nothing more. There was another step, apparently, that he had to take but could not yet imagine.

He followed the perimeter fence all the way around the farm without meeting any living sign of neighbours. In a trough covered with a sheet of iron he found mouldering sheep-feed; he picked out a handful of mealies and put them in his pocket. He returned to the pump and fiddled with it till he discovered how the brake mechanism worked. He rejoined the broken cable and stopped the crazy dry spinning of the wheel.

Though he continued to sleep in the house he was not at ease there. Roaming from one empty room to another he felt as insubstantial as air. He sang to himself and heard his voice echo from walls and ceiling. He shifted his bed to the kitchen, where he could at least see stars through the hole in the roof.

His days he spent at the dam. One morning he took off all his clothes and washed them, standing chest-deep in the water and pounding them against the wall; for the rest of the day, while the clothes dried, he dozed in the shade of a tree.

The time came to return his mother to the earth. He tried to dig a hole on the crest of the hill west of the dam, but an inch from the surface the spade met solid rock. So he moved to the edge of what had been cultivated land below the dam and dug a hole as deep as his elbow. He laid the packet of ash in the hole and dropped the first spadeful of earth on top of it. Then he had misgivings. He closed his eyes and concentrated, hoping that a voice would speak reassuring him that what he was doing was right – his mother's voice, if she still had a voice, or a voice belonging to no one in particular, or even his own voice as it sometimes spoke telling him what to do. But no voice came. So he extracted the packet from the hole, taking the respon-sibility on himself, and set about clearing a patch a few metres square in the middle of the field. There, bend-ing low so that they would not be carried away by the wind, he distributed the fine grey flakes over the earth, afterwards turning the earth over spadeful by spadeful.

This was the beginning of his life as a cultivator. On a shelf in the shed he had found a packet of pumpkin seeds, some of which he had already idly roasted and eaten; he still had the mealie kernels; and on the pantry floor he had even picked up a solitary bean. In the space of a week he cleared the land near the dam and restored the system of furrows that irrigated it. Then he planted a small patch of pumpkins and a small patch of mealies; and some distance away on the river bank, where he would have to carry water to it, he planted his bean, so that if it grew it could climb into the thorntrees.

For the most part he was living on birds that he killed with his catapult. His days were divided between this form of hunting, which he carried on nearer the farmhouse, and the tilling of the soil. His deepest pleasure came at sunset when he turned open the cock at the dam wall and watched the stream of water run down its channels to soak the earth, turning it from fawn to deep brown. It is because I am a gardener, he thought, because that is my nature. He sharpened the blade of his spade on a stone, the better to savour the instant when it clove the earth. The impulse to plant had been reawoken in him; now, in a matter of weeks, he found his waking life bound tightly to the patch of earth he had begun to cultivate and the seeds he had planted there.

There were times, particularly in the mornings,

when a fit of exultation would pass through him at the thought that he, alone and unknown, was making this deserted farm bloom. But following upon the exultation would sometimes come a sense of pain that was obscurely connected with the future; and then it was only brisk work that could keep him from lapsing into gloominess.

The borehole, pumped dry, yielded only a weak and intermittent stream. It became K's deepest wish for the flow of water from the earth to be restored. He pumped only as much as his garden needed, allowing the level in the dam to drop to a few inches and watching without emotion as the marsh dried up, the mud caked, the grass withered, the frogs turned on their backs and died. He did not know how underground waters replenished themselves but knew it was bad to be prodigal. He could not imagine what lay beneath his feet, a lake or a running stream or a vast inner sea or a pool so deep it had no bottom. Every time he released the brake and the wheel spun and water came, it seemed to him a miracle; he hung over the dam wall, closed his eyes, and held his fingers in the stream.

He lived by the rising and setting of the sun, in a pocket outside time. Cape Town and the war and his passage to the farm slipped further and further into forgetfulness.

Then one day, returning to the house at noontime, he saw the front door wide open; and while he still stood confounded a figure emerged from the interior into the sunlight, a pale plump young man in khaki uniform. 'Do you work here?' were this stranger's first words. He stood at the head of the steps as if he owned the house. There was nothing for K to do but nod. 'I have never seen you before,' said the stranger. 'Are you looking after the farm?' K nodded. 'When did the kitchen fall in like that?' he asked. Trying to bring out words, K stumbled. The stranger did not shift his gaze from K's bad mouth. Then he spoke again. 'You don't know who I am, do you?' he said. 'I am boss Visagie's grandson.'

K removed his sacks from the kitchen to one of the rooms on the hillside and yielded the house to the new Visagie. He felt the old hopeless stupidity invading him, which he tried to beat back. Perhaps he will stay only a day or two, he thought, when he sees that there is nothing good enough for him here; perhaps he will be the one to go and I will be the one to stay.

But the grandson, it emerged, was not able to go. That same evening, when K had made a fire up on the hillside and was broiling a pair of bushdoves for his supper, the grandson appeared out of the dusk and hung around so long that K felt obliged to offer him a share. He ate like a hungry boy. There was not enough for both of them. Then his story came out. 'When you go to Prince Albert, I want you to take care not to mention it to anyone that I am here,' he began. He was, it turned out, a deserter from the army. He had slipped off a troop train at Kruidfontein siding the previous evening and walked across country all night, arriving at last at the farm he remembered from his schoolboy days. 'Our family used to spend every Christmas here,' he said. 'Family would keep coming till the house was bursting at the seams. I've never seen such eating as we used to do. Day after day my grandmother would pile the table with food, good country food, and we would eat every last scrap. Karoo lamb like you never taste any more.' K sat on his heels poking the fire, barely listening, thinking: I let myself believe that this was one of those islands without an owner. Now I am learning the truth. Now I am learning my lesson.

Meanwhile the more he talked the more vehement the grandson became. He was anaemic, he said, he had a weak heart, it was in his papers, no one contested it, yet here they were sending him to the front. They were reassigning clerks and sending them to the front. Did they think they could do without clerks? Did they think they could run the war without a paymaster's office? If they came looking for him, the regular police or the military police, to take him back and make an example of him, K must play dumb. He must play the idiot and reveal nothing. Meanwhile he, the grandson, would make a hiding-place for himself. He knew the farm, he would find a place where they would never dream of looking. It would be better if K did not know the hiding-place. Could K find him a saw? He needed a saw, he wanted to begin work first thing in the morning.

K agreed to look. Then followed a long silence. 'Is this all you eat?' asked the grandson. K nodded. 'You should plant potatoes,' said the grandson. 'Potatoes, onions, mealies – anything will grow here if you give it enough water. This is good soil. I'm surprised you don't grow a few things for yourself down by the dam.' A pang of disappointment cut through K: even the dam was known about. 'My grandparents were lucky to find you,' the grandson went on. 'People have a hard time finding good farm servants nowadays. What is your name?' 'Michael,' answered K. It was dark now. The grandson stood up uncertainly. 'You haven't got a torch?' he asked. 'No,' said K; and watched him pick his way down the hillside in the moonlight.

Morning came and there was no longer anything for him to do. He could not go to the dam without betraying his garden. He sat on his heels against the wall of the room, feeling the sun warm his body, feeling time pass, till the grandson came climbing the hill again. He is ten years younger than me, K thought. The climb brought a flush to his skin.

'Michael, there is nothing to eat!' the grandson complained. 'Don't you ever go to the shop?' Without waiting for a reply he pushed open the door of the room and peered inside. He seemed about to pass a comment, but then stopped himself.

'How much do they pay you, Michael?' he said.

He thinks I am truly an idiot, thought K. He thinks I am an idiot who sleeps on the floor like an animal and lives on birds and lizards and does not know there is such a thing as money. He looks at the badge on my beret and asks himself what child gave it to me out of what lucky packet.

'Two rand,' said K. 'Two rand a week.'

'So what news do you have of my grandparents? Don't they ever visit?'

K was silent.

'Where do you come from? You are not from here, are you?'

'I have been all over,' said K. 'I have been in the Cape too.'

'Aren't there sheep on the farm?' said the grandson. 'Aren't there goats? Didn't I see goats yesterday, ten or twelve goats out beyond the dam?' He looked at his watch. 'Come, let's go and find the goats.'

K remembered the goat in the mud. 'Those are goats that have gone wild,' he said. 'You will never catch them.'

'We'll catch them at the dam. The two of us will manage.'

'They come to the dam at night,' said K. 'During the day they are out in the veld.' To himself he thought: A soldier without a gun. A boy on an adventure. To him the farm is just a place of adventure. He said: 'Leave the goats, I'll get you something to eat.'

So while the sound of sawing came from the house, K took his catapult and walked down to the river and in an hour had killed three sparrows and a dove. He brought the dead birds to the front door and knocked. The grandson, stripped to the waist and sweating, came to meet him. 'Very good,' he said. 'Can you clean them quickly? I would appreciate that.'

K held up the four dead birds, their feet together in a tangle of claws. There was a pearl of blood at the beak of one of the sparrows. 'So small you don't taste it as it goes down,' he said. 'You wouldn't get yourself dirty, not even your little finger.'

'What the hell does that mean?' said the Visagie grandson. 'What the fuck do you mean? If you want to say something, say it! Put those things down, I'll take care of them!' So K laid the four birds down on the stoep at the front door and departed.

The first stubby pumpkin leaves were pushing through the earth, one here, one there. K opened the sluice for the last time and watched the water wash slowly across the field, turning the earth dark. Now when I am most needed, he thought, I abandon my children. He closed the sluice and bent the stem of the ball down till the cock was jammed shut, cutting the flow to the trough from which the goats drank.

He brought four jars of water back and set them on the steps. The grandson, wearing his shirt again, stood with his hands in his pockets staring into the distance. After a long silence he spoke. 'Michael,' he said, 'I'm not the one who pays you, I can't put you off the farm just like that. But we have to work together, other-wise – ' He turned his gaze on K.

The words, whatever they stood for, accusation, threat, reprimand, seemed to K to smother him. It is nothing but a manner, he told himself: be calm. Nevertheless he felt stupidity creep over him like a fog again. He no longer knew what to do with his face. He rubbed his mouth and stared at the grandson's brown boots, thinking: You can't buy boots like that in the shops any more. He tried to hold to the thought to steady himself.

'I want you to go to Prince Albert for me, Michael,' said the grandson. 'I will give you a list of things I want, and money. I will give you something for yourself too. Just don't talk to anyone. Don't say you have seen me, don't say who you are getting the things for. Don't say you are getting them for anyone. Don't get everything at the same shop. Get half at Van Rhyn's and half at the café. Don't stop and talk – pretend you are in a hurry. Do you understand?'

Let me not lose my way, K thought. He nodded. The grandson went on.

'Michael, I am speaking to you as one human being to another. There is a war on, there are people dying. Well, I am at war with no one. I have made my peace. Do you understand? I make my peace with everyone. There is no war here on the farm. You and I can live here quietly till they make peace everywhere. No one will disturb us. Peace has got to come one of these days.

'Michael, I worked in the paymaster's office, I know

88

what is going on. I know how many men are going eleven-63 every month, whereabouts unknown, pay stopped, docket opened. Do you know what I mean? I could give you figures that would shock you. I'm not the only one. Soon they are not going to have enough men, I'm telling you, they are not going to have enough men to track down the men who are running away! This is a big country! Just look around you! Lots of places to go! Lots of places to hide!

'I just want to keep out of sight for a little while. They will soon give up. I'm just a little fish in a big ocean. But I need your co-operation, Michael. You must help me. Otherwise there is no future for either of us. Do you see?'

So K left the farm carrying the list of things the grandson needed and forty rand in notes. He picked up an old tin by the roadside, and at the gate of the farm buried the money in the tin under a stone. Then he cut across country, keeping the sun on his left and avoiding all habitation. In the afternoon he began to climb, till the neat white houses of the town of Prince Albert emerged below him to the west. Keeping to the slopes, he skirted the town and joined the road that led up into the Swartberg. He tramped uphill in dark shadow wearing his mother's coat against the chill.

High above the town he cast around for a place to sleep and found a cave that had evidently been used before by campers. There was a stone fireplace, and a bed of fragrant dry thymebush was spread over the floor. He made a fire and roasted a lizard he had killed with a stone. The funnel of the sky above turned a darker blue and stars emerged. He curled up, tucked his hands into his sleeves, and drifted towards sleep. Already it was hard to believe that he had known someone called the Visagie grandson who had tried to turn him into a body-servant. In a day or two, he told himself, he would forget the boy and remember only the farm.

He thought of the pumpkin leaves pushing through the earth. Tomorrow will be their last day, he thought: the day after that they will wilt, and the day after that they will die, while I am out here in the mountains. Perhaps if I started at sunrise and ran all day I would not be too late to save them, them and the other seeds that are going to die underground, though they do not know it, that are never going to see the light of day. There was a cord of tenderness that stretched from him to the patch of earth beside the dam and must be cut. It seemed to him that one could cut a cord like that only so many times before it would not grow again.

He spent a day in idleness, sitting in the mouth of his cave gazing up at the farther peaks on which there were still patches of snow. He felt hungry but did nothing about it. Instead of listening to the crying of his body he tried to listen to the great silence about him. He went to sleep easily and had a dream in which he was running as fast as the wind along an open road with the cart floating behind him on tyres that barely skimmed the ground.

The sides of the valley were so steep that the sun did not emerge till noon and had gone behind the western peaks by mid-afternoon. He was cold all the time. So he climbed higher, zigzagging up the slope till the road through the pass disappeared from sight and he was looking over the vast plain of the Karoo, with Prince Albert itself miles below. He found a new cave and cut bushes for the floor. He thought: Now surely I have come as far as a man can come; surely no one will be mad enough to cross these plains, climb these mountains, search these rocks to find me; surely now that in all the world only I know where I am, I can think of myself as lost.

Everything else was behind him. When he awoke in the morning he faced only the single huge block of the day, one day at a time. He thought of himself as a termite boring its way through a rock. There seemed nothing to do but live. He sat so still that it would not have startled him if birds had flown down and perched on his shoulders.

Straining his eyes he could sometimes make out the dot of a vehicle crawling down the main street of the toy town on the plain below; but even on the stillest of days no sound reached him save the scurrying of insects across the ground, and the buzz of the flies that had not forgotten him, and the pulse of blood in his ears.

He did not know what was going to happen. The story of his life had never been an interesting one; there had usually been someone to tell him what to do next; now there was no one, and the best thing seemed to be to wait.

His thoughts went to Wynberg Park, one of the places where he had worked in the old days. He remembered the young mothers who had brought their children to play on the swings and the couples lying together in the shade of the trees and the green and brown mallards in the pond. Presumably the grass had not stopped growing in Wynberg Park because there was a war, and the leaves had not stopped falling. There would always be a need for people to mow the grass and sweep up the leaves. But he was no longer sure that he would choose green lawns and oak-trees to live among. When he thought of Wynberg Park he thought of an earth more vegetal than mineral, composed of last year's rotted leaves and the year before's and so on back till the beginning of time, an earth so soft that one could dig and never come to the end of the softness; one could dig to the centre of the earth from Wynberg Park, and all the way to the centre it would be cool and dark and damp and soft. I have lost my love for that kind of earth, he thought, I no longer care to feel that kind of earth between my fingers. It is no longer the green and the brown that I want but the yellow and the red; not the wet but the dry; not the dark but the light; not the soft but the hard. I am becoming a different kind of man, he thought, if there are two kinds of man. If I were cut, he thought, holding his wrists out, looking at his wrists, the blood would no longer gush from me but seep, and after a little seeping dry and heal. I am becoming smaller and harder and drier every day. If I were to die here, sitting in the mouth of my cave looking out over the plain with my knees under my chin, I would be dried out by the wind in a day, I would be preserved whole, like someone in the desert drowned in sand.

In his first days in the mountains he went for walks, turned over stones, nibbled at roots and bulbs. Once he broke open an ant-nest and ate grubs one by one. They tasted like fish. But now he ceased to make an adventure of eating and drinking. He did not explore his new world. He did not turn his cave into a home or keep a record of the passage of the days. There was nothing to look forward to but the sight, every morning, of the shadow of the rim of the mountain chasing faster and faster toward him till all of a sudden he was bathed in sunlight. He would sit or lie in a stupor at the mouth of the cave, too tired to move or perhaps too lackadaisical. There were whole afternoons he slept through. He wondered if he were living in what was known as bliss. There was a day of dark cloud and rain, after which tiny pink flowers sprang up all over the mountainside, flowers without any leaf that he could see. He ate handfuls of flowers and his stomach hurt. As the days became hotter the streams ran faster, he could not see why. In this crisp mountain water he missed the bitter savour of water from under the earth. His gums bled; he drank the blood.

As a child K had been hungry, like all the children of Huis Norenius. Hunger had turned them into animals who stole from each other's plates and climbed the kitchen enclosure to rifle the garbage cans for bones and peelings. Then he had grown older and stopped wanting. Whatever the nature of the beast that had howled inside him, it was starved into stillness. His last years at Huis Norenius were the best, when there were no big boys to torment him, when he could slip off to his place behind the shed and be left alone. One of the teachers used to make his class sit with their hands on their heads, their lips pressed tightly together and their eyes closed, while he patrolled the rows with his long ruler. In time, to K, the posture grew to lose its meaning as punishment and became an avenue of reverie; he remembered sitting hands on head through hot afternoons with doves cooing in the gum trees and the chant of the tables coming from other classrooms, struggling with a delicious drowsiness. Now, in front of his cave, he sometimes locked his fingers behind his head, closed his eyes, and emptied his mind, wanting nothing, looking forward to nothing.

There were other times when his mind would return to the Visagie boy in his hiding-place, wherever that was, in darkness under the floor among the mouse-droppings, or shut up in a cupboard in the attic, or out in his grandfather's veld behind a bush. He thought of the nice pair of boots: they seemed wasted on someone who lived in a hole.

It became an effort not to shut his eyes against the glare of the sun. There was a throbbing that would not leave him; lances of light pierced his head. Then he could keep nothing down, even water made him retch. There was a day when he was too tired to get up from his bed in the cave; the black coat lost its warmth and he shivered continually. It came home to him that he might die, he or his body, it was the same thing, that he might lie here till the moss on the roof grew dark before his eyes, that his story might end with his bones growing white in this faroff place.

It took him all of a day to creep down the mountain-side. His legs were weak, his head hammered, every time he looked downward he grew dizzy and had to grip the earth till the whirling stopped. When he reached the level of the road the valley was in deep shadow; the last light was fading by the time he entered the town. The smell of peach-blossom enveloped him. There was a voice too, coming from all sides, the calm even voice he had heard the first day he saw Prince Albert. He stood at the head of the High Street among the verdant gardens unable to make out a word, though he listened hard, of the distant monotone that after a while blended with the twitter of the birds in the trees and then gave way to music.

There was no one on the streets. K made his bed in the doorway of the Volkskas office with a rubber door-mat under his head. When his body had cooled he began to shiver. He slept in fits, clenching his jaws against the pain in his head. A flashlight woke him but he could not separate it from the dream in which he was involved. To the questions of the police he gave unclear answers, shouts and gasps. 'Don't! . . . Don't! . . . Don't! . . .' he said, the word coming out like a cough from his lungs. Understanding nothing, repelled by his smell, they pushed him into their van, took him back to the station, and locked him in a cell with five other men, where he resumed his shivering and his delirious sleep.

In the morning, when they led the prisoners out for ablutions and breakfast, K was rational but unable to stand. He apologized to the constable at the door. 'It is cramp in my legs, it will go away,' he said. The constable called the duty officer. For a while they watched the skeletal figure that sat with its back to the wall rubbing its exposed calves; then together they bore K bodily into the yard, where he cringed from the brilliant sunlight, and motioned to another of the prisoners to give him food. K accepted a thick slab of mealie-porridge but, even before the first spoonful had reached his mouth, had begun his retching.

No one knew where he was from. He had no papers on him, not even a green card. On the charge sheet he was listed 'Michael Visagie – CM – 40 – NFA – Unemployed', and charged with leaving his magisterial district without authorization, not being in possession of an identification document, infringing the curfew, and being drunk and disorderly. Attributing his debilitation and incoherence to alcohol poisoning, they permitted him to stay in the yard while the other prisoners were returned to the cells, then at noon took him in the back of the van to the hospital. There he was stripped of his clothes and lay naked on a rubber sheet while a young nurse washed and shaved him and dressed him in a white smock. He felt no shame. 'Tell me, I have always wanted to know, who is Prince Albert?' he asked the nurse. She paid no attention. 'And who is Prince Alfred? Isn't there a Prince Alfred too?' He waited for the soft warm rag to touch his face, closing his eyes, willing it to come.

So he lay again between clean sheets, not in the main ward but in a long wood-and-iron extension at the rear of the hospital, housing, as far as he could see, only children and old men. A row of light bulbs hung on long cords from the bare rafters swaying out of time with one another. A tube ran out of his arm to a bottle on a rack; out of the corner of his eye he could watch the level fall hour by hour, if he wanted to.

Once when he awoke there were a nurse and a policeman in the doorway looking in his direction, murmuring together. The policeman carried his cap under his arm.

The afternoon sun glared through the window. A fly settled on his mouth. He waved it away. It circled and settled again. He yielded; his lip underwent the tiny cold searching of its proboscis.

An orderly came in with a trolley. Everyone got a tray except K. Smelling the food, he felt the saliva seep in his mouth. It was the first hunger he had known for a long time. He was not sure that he wanted to become a servant to hunger again; but a hospital, it seemed, was a place for bodies, where bodies asserted their rights.

Dusk fell, and then darkness. Someone switched on the lights, in two banks of three. K closed his eyes and slept. When he opened them again the lights were still on. Then as he watched they faded and went off. Moonlight fell in four silver slabs through the four windows. Somewhere nearby a diesel motor sputtered. The lights came on dimly. He fell asleep.

In the morning he ate and kept down a breakfast of baby cereal and milk. He felt strong enough to get up, but was too shy to do so till he saw an old man wrap a dressing-gown over his pyjamas and leave the room. After that he walked up and down beside his bed for a while, feeling odd in the long smock.

In the next bed was a young boy with a bandaged stump of an arm. 'What happened?' said K. The boy turned away and did not reply.

If I could find my clothes, K thought, I would leave. But the cupboard beside his bed was empty.

He ate again at midday. 'Eat while you can,' said the orderly who brought his food, 'the great hunger is still to come.' Then he moved on, pushing the trolley of food before him. It seemed a strange thing to say. K kept an eye on him as he went his round. From the far end of the ward the orderly felt K's gaze, and gave him a mysterious smile; but when he returned to fetch the tray he would say nothing more.

The sun beating down on the iron roof turned the ward into an oven. K lay with his legs spread, dozing. From one of his spells he awoke to see the same policeman and nurse standing over him. He shut his eyes; when he opened them they were gone. Night fell.

In the morning a nurse fetched him and led him to a bench in the main building, where he waited an hour till it was his turn. 'How are you feeling today?' asked the doctor. K hesitated, not knowing what to say, and the doctor stopped listening. He told K to breathe and listened to his chest. He examined him for venereal infection. In two minutes it was over. He wrote something in the brown folder on his desk. 'Have you ever seen a doctor about your mouth?' he asked while he wrote. 'No,' said K. 'You could get it corrected, you know,' said the doctor, but did not offer to correct it.

K returned to his bed and waited with his hands under his head till the nurse brought him clothes: underpants and a khaki shirt and shorts, neatly ironed. 'Put these on,' she said, and busied herself elsewhere. Sitting up in bed, K put them on. The shorts were too big. When he stood up he had to hold the waist-band to stop them from slipping down. Then he saw the policeman at the door. 'These are too big,' he said to

99

the nurse. 'Can't I have my own clothes?' 'You will get your own clothes back at the desk,' she told him. The policeman led him down the corridor to the reception desk and there took charge of a brown paper parcel. No words passed. There was a blue van in the parking lot. K waited for the back to be unlocked; the tarmac was so hot under his bare soles that he had to dance where he stood.

He expected to be taken back to the police station, but instead they drove all the way through the town and then five kilometres down a dirt road to a camp in the bare veld. K had seen the ochre rectangle of Jakkalsdrif from his perch in the mountains but had thought it was a construction site. Not for a moment had he guessed that it might be one of the resettlement camps, that the tents and unpainted wood-and-iron buildings might house people, that its perimeter might be a three-metre fence surmounted with a strand of barbed wire. When he climbed out of the van holding up his pants, he did so under the eyes of a hundred curious inmates, adults and children, lining the fence on either side of the gate.

By the gate stood a little hut with a covered porch on which identical grey-green succulents grew out of two tubs of earth. On the porch waited a stout man in military uniform. K recognized the blue beret of the Free Corps. The policeman greeted him and they retired together into the hut. With his parcel under his arm K was left to endure the inspection of the crowd.

He stared first into the distance, then at his feet; he did not know what expression to wear. 'Where did you steal those pants?' called out someone. 'Off Sarge's line!' came another voice, and there was a ripple of laughter.

Then a second Free Corps man emerged from the hut. He unlocked the camp gate and conducted K through the crowd, crossing the bare earth of the assembly square to one of the wood-and-iron buildings. It was dark inside, there were no windows. He indicated an empty bunk. 'That's your home from now on,' he said. 'It's the only home you've got, keep it clean.' K clambered up and stretched out on the bare foam rubber no more than an armslength from the iron roof. In the dim light, in the stifling heat he waited for the guard to leave.

All afternoon he lay on his bunk listening to the sounds of camp life outside. Once a troop of children rushed in and chased one another noisily over and under the bunks; when they left they slammed the door shut. He tried to sleep but could not. His throat was parched. He thought of the cool of his cave up in the mountains, of the streams that never stopped running. This is like Huis Norenius, he thought: I am back in Huis Norenius a second time, only now I am too old to bear it. He took off the khaki shirt and shorts and opened the package; but the clothes whose smell used to be simply his own smell had in the space of a few days grown stale and frowzy and alien. Spreadeagled on the

101

hot mattress in his undershorts, he waited for the afternoon to pass.

Someone opened the door and tiptoed across the floor. K pretended to be asleep. Fingers touched his bare arm. He flinched at the touch. 'Are you all right?' said a man's voice. Against the dazzle of light from the doorway he could not make out the face. 'I'm fine,' he said: the words seemed to come from far away. The stranger tiptoed off again. K thought: I needed more warning, I should have been told I was going to be sent back amongst people.

Later he put on the khaki clothes and went outside. The sun baked down, there was no breath of wind. Two women lay together on a blanket in the shade of a tent. One was asleep, the other had a sleeping child at her breast. She gave K a smile; he nodded and passed. He found the cistern and drank copiously. On his return he addressed her. 'Is there anywhere I can wash some clothes?' he asked. She pointed out the washhouse. 'Have you got soap?' she said. 'Yes,' he lied.

In the washhouse were two basins and two showers. He wanted to have a shower, but when he tried the shower tap there was no water. He washed the white St John's jacket, the black trousers, the yellow shirt and the underpants with the sagging elastic; he found pleasure in soaking and wringing, in standing with his eyes shut and his arms plunged to the elbows in cold water. He put on his own shoes. Afterwards, when he went to drape his clothes over the washline, he saw the

102

painted sign against the wall: JAKKALSDRIF RELOCATION CAMP/BATH TIMES/MALES 6–7 AM/FEMALES 7.30–8.30 AM/ BY ORDER/SAVE WATER/BE SPARING. Following the line of the waterpipe from the cistern, he saw it run under the camp fence and then on to a pump on high ground some distance away.

The woman with the baby stopped him as he passed. 'You leave your clothes there,' she warned, 'they'll be gone in the morning.' So he fetched the damp clothing back and spread it over his bunk.

The sun was setting; there were more people about now, and children everywhere. Three old men were playing cards outside the next hut. For a while he stood and watched.

He counted thirty tents evenly spaced over the camp terrain, and seven huts besides the bathhouse and latrines. Foundations for a second row of huts had been laid, and rusty bolts jutted from the concrete.

He walked over to the gate. On the guardhouse porch one of the two Free Corps sentries sat in a deck-chair dozing, his shirt open to the waist. K leaned his head against the mesh, willing the guard to wake. 'Why have I been sent here?' he wanted to say. 'How long do I have to stay?' But the guard went on sleeping, and K lacked the courage to shout.

He wandered back to the hut, and from the hut to the cistern. He did not know what to do with himself. A young girl came with a bucket to fill, but stopped when she saw him and went away. He retreated to the

103

back fence of the camp and stared out over the empty veld.

In one or two of the stone fireplaces amongst the tents there were now fires burning; there was a bustle of people coming and going; the camp was coming to life.

A blue police van arrived in a cloud of dust and pulled up at the gate, followed by an open truck with men standing packed together in the back. Every child in the camp rushed to the gate. The guard let the van through, and it drove slowly to the fourth in the row of huts, the one with the stovepipe. Two women got out and unlocked the hut; behind them followed the police driver carrying a cardboard box. From the back fence K could faintly hear the crackling of the radio in the van. Soon a first puff of black smoke came from the pipe.

Men from the truck were unloading bundles of firewood and stacking them inside the gate.

The policeman returned to his van and sat in the cab combing his hair. One of the women, the large one in slacks, emerged from the hut and beat on a triangle. Before the last note had died away there was a crowd of children jostling at the door, carrying mugs or plates or tin cans, and mothers with infants. The woman cleared a space and began to let the children in two by two. K wandered over and joined the back of the crowd. When the children emerged, he saw, they had soup and slices of bread.

A little boy, bumped as he came out, spilled his soup over his legs. Walking gingerly, as though he had wet himself, he rejoined the line. Some of the children sat down on the bare ground outside the hut to eat, others carried their supper back to the tents.

K approached the woman at the door. 'Excuse me,' he said, 'can I have something to eat? I haven't got a plate. I come from the hospital.'

'It's for the children only,' replied the woman, and looked away.

He went back to his hut and put on the black trousers, which were still damp. The khaki shorts he tossed under a bunk.

He spoke to the policeman in the van. 'Where do I get something to eat?' he said. 'I didn't ask to come here. Now where must I get food?'

'This isn't jail,' said the policeman, 'this is a camp, you work for your food like everyone else in the camp.'

'How can I work when I am locked up? Where is the work I must do?'

'Fuck off,' said the policeman. 'Ask your friends. Who do you think you are that I should give you a free living?'

It was better in the mountains, K thought. It was better on the farm, it was better on the road. It was better in Cape Town. He thought of the hot dark hut, of strangers lying packed about him on their bunks, of air thick with derision. It is like going back to childhood, he thought: it is like a nightmare.

There were more fires burning now, and a smell of cooking, even of meat grilling. The woman in slacks beckoned him over to the kitchen and handed him a plastic bucket. 'Wash this,' she said, 'and put it inside here. Lock the door. You know how a padlock works?' K nodded. There was a layer of soup mush at the bottom of the bucket. The two women got into the van with the policeman; as they drove off, K noticed, they looked straight ahead of them as though there were nothing left to be curious about in the camp.

Darkness fell. Around the fires there were groups eating and talking; later on someone began to play a guitar and there was dancing. At first K hung about in the shadows looking on; then, feeling foolish, he went and lay down on his bunk in the empty hut.

Someone entered: he turned as the dark shape approached him. 'Want a cigarette?' said a voice. K accepted the cigarette and sat up hunched against the wall. By the light of the match he saw a man older than himself.

'Where are you from?' said the man.

'I walked around the back fence this afternoon,' said K. 'Anyone can climb it. A child could climb it in a minute. Why do people stay here?'

'This isn't a prison,' said the man. 'Didn't you hear the policeman tell you it isn't a prison? This is Jakkalsdrif. This is a camp. Don't you know what a camp is? A camp is for people without jobs. It is for all the people who go around from farm to farm begging

106

for work because they haven't got food, they haven't got a roof over their heads. They put all the people like that together in a camp so that they won't have to beg any more. You say why don't I run away. But why should people with nowhere to go run away from the nice life we've got here? From soft beds like this and free wood and a man at the gate with a gun to stop the thieves from coming in the night to steal your money? Where do you come from that you don't know these things?'

K was silent. He did not understand who was being blamed.

'You climb the fence,' the man said, 'and you have left your place of abode. Jakkalsdrif is your place of abode now. Welcome. You leave your place of abode, they pick you up, you are a vagrant. No place of abode. First time, Jakkalsdrif. Second time, Brandvlei. You want to go to Brandvlei, penal servitude, hard labour, brickfields, guards with whips? You climb the fence, they pick you up, it's a second offence, you go to Brandvlei. Remember that, it's your choice. Where do you want to go, anyway?' He dropped his voice. 'You want to go to the mountains?'

K did not know what he meant. The man slapped him on the leg. 'Come out and join the party,' he said. 'You see them searching people at the gate? Searching for liquor. No liquor in the camp, by order. So come out and have a drink.'

Thus K allowed himself to be led out to the group

107

gathered around the guitar-player. The music stopped. 'This is Michael,' the man said. 'He has come all the way to Jakkalsdrif for his holiday. Let's make him welcome.' K was pressed to sit down, offered wine out of a bottle wrapped in brown paper, and besieged with questions: Where did he come from? What was he doing in Prince Albert? Where had he been picked up? No one could understand why he should have left the city and come to this lonely part of the world where there was no work and where entire families had been turned off farms they had lived on for generations.

'I was bringing my mother to live in Prince Albert,' K tried to explain. 'She was sick, her legs were giving her trouble. She wanted to live in the country, to get away from the rain. It was raining all the time where we lived. But she died on the way, in Stellenbosch, in the hospital there. So she never saw Prince Albert. She was born here.'

'Poor lady,' said a woman. 'But haven't you got Welfare in the Cape?' She did not wait for K's answer. 'There is no Welfare here. This is our Welfare.' She waved an arm to embrace the camp.

K pressed on. 'Then I worked on the railways,' he said. 'I helped to clear the line when there was a blockage. Then I came here.'

There was a silence. Now I must speak about the ashes, thought K, so as to be complete, so as to have told the whole story. But he found that he could not, or could not yet. The man with the guitar began to pick out a new melody. K felt the attention of the group drift away from him to the music. 'There is no Welfare in Cape Town either,' he said. 'The Welfare stopped.' The tent next door glowed, lit from within by a candle; figures moved in silhouette against the walls larger than life. He reclined and stared up at the stars.

'We've been in for five months now,' said a voice beside him. It was the man from the hut. His name was Robert. 'My wife, my children, three girls and a boy, my sister and her children. I had work near Klaarstroom, on a farm. I'd been there a long time, twelve years. Then suddenly there was no wool market. Then they started the quota system – only so much wool per farmer. Then they closed the one road to Oudtshoorn, then they closed the other one, then they opened them both, then they closed them for good. So one day he came to me, this farmer, and he said, "I've got to let you go. Too many mouths to feed, I can't afford it." "Where must I go?" I said: "you know there are no jobs." "Sorry," he said, "nothing personal, I just can't afford it any more." So he let me go, me with a family, and he kept on a man who had been there only a short time, a young man, single. Just one mouth to feed – he could afford that. I said to him, "I've got no work now, what can *I* afford?" Anyway, we packed everything and left; and on the road, I'm not lying, *on the road* the police picked us up, he had phoned them, they picked us up and that same night we were here in Jakkalsdrif behind the wire. "No fixed abode?" I said to them, "Last night I had a fixed abode, how do you know tonight I won't have a fixed abode?" They said, "Where would you rather sleep, out in the veld under a bush like an animal or in a camp with a proper bed and running water?" I said, "Do I get a choice?" They said, "You get a choice and you choose Jakkalsdrif. Because we are not going to have people wandering around being a nuisance." But I'll tell you the real reason, I'll tell you why they were so quick to pick us up. They want to stop people from disappearing into the mountains and then coming back one night to cut their fences and drive their stock away. Do you know how many men there are in this camp – young men?' He leaned towards K and dropped his voice. 'Thirty. You are thirty-one. And how many women and children and old people? Look around, count for yourself. So I ask you, where are the men who aren't here with their families?'

'I was in the mountains,' said K. 'I didn't see anyone.'

'But you ask any of these women where their menfolk are, they will say, "He has got a job, he sends me money every month," or, "He ran away, he left me." So who knows?'

There was a long silence. A tiny light flashed across the heavens. K pointed. 'A shooting star,' he said.

The next morning K went out to work. The Railways Administration had first call on the men from Jakkalsdrif, followed by the Prince Albert Divisional Council, followed by the local farmers. The truck came to fetch them at six-thirty, and by seven-thirty they were at work north of Leeu-Gamka, clearing under-growth from the river-bed upstream and downstream from a railway bridge, digging holes and mixing cement for a security fence. The work was hard; by mid-morning K was flagging. The time in the mountains has turned me into an old man, he thought.

Robert paused beside him. 'Before you break your back, my friend,' he said, 'remember what they pay you. You get the standard wage, one rand a day. I get one rand fifty because I have dependants. So don't kill yourself. Go and take a pee. You've been in hospital, you're not well.'

Later, when the midday break came, he offered K one of his sandwiches and stretched out beside him in the shade of a tree. 'Out of your five–six rand a week,' he told him, 'you have to provide your own food. The camp is just a place to sleep. The ACVV ladies – you saw them yesterday – they visit three times a week, but that is charity work for the children only. My wife has a job in the town three half-days a week as a domestic. She takes the baby with her and leaves the other children with my sister. So we bring in maybe twelve rand a week. From that we have to feed nine people, three grownups, six children. Other people have it harder. When there isn't work, too bad, we sit behind the wire and tighten our belts.

'Now the money you earn, there is only one place to spend it, that is Prince Albert. And when you go into a shop in Prince Albert, all of a sudden prices go up. Why? Because you are from the camp. They don't want a camp so near their town. They never wanted it. They ran a big campaign against the camp at the beginning. We breed disease, they said. No hygiene, no morals. A nest of vice, men and women all together. The way they talked, there should be a fence down the middle of the camp, men on one side, women on the other, dogs to patrol it at night. What they would really like – this is my opinion – is for the camp to be miles away in the middle of the Koup out of sight. Then we could come on tiptoe in the middle of the night like fairies and do their work, dig their gardens, wash their pots, and be gone in the morning leaving everything nice and clean.

'So I hear you ask who is in favour of the camp? I'll tell you. First, the Railways. The Railways would like to have a Jakkalsdrif every ten miles along the line. Second, the farmers. Because from a gang from Jakkalsdrif a farmer gets a day's work blood cheap, and at the end of the day the truck fetches them and they are gone and he doesn't have to worry about them or their families, they can starve, they can be cold, he knows nothing, it's none of his business.'

A short distance away, out of earshot, sat the gang foreman on a little folding stool. K watched him pour coffee out of his vacuum flask. His long flat fingers could not all find a place on the ear of the mug. With two fingers in the air he raised it and drank. Over the rim his eyes met K's. What does he see? thought K.

112

What am I to him? The foreman set down the mug, raised his whistle to his lips, and, still sitting, blew a long blast.

Later that afternoon, while he was chopping at the roots of a thornbush, the same foreman came and stood behind him. Glancing under his arm, he saw the two black shoes and the rattan stick tapping idly in the dust, and felt himself trembling with the old nervousness. He went on chopping, but there was no strength in his arms. Only when the foreman moved off could he begin to collect himself.

In the evening he was too tired to eat. He took his mattress outside and lay watching the stars appear one by one out of the violet sky. Then someone on the way to the latrines stumbled over him. There was a commotion, from which he retreated. Moving the mattress back to the hut, he lay on his bunk in the dark under the roofplates.

On Saturday they were paid and the commissary lorry came. On Sunday a pastor visited the camp to conduct a prayer service, after which the gates were thrown open till curfew time. K went to the service. Standing among the women and children, he joined in the singing. Then the pastor bent his head and prayed. 'Let peace enter our hearts again, O Lord, and grant it to us to return to our homes cherishing bitterness against no man, resolved to live together in fellowship in Thy name, obeying Thy commandments.' Afterwards he spoke to some of the old people, then climbed into the blue van that had waited for him at the gate and was driven off.

Now they were free to go to Prince Albert, or visit friends, or simply take a walk in the veld. K saw a family of eight, the man and wife in their best sober black, the girls in pink and white dresses with white hats, the boys in grey suits and ties with their feet stuffed into shiny black shoes, set off down the long road to the town. Others followed: a band of girls, laughing, arm in arm; the man with the guitar together with his sister and his girlfriend. 'Why don't we go?' suggested K to Robert. 'Let the youngsters go if they want to,' replied Robert. 'What's so special about Prince Albert on a Sunday? I've seen it before, it's nothing to me. Go with them if you want to. Buy yourself a cool drink and sit outside the café and scratch your fleabites. There is nothing else to do. I say, if we are going to be in jail, let's be in jail, let's not pretend.'

Nevertheless K left the camp. He strolled down the Jakkalsrivier till the wire and the huts and the pump were out of sight. Then he lay down in the warm grey sand with his beret over his face and fell asleep. He awoke sweating. He lifted the beret and squinted into the sun. Striking all the colours of the rainbow from his eyelashes, it filled the sky. I am like an ant that does not know where its hole is, he thought. He dug his hands into the sand and let it pour through his fingers over and over again.

114

The moustache they had shaved off at the hospital was beginning to cover his lip again. Still, he found it hard to relax with Robert and his family around the fire where the eyes of the children were continually upon him. There was one little boy in particular who pursued him wherever he sat, clutching at his face. The child's mother, embarrassed, would fetch him away, where-upon he would wriggle and whine to be let loose till K did not know what to do or where to look. He suspected that the older girls laughed at him behind his back. He had never known how to behave with women. The Vrouevereniging ladies, perhaps because he was so thin, perhaps because they had decided he was simple, regularly allowed him to clean the soup-bucket: three times a week this made up his meal. He gave half his wages to Robert and carried the other half about in his pocket. There was nothing he wanted to buy; he never went to town. Robert still looked after him in various ways but spared him his speeches about the camp. 'I have never seen anyone as asleep as you,' Robert said. 'Yes,' replied K, struck that Robert too had seen it.

The work around the bridge was finished. For two days the men were laid off, then the Council truck came to fetch them to do road grading. K lined up at the gate with the other men, but at the last moment declined to board the truck. 'I'm sick, I can't work,' he told the guard. 'Suit yourself, but you won't be paid,' said the guard.

So K brought his mattress out and lay next to the

hut in the shade with an arm over his face while the camp lived its life around him. He lay so still that the smaller children, having first kept their distance, next tried to rouse him, and, when he would not be roused, incorporated his body into their game. They clambered over him and fell upon him as if he were part of the earth. Still hiding his face, he rolled over and found that he could doze even with little bodies riding on his back. He found unexpected pleasure in these games. It felt to him that he was drawing health from the children's touch; he was sorry when men from the Council arrived to spread lime in the latrine pits and they rushed off to watch.

Through the fence K spoke to the guard: 'Can I go out?'

'I thought you were sick. This morning you told me you were sick.'

'I don't want to work. Why do I have to work? This isn't a jail.'

'You don't want to work but you want other people to feed you.'

'I don't need to eat all the time. When I need to eat, I'll work.'

The guard sat in his deckchair on the porch of the tiny guardhouse with his rifle leaning at his side against the wall. He smiled into the distance.

'So can you open the gate?' said K.

'The only way to leave is with the work party,' said the guard.

'And if I climb the fence? What will you do if I climb the fence?'

'You climb the fence and I'll shoot you, I swear to God I won't think twice, so don't try.'

K caressed the wire as if weighing the risk.

'Let me tell you something, my friend,' said the guard, 'for your own good, because you're new here. If I let you out now, in three days you'll be back pleading to be let in. I know. In three days. You'll be standing at the gate here with tears in your eyes pleading with me to let you back. Why do you want to run away? You've got a home here, you've got food, you've got a bed. You've got a job. People are having a hard time out there in the world, you've seen it, I don't need to tell you. For what do you want to join them?'

'I don't want to be in a camp, that's all,' said K. 'Let me climb the fence and go. Turn your back. Nobody will notice I'm gone. You don't even know how many people you've got here.'

'You climb the fence and I'll shoot you dead, mister. No hard feelings. I'm just telling you.'

The next morning K lay in bed while the other men went to work. Later he walked over to the gate again. The same guard was on duty. He and K talked about football. 'I've got diabetes,' said the guard. 'That's the reason they never sent me north. Three years now I've been on paperwork, stores, guard duties. You think it's bad in the camp, you try sitting out here twelve hours a day with nothing to do but look at the thornbushes.

Still, I'll tell you one thing, my friend, and this is the truth: the day I get orders to go north I walk out. They'll never see me again. It's not my war. Let them fight it, it's their war.'

He wanted to know about K's mouth ('Just curious,' he said), and K told him. He nodded. 'I thought so. But then I thought maybe someone cut you.'

In the guardhouse he had a small paraffin-fuelled refrigerator. He brought out a lunch of cold chicken and bread and shared it with K, passing the food through the mesh. 'We live pretty well, I suppose,' he said, 'considering there's a war on.' He gave a sly smile.

He spoke about the women in the camp, about the visits he and his colleague received at night. 'They're starved for sex,' he said. Then he yawned and returned to his deckchair.

The next morning K was shaken awake by Robert. 'Get dressed, you've got to work,' Robert said. K pushed his arm away. 'Come on,' said Robert, 'they want everyone today, no excuses, no arguments, you've got to come.' Ten minutes later K was standing out-side the gate in the chilly early-morning wind, being counted, waiting for the truck. They were driven through the streets of Prince Albert and then out in the direction of Klaarstroom; they took a farm road past a sprawling shaded homestead and halted beside a lush field of lucerne where two police reservists with armbands and rifles stood waiting. As they climbed down they were handed sickles by a farm-worker who did not speak or meet their eyes. A tall man in freshly-pressed khaki slacks appeared. He held up a sickle. 'You all know how to use a sickle,' he called out. 'You've got two morgen to cut. So get down to it!'

Lined up three paces apart, the men began to work their way across the field, bending, gathering, cutting, taking half a step forward, in a rhythm that soon had K sweating and dizzy. 'Cut clean, cut clean!' bellowed a voice right behind him. K turned and faced the farmer in khaki; he could smell the sweet deodorant he used. 'Where were you brought up, monkey?' shouted the farmer. 'Cut low, cut clean!' He took the sickle from K's hand, pushed him aside, gathered the next tuft of lucerne, and cut it clean and low. 'See?' he shouted. K nodded. 'Then do it, man, do it!' he shouted. K bent and sawed the next tuft off close to the earth. 'Where do they pick up rubbish like that?' he heard the farmer call to one of the reservists. 'He's half-dead! They'll be digging up corpses for us next!'

'I can't go on!' K gasped to Robert at the first break. 'My back is breaking, every time I stand straight the world spins.'

'Just go slow,' said Robert. 'They can't make you do what you can't do.'

K looked at the ragged swathe he had cut.

'You want to know who this is?' murmured Robert. 'This guy is the brother-in-law of the captain of police, Oosthuizen. His machine breaks down, so what happens? He picks up the phone, calls the police station,

119

and first thing in the morning he has thirty pairs of hands to cut his lucerne for him. That's how it works here, the system.'

They finished cutting the field in near-darkness, leaving the baling for the next day. K was reeling with exhaustion. Sitting in the truck he closed his eyes and felt as if he were hurtling through endless empty space. Back in the hut he fell into a dead sleep. Then in the middle of the night he was woken by the crying of a baby. There were discontented murmurs from around him; everyone seemed to be awake. For what seemed hours they lay and listened as the baby somewhere in the tents went through cycles of whimpering, wailing, and shrieks that left it gasping for breath. Aching to sleep, K felt anger mount inside himself. He lay with his fists clenched against his breast wishing the child annihilated.

In the back of the truck, with the slipstream roaring on them, K mentioned the crying in the night. 'You want to know how they shut that child up in the end?' said Robert. 'Brandy. Brandy and aspirin. That's the only medicine. No doctor in the camp, no nurse.' He paused. 'Let me tell you what happened when they opened the camp, when they opened the new home they had built for all the homeless people, the squatters from Boontjieskraal and the Onderdorp, the beggars off the streets, the unemployed, the vagrants who sleep on the mountain, the people chased off the farms. Not a month after they opened the gates everyone was sick.

Dysentery, then measles, then 'flu, one on top of the other. From being shut up like animals in a cage. The district nurse came in, and you know what she did? Ask anyone who was here, they will tell you. She stood in the middle of the camp where everyone could see, and she cried. She looked at children with the bones sticking out of their bodies and she didn't know what to do, she just stood and cried. A big strong woman. A district nurse.

'Anyway,' said Robert, 'they got a big fright. After that they started dropping pellets in the water and digging latrines and spraying for flies and bringing buckets of soup. But do you think they do it because they love us? Not a hope. They prefer it that we live because we look too terrible when we get sick and die. If we just grew thin and turned into paper and then into ash and floated away, they wouldn't give a stuff for us. They just don't want to get upset. They want to go to sleep feeling good.'

'I don't know,' said K. 'I don't know.'

'You don't look deep enough,' said Robert. 'Take a good look in their hearts, then you'll see.'

K shrugged.

'You're a baby,' said Robert. 'You've been asleep all your life. It's time to wake up. Why do you think they give you charity, you and the children? Because they think you are harmless, your eyes aren't opened, you don't see the truth around you.'

Two days later the baby that had cried in the night

was dead. Because it was an iron rule from above that under no circumstances was a graveyard to be established within or in close proximity to any camp of any type, the child was buried in the back block of the town cemetery. The mother, a girl of eighteen, returned from the burial service and refused to eat. She did not weep, merely sat beside her tent staring out in the direction of Prince Albert. The friends who came to console her she did not hear; when they touched her she pushed their hands away. Michael K spent hours standing against the fence where she could not see him, watching her. Is this my education? he wondered. Am I at last learning about life here in a camp? It seemed to him that scene after scene of life was playing itself out before him and that the scenes all cohered. He had a presentiment of a single meaning upon which they were converging or threatening to converge, though he did not know yet what that might be.

For a night and a day the girl kept her vigil, then retired into the tent. She still would not cry, word went about, nor would she eat. K's first thought each morning was: Will I see her today? She was short and fat; no one knew for sure who the father of the child had been, though it was rumoured that he was away in the mountains. K wondered whether he was at last in love. Then after three days the girl re-emerged and resumed her life. Seeing her in the midst of other people, K could detect no sign that she was different from them. He never spoke to her.

One night in December, woken by excited shouts, the people of the camp stumbled from their beds to behold on the horizon in the direction of Prince Albert a vast and beautiful orange blossom unfolding itself against the murk of the sky. There were gasps and whistles of amazement. 'What's the bet it's the police station!' someone shouted. For an hour they stood and watched while the fire poured out like a fountain consuming itself and being consumed. There were moments when they were sure they could hear shouts and cries and the roar of the flames across the miles of empty veld. Then by degrees the flower grew redder and duller, the fountain lost its strength, till at last, with some of the children asleep in arms and others rubbing their eyes, and with nothing left to see but a smoky glow in the distance, it was time to go back to bed.

The police struck at dawn. In a squad of twenty, regular police and schoolboy reservists, with dogs and guns, with an officer standing on the roof of a van shouting commands through a megaphone, they moved down the rows pulling out the pegs, collapsing the tents, beating at the shapes struggling in the folds. They burst into the huts and beat the sleepers in their beds. A youth who dodged them and ran away was chased into a corner behind the latrines and kicked into insensibility; a small boy was knocked over by a dog and rescued screaming with fright, his scalp lacerated and bleeding. Half-dressed, some wailing, some praying, some stunned with fear, men, women and children were herded on to the open terrain before the huts and ordered to sit down. From there, under the eye of dogs and men with cocked guns, they watched while the rest of the squad moved like a swarm of locusts through the lines of tents, turning them inside out, hurling everything they had contained into the open, emptying suitcases and boxes, till the site looked like a trash-heap, with clothes, bedding, food, cooking utensils, crockery, toiletries scattered everywhere; after a while they moved on to the huts and turned them to chaos too.

Through all this K sat with his beret pulled over his ears against the early-morning wind. The woman beside him had a crying baby with a bare bottom and two little girls who clung tightly to her, one to each arm. 'Come and sit here with me,' whispered K to the smaller of the girls. Without taking her eyes from the destruction being visited on them, she stepped over his legs and stood within the protective circle of his arms sucking her thumb. Her sister joined her. The two stood pressed together; K closed his eyes; the baby continued to kick and whine.

They were made to line up at the gate and file out one by one. Everything they had with them they were forced to leave behind, even the blankets some of them wore wrapped over their nightclothes. A dog-handler plucked a little radio out of the hands of a woman in front of K: he dropped it to the earth and stamped on it. 'No radios,' he explained.

Outside the gate the men were herded left, the women and children right. The gates were locked and the camp stood empty. Then the captain, the big blond man who had shouted orders, brought the two Free Corps guards out to face the men where they stood in a row against the fence. The guards were unarmed and dishevelled: K wondered what had gone on in the guardhouse. 'Now,' said the captain, 'tell us who is missing.'

There were three missing, three men who slept in one of the other huts, with whom K had never exchanged a word.

The captain was shouting at the guards, who had come to attention before him. At first K thought he shouted because he was used to the megaphone; but soon the rage behind the shouting became too clear to be missed. 'What are we keeping here in our back yard!' he shouted. 'A nest of criminals! Criminals and saboteurs and idlers! And you! The two of you! You eat and sleep and get fat and from one day to the next you don't know where the people are you are supposed to be guarding! What do you think you are doing here – running a holiday camp? It's a work camp, man! It's a camp to teach lazy people to work! *Work*! And if they don't work we close the camp! We close it down and chase all these vagrants away! Get out and don't come back! You've had your chance!' He turned to the group of men. 'Yes, you, you ungrateful bastards, you, I'm talking about you!' he shouted. 'You appreciate nothing!

Who builds houses for you when you have nowhere to live? Who gives you tents and blankets when you are shivering with cold? Who nurses you, who takes care of you, who comes here day after day with food? And how do you repay us? Well, from now on you can starve!'

He drew a deep breath. Over his shoulder the sun made its appearance like a ball of fire. 'Do you hear me?' he shouted. 'I want everyone to hear me! You ask for war, you get war! I'm putting my own men on guard here – fuck the Army! – I'm putting my own men on guard, and I'm locking the gates, and if my men see any of you, man, woman or child, outside the wire, they have orders to shoot, no questions asked! No one leaves the camp except on labour calls. No visits, no outings, no picnics. Roll-calls morning and evening, with everyone present to answer. We've been kind to you long enough.

'And I'm locking up these monkeys with you!' He raised an arm and pointed dramatically at the two guards, still standing to attention. 'I'm putting them in to teach them who runs things here! You! You think I haven't kept an eye on the two of you? You think I don't know about the nice life you lead? You think I don't know about all the pussy-fucking that goes on when you should be on guard?' The thought seemed to inflame him further, for suddenly he wheeled, stormed into the guardhouse, and a moment later reappeared in the doorway bearing a small white-enamelled refrigerator clutched to his belly. His face glowed with the strain; his cap, brushing against the lintel, fell off. He stepped to the edge of the porch, raised the refrigerator as high as he could, and flung it down. It hit the ground with a crash; paraffin began to seep from the motor. 'You see?' he panted. He tipped the refrigerator on to its side. The door fell open and with a clatter disgorged a one-litre bottle of ginger beer, a tub of margarine, a loop of sausage, loose peaches and onions, a plastic water-flask, and five bottles of beer. 'You see!' he panted again, glaring.

All morning they sat waiting in the sun while two young policemen and a helper in a blue T-shirt with the legend SAN JOSE STATE on front and back searched with officious slowness through the debris. In the huts they found caches of wine, which they emptied into the earth. They threw all the weapons they found in a pile: a *kierie*, an iron bar, a length of piping, a pair of sheep-shears, several folding knives. Then at midday the search was declared over. The police shepherded the inmates back in, locked the gates, and in a few minutes were gone, leaving behind two of their number, who sat all afternoon under the awning watching the people of Jakkalsdrif scratch in the mess for their belongings.

From one of the new guards they later learned what had brought down Oosthuizen's wrath upon them. In the middle of the night a loud explosion had come from the welding shop on the High Street, followed by an uncontrollable fire that had spread to the building next door and thence to the town's cultural history museum. The museum, with its thatched roof and yellowwood ceilings and floors, had been gutted in an hour, though some of the antique farming equipment on display in the courtyard had been rescued. Searching by torchlight in the smoking rubble of the welding shop, the police had found evidence of forced entry; and when one of their own drivers recollected that at dusk the previous evening he had stopped three strange men on two bicycles near the Jakkalsdrif turnoff (he had warned them that they were on the point of infringing the curfew; they had pleaded that they were hurrying back as fast as they could to the Onderdorp, where they lived; he had thought no more of it), it seemed clear that camp people were implicated in an act of arson against the town.

It cost K little trouble to gather his few belongings together; but other men from the huts who had had trunks or suitcases wandered moodily through the debris searching for what was theirs. A fight broke out over no more than a plastic comb. K retreated.

Though it was a Wednesday, the ladies with the soup did not arrive. A deputation of women went to the gate to ask permission to use the stove in the camp kitchen; but the guards claimed not to have the key. Someone, perhaps a child, threw a rock through the kitchen window.

Nor did the truck come the next day to fetch the work gang. In mid-morning the police guards were replaced by two new men. 'They are going to starve us,' said Robert, loudly enough for others to hear. 'That fire was the excuse they were looking for. Now they are going to do what they always wanted – lock us up and wait for us to die.'

Standing against the wire looking out over the veld, K brooded on Robert's words. He no longer found it so strange to think of the camp as a place where people were deposited to be forgotten. It no longer seemed an accident that the camp lay out of sight of the town on a road that led nowhere else. But he could not yet believe that the two young men on the guardhouse porch would sit and watch with equanimity, yawning, smoking, going indoors every now and again for a nap, while people were dying before their eyes. When people died they left bodies behind. Even people who died of starvation left bodies behind. Dead bodies could be as offensive as living bodies, if it was true that a living body could be offensive. If these people really wanted to be rid of us, he thought (curiously he watched the thought begin to unfold itself in his head, like a plant growing), if they really wanted to forget us forever, they would have to give us picks and spades and command us to dig; then, when we had exhausted ourselves digging, and had dug a great hole in the middle of the camp, they would have to order us to climb in and lay ourselves down; and when we were lying there, all of us, they would have to break down the huts and tents and tear down the fence and throw

129

the huts and the fence and the tents as well as every last thing we had owned upon us, and cover us with earth, and flatten the earth. *Then*, perhaps, they might begin to forget about us. But who could dig a hole as big as that? Not thirty men, even with women and children and old people to help, not in our present state, with nothing but picks and spades, here in the stone-hard veld.

It seemed more like Robert than like him, as he knew himself, to think like that. Would he have to say that the thought was Robert's and had merely found a home in him, or could he say that though the seed had come from Robert, the thought, having grown up inside him, was now his own? He did not know.

Then on Monday morning the Divisional Council truck arrived as usual to take them to work. Before they climbed aboard, the guards checked their names on a list; otherwise nothing seemed to have changed. They were dropped off at various farms in the district according to a roster the driver kept. With two comrades K found himself at the job of repairing fences. The work was slow, for they were using not new wire but lengths of old wire which when joined together coiled in inconsistent directions. K liked the leisureliness of the work and its repetitiveness. Coming in the mornings and going in the evenings, they spent a week on the same farm, on some days doing no more than a few hundred metres of fencing. Once the farmer took K aside, gave him a cigarette, and commended him.

'You have a feel for wire,' he said. 'You should go into fencing. There will always be a need for good fencers in this country, no matter what. If you carry stock, you need fences: it's as simple as that.' He too loved wire, he went on. It pained him to have to use ragtag materials, but what else was there? At the end of the week he paid the three men the standard rate for their labour, but gave them in addition packets of fruit and green mealies, and used clothes. For K he had an old sweater, for the other men a carton of castoffs for their wives and children. On the way back, on the truck, one of K's companions, picking around in the box, came up with a large pair of cotton panties. He held it at a distance between his fingertips, wrinkled his nose, and let it go. The slipstream caught it and whirled it away. Then he pitched the whole box over the side.

That night there was liquor in the camp and a fight broke out. When K looked again, one of the Free Corps men, the one who said he had diabetes, was standing in the firelight gripping his thigh and calling for help. His hands glistened with blood, his trouser-leg was wet. 'What is going to happen to me?' he cried, over and over. One could even see the blood oozing between his fingers, thick as oil. People came running from all quarters to stare.

K rushed to the gate, where the two police guards stood peering in the direction of the commotion. 'That man has been stabbed,' he stammered – 'he is bleeding, you must take him to the hospital.'

131

The guards exchanged glances. 'Bring him over,' said one, 'then we'll see.'

K ran back. The wounded man was sitting with his trousers around his ankles, talking without cease, gripping his thigh from which blood continued to gush. 'We must take him to the gate!' K shouted. It was the first time he had raised his voice in the camp, and people looked at him curiously. 'Take him to the gate, then they will take him to hospital!' The man on the ground nodded vigorously. 'Take me to hospital, look how I'm bleeding!' he cried.

His comrade, the other Free Corps man, pushed his way to his side, bringing a towel which he tried to tie around the wound. Someone nudged K: it was one of the men from the other huts. 'Leave them, let them look after each other,' he said. The crowd began to break up. Soon there were only children left, and K, watching the younger man bind the older man's thigh in the flickering light.

K never discovered who had stabbed the guard or whether he recovered, for this was his last night in the camp. While everyone else was going to bed, K quietly bundled his belongings in the black coat, slipped out, and settled down behind the cistern to wait till the last embers had died, till there was nothing to hear but the wind across the veld. He waited an hour longer, shivering from sitting still so long. Then he took off his shoes, hung them about his neck, tiptoed to the fence behind the latrines, tossed the bundle over, and climbed.

There was a moment when, straddling the fence, his trousers hooked on a barb, he was an easy shot against the silver-blue sky; then he unpicked himself and was away, tiptoeing across ground surprisingly like the ground inside the fence.

He walked all night, feeling no fatigue, trembling sometimes with the thrill of being free. When it began to grow light he left the road and moved across open country. He saw no human being, though more than once he was startled by buck leaping from cover and racing away into the hills. The dry white grass waved in the wind, the sky was blue, his body was overflowing with vigour. Walking in great loops, he skirted first one farmhouse, then another. The landscape was so empty that it was not hard to believe at times that his was the first foot ever to tread a particular inch of earth or disturb a particular pebble. But every mile or two there was a fence to remind him that he was a trespasser as well as a runaway. Ducking through the fences, he could feel a craftsman's pleasure in wire spanned so taut that it hummed when it was plucked. Nonetheless, he could not imagine himself spending his life driving stakes into the ground, erecting fences, dividing up the land. He thought of himself not as something heavy that left tracks behind it, but if anything as a speck upon the surface of an earth too deeply asleep to notice the scratch of ant-feet, the rasp of butterfly teeth, the tumbling of dust.

He climbed the last rise, his heart beating faster. As

he reached the crest the house came into sight below, first the roof and the broken gable, then the white-washed walls, everything as it had been before. Surely, he thought, surely now I have outlasted the last of the Visagies; surely every day I spent living on air in the mountains or being devoured by time in the camp was as long a day for that boy to endure, eating or starving, sleeping or waking in his hiding-hole.

The back door was unlocked. As K pushed open the top flap something leapt out nearly into his face and raced away around a corner: a cat, a huge cat with mottled black and ginger fur. He had never seen a cat on the farm before.

The house smelled of heat and dust, but also of old fat and uncured leather. The smell grew worse as he approached the kitchen. At the kitchen door he hesitated. There is still time, he thought, time to brush away my footprints and tiptoe out. Because whatever I have returned for, it is not to live as the Visagies lived, sleep where they slept, sit on their stoep looking out over their land. If this house were to be abandoned as a home for the ghosts of all the generations of the Visagies, it would not matter to me. It is not for the house that I have come.

The kitchen, into which a beam of sunlight shone from the hole in the roof, was empty; the smell came from the pantry, where, peering into shadow, K made out a side of sheep or goat hanging from a hook. Though there was little left of the carcase but bones held together by a dry grey parchment, green-bellied flies still buzzed about it.

He left the kitchen and went through the rest of the house seeking in the gloom for signs of the Visagie boy or clues to his hiding-place. He found nothing. The floors were covered in a fresh film of dust. The attic door was padlocked on the outside. Furniture stood where it had always stood, there were no telltale marks. He stood in the middle of the dining-room and held his breath, listening for the faintest stirring from above or below; but the very heart of the grandson, if there were a grandson and he were alive, beat in time with his own.

He emerged into sunlight and took the track across the veld to the dam and the field where once he had scattered his mother's ashes. Every stone, every bush along the way he recognized. He felt at home at the dam as he had never felt in the house. He lay down and rested with the black coat rolled under his head, watching the sky wheel above. I want to live here, he thought: I want to live here forever, where my mother and my grandmother lived. It is as simple as that. What a pity that to live in times like these a man must be ready to live like a beast. A man who wants to live cannot live in a house with lights in the windows. He must live in a hole and hide by day. A man must live so that he leaves no trace of his living. That is what it has come to.

The dam itself was dry, the once lush grass around it

brittle, white, dead. There was no trace of the pumpkins and mealies he had sown. Veld-grasses had taken over the patch he had dug and were growing briskly.

He released the brake of the pump. The wheel creaked and swung and shuddered and began to turn. The piston plunged and came up. Water gushed, in rust-brown gouts at first, then clear. All was as it had been before, as he had remembered it in the mountains. He held his hand in the flow and felt the force beat his fingers back; he climbed into the dam and stood under the stream, turning his face up like a flower, drinking and being bathed; he could not get enough of the water.

He slept in the open, and awoke from a dream in which the Visagie boy, crouched in a ball in the dark beneath the floorboards, with spiders walking over him and the great weight of the wardrobe pressing down above his head, mouthed words, pleas or cries or orders, he did not know, that he could not hear or understand. He sat up feeling stiff and exhausted. Let him not steal my first day from me! he groaned to himself. I did not come back to be a nursemaid! He has looked after himself all these months, let him look after himself a while longer! Wrapped in the black coat he clenched his jaw and waited for dawn, aching after the pleasures of digging and planting he had promised himself, impatient to be through with the business of making a dwelling.

All morning he tramped the veld, searching along

the shallow gullies that led from the hillsides and along the faults where the rock broke in sheer lines. Three hundred yards from the dam two low hills, like plump breasts, curved towards each other. Where they met, their sides formed a sloping crevice as deep as a man's waist three or four yards long. The bed of the crevice was of a fine dark blue gravel; the same gravel could be chipped from the sides. This was the site K settled on. From the shed beside the farmhouse he fetched his tools, a spade and chisel. From the roof of a sheep-pen he removed a five-foot sheet of corrugated iron. Laboriously he freed three fenceposts from the tangle of broken fencing below the dead orchard. All this he carried back to the dam, and set to work.

His first step was to hollow out the sides of the crevice till it was wider at the bottom than the top, and to flatten the gravel bed. The narrower end he blocked with a heap of stones. Then he laid the three fenceposts across the crevice, and upon them the iron sheet, with slabs of stone to hold it down. He now had a cave or burrow five feet deep. When he backed away toward the dam to inspect it, however, his eye at once picked out the dark hole of the entrance. So he spent the rest of the afternoon looking for ways to disguise it. When dusk fell he realized with surprise that he had spent a second day without eating.

The next morning he dragged in bagfuls of river sand to spread over the floor. He split flat stones from the hillside strata and built up the front wall, leaving

137

himself only an irregular slit through which to wriggle. He made a paste of mud and dry grass which he stuffed into the cracks between roof and walls. Over the roof he spread gravel. All day he did not eat or feel any need to eat; but he noticed that he was working more slowly, and that there were spells when he simply stood or knelt before his handiwork, his mind elsewhere.

As he was prodding mud into the cracks and smoothing it flat, it occurred to him that at the next hard rain all his careful mortarwork would be washed out; indeed, rainwater would come pouring down the gully through his house. I should have laid a bed of stones beneath the sand, he thought; and I should have allowed myself an eave. But then he thought: I am not building a house out here by the dam to pass on to other generations. What I make ought to be careless, makeshift, a shelter to be abandoned without a tugging at the heartstrings. So that if ever they find this place or its ruins, and shake their heads and say to each other: What shiftless creatures, how little pride they took in their work! it will not matter.

In the shed there remained a last handful of pumpkin and melon seed. On the fourth day of his return K set about planting these, clearing a spot of ground for each individual seed in the sea of veld-grass that waved over the cemetery of the earlier crop. He no longer dared to irrigate the entire acre, for the greenness of new grass would betray him. So he watered the seeds one by one, carrying water from the dam in an old paint-tin. After this labour there was nothing to do but wait for the seed to shoot, if it would. In his burrow he lay thinking of these poor second children of his beginning their struggle upward through the dark earth toward the sun. His one misgiving was that by planting them in the latter days of summer he had not provided well.

As he tended the seeds and watched and waited for the earth to bear food, his own need for food grew slighter and slighter. Hunger was a sensation he did not feel and barely remembered. If he ate, eating what he could find, it was because he had not yet shaken off the belief that bodies that do not eat die. What food he ate meant nothing to him. It had no taste, or tasted like dust.

When food comes out of this earth, he told himself, I will recover my appetite, for it will have savour.

After the hardships of the mountains and the camp there was nothing but bone and muscle on his body. His clothes, tattered already, hung on him without shape. Yet as he moved about his field he felt a deep joy in his physical being. His step was so light that he barely touched the earth. It seemed possible to fly; it seemed possible to be both body and spirit.

He returned to eating insects. Since time was poured out upon him in such an unending stream, there were whole mornings he could spend lying on his belly over an ant-nest picking out the larvae one by one with a grass-stalk and putting them in his mouth. Or he would peel the bark from dead trees looking for

139

beetle-grubs; or knock grasshoppers out of the air with his jacket, tear off their heads and legs and wings, and pound their bodies to a pulp which he dried in the sun.

He also ate roots. He had no fear of being poisoned, for he seemed to know the difference between a benign bitterness and a malign one, as though he had once been an animal and the knowledge of good and bad plants had not died in his soul.

His retreat was little more than a mile from the track that passed through the farm and then looped back to rejoin the secondary road leading into the farther reaches of the Moordenaarsvallei. Little frequented though the track was, there was still reason to be wary. Several times, hearing the faroff drone of a motor, K had to duck and hide. Once, walking idly in the river-bed, he chanced to look up and saw a donkey-cart passing within hailing distance, driven by an old man with someone else, a woman or child, beside him. Had they seen him? Afraid to stir and draw attention to himself, he stood frozen in his tracks in full view of whoever cared to see, watching the gentle progress of the cart down the track and behind the next hill.

As irksome as this incessant watchfulness was the restraint on the use of water. The vanes of the pump must never be seen to be moving, the dam must always seem to be empty; therefore it was only by moonlight, or else anxiously at dusk, that he dared release the brake, pump a few inches, and carry water to his plants.

Once or twice he came across hoofprints of buck in the damp soil, but gave no thought to them. Then one night he was woken by snorts and a clatter of hooves. He crawled out of his house, smelling them before he saw them: the goats he had thought fled forever when the dam dried up. Stumbling after them, shouting abuse, throwing stones, fuddled with sleep but driven by a desire to save his garden, he fell and drove a thorn deep into his palm. All night he patrolled the acre. The goats emerged in the early morning light dotting the hillsides in twos and threes, waiting for him to go; and all day he had to remain on guard, making sorties after them with stones.

It was these wild goats, which not only threatened his crop but by their presence rendered the acre conspicuous, that decided him: henceforth he would rest by day and stay up at night to protect his land and till it. At first he could work only on moonlit nights: in the dense blackness when there was no moon he would stand rooted, stretching out his hands, fearful of the looming shapes he imagined about him. But as time passed he began to acquire the confidence of a blind man: with a switch held before him he would make his way along the track he had worn between his house and the field, release the brake on the pump, open the cock, fill his can, and carry water to one vine after another, folding the grass aside to find them. Gradually he lost all fear of the night. Indeed, waking sometimes in the daytime and peering outdoors, he would wince at the sharpness of the light and withdraw to his bed with a strange green glow behind his eyelids.

It had grown to be late summer, and over a month since he had left the camp at Jakkalsdrif. He had not searched for the Visagie boy, nor did it seem he would ever do so. He tried not to think of him, but sometimes found himself wondering whether the boy might not have dug a hole for himself in the veld, and somewhere else on the farm be living a life parallel to his own, eating lizards, drinking dew, waiting for the army to forget him. It seemed unlikely.

He avoided the farmhouse as a place of the dead, except when he had to visit it to hunt for necessities. He needed means of making fire, and in the suitcase of broken toys had the good fortune to find a red plastic telescope, one of whose lenses would focus the rays of the sun sharply enough to coax smoke out of a handful of dry grass. From a buckskin he found in the shed he cut strips and used them in making a catapult to replace the one he had lost.

There was much else he could have taken to make life easier for himself: a grid, a cooking-pot, a folding chair, slabs of foam rubber, more of the feed-sacks. He scratched among the odds and ends in the shed and there was nothing for which he could not imagine a use. But he was wary of conveying the Visagies' rubbish to his home in the earth and setting himself on a trail that might lead to the re-enactment of their mis-fortunes. The worst mistake, he told himself, would be to try to found a new house, a rival line, on his small beginnings out at the dam. Even his tools should be of wood and leather and gut, materials the insects would eat when one day he no longer needed them.

He stood leaning against the frame of the pump, feeling the tremor that passed through it each time the piston reached the bottom of its stroke, hearing the great wheel above his head cut through the dark on its greased bearings. How fortunate that I have no children, he thought: how fortunate that I have no desire to father. I would not know what to do with a child out here in the heart of the country, who would need milk and clothes and friends and schooling. I would fail in my duties, I would be the worst of fathers. Whereas it is not hard to live a life that consists merely of passing time. I am one of the fortunate ones who escape being called. He thought of the camp at Jakkalsdrif, of parents bringing up children behind the wire, their own children and the children of cousins and second cousins, on earth stamped so tight by the passage of their footsteps day after day, baked so hard by the sun, that nothing would ever grow there again. My mother was the one whose ashes I brought back, he thought, and my father was Huis Norenius. My father was the list of rules on the door of the dormitory, the twenty-one rules of which the first was 'There will be silence in the dormitories at all times', and the woodwork teacher with the missing fingers who twisted my ear when the line was not straight, and the Sunday mornings when we put on our khaki shirts and our khaki shorts and our black socks and our black shoes and marched two abreast to the church on Papegaai Street to be forgiven. They were my father, and my mother is buried and not yet risen. That is why it is a good thing that I, who have nothing to pass on, should be spending my time here where I am out of the way.

In the month since his return there had been no visitor K knew of. The only fresh footprints in the dust on the farmhouse floor were his own and those of the cat, which came and went as it pleased, he did not know how. Then, passing the house one day on a dawn walk, he was thunderstruck to see the front door, which was always closed, standing ajar. He halted not thirty paces from the open eye of the door feeling suddenly as naked as a mole in daylight. On tiptoe he retreated to the cover of the river-bed, then stole back to his burrow.

For a week he did not go near the farmhouse but crept about in the dark tending his acre, fearful that the merest clatter of pebble against pebble would echo across the veld and give him away. The young pumpkin leaves now seemed nothing so much as vivid green flags proclaiming his occupation of the dam: he spread grass painstakingly over the vines, he even considered cutting them back. He could not sleep but lay on his bed of grass beneath the oven-heat of the roof straining his ears for the noises that would herald his discovery.

Yet there were times when his fears seemed absurd,

spells of clarity in which he would recognize that, cut off from human society, he was in danger of becoming more timorous than a mouse. What grounds had he for thinking that the open door meant the return of the Visagies or the arrival of the police come to consign him to the notorious Brandvlei? In a vast country across whose face hundreds of thousands of people were daily following their cockroach pilgrimages in flight from the war, why should he be alarmed if some refugee or other hid away in an empty farmhouse in a desolate strip of country? Surely he, or they (K had a vision of a man pushing a barrow loaded with household goods, and a woman trudging behind him, and two children, one holding the woman's hand, the other seated on top of the pile in the barrow clutching a mewling kitten, all dead tired, the wind blowing dust in their faces and sending grey clouds scudding across the sky) – surely such people had more cause to fear him, a wild man all skin and bone and rags rising up out of the earth at the hour of batflight, than he had to fear them?

But then he would think: Yet what if they are of the other kind, runaway soldiers, off-duty policemen come to shoot the goats for sport, hefty men who would hold their sides laughing at my pathetic tricks, my pumpkins hidden in the grass, my burrow disguised with mud, and kick my backside and tell me to pull myself together and turn me into a servant to cut wood and carry water for them and chase the goats towards their guns so that they could eat grilled chops while I squatted behind a bush with my plate of offal? Would it not be better to hide day and night, would it not be better to bury myself in the bowels of the earth than become a creature of theirs? (And would the idea of turning me into a servant even cross their minds? Seeing a wild man making his way towards them across the veld, would they not start laying bets on who could put a bullet through the brass badge on his headgear?)

The days passed and nothing happened. The sun shone, the birds skipped from bush to bush, the great silence reverberated from horizon to horizon, and K's confidence came back. He spent a whole day lying under cover watching the farmhouse, while the sun moved in its arc from left to right and the shadows moved across the stoep from right to left. Was the strip of deeper darkness in the centre an open doorway or the door itself? It was too far to see. When night came and the moon rose, he approached as far as the dead orchard. There was no light in the house, no sound. He tiptoed into the open, across the yard, to the very foot of the steps, from where he could finally see that the door was open, as it must have been all the time. He climbed the steps and entered the house. In the pitch darkness of the hallway he stood listening. All was silence.

He spent the rest of the night lying on a sack in the shed, waiting. He even slept, though he was not used to sleeping by night. In the morning he re-entered the house. The floor had been freshly swept, as had the grate. A faint smell of smoke still hung in the corners. In the rubbish tip behind the shed he found six new shiny unlabelled corned-beef cans.

He went back to his burrow and spent the day in hiding, shaken by the certainty that soldiers had been on the farm and that they had come on foot. If they were hunting rebels in the mountains or tracking down deserters or simply making a tour of inspection, why had they not come in jeeps or trucks? Why were they being stealthy, why were they hiding their tracks? There might be many explanations, there might be a thousand explanations, he could not read their minds; all he knew was that it was the merest luck that had preserved him.

He did not pump water that night, hoping the sun and wind would dry out the floor of the dam. He pulled out more grass, armfuls of grass, and spread it over the telltale pumpkin vines. He lay low and breathed quietly.

A day passed, and another day. Then, as the sun was going down and K had emerged from his house to stretch his limbs, shapes moving across the flats caught his eye. He dropped to the earth. He had seen a man on horseback heading towards the dam, and another man on foot beside him; he had also clearly seen the barrel of the gun poking over the horseman's shoulder. Like a worm he began to slither toward his hole, thinking only: Let darkness fall soon, let the earth swallow me up and protect me.

From behind the swell of the hillock near the mouth of the hole he raised his head for a last look.

It was not a horse but a donkey, a donkey so tiny that its rider's feet almost touched the ground. Further back there was a second donkey, riderless but with two bulky grey packs strapped to its sides; and between the two donkeys he counted eight men, with a ninth at the tail of the train. All of them had guns; some seemed to carry packs as well. One wore blue trousers, another yellow, but otherwise they were in camouflage uniform.

As quietly as he could K slid backwards into the hole. From the doorway he could no longer see anything of them, but on the windless air he heard them dismount at the dam, heard the rattle of the chain as they released the brake on the pump, even heard a murmur of words. Someone climbed the ladder to the platform high above the ground, then climbed down again.

It grew darker, till it was only the snorting of the donkeys that revealed how nearby the strangers were. K heard the thud of an axe down in the river-bed; later the contour of the ridge above him began to be visible against the faint orange glow of their fire. There was a puff of wind; the rudder swung, metal groaned, the wheel of the pump turned once and stopped. 'Why no water?' – he heard the words clearly. There were more

148

words he could not make out, followed by a burst of laughter. Then the wind stirred again, the pump groaned and turned, and through the palms of his hands and the soles of his feet K heard the first boom of the piston deep in the earth. There was a muted cheer. On the wind came the smell of roasting meat.

K closed his eyes and rested his face on his hands. It was clear to him now that it was not soldiers who were camping at the dam, who had earlier camped in the house, but men from the mountains, men who blew up railway tracks and mined roads and attacked farmhouses and drove off stock and cut one town off from another, whom the radio reported exterminated in scores and the newspapers published pictures of sprawling gape-mouthed in pools of their own blood. That was who his visitors were. Yet they seemed to him like nothing so much as a football team: eleven young men come off the field after a hard game, tired, happy, hungry.

His heart was pounding. When they leave in the morning, he thought to himself, I could come out of hiding and trot along behind them like a child following a brass band. After a while they would notice me and stop to ask what I wanted. And I could say: Give me a pack to carry; let me chop wood and build the fire at the end of the day. Or I could say: Be sure to come back to the dam next time, and I will feed you. I will have pumpkins and squashes and melons by then, I will have peaches and figs and prickly pears, you will lack nothing. And they would come next time on their way to the mountains or wherever it is they go by night, and I would feed them and afterwards sit with them around the fire drinking in their words. The stories they tell will be different from the stories I heard in the camp, because the camp was for those left behind, the women and children, the old men, the blind, the crippled, the idiots, people who have nothing to tell but stories of how they have endured. Whereas these young men have had adventures, victories and defeats and escapes. They will have stories to tell long after the war is over, stories for a lifetime, stories for their grandchildren to listen to open-mouthed.

Yet in the same instant that he reached down to check that his shoelaces were tied, K knew that he would not crawl out and stand up and cross from darkness into firelight to announce himself. He even knew the reason why: because enough men had gone off to war saying the time for gardening was when the war was over; whereas there must be men to stay behind and keep gardening alive, or at least the idea of gardening; because once that cord was broken, the earth would grow hard and forget her children. That was why.

Between this reason and the truth that he would never announce himself, however, lay a gap wider than the distance separating him from the firelight. Always, when he tried to explain himself to himself, there remained a gap, a hole, a darkness before which his understanding baulked, into which it was useless to pour words. The words were eaten up, the gap remained. His was always a story with a hole in it: a wrong story, always wrong.

He remembered Huis Norenius and the classroom. Numb with terror he stared at the problem before him while the teacher stalked the rows counting off the minutes till it should be time for them to lay down their pencils and be divided, the sheep from the goats. Twelve men eat six bags of potatoes. Each bag holds six kilograms of potatoes. What is the quotient? He saw himself write down 12, he saw himself write down 6. He did not know what to do with the numbers. He crossed both out. He stared at the word *quotient*. It did not change, it did not dissolve, it did not yield its mystery. I will die, he thought, still not knowing what the quotient is.

He lay awake much of the night listening to the dam slowly fill, peering out occasionally into the starlight to see whether the donkeys had settled or were still browsing on his pumpkins. Then he must have dozed, for the next thing he knew someone was stamping heavily through the grass below him, clapping his hands, chasing the donkeys, and the mountains were already outlined blue on pink against the sky. The wind was still, on the air came faint sounds: the tinkle of a buckle, the clash of a spoon on a mug, the splash of water.

Now, he thought, waking fully, now is my last

chance: now. He slid out of the burrow into the open, crept forward on hands and knees, and peered over the shoulder of the ridge.

There was a man clambering out of the dam. Out of the cold night-water he came, lifted himself on to the wall, and stood there drying himself with a white towel, the first soft light of day shining from his wet naked body.

Two men were loading a donkey, one holding the bridle, the other settling and strapping two bulky canvas bags over its back, and a long tubular parcel also tied in canvas.

The rest of the party were behind the dam wall; sometimes K saw a head move.

The man who had stood on the wall reappeared, dressed now. He bent down and opened the cock. Water gushed out along the old furrows K had dug during his first stay, flowing into the field.

That is a mistake, thought K, that is a sign.

The same man fastened the brake on the pump.

In a long straggling line they began moving out eastward across the veld heading for the mountains, one donkey at the head of the line, the other at the tail, the sun, now over the rim of the world, catching them full in the face. K watched from behind the ridge till they were nothing but bobbing specks against the yellow of the grass, thinking: It is not too late to run after them, it is not too late yet. Then when they were finally gone he came out and made a tour of the flooded acre to see the devastation the donkeys had done.

Their marks were everywhere. They had not only cropped the vines but in many places trampled them. There were long severed creepers winding through the grass whose leaves were already furling and drooping; the few kernels that had shot, little green nuts no bigger than marbles, were devoured. He had lost half his crop. Otherwise the strangers had left behind no trace of their passing. Over the site of the fire they had spread soil and pebbles so painstakingly that it was only by its warmth that he could detect the spot. The dam had long emptied itself; he closed the cock.

He climbed the hillside above his burrow and, lying on the crest, peered into the sun. There was nothing to be seen. They had merged into the hills.

I am like a woman whose children have left the house, he thought: all that remains is to tidy up and listen to the silence. I would have liked to give them food, but all I fed were their donkeys, that could have eaten grass. He crept into the burrow, stretched out listlessly, and closed his eyes.

He was woken later in the morning by the clatter of a helicopter. It passed overhead, following the course of the river. Fifteen minutes later it was back, sweeping further to the north.

They will see that the land has been flooded, he thought. They will see that the grass is greener. They will see the green of the pumpkins. The leaves are like flags waving to them. They can see everything from the air, everything that by its nature does not hide underground. I should be growing onions.

There is still time to run away to the mountains, he thought, even if all I do is hide in a cave. But the listlessness would not leave him. Let them come, he thought, what does it matter. He went back to sleep.

For a week K was more cautious than ever. He did not emerge from the burrow at all during daylight hours, and he watered the surviving vines so meagrely that the leaves drooped and the tendrils withered. The vines that had been cropped he tore out. If every flower turns to fruit, he told himself, looking at what was left, I shall not have forty pumpkins; if they bring their donkeys back this way I shall have none. It was no longer a matter of growing a fat crop, only of growing enough for the seed not to die out. There will be another year, he consoled himself, another summer in which to try again.

It was the last of summer. After days of sultriness and heavy cloudbanks there was a thunderstorm. The gully came washing down and K was flooded out of his house. He crouched in the lee of the dam wall, sodden, feeling like a snail without its shell. After an hour the rain stopped, the birds began singing, a rainbow appeared in the west. He dragged the mat of sodden grass out of his burrow and waited for the stream to stop running. Then he made mud and set about plastering the roof and walls again.

The donkeys did not come back, nor did the eleven men, nor did the helicopter. The pumpkins grew. In the night K would creep about stroking the smooth shells. Every night they were palpably larger. As time passed he permitted the hope to grow up again in his breast that all would be well. He woke during the day and peered out over the acre; from under the camouflage of grass a shell here and there glinted quietly back at him.

Among the seeds he had sown had been a melon seed. Now two pale green melons were growing on the far side of the field. It seemed to him that he loved these two, which he thought of as two sisters, even more than the pumpkins, which he thought of as a band of brothers. Under the melons he placed pads of grass so that their skins should not bruise.

Then came the evening when the first pumpkin was ripe enough to cut. It had grown earlier and faster than the others, in the very centre of the field; K had marked it out as the first fruit, the firstborn. The shell was soft, the knife sank in without a struggle. The flesh, though still rimmed with green, was a deep orange. On the wire grid he had made he laid strips of pumpkin over a bed of coals that glowed brighter and brighter as the dark came on. The fragrance of the burning flesh rose into the sky. Speaking the words he had been taught, directing them no longer upward but to the earth on which he knelt, he prayed: 'For what we are about to receive make us truly thankful.' With two wire skewers he turned the strips, and in mid-act felt his heart suddenly flow over with thankfulness. It was exactly as they had described it, like a gush of warm water. Now it is completed, he said to himself. All that remains is to live here quietly for the rest of my life, eating the food that my own labour has made the earth to yield. All that remains is to be a tender of the soil. He lifted the first strip to his mouth. Beneath the crisply charred skin the flesh was soft and juicy. He chewed with tears of joy in his eyes. The best, he thought, the very best pumpkin I have tasted. For the first time since he had arrived in the country he found pleasure in eating. The aftertaste of the first slice left his mouth aching with sensual delight. He moved the grid off the coals and took a second slice. His teeth bit through the crust into the soft hot pulp. Such pumpkin, he thought, such pumpkin I could eat every day of my life and never want anything else. And what perfection it would be with a pinch of salt – with a pinch of salt, and a dab of butter, and a sprinkling of sugar, and a little cinnamon scattered over the top! Eating the third slice, and the fourth and fifth, till half the pumpkin was gone and his belly was full, K wallowed in the recollection of the flavours of salt, butter, sugar, cinnamon, one by one.

But the ripening of the pumpkins brought a new anxiety. For while it had been possible to conceal the vines, the pumpkins themselves created hollows which even at a distance gave the field an odd look, as though a flock of lambs were sleeping in the knee-high grass. K did what he could to fold the grass back over the pumpkins but dared not cover them wholly, for it was the precious late-summer sun that was ripening them. All he could do was pick them as early as possible, before the stems withered, sometimes even when there were green flecks left on the shell, and bear them away.

The days were growing shorter, the nights colder. Sometimes K had to wear his black coat to work in the field; he slept with his feet wrapped in a bag and his hands between his thighs. He slept more and more. He no longer sat outside when his tasks were finished, looking at the stars, listening to the night, or walked about in the veld, but crept into his hole and fell into deep sleep. All morning he would sleep. At noon he would begin to emerge into an interval of languor and waking dreams, bathed in a gentle warmth that radiated down from the roof; then as the sun set he would come out, stretch himself, and go down to the river-bed to chop wood till he could no longer see his mark.

He had dug a pit for his fire so that it should not be seen at a distance, and constructed a vent-tunnel. After he had eaten he would lay two stone slabs over the pit and sprinkle them with earth. The embers would then continue to smoulder till the next night. In the earth around the pit there grew up a multifarious insect life drawn by the benign, continuous warmth.

He did not know what month it was, though he guessed it was April. He had kept no tally of the days nor recorded the changes of the moon. He was not a prisoner or a castaway, his life by the dam was not a sentence that he had to serve out.

He had become so much a creature of twilight and night that daylight hurt his eyes. He no longer needed to keep to paths in his movements around the dam. A sense less of sight than of touch, the pressure of presences upon his eyeballs and the skin of his face, warned him of any obstacle. His eyes remained unfocussed for hours on end like those of a blind person. He had learned to rely on smell too. He breathed into his lungs the clear sweet smell of water brought up from inside the earth. It intoxicated him, he could not have enough of it. Though he knew no names he could tell one bush from another by the smell of their leaves. He could smell rain-weather in the air.

But most of all, as summer slanted to an end, he was learning to love idleness, idleness no longer as stretches of freedom reclaimed by stealth here and there from involuntary labour, surreptitious thefts to be enjoyed sitting on his heels before a flower-bed with the fork dangling from his fingers, but as a yielding up of himself to time, to a time flowing slowly like oil from horizon to horizon over the face of the world, washing over his body, circulating in his armpits and his groin, stirring his eyelids. He was neither pleased nor displeased when there was work to do; it was all the same. He could lie all afternoon with his eyes open staring at the corrugations in the roof-iron and the tracings of rust:

his mind would not wander, he would see nothing but the iron, the lines would not transform themselves into pattern or fantasy: he was himself, lying in his own house, the rust was merely rust, all that was moving was time, bearing him onward in its flow. Once or twice the other time in which the war had its existence reminded itself to him as the jet fighters whistled high overhead. But for the rest he was living beyond the reach of calendar and clock in a blessedly neglected corner, half awake, half asleep. Like a parasite dozing in the gut, he thought; like a lizard under a stone.

Parasite was the word the police captain had used: the camp at Jakkalsdrif, a nest of parasites hanging from the neat sunlit town, eating its substance, giving no nourishment back. Yet to K lying idle in his bed, thinking without passion (What is it to me, after all? he thought), it was no longer obvious which was host and which parasite, camp or town. If the worm devoured the sheep, why did the sheep swallow the worm? What if there were millions, more millions than anyone knew, living in camps, living on alms, living off the land, living by guile, creeping away in corners to escape the times, too canny to put out flags and draw attention to themselves and be counted? What if the hosts were far outnumbered by the parasites, the parasites of idleness and the other secret parasites in the army and the police force and the schools and factories and offices, the parasites of the heart? Could the parasites then still be called parasites? Parasites too had flesh and substance; parasites too could be preyed upon. Perhaps in truth whether the camp was declared a parasite on the town or the town a parasite on the camp depended on no more than on who made his voice heard loudest.

He thought of his mother. She had asked him to bring her back to her birthplace and he had done so, though perhaps only by a trick of words. But what if this farm was not her true birthplace? Where were the stone walls of the wagonhouse she had spoken of? He made himself pay a daylight visit to the farmyard and to the cottages on the hillside and the rectangle of bare earth beside them. If my mother ever lived here I will surely know, he told himself. He closed his eyes and tried to recover in his imagination the mud-brick walls and reed roof of her stories, the garden of prickly pear, the chickens scampering for the feed scattered by the little barefoot girl. And behind that child, in the door-way, her face obscured by shadow, he searched for a second woman, the woman from whom his mother had come into the world. When my mother was dying in hospital, he thought, when she knew her end was coming, it was not me she looked to but someone who stood behind me: her mother or the ghost of her mother. To me she was a woman but to herself she was still a child calling to her mother to hold her hand and help her. And her own mother, in the secret life we do not see, was a child too. I come from a line of children without end.

He tried to imagine a figure standing alone at the

head of the line, a woman in a shapeless grey dress who came from no mother; but when he had to think of the silence in which she lived, the silence of time before the beginning, his mind baulked.

Now that he slept so much, animals came back to prey on his field, hares and little grey steenbok. He would not have minded if they had merely nibbled the tips of the vines; but he lapsed into fits of gloomy anger when they bit through a vine and left the fruit to wither. He did not know what he would do if he lost his two beloved melons. He spent hours trying to construct a game-trap out of wire but could not get it to work. One night he made his bed in the middle of the field. The glare of the moon kept him awake, he started at every rustle, the cold numbed his feet. How much easier it would all be, he thought, if there were a fence around the dam, a fence of stout wire mesh with its bottom edge staked a foot underground to stop the burrowers.

There was a continual taste of blood in his mouth. His bowels ran and there were moments of giddiness when he stood up. Sometimes his stomach felt like a fist clenched in the centre of his body. He forced himself to eat more of the pumpkin than he had appetite for; it relieved the tightness in his stomach but did not make him better. He tried to shoot birds but had lost his skill with the catapult as well as his old patience. He killed and ate a lizard.

The pumpkins were ripening all together, the vines

turning yellow and withering. K had not thought of how he could store them. He tried cutting the flesh in strips and drying it in the sun, but it rotted and attracted ants. He piled the thirty pumpkins in a pyramid near his burrow; it looked like a beacon. They could not be buried, they needed warmth and dryness, they were creatures of the sun. Eventually he deposited them fifty paces apart up and down the river-bed in the undergrowth; to disguise them he made a paste of mud and painted each shell in a mottled pattern.

Then the melons ripened. He ate these two children on successive days, praying that they would make him well. He thought he felt better afterwards, though he was still weak. Their flesh was the colour of orange river-silt, but deeper. He had never tasted fruit so sweet. How much of that sweetness came from the seed, how much from the earth? He scraped their seeds together and spread them to dry. From one seed a whole handful: that was what it meant to say *the bounty of the earth*.

The first day passed when K did not come out of his burrow at all. He awoke in the afternoon feeling no hunger. There was a cold wind blowing, there was nothing that needed his attention, his work for the year was done. He turned over and went to sleep again. When next he knew, it was dawn and birds were singing.

He lost track of time. Sometimes, waking stifled under the black coat with his legs swaddled in the bag,

162

he knew that it was day. There were long periods when he lay in a grey stupor too tired to kick himself free of sleep. He could feel the processes of his body slowing down. You are forgetting to breathe, he would say to himself, and yet lie without breathing. He raised a hand heavy as lead and put it over his heart: far away, as if in another country, he felt a languid stretching and closing.

Through whole cycles of the heavens he slept. Once he dreamed that he was being shaken by an old man. The old man wore filthy tattered clothing and smelled of tobacco. He bent over K gripping his shoulder. 'You must get off the land!' he said. K tried to shrug him off but the claw gripped tighter. 'You will get into trouble!' the old man hissed.

He also dreamed of his mother. He was walking with her in the mountains. Though her legs were heavy, she was young and beautiful. With great sweeps he was gesturing from horizon to horizon: he was happy and excited. The green lines of river-courses stood out against the fawn of the earth; there were no roads or houses anywhere; the air was still. In his wild gesturings, in the great windmill sweeps of his arms, he realized he was in danger of losing his footing and being carried over the edge of the rock-face into the vast airiness of space between the heavens and the earth; but he had no fear, he knew he would float.

Sometimes he would emerge into wakefulness unsure whether he had slept a day or a week or a month.

It occurred to him that he might not be fully in possession of himself. You must eat, he would say, and struggle to get up and look for a pumpkin. But then he would relax again, and stretch his legs and yawn in sensual pleasure so sweet that he wished for nothing but to lie and let it ripple through him. He had no appetite; eating, picking up things and forcing them down his gullet into his body, seemed a strange activity.

Then step by step his sleep grew to be lighter and the periods of wakefulness more frequent. He began to be visited by trains of images so rapid and unconnected that he could not follow them. He tossed and turned, unsatisfied by sleep but too drained of strength to rise. He began to have headaches; he gritted his teeth, wincing with every pulse of blood in his skull.

There was a thunderstorm. As long as the thunder rolled far away K barely noticed it. But then a clap burst directly over him and it began to pour. Water seeped down the sides of the burrow; streaming down the gully, it washed away the mud plaster and flooded through his sleeping-place. He sat up, head and shoulders bowed under the roof-plates. There was nowhere better to go. Propped in a corner in the rushing water with the sodden coat pulled tight around him, he slept and woke.

He emerged into daylight shivering with cold. The sky was overcast, he had no way of making a fire. One cannot live like this, he thought. He wandered about the field and past the pump. Everything was familiar, yet he felt like a stranger or a ghost. There were pools of water on the ground and water in the river for the first time, a swift brown stream yards wide. On the far side something pale stood out against the gun-blue gravel. What is it, he marvelled, a great white mushroom brought out by the rain? With a start he recognized it as a pumpkin.

The shivering would not stop. He had no strength in his limbs; when he set one foot in front of the other it was tentatively, like an old man. Needing to sit all of a sudden, he sat down on the wet earth. The tasks that awaited him seemed too many and too great. I have woken too early, he thought, I have not finished my sleeping. He suspected that he ought to eat to stop the swimming in front of his eyes, but his stomach was not ready. He forced himself to imagine tea, a cup of hot tea thick with sugar; on hands and knees he drank from a puddle.

He was still sitting when they discovered him. He heard the drone of the vehicles when they were far off but thought it was distant thunder. Only when they had reached the gate below the farmhouse did he see them and realize what they were. He stood up, grew dizzy, sat down again. One of the vehicles stopped before the house, the other, a jeep, bumped across the veld towards him. It held four men; he watched them come; hopelessness settled over him.

At first they were ready to believe he was simply a vagrant, a lost soul the police would have picked up in the course of time and found a home for in Jakkalsdrif. 'I live in the veld,' he said, replying to their question; 'I live nowhere.' Then he had to rest his head on his knees: there was a hammering inside his skull and a taste of bile in his mouth. One of the soldiers picked up an arm between two fingers and dangled it. K did not pull away. The arm felt like something alien, a stick protruding from his body. 'What do you think he lives on?' the soldier asked – 'Flies? Ants? Locusts?' K could see nothing but their boots. He closed his eyes; for a while he was absent. Then someone gave his shoulder a slap and pushed something at him: a sandwich, two thick slices of white bread with polony between them. He pulled back and shook his head. 'Eat, man!' his benefactor said. 'Get some strength into yourself!' He took the sandwich and bit into it. Before he could chew his stomach began to retch drily. With his head between his knees he spat out the mouthful of bread and meat and handed the sandwich back. 'He's sick,' said one voice. 'He's been drinking,' said another.

But then they found his house, the stonework of the front wall nakedly visible after the rain. First they took turns on hands and knees to peer inside. Then they lifted off the roof and uncovered the neat interior, the spade and axe, the knife and spoon and plate and mug on a shelf cut into the gravel, the magnifying glass, the bed of wet grass. They brought K over to confront his handiwork, holding him upright, no longer disposed to be kindly. Tears ran down his face. 'Did you make

166

this?' they asked. He nodded. 'Are you alone here?' He nodded. The soldier holding him brought his arm up sharply behind his back. K hissed with pain. 'The truth!' said the soldier. 'It is the truth,' said K.

The truck arrived too; the air was loud with voices and the squawks and rasps of the two-way radio; soldiers were crowding around to see K and the house he had built. 'Spread out!' one of them shouted: 'I want the whole area searched! We are looking for footpaths, we are looking for holes and tunnels, we are looking for any kind of storage site!' He dropped his voice. He was dressed in camouflage uniform like everyone else; there was no badge K could see to tell he was in charge. 'You see what kind of people they are,' he said: his eyes moved around restlessly, he did not seem to be speaking to anyone in particular. 'You think there is nothing and all the time the ground beneath your feet is rotten with tunnels. Look around a place like this and you would swear there wasn't a living soul in miles. Then turn your back and they come crawling out of the ground. Ask him how long he's been here.' He turned on K and raised his voice. 'You! How long have you been here?'

'Since last year,' K said, not knowing whether it was a good lie or a bad lie.

'So when are your friends coming? When are your friends coming again?'

K shrugged.

'Ask him again,' said the officer, turning away. 'Keep asking him. Ask him when his friends are coming. Ask

167

him when they were last here. See if he's got a tongue. See if he is such an idiot as he looks.'

The soldier who was holding K gripped the nape of his neck between thumb and forefinger and guided him down till he was kneeling, till his face was touching the earth. 'You heard what the officer said,' he said, 'so tell me. Tell me your story.' He flicked the beret away and pressed K's face hard into the earth. With nose and lips squashed flat, K tasted the damp soil. He sighed. They lifted him and held him up. He did not open his eyes. 'So tell us about your friends,' the soldier said. K shook his head. He was hit a terrific blow in the pit of the stomach and fainted.

They spent the afternoon hunting for the stocks of food and arms they were convinced were hidden there. First they scoured the area around the dam, then they explored further up and down the river. There was an instrument with earphones and a black box that one of them used: K watched him move slowly along the shoulder of the river-bank, where the earth was soft, prodding his rod into the earth. Many of the pumpkins, perhaps all of them, were discovered: young men kept returning bearing pumpkins, which they tossed in a heap at the edge of the field. The pumpkins only made them more certain that there were stores hidden ('Otherwise why would they leave this monkey here?' K overheard).

They wanted to interrogate him again but he was plainly too weak. They gave him tea, which he drank, and tried to reason with him. 'You're sick, man,' they said. 'Look at you. Look at how your friends treat you. They don't care what happens to you. You want to go home? We'll take you home and give you a new start in life.'

They sat him up against a wheel of the jeep. One of them fetched the beret and dropped it in his lap. They offered him a slice of soft white bread. He swallowed a mouthful, leaned sideways, and brought it up, together with the tea. 'Leave him alone, he's finished,' someone said. K wiped his mouth on his sleeve. They stood in a circle about him; he had a feeling they did not know what to do.

He spoke. 'I'm not what you think,' he said. 'I was sleeping and you woke me, that's all.' They gave no sign of understanding.

They quartered themselves in the farmhouse. In the kitchen they set up their own stove; soon K could smell tomatoes cooking. Someone had hung a radio on a hook on the stoep; the air was full of nervous electric rhythms that unsettled him.

They put him in the bedroom at the end of the corridor, on a tarpaulin folded in four, with a blanket over him. They gave him warm milk and two pills which they said were aspirin and which he kept down. Later, after dark, a boy brought him a plate of food. 'See if you can eat just a mouthful,' he said. He shone a flashlight on the plate. K saw two sausages in a thick gravy, and mashed potato. He shook his head and turned to the wall. The boy left the plate at the bedside

('In case you change your mind'). After that they did not disturb him. He drowsed uneasily for a while, troubled by the smell of the food. At last he got up and put the plate in a corner. Some of the soldiers were on the stoep, some in the living-room. There was talk and laughter but no light.

The next morning the police arrived from Prince Albert with dogs to help in the search for tunnels and hidden supplies. Captain Oosthuizen recognized K at once. 'How could I forget a face like that?' he said. 'This joker ran away from Jakkalsdrif in December. His name is Michaels. What name did he give you?' 'Michael,' said the army officer. 'It's Michaels,' said Captain Oosthuizen. He poked K in the ribs with his boot. 'He's not sick, he always looks like this. Hey, Michaels?'

So they took K back to the dam, where he watched the dogs drag their handlers back and forth across the acre of grass and up and down the river banks, whining with eagerness, tugging at the leash, but finally able to lead them to nothing better than old porcupine burrows and hare sets. Oosthuizen gave K a cuff on the side of the head. 'So what's this about, monkey?' he said. 'You playing games with us?' The dogs were loaded back into the van. Everyone was losing interest in the search. The young soldiers stood about in the sun talking, drinking coffee.

K sat with his head between his knees. Though his mind was clear, he could not control the dizziness. A string of spittle drooled from his mouth; he did not bother to stop it. Every grain of this earth will be washed clean by the rain, he told himself, and dried by the sun and scoured by the wind, before the seasons turn again. There will be not a grain left bearing my marks, just as my mother has now, after her season in the earth, been washed clean, blown about, and drawn up into leaves of grass.

So what is it, he thought, that binds me to this spot of earth as if to a home I cannot leave? We must all leave home, after all, we must all leave our mothers. Or am I such a child, such a child from such a line of children, that none of us can leave, but have to come back to die here with our heads upon our mothers' laps, I upon hers, she upon her mother's, and so back and back, generation upon generation?

There was a heavy explosion, and at once a second explosion. The air shook, there was a clamour of birds, the hills rumbled and echoed. K stared around wildly. 'Look!' said a soldier, and pointed.

Where the Visagie house had once stood there was now a cloud of grey and orange, not mist but dust, as if a whirlwind were carrying the house away. Then the cloud stopped growing, its substance thinned, and a skeleton began to emerge: part of the back wall with the chimney; three of the supports that had held up the verandah. A sheet of roofing swooped out of the air and hit the ground noiselessly. The reverberations went on, but K did not know any more if they were in the hills or in his head.

Swallows flew past, so low above the ground he could have touched them had he stretched out a hand.

Afterwards there were more explosions, for which he did not look up, guessing that the outbuildings had gone. He thought: No longer do the Visagies have anywhere to hide.

The jeep came bumping back across the veld. All around him they were clearing and packing up. In the acre itself, however, a lone soldier was still at work. He was digging up tufts of grass and laying them carefully to one side. With some anxiety K rose to his feet and stumbled across. 'What are you doing?' he called. The soldier did not answer. He began to shape a shallow pit, laying the earth on a black plastic sheet. This was the third hole he had dug, K saw: both of the others had neat piles of earth on plastic sheets beside them, and tufts of grass with the earth still clinging to their roots. 'What are you doing?' he asked again. The sight of the stranger digging up his earth agitated him more than he would have guessed. 'Let me do it,' he offered – 'I am used to digging.' But the soldier waved him away. Completing the third hole, he stepped off eight paces and laid down another plastic sheet. As the spade bit into the earth, K squatted and covered the grass with his hands. 'Please, my friend!' he said. The soldier stood back, exasperated. Someone hauled K back by the scruff of the neck. 'Just keep him out of my way,' said the soldier.

K stood by the pump and watched. When he had

dug five holes in a zigzag pattern, the soldier unrolled a long white cord to mark off the area. Two of his comrades brought a crate from the truck and began to lay the mines. As they laid each and primed it, the first soldier planted the grass and poured the earth back handful by handful, patted the surface down, and brushed away all their prints with a hand-broom, moving backward on hands and knees.

'Get out of the way here,' said someone behind K. 'Go and wait there by the truck.' It was the officer. Retreating, K heard the instructions he was giving: 'Tape two inside the struts at about waist height. Put another under the platform. When they trip it, I want the whole thing to go.'

Everything was packed in, they were about to drive off, with K in the back of the truck among the soldiers, when someone pointed to the heap of pumpkins they had left by the side of the field. 'Load them!' shouted the officer from the jeep. They loaded the pumpkins. 'And fix up that kennel of his so that it looks just the same!' he ordered. They all waited while the roof was replaced. 'Stones to hold it down, like it was! Hurry up!'

They drove off, bumping and jostling on the dirt road, following the jeep. K clutched the strap above his head; he could feel his neighbours holding their bodies stiff to avoid being thrown against him. A cloud of dust billowed up till he could see nothing of what he was leaving behind.

He leaned nearer to the young soldier facing him. 'You know,' he said, 'there was a boy hiding in that house.'

The soldier did not understand. K had to repeat himself.

'What does he say?' asked someone.

'He says there was another boy hiding in the house.'

'Tell him he's dead now. Tell him he's in paradise.'

Then after a while they reached the turnoff. The truck picked up speed, the tyres began to hum, the soldiers relaxed, and the dust blew away to reveal behind them the long straight line of the road to Prince Albert.

II

THERE IS A NEW PATIENT IN THE WARD, A LITTLE OLD man who collapsed during physical training and was brought in with very low respiration and heartbeat. There is every evidence of prolonged malnutrition: cracks in his skin, sores on his hands and feet, bleeding gums. His joints protrude, he weighs less than forty kilos. The story is that he was picked up all by himself in the middle of nowhere in the Karoo running a staging post for guerrillas operating out of the mountains, caching arms and growing food, though obviously not eating it. I asked the guards who brought him why they made someone in his condition do physical exercise. It was an oversight, they said: he came with the new intake, the processing was taking a long time, the sergeant in charge wanted to give them something to do while they waited, so he made them run on the spot. Couldn't he see this man was incapable? I asked. The prisoner didn't complain, they replied: he said he was fine, he had always been thin. Can't you tell the difference between a thin man and a skeleton? I asked. They shrugged.

*   *

Have been struggling with the new patient Michaels. He insists there is nothing wrong with him, he only wants something for his headache. Says he is not hungry. In fact he cannot hold his food down. Am keeping him on a drip, which he fights against feebly.

Though he looks like an old man, he claims to be only thirty-two. Perhaps it is the truth. He comes from the Cape and knows the racecourse from the days when it was still a racecourse. It amused him to hear that this used to be the jockeys' dressing-room. 'I could become a jockey too, at my weight,' he said. He worked for the Council as a gardener, but lost his job and went to seek his fortune in the countryside, taking his mother with him. 'Where is your mother now?' I asked. 'She makes the plants grow,' he replied, evading my eyes. 'You mean she has passed away?' I said (pushing up the daisies?). He shook his head. 'They burned her,' he said. 'Her hair was burning round her head like a halo.'

He makes a statement like that as impassively as if talking about the weather. I am not sure he is wholly of our world. One tries to imagine him running a staging post for insurgents and one's mind boggles. More likely someone came along and offered him a drink and asked him to look after a gun and he was too stupid or too innocent to refuse. He is locked up as an insurgent, but he barely knows there is a war on.

*   *

Now that Felicity has shaved him I have had a chance to examine his mouth. A simple incomplete cleft, with some displacement of the septum. The palate intact. I asked him whether there had ever been an attempt to correct the condition. He did not know. I pointed out that the operation is a slight one, even at his age. Would he agree to such an operation if it could be arranged? He replied (I quote): 'I am what I am. I was never a great one for the girls.' I felt like telling him that, never mind the girls, he would find it easier to get along if he could talk like everyone else; but said nothing, not wanting to hurt him.

I mentioned him to Noël. 'He couldn't run a darts game, much less a staging post,' I said. 'He is a person of feeble mind who drifted by chance into a war zone and didn't have the sense to get out. He ought to be in a protected environment weaving baskets or stringing beads, not in a rehabilitation camp.'

Noël brought out the register. 'According to this,' he said, 'Michaels is an arsonist. He is also an escapee from a labour camp. He was running a flourishing

179

garden on an abandoned farm and feeding the local guerrilla population when he was captured. That is the story of Michaels.'

I shook my head. 'They have made a mistake,' I said. 'They have mixed him up with some other Michaels. This Michaels is an idiot. This Michaels doesn't know how to strike a match. If this Michaels was running a flourishing garden, why was he starving to death?'

'Why didn't you eat?' I asked Michaels back in the ward. 'They say you had a garden. Why didn't you feed yourself?' His reply: 'They woke me in the middle of my sleep.' I must have looked blank. 'I don't need food in my sleep.'

He says his name is not Michaels but Michael.

*   *

Noël is putting pressure on me to speed up the turnaround. There are eight beds in the infirmary and, at the moment, sixteen patients, the other eight being housed in the old weighing room. Noël asks whether I cannot treat and release them faster. I reply that there is no point in discharging a patient with dysentery into camp life unless he wants an epidemic. Of course he doesn't want an epidemic, he says; but in the past there have been cases of malingering, and he wants to stamp that out. His responsibility is to his programme, I reply, mine to my patients, that is what being medical officer entails. He pats me on the shoulder. 'You are doing a fine job, I'm not questioning that,' he says.

'All I ask is that they shouldn't get the idea we are soft.'

A silence falls between the two of us; we watch the flies on the windowpane. 'But we are soft,' I suggest.

'Perhaps we are soft,' he replies. 'Perhaps we are even scheming a bit, at the back of our minds. Perhaps we think that if one day they come and put everyone on trial, someone will step forward and say, "Let those two off, they were soft." Who knows? But that isn't what I am talking about. I am talking about flow. At the moment you have got more patients flowing into your infirmary than flowing out, and my question is, are you going to do something about it?'

When we emerged from his office it was to behold a corporal raising the orange, white and blue on a flagpole in the middle of the track, a five-piece band playing '*Uit die blou*', the cornet out of key, and six hundred sullen men standing to attention, barefoot, in their tenth-hand khakis, having their thinking set right. A year ago we were still trying to make them sing; but we have given up on that.

* *

Felicity took Michaels outdoors for some fresh air this morning. I passed him sitting on the grass holding his face up to the sun like a lizard basking, and asked him how he liked it in the infirmary. He was un-expectedly talkative. 'I'm glad there isn't a radio,' he said. 'The other place I stayed there was a radio playing all the time.' At first I thought he was referring to another camp, but it turned out that he meant the godforsaken institution where he spent his childhood. 'There was music all afternoon and all evening, till eight o'clock. It was like oil over everything.' 'The music was to keep you calm,' I explained. 'Otherwise you might have beaten each other's faces in and thrown chairs through the windows. The music was to soothe your savage breast.' I don't know whether he understood, but he smiled his lopsided smile. 'The music made me restless,' he said. 'I used to fidget, I couldn't think my own thoughts.' 'And what were the thoughts you wanted to think?' He: 'I used to think about flying. I always wanted to fly. I used to stretch out my arms and think I was flying over the fences and between the houses. I flew low over people's heads, but they couldn't see me. When they switched on the music I became too restless to do it, to fly.' And he even named one or two of the tunes that had disturbed him most.

I have moved him to the bed by the window, away from the boy with the broken ankle who has taken a dislike to him, God knows why, and lies and hisses at him all day. When he sits up he can now at least see the sky and the top of the flagpole. 'Eat a little more and you can go for a walk,' I coax him. What he really needs, however, is physiotherapy, which we cannot provide. He is like one of those toys made of sticks held together with rubber bands. He needs a graduated diet, gentle exercise, and physiotherapy, so that one day soon he can rejoin camp life and have a chance to march back and forth across the racetrack and shout slogans and salute the flag and practise digging holes and filling them again.

*　　*

Overheard in the canteen: 'The children are finding it so hard to adapt to life in a flat. They really miss the big garden and their pets. We had to evacuate just like that: three days' notice. I can cry when I think of what we left behind.' The speaker a florid-faced woman in a polka-dot dress, the wife, I think, of one of the NCOs. (In her dreams of her abandoned home a strange man sprawls on the sheets with his boots on, or opens the deep-freeze and spits into the ice-cream.) 'Don't tell me not to feel bitter,' she said. Her companion a slim little woman I did not recognize, with her hair combed back like a man's.

Do any of us believe in what we are doing here? I doubt it. Her NCO husband least of all. We are given an old racetrack and a quantity of barbed wire and told to effect a change in men's souls. Not being experts on the soul but assuming cautiously that it has some connection with the body, we set our captives to doing pushups and marching back and forth. We also ply them with items from the brass band repertoire and show them films of young men in neat uniforms demonstrating to grizzled village elders how to eradicate mosquitoes and plough along the contour. At the end of the process we certify them cleansed and pack them off to the labour battalions to carry water and dig latrines. At the big military parades there is always a company from the labour battalions marching past the cameras among all the tanks and rockets and field artillery to prove that we can turn enemies into friends; but they march with spades on their shoulders, I notice, not guns.

* *

Returning to camp after a Sunday off, I present myself at the gate feeling like a punter paying admission. ENCLOSURE A, reads the sign over the main gate. MEMBERS AND OFFICIALS ONLY, reads the sign over the gate to the infirmary. Why have they not taken them down? Do they believe the track will be re-opened one of these days? Are there still people training racehorses some-where, convinced that after all the fuss the world will settle down to being as it was?

* *

We are down to twelve patients. Michaels, however, makes no progress. There has obviously been de-generation of the intestinal wall. I have put him back on skimmed milk.

He lies looking up at the window and the sky, with his ears sticking out of his bare skull, smiling his smile. When he was brought in he had a brown paper packet which he put away under his pillow. Now he has taken to holding the packet against his chest. I asked him whether it contained his *muti*. No, he said, and showed me dried pumpkin seeds. I was quite affected. 'You must go back to your gardening when the war is over,' I told him. 'Will you go back to the Karoo, do you think?' He looked cagey. 'Of course there is good soil in the Peninsula too, under all the rolling lawns,' I said. 'It would be nice to see market gardening carried on in the Peninsula again.' He made no reply. I took the packet out of his hand and tucked it under the pillow 'for safety'. When I passed an hour later he was asleep, his mouth nudging the pillow like a baby's.

He is like a stone, a pebble that, having lain around quietly minding its own business since the dawn of time, is now suddenly picked up and tossed randomly from hand to hand. A hard little stone, barely aware of its surroundings, enveloped in itself and its interior life. He passes through these institutions and camps and hospitals and God knows what else like a stone. Through the intestines of the war. An unbearing, unborn creature. I cannot really think of him as a man, though he is older than me by most reckonings.

*   *

His condition is stable, the diarrhoea under control. Pulse rate low, however, blood pressure low. Last night he complained of being cold, though in fact the nights are getting warmer, and Felicity had to give him a pair of socks. This morning when I tried to be friendly

185

he shook me off. 'Do you think if you leave me alone I am going to die?' he said. 'Why do you want to make me fat? Why fuss over me, why am I so important?' I was in no mood to argue. I tried to take his wrist; he pulled away with surprising strength, waving an arm like an insect's claw. I left him till I had done my round, then came back. I had something I wanted to say. 'You ask why you are important, Michaels. The answer is that you are not important. But that does not mean you are forgotten. No one is forgotten. Remember the sparrows. Five sparrows are sold for a farthing, and even they are not forgotten.'

He gazed up at the ceiling for a long while, like an old man consulting the spirits, then spoke. 'My mother worked all her life long,' he said. 'She scrubbed other people's floors, she cooked food for them, she washed their dishes. She washed their dirty clothes. She scrubbed the bath after them. She went on her knees and cleaned the toilet. But when she was old and sick they forgot her. They put her away out of sight. When she died they threw her in the fire. They gave me an old box of ash and told me, "Here is your mother, take her away, she is no good to us."'

The boy with the broken ankle lay pricking his ears, pretending to be asleep.

I answered Michaels as abruptly as I could; there seemed no point in humouring his self-pity. 'We do for you what we have to do,' I told him. 'There is nothing special about you, you can rest easy about that. When

186

you are better there are plenty of floors waiting to be scrubbed and plenty of toilets to clean. As for your mother, I am sure you have not told the full story and I am sure you know that.'

Nevertheless, he is right: I do indeed pay too much attention to him. Who is he, after all? On the one hand we have a flood of refugees from the countryside seeking safety in the towns. On the other hand we have people tired of living five to a room and not getting enough to eat who slip out of the towns to scratch a living in the abandoned countryside. Who is Michaels but one of a multitude in the second class? A mouse who quit an overcrowded, foundering ship. Only, being a city mouse, he did not know how to live off the land and began to grow very hungry indeed. And then was lucky enough to be sighted and hauled aboard again. What has he to be so piqued about?

*   *

Noël has had a phone call from the police at Prince Albert. There was an attack on the town's water supply last night. The pump was blown up as well as a section of the pipe. While they wait for the engineers they will have to make do with borehole water. The overland power lines are down as well. Evidently yet another of the little ships is sinking, while the big ships plough on through the darkness, more and more lonely, groaning under their weight of human cargo. The police would like another chance to talk to Michaels about those responsible, namely his friends from the mountains. Alternatively they want us to put certain questions to him. 'Haven't they been over him once already?' I protested to Noël. 'What is the point of interrogating him a second time? He is too sick to travel, and anyhow not responsible for himself.' 'Is he too sick to talk to us?' Noël asked. 'Not too sick, but you won't get sense out of him,' I said. Noël brought out Michaels' papers again and showed them to me. Under *Category* I read *Opgaarder* in neat country-policeman copperplate. 'What is an *opgaarder*?' I said. Noël: 'Like a squirrel or an ant or a bee.' 'Is that a new rank?' I said. 'Did he go to *opgaarder* school and get an *opgaarder*'s badge?'

We took Michaels in his pyjamas, with a blanket over his shoulders, to the store-room at the far end of the stand. Paint cans and cardboard boxes piled against the wall, cobwebs in every corner, dust thick on the floor, and nowhere to sit. Michaels confronted us crossly, holding the blanket tight, resolute on his two stick-feet.

'You're in the shit, Michaels,' said Noël. 'Your friends from Prince Albert have been misbehaving. They are making a nuisance of themselves. We need to catch them, have a talk to them. We don't think you are giving us all the help you can. So you are getting a second chance. We want you to tell us about your friends: where they hide out, how we can get to meet them.' He lit a cigarette. Michaels did not stir or take his eyes off us.

'Michaels,' I said, 'Michael – some of us are not even

sure you had anything to do with the insurgents. If you can persuade us you were not working for them, you can save us a lot of trouble and save yourself a lot of unhappiness. So tell me, tell the Major: what were you actually doing on that farm when they caught you? Because all we know is what we read in these papers from the police at Prince Albert, and, frankly, what they say doesn't make sense. Tell us the truth, tell us the whole truth, and you can go back to bed, we won't bother you any more.'

Now he crouched perceptibly, clutching the blanket about his throat, glaring at the two of us.

'Come on, my friend!' I said. 'No one is going to hurt you, just tell us what we want to know!'

The silence lengthened. Noël did not speak, passing the whole burden to me. 'Come on, Michaels,' I said, 'we haven't got all day, there is a war on!'

At last he spoke: 'I am not in the war.'

Irritation overflowed in me. 'You are not in the war? Of course you are in the war, man, whether you like it or not! This is a camp, not a holiday resort, not a convalescent home: it is a camp where we rehabilitate people like you and make you work! You are going to learn to fill sandbags and dig holes, my friend, till your back breaks! And if you don't co-operate you will go to a place that is a lot worse than this! You will go to a place where you stand baking in the sun all day and eat potato-peelings and mealie-cobs, and if you don't survive, tough luck, they cross your number off the list

189

and that is the end of you! So come on, talk, time is running out, tell us what you were doing so that we can write it down and send it to Prince Albert! The Major here is a busy man, he isn't used to wasting time, he came out of retirement to run this nice camp and help people like you. You must co-operate.'

Still crouching, ready to evade me if I should spring, he made his reply. 'I am not clever with words,' he said, nothing more. He moistened his lips with his lizard-tongue.

'We don't want you to be clever with words or stupid with words, man, we just want you to tell the truth!'

He smiled back craftily.

'This garden you had,' said Noël: 'what did you grow there?'

'It was a vegetable garden.'

'Who were these vegetables for? Who did you give them to?'

'They weren't mine. They came from the earth.'

'I asked, who did you give them to?'

'The soldiers took them.'

'Did you mind it that the soldiers took your vegetables?'

He shrugged. 'What grows is for all of us. We are all the children of the earth.'

Now I intervened. 'Your own mother is buried on that farm, isn't she? Didn't you tell me your mother is buried there?'

190

His face closed like a stone, and I pressed on, scenting the advantage. 'You told me the story of your mother, but the Major has not heard it. Tell the Major the story of your mother.'

Again I noted how distressed he becomes when he has to talk about his mother. His toes curled on the floor, he licked at the lip-cleft.

'Tell us about your friends who come in the middle of the night and burn down farms and kill women and children,' said Noël. 'That's what I want to hear.'

'Tell us about your father,' I said. 'You talk a lot about your mother but you never mention your father. What became of your father?'

He closed his mouth obstinately, the mouth that would never wholly shut, and glowered back.

'Don't you have children, Michaels?' I said. 'A man of your age – don't you have a woman and children tucked away somewhere? Why is it just you by yourself? Where is your stake in the future? Do you want the story to end with you? That would make it a sad story, don't you think?'

There was a silence so dense that I heard it as a ringing in my ears, a silence of the kind one experiences in mine shafts, cellars, bomb shelters, airless places.

'We brought you here to talk, Michaels,' I said. 'We give you a nice bed and lots of food, you can lie in comfort all day and watch the birds fly past in the sky, but we expect something in return. It is time to deliver, my friend. You've got a story to tell and we want to hear it. Start anywhere. Tell us about your mother. Tell us about your father. Tell us your views on life. Or if you don't want to tell us about your mother and your father and your views on life, tell us about your recent agricultural enterprise and the friends from the mountains who drop in for a visit and a meal every now and again. Tell us what we want to know, then we will leave you alone.'

I paused; he stared stonily back. '*Talk*, Michaels,' I resumed. 'You see how easy it is to talk, now *talk*. Listen to me, listen how easily I fill this room with words. I know people who can talk all day without getting tired, who can fill up whole worlds talking.' Noël caught my eye but I pressed on. 'Give yourself some substance, man, otherwise you are going to slide through life absolutely unnoticed. You will be a digit in the units column at the end of the war when they do the big subtraction sum to calculate the difference, nothing more. You don't want to be simply one of the perished, do you? You want to live, don't you? Well then, *talk*, make your voice heard, tell your story! We are listening! Where else in the world are you going to find two polite civilized gentlemen ready to listen to your story all day and all night, if need be, and take notes too?'

Without warning, Noël left the room. 'Wait here, I'll be back,' I ordered Michaels, and followed in haste.

In the murky passageway I stopped Noël and pleaded with him. 'You are never going to get sense out of him,'

192

I said, 'surely you see that. He is a simpleton, and not even an interesting simpleton. He is a poor helpless soul who has been permitted to wander out on to the battlefield, if I may use that word, the battlefield of life, when he should have been shut away in an institution with high walls, stuffing cushions or watering the flowerbeds. Listen to me, Noël, I have a serious request to make. Let him go. Don't try beating a story out of him . . .'

'Who spoke about beating?'

'. . . Don't try twisting a story out of him, because truly there is no story to be had. In the profoundest sense he does not know what he is doing: I have watched him for days and I am sure of it. *Make up something for the report.* How big is this Swartberg insurgent gang, do you think? Twenty men? Thirty men? Say that he told you there were twenty men, always the same twenty. They came to the farm every four, five, six weeks, they never told him when they would be coming next. He knew their names, but only their first names. Make up a list of their first names. Make up a list of the arms they carried. Say they had a camp in the mountains somewhere, they never told him exactly where, except that it was high up, that it took two days to get there from the farm on foot. Say that they slept in caves and had women with them. Children too. That's enough. Put it in a report and send it off. It's enough to keep them off our backs, so that we can get on with our jobs.'

We stood outside in the sunlight under the blue spring sky.

'So you want me to make up a lie and sign my name to it.'

'It's not a lie, Noël. There is probably more truth in the story I told you than you would ever get out of Michaels if you used thumbscrews on him.'

'And what if this gang doesn't live in the mountains at all? What if they live around Prince Albert, quietly doing their jobs by day like they are told, and then when the children are asleep take out guns from under the floorboards and roam around in the dark blowing up things, setting fires, terrorizing people? Have you thought of that possibility? Why are you so keen to protect Michaels?'

'I am not protecting him, Noël! Do you want to spend the rest of today in that filthy hole twisting a story out of a poor idiot who doesn't know his arse from his elbow, who quakes in his pants when he thinks of a mother with flaming hair who visits him in his dreams, who believes that babies are found under cabbage bushes? Noël, we have got better things to do! *There is nothing there*, I'm telling you, and if you handed him over to the police they would come to the same conclusion: there is nothing there, no story of the slightest interest to rational people. I have watched him, I know! He is not of our world. He lives in a world all his own.'

So, Michaels, the long and the short of it is that by

my eloquence I saved you. We will make up a story to satisfy the police, and instead of travelling back to Prince Albert handcuffed in the back of a van in a pool of urine you can lie in clean sheets listening to the cooing of the doves in the trees, dozing, thinking your own thoughts. I hope you will be grateful one day.

Extraordinary, though, that you should have survived thirty years in the shadows of the city, followed by a season footloose in the war zone (if one is to believe your story), and come out intact, when keeping you alive is like keeping the weakest pet duckling alive, or the runt of the cat's litter, or a fledgling expelled from the nest. No papers, no money; no family, no friends, no sense of who you are. The obscurest of the obscure, so obscure as to be a prodigy.

*　　*

The first warm day of the summer, a day for the beach. Instead of which a new patient has been brought in exhibiting a high fever, dizziness, vomiting, swelling of the lymph nodes. I isolated him in the old weighing room and sent off blood and urine samples to Wynberg for analysis. Half an hour ago, passing the mail room, I noticed the package still lying there with the red cross and the URGENT stamp clear for all to see. The mail van doesn't come today, the clerk explained. Couldn't he have sent it with a messenger on a bicycle? No messenger to send, he replied. It's not a matter of one prisoner, I said, it's a matter of the health of the whole camp. He shrugged. *Môre is nog 'n dag*. What's the hurry? On his desk an open girlie magazine.

Behind the west wall, behind the brick and barbed wire, the oaks along Rosmead Avenue have exploded these last few days into dense emerald green. From the avenue comes the clip-clop of horses' hooves, and now from the other direction, from the exercise terrain, the strains of the little choir from the church in Wynberg who come every second Sunday, with their accordionist, to sing to the prisoners. '*Loof die Heer*' they are singing, their closing number, after which the prisoners will be marched back to Block D for their meal of *pap* and beans and gravy. For their souls they have a choir and a pastor (there is no shortage of pastors), for their bodies a medical officer. Thus they lack for nothing. In a few weeks they will pass out certified pure of heart and willing of hand, and there will be six hundred bright new faces coming in. 'If I don't do it, somebody else will,' says Noël, 'and that somebody will be worse than me.' 'At least prisoners have stopped dying of unnatural causes since I took over,' says Noël. 'The war can't go on forever,' says Noël, 'it will have to end one day, like all things.' The sayings of Major van Rensburg. 'Nevertheless,' I say, when it is my turn to speak, 'when the shooting stops and the sentries are fled and the enemy walk through the gates unchallenged, they will expect to find the camp commandant at his desk with a revolver in his hand and a bullet through his head. That is the gesture they will expect, despite everything.'

Noël makes no response, though I presume he has thought it all out.

*　　*

Yesterday I discharged Michaels. On the discharge slip I clearly specified exemption from physical exercise for a minimum of seven days. Yet when I emerged from the grandstand this morning the first thing I saw was Michaels slogging it out around the track with the rest of them, stripped to the waist, a skeleton trailing behind forty vigorous human bodies. I remonstrated with the duty officer. His reply: 'When he can't take any more, he can drop out.' I protested: 'He will drop dead. His heart will stop.' 'He has been telling you stories,' he replied. 'You mustn't believe all the stories these buggers tell you. There's nothing wrong with him. Why are you so interested anyway? Look.' He pointed. Michaels passed us, his eyes shut, breathing deeply, his face relaxed.

Perhaps I do indeed believe too many of his stories. Perhaps the truth is simply that he needs to eat less than other people.

*　　*

I was wrong. I should not have doubted. After two days he is back. Felicity went to the door, and there he was, supported between two guards, unconscious. She asked what had happened. They pretended not to know. Ask Sergeant Albrechts, they said.

197

His hands and feet were cold as ice, his pulse very weak. Felicity wrapped him in blankets with hot water bottles. I gave him an injection, and later fed him glucose and milk through a tube.

Albrechts sees the case as one of simple insubordination. Michaels refused to participate in prescribed activities. As punishment he was made to do exercises: squats and star-jumps. After half a dozen of these he collapsed and could not be revived.

'What was it that he was refusing to do?' I asked.

'Sing,' he said.

'Sing? He's not right in the head, man, he can't speak properly – how do you expect him to sing?'

He shrugged. 'It won't hurt him to try,' he said.

'And how can you punish him with physical exercise? He's as weak as a baby, you can see that.'

'It's in the book,' he replied.

*   *

Michaels is conscious again. His first act was to pull the tube out of his nose, Felicity coming too late to stop him. Now he lies near the door under his heap of blankets looking like a corpse, refusing to eat. With his stick-arm he pushes away the feed bottle. 'It's not my kind of food' is all he will say.

'What the hell *is* your kind of food?' I ask him. 'And why are you treating us like this? Don't you see we are trying to help you?' He gives me a serenely indifferent look that really rouses my ire. 'There are hundreds of

198

people dying of starvation every day and you won't eat! Why? Are you fasting? Is this a protest fast? Is that what it is? What are you protesting against? Do you want your freedom? If we turned you loose, if we put you out on the street in your condition, you would be dead within twenty-four hours. You can't take care of yourself, you don't know how. Felicity and I are the only people in the world who care enough to help you. Not because you are special but because it is our job. Why can't you co-operate?'

This open row caused a great stir in the ward. Everyone listened. The boy I had suspected of meningitis (and whom I caught yesterday with his hand up Felicity's skirt) knelt on his bed craning to see, a broad smile on his face. Felicity herself dropped all pretence of pushing the broom.

'I never asked for special treatment,' croaked Michaels. I turned my back and walked out.

You have never asked for anything, yet you have become an albatross around my neck. Your bony arms are knotted behind my head, I walk bowed under the weight of you.

Later, when things had calmed down in the ward, I returned and sat down at your bedside. For a long while I waited. Then at last you opened your eyes and spoke. 'I am not going to die,' you said. 'I can't eat the food here, that's all. I can't eat camp food.'

'Why don't you write out a discharge for him,' I pressed Noël. 'I'll take him to the gate tonight and put a few rand in his pocket and chuck him out. Then he can start fending for himself like he wants to. You write a discharge and I'll make out a report for you: "Cause of decease pneumonia, consequent on chronic malnutrition predating admission." We can cross him off the list and we won't have to think about him any more.'

'I am baffled by this interest you have in him,' said Noël. 'Don't ask me to tamper with records, I am not going to do it. If he is going to die, if he is starving himself to death, let him die. It's simple enough.'

'It's not a question of dying,' I said. 'It's not that he wants to die. He just doesn't like the food here. Profoundly does not like it. He won't even take babyfood. Maybe he only eats the bread of freedom.'

An awkward silence fell between us.

'Maybe you and I wouldn't like camp food either,' I persisted.

'You saw him when they brought him in,' said Noël. 'He was a skeleton even then. He was living by himself on that farm of his free as a bird, eating the bread of freedom, yet he arrived here looking like a skeleton. He looked like someone out of Dachau.'

'Maybe he is just a very thin man,' I said.

*   *

The ward was in darkness, Felicity asleep in her room. I stood over Michaels' bed with a flashlight, shaking him till he woke and shielded his eyes. I spoke in a whisper, bending so close that I could smell the odour of smoke he somehow carries with him despite his ablutions.

'Michaels, there is something I want to tell you. If you don't eat, you are truly going to die. It is as simple as that. It will take time, it will not be pleasant, but in the end you will certainly die. And I am going to do nothing to stop you. It would be easy for me to tie you down and strap your head and put a tube down your throat and feed you, but I am not going to do that. I am going to treat you like a free man, not a child or an animal. If you want to throw your life away, so be it, it is your life, not mine.'

He took his hand away from his eyes and cleared his throat deeply. He seemed about to speak, then shook his head instead and smiled. In the torchlight his smile was repulsive, sharklike.

'What sort of food do you want?' I whispered. 'What sort of food would you be prepared to eat?'

Reaching out a slow hand he pushed the flashlight aside. Then he turned over and went back to sleep.

*   *

The training period for September's intake is over, and this morning the long column of barefoot men, headed by a drummer and flanked by armed guards, set out on the twelve-kilometre march to the railway yards and dispatch up-country. They leave behind half a dozen of their number classed as intractable and

201

locked up waiting to be shipped to Muldersrus, plus three in the infirmary not fit to walk. Michaels is among the latter: nothing has passed his lips since he refused to be fed by tube.

There is a smell of carbolic soap on the breeze and a pleasant stillness. I feel lightened, almost happy. Is this how it will be when the war is over and the camp is closed down? (Or will the camp not close down even then, camps with high walls always having their uses?) Everyone save a skeleton staff is off on a weekend pass. On Monday the November intake is due to arrive. Rail services have deteriorated so badly, however, that we can plan ahead only day by day. There was an attack on De Aar last week, with significant damage to the yards. It did not get into the news bulletins but Noël heard of it reliably.

*   *

I bought a butternut squash from a hawker on the Main Road today, which I cut into thin slices and grilled under the toaster. 'It's not pumpkin,' I told Michaels, propping him up with pillows, 'but it tastes nearly the same.' He took a bite, and I watched him mumble it around in his mouth. 'Do you like it?' I asked. He nodded. I had sprinkled the squash with sugar but had not been able to find cinnamon. After a while, to spare him embarrassment, I left. When I came back he was lying down, the plate empty beside him. I presume that when Felicity next sweeps she will find the squash under the bed covered in ants. A pity.

'What would persuade you to eat?' I asked him later on.

He was silent so long that I thought he had gone to sleep. Then he cleared his throat. 'No one was interested before in what I ate,' he said. 'So I ask myself why.'

'Because I don't want to see you starve yourself to death. Because I don't want anyone here to starve to death.'

I doubt that he heard me. The cracked lips went on moving as though there were some train of thought he was afraid of losing. 'I ask myself, What am I to this man? I ask myself, What is it to this man if I live or die?'

'You might as well ask why we don't shoot prisoners. It is the same question.'

He shook his head from side to side, then without warning opened the great dark pools of his eyes on me. There was something more I had wanted to say, but I could not speak. It seemed foolish to argue with someone who looked at you as if from beyond the grave.

For a long while we stared at each other. Then I found myself speaking, in no more than a whisper. As I spoke I thought: Surrender. This is how surrender will feel. 'I might ask the same question of you,' I said, 'the same question you asked: What am I to this man?' Even softer I whispered, my heart hammering: 'I did not ask you to come here. Everything was well with me before you came. I was happy, as happy as one can be in a place like this. Therefore I too ask: Why me?'

He had closed his eyes again. My throat was dry. I left him, went to the washroom, drank, and for a long while stood leaning on the basin, full of regret, thinking of the trouble to come, thinking, I am not ready. I returned to him with a glass of water. 'Even if you don't eat, you must drink,' I said. I helped him to sit up and take a few mouthfuls.

*   *

Dear Michaels,

The answer is: because I want to know your story. I want to know how it happened that you of all people have joined in a war, a war in which you have no place. You are no soldier, Michaels, you are a figure of fun, a clown, a wooden man. What is your business in this camp? There is nothing we can do here to rehabilitate you from the vengeful mother with flaming hair who comes to you in your dreams. (Do I understand that part of the story correctly? That is how I understand it anyhow.) And what is there for us to rehabilitate you into? Basketwork? Lawnmowing? You are like a stick insect, Michaels, whose sole defence against a universe of predators is its bizarre shape. You are like a stick insect that has landed, God knows how, in the middle of a great wide flat bare concrete plain. You raise your slow fragile stick-legs one at a time, you inch about looking for something to merge with, and there is nothing. Why did you ever leave the bushes, Michaels? That was where you belonged. You should have stayed all your life clinging to a nondescript bush in a quiet corner of an obscure garden in a peaceful suburb, doing whatever it is that stick insects do to maintain life, nibbling a leaf here and there, eating the odd aphid, drinking dew. And – if I may be personal – you should have got away at an early age from that mother of yours, who sounds like a real killer. You should have found yourself another bush as far as possible from her and embarked on an independent life. You made a great mistake, Michaels, when you tied her on your back and fled the burning city for the safety of the countryside. Because when I think of you carrying her, panting under her weight, choking in the smoke, dodging the bullets, performing all the other feats of filial piety you no doubt performed, I also think of her sitting on your shoulders, eating out your brains, glaring about triumphantly, the very embodiment of great Mother Death. And now that she is gone you are plotting to follow her. I have wondered what it is you see, Michaels, when you open your eyes so wide – for you certainly do not see me, you certainly do not see the white walls and the empty beds of the infirmary, you do not see Felicity in her snow-white turban. What do you see? Is it your mother in her circle of flaming hair grinning and beckoning to you with crooked finger to pass through the curtain of light and join her in the world beyond? Does that explain your indifference to life?

Another thing I would like to know is what the food was that you ate in the wilderness that has made all other food tasteless to you. The only food you have ever mentioned is pumpkin. You even carry pumpkin seeds with you. Is pumpkin the only food they know in the Karoo? Am I to believe that you lived for a year on pumpkin? The human body is not capable of that, Michaels. What else did you eat? Did you hunt? Did you make yourself a bow and arrows and hunt? Did you eat roots and berries? Did you eat locusts? Your papers say that you were an *opgaarder*, a storage man, but they do not say what it was you stored. Was it manna? Did manna fall from the sky for you, and did you store it away in underground bins for your friends to come and eat in the night? Is that why you will not eat camp food – because you have been spoiled forever by the taste of manna?

You should have hidden, Michaels. You were too careless of yourself. You should have crept away in the darkest reach of the deepest hole and possessed yourself in patience till the troubles were over. Did you think you were a spirit invisible, a visitor on our planet, a creature beyond the laws of nations? Well, the laws of nations have you in their grip now: they have pinned you down in a bed beneath the grandstand of the old Kenilworth racecourse, they will grind you in the dirt if necessary. The laws are made of iron, Michaels, I hope you are learning that. No matter how thin you make yourself, they will not relax. There is no home left for universal souls, except perhaps in Antarctica or on the high seas.

If you will not compromise you are going to die, Michaels. And do not think you are simply going to waste away, grow more and more insubstantial till you are all soul and can fly away into the aether. The death you have chosen is full of pain and misery and shame and regret, and there are many days to endure yet before release comes. You are going to die, and your story is going to die too, for ever and ever, unless you come to your senses and listen to me. Listen to me, Michaels. I am the only one who can save you. I am the only one who sees you for the original soul you are. I am the only one who cares for you. I alone see you as neither a soft case for a soft camp nor a hard case for a hard camp but a human soul above and beneath classification, a soul blessedly untouched by doctrine, untouched by history, a soul stirring its wings within that stiff sarcophagus, murmuring behind that clownish mask. You are precious, Michaels, in your way; you are the last of your kind, a creature left over from an earlier age, like the coelacanth or the last man to speak Yanqui. We have all tumbled over the lip into the cauldron of history: only you, following your idiot light, biding your time in an orphanage (who would have thought of *that* as a hiding-place?), evading the peace and the war, skulking in the open where no one dreamed of looking, have managed to live in the old way, drifting through time, observing the seasons, no more trying to change the course of history than a grain of sand does. We ought to value you and celebrate you, we ought to put your clothes on a maquette in a museum, your clothes and your packet of pumpkin seeds too, with a label; there ought to be a plaque nailed to the racetrack wall commemorating your stay here. But that is not the way it is going to be. The truth is that you are going to perish in obscurity and be buried in a nameless hole in a corner of the racecourse, transport to the acres of Woltemade being out of the question nowadays, and no one is going to remember you but I, unless you yield and at last open your mouth. I appeal to you, Michaels: *yield*!

A friend.

* * *

After a flurry of rumours, definite word at last about this month's intake. The main batch is held up on the line at Reddersburg waiting for transport. As for the batch from the Eastern Cape, it will not be coming at all: the staging camp at Uitenhage no longer has the staff to separate prisoners into hard and soft, and all detainees in that sector are being committed to high-security camps until further notice.

So the holiday-camp atmosphere at Kenilworth lingers on. A cricket match has been arranged for tomorrow between camp personnel and a team from the Quartermaster-General's. Great activity out in the middle of the course, where they are mowing and rolling a pitch. Noël is to captain the team. It is thirty years since he last played, he says. He cannot find a pair of white trousers to fit him.

Maybe if tracks continue to be blown up and the transports are halted everywhere, the Castle will forget about us and leave us to play out the duration of the war in quiet oblivion behind our walls.

Noël came over on an inspection. There were only two prisoners in the ward, Michaels and the concussion case. We spoke about Michaels, keeping our voices low though he was asleep. I could still save him if I used a tube, I told Noël, but was reluctant to force anyone to live who did not want to. The regulations are clearly behind me: No force-feeding, no artificial prolongation of life. (Also: No publicity to hunger strikes.) 'How much longer will he last?' asked Noël. Perhaps two weeks, perhaps as long as three, I told him. 'At least it is a quiet end,' he said. 'No,' I said, 'it is a painful and distressing end.' 'Isn't there some kind of injection you can give?' he asked. 'To put him down?' I said. 'No, I don't mean to put him down,' he said, 'just to make the going easier for him.' I refused. I cannot take on that responsibility while there is still a chance he might change his mind. We left it at that.

*   *

209

The cricket match is played and lost, with the ball shooting through off the uneven grass and batsmen jumping about to avoid being hit. Noël, playing in a white track-suit with red piping that made him look like Father Christmas in thermal underwear, batted number eleven and was bowled first ball. 'Where did you learn your cricket?' I asked. 'Moorreesburg, in the 1930s, in the school playground, in the lunch break,' he replied.

He strikes me as the best kind of person we have.

Partying deep into the night after the game. A return match promised for February, at Simonstown, if we are all still around.

*   *

Noël very despondent. He heard today that Uitenhage was just the beginning, that the distinction between rehabilitation camps and internment camps is to be abolished. Baardskeerdersbos is to be closed down and the remaining three, including Kenilworth, will be converted into straight internment camps. Rehabilitation, it would seem, is an ideal that has failed to prove itself; as for the labour battalions, they can be supplied just as well from the internment camps. Noël: 'You mean you are going to intern battle-hardened soldiers here in Kenilworth, in the heart of a residential area, behind a brick wall and two strands of barbed wire, with nothing but a handful of old men and boys and heart cases to guard them?' The reply: The drawbacks of

210

the Kenilworth camp have been taken note of. There will be physical modifications, including lights and guard towers, before it is re-opened.

To me Noël confides that he is thinking of resigning: he is sixty, he has given enough of his life to the service, he has a widowed daughter who is pressing him to come and live with her in Gordon's Bay. 'You need an iron man to run an iron camp. I am not that kind of man.' I could not disagree. Not being iron is his greatest virtue.

*   *

Michaels is gone. He must have escaped during the night. Felicity noticed that his bed was empty when she arrived this morning but did not report it ('I thought he had gone to the toilet' – !). It was ten o'clock before I found out. Now, in retrospect, one can see how easy it must have been, or would be for anyone in normal health. With the camp nearly empty, the only sentries on duty were at the main gate and the gate to the personnel compound. There were no perimeter patrols and the side gate was simply locked. There was no one inside to break out, and who would want to break in? Well, we forgot about Michaels. He must have tiptoed out, climbed the wall – God knows how – and stolen away. The wire does not seem to have been cut; but then Michaels is enough of a wraith to slip through anything.

Noël is in a quandary. The specified procedure is to

211

report the escape and pass responsibility to the civil police. But in that case there will be an investigation, and the happy-go-lucky state of affairs here will undoubtedly emerge: half the personnel out on overnight passes, foot patrols discontinued, etc. The alternative is to concoct a death report and let Michaels go. I have been urging this course on Noël. 'For God's sake close the story of Michaels here and now,' I told him. 'The poor simpleton has gone off like a sick dog to die in a corner. Let him be, don't haul him back and force him to die here under a spotlight with strangers looking on.' Noël smiled. 'You smile,' I said, 'but what I say is true: people like Michaels are in touch with things you and I don't understand. They hear the call of the great good master and they obey. Haven't you heard of elephants?

'Michaels should never have come to this camp,' I went on. 'It was a mistake. In fact his life was a mistake from beginning to end. It's a cruel thing to say, but I will say it: he is someone who should never have been born into a world like this. It would have been better if his mother had quietly suffocated him when she saw what he was and put him in the trash can. Now at least let him go in peace. I'll write out a death certificate, you countersign it, some clerk in the Castle will file it away without giving it a glance, and that will be the end of the story of Michaels.'

'He is wearing camp-issue khaki pyjamas,' said Noël. 'The police will pick him up, they will ask where he comes from, he will tell them he comes from Kenilworth, they will check and find there has been no escape reported, and there will be hell to pay.'

'He was not wearing pyjamas,' I replied. 'What he found to wear I don't yet know, but he left his pyjamas behind. As for admitting he comes from Kenilworth, he won't do that for the simple reason that he doesn't want to be returned to Kenilworth. He will tell them one of his other stories, for example that he comes from the Garden of Paradise. He will bring out his packet of pumpkin seeds and rattle them, and give them one of his smiles, and they will pack him straight off to the madhouse, if the madhouses haven't all been closed down yet. You have heard the last of Michaels, Noël, I swear it. Besides, do you know what he weighs? Thirty-five kilos, all skin and bone. For two weeks he has eaten nothing whatever. His body has lost the ability to digest ordinary foodstuffs. I am amazed he had the strength to stand up and walk; it is a miracle that he climbed the wall. How long can he possibly last? One night in the open and he will be dead of exposure. His heart will stop.'

'Speaking of which,' said Noël: 'has anyone checked that he is not lying outside somewhere – that he didn't climb the wall and fall straight down the other side?' I stood up. 'Because the last advertisement we need,' he went on, 'is a body lying outside the camp with flies all over it. It isn't your job, but if you want to check by all means do so. You can take my car.'

I did not take the car, but made a circuit of the camp on foot. There were weeds growing thickly all around the perimeter; along the back wall I had to struggle through knee-high grass. I saw no body nor any break in the wire. In half an hour I was back where I had started, a little surprised at how small a camp can seem from the outside that is, to those who dwell within, an entire universe. Then, instead of returning to report to Noël, I wandered down Rosmead Avenue in the dappled shade of the oak-trees, enjoying the midday stillness. An old man passed me riding a bicycle that creaked with every stroke of the pedals. He raised a hand in greeting. It occurred to me that if I followed after him, proceeding down the avenue in a straight line, I could be at the beach by two o'clock. Was there any reason, I asked myself, why order and discipline should not crumble today rather than tomorrow or next month or next year? What would yield the greater benefit to mankind: if I spent the afternoon taking stock in the dispensary, or if I went to the beach and took off my clothes and lay in my underpants absorbing the benign spring sun, watching the children frolic in the water, later buying an ice cream from the kiosk on the parking lot, if the kiosk is still there? What did Noël ultimately achieve labouring at his desk to balance the bodies out against the bodies in? Would he not be better off taking a nap? Maybe the universal sum of happiness would be increased if we declared this afternoon a holiday and went down to the beach, commandant, doctor, chaplain, PT instructors, guards, dog handlers all together with the six hard cases from the detention block, leaving behind the concussion case to look after things. Perhaps we might meet some girls. For what reason were we waging the war, after all, but to augment the sum of happiness in the universe? Or was I misremembering, was that another war I was thinking of?

'Michaels is not lying outside the wall,' I reported. 'Nor is he wearing clothes that will incriminate us. He is wearing royal blue overalls with the legend TREEFELLERS emblazoned on back and front that have been hanging on a nail in the grandstand toilets since God knows when. Therefore we can safely disclaim him.'

Noël looked tired: an old and tired man.

'Also,' I said, 'can you remind me why we are fighting this war? I was told once, but that was long ago and I seem to have forgotten.'

'We are fighting this war,' Noël said, 'so that minorities will have a say in their destinies.'

We exchanged empty looks. Whatever my mood was, I could not get him to share it.

'Let me have that certificate you promised,' he said. 'Don't fill in the date, leave it blank.'

Then as I sat at the nurse's table in the evening, with nothing to do and the ward in darkness and the south-easter beginning to stir outside and the concussion case breathing away quietly, it came to me with

215

great force that I was wasting my life, that I was wasting it by living from day to day in a state of waiting, that I had in effect given myself up as a prisoner to this war. I went outside and stood on the empty racetrack staring up into a sky swept clean by the wind, hoping that the spirit of restlessness would pass and the old calm return. War-time is a time of waiting, Noël once said. What was there to do in camp but wait, going through the motions of living, fulfilling one's obligations, keeping an ear tuned all the time to the hum of the war beyond the walls, listening for its pitch to change? Still, it occurred to me to wonder whether Felicity, to name only Felicity, thought of herself as living in suspension, alive but not alive, while history hesitated over what course it would take. Felicity, if I am to judge by what has passed between Felicity and me, has never conceived of history as anything but a childhood catechism ('When was South Africa discovered?' '1652.' 'Where is the biggest man-made hole in the world?' 'Kimberley.'). I doubt that Felicity pictures to herself currents of time swirling and eddying all about us, on the battlefields and in the military headquarters, in the factories and on the streets, in boardrooms and cabinet chambers, murkily at first, yet tending ever towards a moment of transfiguration in which pattern is born from chaos and history manifests itself in all its triumphant meaning. Unless I mistake her, Felicity does not think of herself as a castaway marooned in a pocket of time, the time of waiting, camp time, war-time. To her time is as full as it has ever been, even the time of washing sheets, even the time of sweeping the floor; whereas to me, listening with one ear to the banal exchanges of camp life and with the other to the suprasensual spinning of the gyroscopes of the Grand Design, time has grown empty. (Or do I underestimate Felicity?) Even the concussion case, turned wholly inward, wrapped up in the processes of his own slow extinction, lives in dying more intensely than I in living.

Despite the embarrassment it would cause us, I find myself wishing that a policeman would arrive at the gate holding Michaels by the scruff of the neck like a rag doll, saying, 'You should watch the bastards more carefully,' and deposit him there, and march off. Michaels with his fantasy of making the desert bloom with pumpkin flowers is another of those too busy, too stupid, too absorbed to listen to the wheels of history.

*   *

This morning, without notice, a convoy of trucks arrived bringing four hundred new prisoners, the batch held up first at Reddersburg for a week and then on the line north of Beaufort West. All the time we were playing games here, and spending time with girlfriends, and philosophizing about life and death and history, these men waited in cattle trucks parked in sidings under the November sun, sleeping packed against one another in the cold of the highland nights, let out twice a

217

day to relieve themselves, eating nothing but porridge cooked over thornbush fires beside the tracks, watching cargoes more urgent than themselves rumble past while the spider spun his web between the wheels of their home. Noël says he was going to refuse delivery point-blank, as he might be entitled to do, given the facilities here, until he smelled the prisoners, saw their lassitude and helplessness, and knew that if he created difficulties they would simply be driven back to the railway yards and herded into the same trucks they came in to wait till someone somewhere in the unimaginable bureaucracy above bestirred himself, or else till they died. So we have been working all day, all of us, without a break, to process them: to delouse them and burn their old clothes, to fit them out in camp uniform and feed them and dose them, to separate the sick from the merely starved. The ward and its annexe are bursting at their seams again; some of the new patients are no less fragile than Michaels, who approached, I thought, as near to a state of life in death or death in life, whatever it was, as is humanly possible. All in all, then, we are back in business, and before long there will once again be flag-raising exercises and educative chanting to spoil the peace of the summer afternoons.

There were at least twenty deaths en route, the prisoners told us. The dead were buried in unmarked graves out in the veld. Noël checked the papers. They turn out to be a fresh set drawn up in Cape Town this

218

morning, reflecting nothing but the number of arrivals. 'Why don't you demand the embarkation documents?' I asked him. 'It would be a waste of time,' he replied. 'They would say the papers haven't come through yet. Only the papers will never come through. No one wants an inquiry. Besides, who is to say that twenty in four hundred is an unacceptable rate? People die, people are dying all the time, it's human nature, you can't stop them.'

Dysentery and hepatitis are rife, and of course worms. Felicity and I will plainly not be able to cope. Noël has agreed that I should impress two prisoners as orderlies.

Meanwhile plans go ahead for the upgrading of Kenilworth to high-security status. March 1 is set as the changeover date. There will be major modifications, including the flattening of the grandstand, and huts to house five hundred more prisoners. Noël telephoned the Castle to protest the shortness of the notice and was told: Calm yourself. Everything is taken care of. Help us by setting your men to clearing the ground. If there is grass, burn it. If there are stones, remove them. Every stone casts a shadow. Good luck. Remember, *'n boer maak 'n plan.*

I suspect that Noël is drinking more than usual. Perhaps now would be a good time, for him as for me, to quit the fortress – for that is what the Peninsula is clearly to become – leaving behind the prisoners to guard the prisoners, the sick to cure the sick. Perhaps the two of us should take a leaf out of Michaels' book and go on a trip to one of the quieter parts of the country, the obscurer reaches of the Karoo for example, and set up house there, two gentleman deserters of modest means and sober habits. How to get as far as Michaels did without being picked up is the main difficulty. Perhaps we could make a start by discarding our uniforms and getting dirt under our fingernails and walking a little closer to the earth; though I doubt we will ever look as nondescript as Michaels, or as Michaels must have looked in the days before he turned into a skeleton. With Michaels it always seemed to me that someone had scuffled together a handful of dust, spat on it, and patted it into the shape of a rudimentary man, making one or two mistakes (the mouth, and without a doubt the contents of the head), omitting one or two details (the sex), but coming up nevertheless in the end with a genuine little man of earth, the kind of little man one sees in peasant art emerging into the world from between the squat thighs of its mother-host with fingers ready hooked and back ready bent for a life of burrowing, a creature that spends its waking life stooped over the soil, that when at last its time comes digs its own grave and slips quietly in and draws the heavy earth over its head like a blanket and cracks a last smile and turns over and descends into sleep, home at last, while unnoticed as ever somewhere far away the grinding of the wheels of history continues. What organ of state would play with the idea of recruiting creatures like that as its agents, and what use would they serve except to carry things and die in large numbers? The state rides on the backs of earth-grubbers like Michaels; it devours the products of their toil and shits on them in return. But when the state stamped Michaels with a number and gobbled him down it was wasting its time. For Michaels has passed through the bowels of the state undigested; he has emerged from its camps as intact as he emerged from its schools and orphanages.

Whereas I – if one dark night I were to slip into overalls and tennis shoes and clamber over the wall (cutting the wire, since I am not made of air) – I am the kind who would be snapped up by the first patrol to pass while I yet stood dithering over which way lay salvation. The truth is that the only chance I had is gone, and gone before I knew. The night that Michaels made his break, I should have followed. It is vain to plead that I was not ready. If I had taken Michaels seriously I would always have been ready. I would have had a bundle at hand at all times, with a change of clothing and a purse full of money and a box of matches and a packet of biscuits and a can of sardines. I would never have let him out of my sight. When he slept I would have slept across the door-sill; when he woke I would have watched. And when he stole off I would have stolen off behind him. I would have dodged from shadow to shadow in his tracks, and climbed the wall in the darkest corner, and followed him down the

221

avenue of oaks under the stars, keeping my distance, stopping when he stopped, so that he should never be forced to say to himself, 'Who is this behind me? What does he want?', or perhaps even start running, taking me for a policeman, a plain-clothes policeman in overalls and tennis shoes carrying a bundle with a gun in it. I would have dogged him all night through the side streets till at daybreak we would have found ourselves on the fringes of the wastes of the Cape Flats, plodding fifty paces apart through sand and bush, avoiding the clusters of shanties where here and there a curl of smoke would be climbing into the sky. And here, in the light of day, you would at last have turned and looked at me, the pharmacist turned makeshift medical officer turned foot-follower who before seeing the light had dictated to you when you might sleep and when you might wake, who had pushed tubes up your nose and pills down your throat, who had stood in your hearing and made jokes about you, who above all had unrelentingly pressed food on you that you could not eat. Suspiciously, angrily even, you would have waited in the middle of the track for me to approach and explain myself.

And I would have come before you and spoken. I would have said: 'Michaels, forgive me for the way I treated you, I did not appreciate who you were till the last days. Forgive me too for following you like this. I promise not to be a burden. ('Not to be a burden like your mother was'? That would perhaps be imprudent.)

222

I am not asking you to take care of me, for example by feeding me. My need is a very simple one. Though this is a large country, so large that you would think there would be space for everyone, what I have learned of life tells me that it is hard to keep out of the camps. Yet I am convinced there are areas that lie between the camps and belong to no camp, not even to the catchment areas of the camps – certain mountaintops, for example, certain islands in the middle of swamps, certain arid strips where human beings may not find it worth their while to live. I am looking for such a place in order to settle there, perhaps only till things improve, perhaps forever. I am not so foolish, however, as to imagine that I can rely on maps and roads to guide me. Therefore I have chosen you to show me the way.'

Then I would have stepped closer till I was within touching distance and you could not fail to see into my eyes. 'From the moment you arrived, Michaels,' I would have said, had I been awake and followed you, 'I could see that you did not belong inside any camp. At first I thought of you, I will confess, as a figure of fun. I did indeed urge Major van Rensburg to exempt you from the camp regime, but only because I thought that putting you through the motions of rehabilitation would have been like trying to teach a rat or a mouse or (dare I say it?) a lizard to bark and beg and catch a ball. As time passed, however, I slowly began to see the originality of the resistance you offered. You were not a hero and did not pretend to be, not even a hero of

223

fasting. In fact you did not resist at all. When we told you to jump, you jumped. When we told you to jump again, you jumped again. When we told you to jump a third time, however, you did not respond but collapsed in a heap; and we could all see, even the most unwilling of us, that you had failed because you had exhausted your resources in obeying us. So we picked you up, finding that you weighed no more than a sack of feathers, and set you down before food, and said, Eat, build up your strength so that you can exhaust it again obeying us. And you did not refuse. You tried sincerely, I believe, to do as you were told. You acquiesced in your will (excuse me for making these distinctions, they are the only means I possess to explain myself), your will acquiesced but your body baulked. That was how I saw it. Your body rejected the food we fed you and you grew even thinner. *Why?* I asked myself: why will this man not eat when he is plainly starving? Then as I watched you day after day I slowly began to understand the truth: that you were crying secretly, unknown to your conscious self (forgive the term), for a different kind of food, food that no camp could supply. Your will remained pliant but your body was crying to be fed its own food, and only that. Now I had been taught that the body contains no ambivalence. The body, I had been taught, wants only to live. Suicide, I had understood, is an act not of the body against itself but of the will against the body. Yet here I beheld a body that was going to die rather than change

224

its nature. I stood for hours in the doorway of the ward watching you and puzzling over the mystery. It was not a principle, an idea that lay behind your decline. You did not want to die, but you were dying. You were like a bunny-rabbit sewn up in the carcase of an ox, suffocating no doubt, but starving too, amid all those basketfuls of meat, for the true food.'

Here I might have paused in my discourse on the Flats while from somewhere in the middle distance behind us came the sound of a man coughing and hawking and spitting, and the smell of woodsmoke; but my glittering eye would have held you, for the time being, rooted where you stood.

'I was the only one who saw that you were more than you seemed to be,' I would have proceeded. 'Slowly, as your persistent *No*, day after day, gathered weight, I began to feel that you were more than just another patient, another casualty of the war, another brick in the pyramid of sacrifice that someone would eventually climb and stand straddle-legged on top of, roaring and beating his chest and announcing himself emperor of all he surveyed. You would lie on your bed under the window with only the nightlight shining, your eyes closed, perhaps sleeping. I would stand in the doorway breathing quietly, listening to the groans and rustlings of the other sleepers, waiting; and upon me the feeling would grow stronger and stronger that around one bed among all there was a thickening of the air, a concentration of darkness, a black whirlwind

225

roaring in utter silence above your body, pointing to you, without so much as stirring the edge of the bedclothes. I would shake my head like a man trying to shake off a dream, but the feeling would persist. "This is not my imagination," I would say to myself. "This sense of a gathering meaningfulness is not something like a ray that I project to bathe this or that bed, or a robe in which I wrap this or that patient according to whim. Michaels means something, and the meaning he has is not private to me. If it were, if the origin of this meaning were no more than a lack in myself, a lack, say, of something to believe in, since we all know how difficult it is to satisfy a hunger for belief with the vision of times to come that the war, to say nothing of the camps, presents us with, if it were a mere craving for meaning that sent me to Michaels and his story, if Michaels himself were no more than what he seems to be (what you seem to be), a skin-and-bones man with a crumpled lip (pardon me, I name only the obvious), then I would have every justification for retiring to the toilets behind the jockeys' changing-rooms and locking myself into the last cubicle and putting a bullet through my head. Yet have I ever been more sincere than I am tonight?" And standing in the doorway I would turn my bleakest stare in upon myself, seeking by the last means I knew to detect the germ of dishonesty at the heart of the conviction – the wish, let us say, for example, to be the only one to whom the camp was not just the old Kenilworth racetrack with prefabricated

226

huts dotted across it but a privileged site where meaning erupted into the world. But if such a germ lurked within me it would not raise its head, and if it would not what could I do to compel it? (I am dubious anyhow that one can separate the self that scrutinizes from the self that hides, setting them at odds like hawk and mouse; but let us agree to postpone that discussion for a day when we are not running away from the police.) So I would turn my gaze out again, and, yes, it would still be true, I was not deceiving myself, I was not flattering myself, I was not comforting myself, it was as it had been before, it was the truth, there was indeed a gathering, a thickening of darkness above one bed alone, and that bed was yours.'

At this stage I think you might already have turned your back on me and begun to walk off, having lost the thread of my discourse and anyhow being anxious to put more miles between yourself and the camp. Or perhaps by now, attracted by my voice, a crowd of children from the shanties would have gathered around us, some in their pyjamas, listening open-mouthed to the big passionate words and making you nervous. So now I would have had to hurry after you, keeping close at your heels so as not to have to shout. 'Forgive me, Michaels,' I would have had to say, 'there is not much more, please be patient. I only want to tell you what you mean to me, then I will be through.'

At this moment, I suspect, because such is your nature, you would break into a run. So I would have to run after you, ploughing as if through water through the thick grey sand, dodging the branches, calling out: 'Your stay in the camp was merely an allegory, if you know that word. It was an allegory – speaking at the highest level – of how scandalously, how outrageously a meaning can take up residence in a system without becoming a term in it. Did you not notice how, whenever I tried to pin you down, you slipped away? I noticed. Do you know what thought crossed my mind when I saw you had got away without cutting the wire? "He must be a polevaulter" – that is what I thought. Well, you may not be a polevaulter, Michaels, but you are a great escape artist, one of the great escapees: I take off my hat to you!'

By this time, what with the running and the ex- plaining, I would have begun to gasp for breath, and it is even possible that you might have begun drawing away from me. 'And now, last topic, your garden,' I would have panted. 'Let me tell you the meaning of the sacred and alluring garden that blooms in the heart of the desert and produces the food of life. The garden for which you are presently heading is nowhere and everywhere except in the camps. It is another name for the only place where you belong, Michaels, where you do not feel homeless. It is off every map, no road leads to it that is merely a road, and only you know the way.'

Would I be imagining it, or would it be true that at this point you would begin to throw your most urgent energies into running, so that it would be clear to the meanest observer that you were running to escape the man shouting at your back, the man in blue who must seem to be persecutor, madman, bloodhound, policeman? Would it be surprising if the children, having trotted after us for the sake of entertainment, were now to begin to take your part and harry me from all sides, darting at me, throwing sticks and stones, so that I would have to stop and beat them away while shouting my last words to you as you plunged far ahead into the deepest wattle thickets, running more strongly now than one would ever expect from someone who did not eat – 'Am I right?' I would shout. 'Have I understood you? If I am right, hold up your right hand, if I am wrong hold up your left!'

III

WEAK AT THE KNEES AFTER HIS LONG WALK, screwing up his eyes against the brilliant morning light, Michael K sat on a bench beside the miniature golf course on the Sea Point esplanade, facing the sea, resting, gathering his strength. The air was still. He could hear the slap of waves on the rocks below and the hiss of retreating water. A dog stopped to sniff his feet, then peed against the bench. A trio of girls in shorts and singlets passed, running elbow to elbow, murmuring together, leaving a sweet smell in their wake. From Beach Road came the tinkle of an ice-cream vendor's bell, first approaching, then receding. At peace, on familiar ground, grateful for the warmth of the day, K sighed and slowly let his head sag sideways. Whether he slept or not he did not know;

233

but when he opened his eyes he was well enough again to go on.

More of the windows along Beach Road than he remembered seemed to be boarded shut, particularly at street level. The same cars were parked in the same places, though rustier now; a hulk, stripped of its wheels and burnt out, lay overturned on its side against the sea-wall. He passed along the promenade, conscious of being naked inside the blue overalls, conscious that of all the strollers he was the only one not wearing shoes. But if eyes flickered toward him at all, it was toward his face, not his feet.

He came to a stretch of scorched grass where amid broken glass and charred garbage new points of green were already beginning to shoot. A small boy clambered up the blackened bars of a play apparatus, his soles and palms sooty. K picked his way across the lawn, crossed the road, and passed out of sunlight into the gloom of the unlit entrance hall of the Côte d'Azur, where along a wall in looping black spraypaint he read JOEY RULES. Choosing a place across the passageway from the door with the monitory death's-head where his mother had once lived, he settled down, squatting on his heels against the wall, thinking: It is all right, people will take me for a beggar. He remembered the beret he had lost, that he might have put beside him for alms, to complete the picture.

For hours he waited. No one came. He chose not to get up and try the door, since he did not know what he would do once it opened. In mid-afternoon, when his bones had begun to grow cold, he left the building again and went down to the beach. On the white sand under the warm sun he fell asleep.

He awoke thirsty and confused, sweating inside the overalls. He found a public toilet on the beach, but the taps were not working. The lavatory pans were full of sand; driftsand lay against the far wall a foot deep.

As K stood at the basin thinking what to do next, he saw in the mirror three people enter behind him. One was a woman in a tight white dress wearing a platinum-blonde wig and carrying a pair of silver high-heeled shoes. The other two were men. The taller of them came straight up to K and took him by the arm. 'I hope you are finished your business here,' he said, 'because this place is booked.' He steered K out into the dazzling white light of the beach. 'Plenty of other places to go,' he said, and gave him a slap, or perhaps a light push. K sat down on the sand. The tall man took up position beside the toilet door, keeping an eye on him. He had a check cap, which he wore cocked to one side.

There were bathers dotted over the little beach but no one in the water save a woman standing in the shallow surf, her skirt tucked up, her legs sturdily apart, swinging a baby by its arms, left and right, so that its toes skimmed the waves. The baby screamed in terror and glee.

'That one is my sister,' remarked the man at the

235

door, indicating the woman in the water. 'The one in there' – he pointed over his shoulder – 'is also my sister. Plenty of sisters I have. A big family.'

K's head was beginning to throb. Longing for a hat of his own, or a cap, he closed his eyes.

The other man emerged from the toilet and hurried up the steps to the esplanade without a word.

The rim of the sun touched the surface of the empty sea. K thought: I will give myself time till the sand cools, then I will think of somewhere else to go.

The tall stranger stood over him poking him in the ribs with the toe of his shoe. Behind him were his two sisters, one with the child tied on her back, the other bareheaded now, carrying both wig and shoes. The probing toe found the slit in the side of the overalls and pushed it open, revealing a patch of K's bare thigh. 'Look, this man is naked!' called out the stranger, turning to his two women, laughing. 'A naked man! When did you last eat, man?' He prodded K in the ribs. 'Come, let us give this man something to wake him up!'

From a bag the sister with the baby took a bottle of wine wrapped in brown paper. K sat up and drank.

'So where are you from, man?' said the stranger. 'Do you work for these people?' He pointed a long finger at the overalls, at the gold lettering on the pocket.

K was about to reply when without warning his stomach contracted and the wine came up in a neat golden stream that sank at once into the sand. He closed his eyes while the world spun.

236

'Hey!' said the stranger, and laughed, and patted K on the back. 'That is called drinking on an empty stomach! Let me tell you, when I saw you I said to myself, "That man is definitely undernourished! That man definitely needs a square meal inside him!"' He helped K to his feet. 'Come with us, Mister Treefeller, and we will give you something so that you will not be so thin!'

Together they walked along the esplanade till they found an empty bus shelter. From the bag the stranger produced a new loaf of bread and a can of condensed milk. From his hip pocket came a slim black object which he held up before K's eyes. He did something and the object transformed itself into a knife. With a whistle of astonishment he displayed the glinting blade to all, then laughed and laughed, slapping his knee, pointing at K. The baby, peering wide-eyed over its mother's shoulder, began to laugh too, beating the air with a fist.

The stranger recovered himself and cut a thick slice of bread, which he decorated with loops and swirls of condensed milk and presented to K. With everyone watching, K ate.

They passed an alley with a dripping tap. K broke away to drink. He drank as if he would never stop. The water seemed to pass straight through his body: he had to retire to the end of the alley and squat over a drain, and after that felt so dizzy that he took a long time to find the arms of the overalls.

237

They left the residential area behind and began to climb the lower slopes of Signal Hill. K, at the tail of the group, stopped to catch his breath. The sister with the baby stopped too. 'Heavy!' she remarked, indicating the baby, and smiled. K offered to carry her bag, but she refused. 'It's nothing, I'm used to it,' she said.

They passed through a hole in the fence that marked the boundary of the forest reserve. The stranger and the other sister were ahead of them on a track that zigzagged up the hill; below them the lights of Sea Point began to wink; sea and sky glowed crimson on the horizon.

They halted under a clump of pines. The sister in white disappeared into the gloom. In a few minutes she came back wearing jeans and carrying two bulging plastic packets. The other sister opened her blouse and offered her breast to the baby; K did not know which way to look. The man spread a blanket, lit a candle and stuck it in a can. Then he set out their supper: the loaf of bread, the condensed milk, a whole polony sausage ('Gold!' he said, wagging the sausage in K's direction. 'For this you pay gold!'), three bananas. He screwed the cap off the bottle of wine and passed it over. K took a mouthful and returned it. 'Have you got any water?' he asked.

The man shook his head. 'Wine we have got, milk we have got, two kinds of milk' – casually he indicated the woman with the baby – 'but water, no, my friend, I regret there is no water in this place. Tomorrow, I promise. Tomorrow will be a new day. Tomorrow you will have everything you need to make a new man of you.'

Lightheaded from the wine, gripping the earth every now and again to steady himself, K ate of the bread and condensed milk, even ate half a banana, but refused the sausage.

The stranger spoke of life in Sea Point. 'Do you think it is strange,' he said, 'that we are sleeping on the mountain like tramps? We are not tramps. We have food, we have money, we make a living. Do you know where we used to live? Tell Mister Treefeller where we lived.'

'Normandie,' said the sister in jeans.

'Normandie. 1216 Normandie. Then we got tired of climbing steps and came here. This is our summer resort, where we come for picnics.' He laughed. 'And before that do you know where we lived? Tell him.'

'Clippers,' said the sister.

'Clippers Unisex Hairdressers. So you see, it is easy to live in Sea Point if you know how. But now tell me, where do *you* come from? I have not seen you before.'

K understood that it was his turn to speak. 'I was three months in the camp at Kenilworth, till last night,' he said. 'I was a gardener once, for the Council. That was a long time ago. Then I had to leave and take my mother into the country, for her health. My mother used to work in Sea Point, she had a room here, we passed it on the way.' A wave of sickness came up from

239

his stomach; he struggled to control himself. 'She died in Stellenbosch, on the way up-country,' he said. The world swam, then became stable again. 'I didn't always get enough to eat,' he went on. He was aware of the woman with the baby whispering to the man. The other woman had gone out of range of the wavering candlelight. It struck him that he had not seen the two sisters address each other. It struck him too that his story was paltry, not worth the telling, full of the same old gaps that he would never learn how to bridge. Or else he simply did not know how to tell a story, how to keep interest alive. The nausea passed but the sweat that had broken out on him was turning cold and he had begun to shiver. He closed his eyes.

'I see you are sleepy!' said the strange man, slapping him on the knee. 'Time to go to bed! Tomorrow you will be a new man, you will see.' He slapped K again, more lightly. 'You are all right, my friend,' he said.

They made their bed on the pine needles. For themselves the others seemed to have bedclothes unfolded from their bags and packets. For K they had a sheet of heavy plastic in which they helped him wrap himself. Closed in the plastic, sweating and shivering, troubled by a ringing in his ears, K slept only fitfully. He was awake when in the middle of the night the man whose name he did not yet know knelt over him, blotting out his sight of the treetops and the stars. He thought, I must speak before it is too late, but did not. The strange hand brushed his throat and fumbled with

240

the button of the breast pocket of the overalls. The packet of seed emerged so noisily that K was ashamed to pretend not to hear. So he groaned and stirred. For a moment the hand froze; then the man withdrew into the darkness.

For the rest of the night K lay watching the moon through the branches as it crossed the sky. At daybreak he crawled out of the stiff plastic and went over to where the others lay. The man was sleeping close beside the woman with the baby. The baby itself was awake: fondling the buttons of its mother's jersey, it regarded K with unafraid eyes.

K shook the man by the shoulder. 'Can I have my packet,' he whispered, trying not to wake the others. The man grunted and turned away.

A few yards distant K found the packet. Searching on hands and knees he recovered perhaps half of the scattered seeds. He buttoned them in his pocket, abandoning the rest, thinking: What a pity – in the shade of a pine tree nothing will grow. Then he picked his way down the zigzag track.

He passed through the empty early-morning streets and went down to the beach. With the sun still behind the hill, the sand was cold to his touch. So he walked among the rocks peering into the tidal pools, where he saw snails and anemones living lives of their own. Tiring of that, he crossed Beach Road and spent an hour sitting against the wall before his mother's old door waiting for whoever might live there to emerge

241

and be revealed. Then he returned to the beach and lay on the sand listening to the ringing mount in his ears, the sound of the blood running in his veins or the thoughts running through his head, he did not know which. He had the feeling that something inside him had let go or was letting go. What it was letting go of he did not yet know, but he also had a feeling that what he had previously thought of in himself as tough and rope-like was becoming soggy and fibrous, and the two feelings seemed to be connected.

The sun was high in the sky. It had arrived there in the flicker of an eyelid. He had no recollection of the hours that must have passed. I have been asleep, he thought, but worse than asleep. I have been absent; but where? He was no longer alone on the beach. Two girls in bikinis were sunbathing a few paces from him with hats over their faces, and there were other people too. Hot and confused, he stumbled across to the public toilet. The taps were still dry. Slipping his arms out of the overalls, he sat on the bed of driftsand naked to the waist, trying to collect himself.

He was still sitting there when the tall man entered with the one he thought of as the second of the sisters. He tried to get up and leave, but the man embraced him. 'My friend Mister Treefeller!' he said. 'How happy I am to see you! Why did you leave us so early this morning? Didn't I tell you this is going to be your big day? Look what I have brought you!' From the pocket of his jacket he drew a half-jack of brandy. (How does

he stay so neat, living on the mountain? K marvelled.)
He guided K back on to the driftsand. 'Tonight we are
going to a party,' he whispered. 'There you will meet
lots of people.' He drank and passed the bottle. K took
a mouthful. A languor spread from his heart bringing a
blessed numbness to his head. He lay back swimming
in his own dizziness.

There was whispering; then someone unbuttoned
the last button of the overalls and slipped a cool hand
in. K opened his eyes. It was the woman: she was
kneeling beside him fondling his penis. He pushed her
hand away and tried to struggle to his feet, but the man
spoke. 'Relax, my friend,' he said, 'this is Sea Point, this
is the day when all good things happen. Relax and
enjoy yourself. Help yourself to a drink.' He settled the
bottle in the sand beside K and was gone.

'Who is your brother?' asked K with a thick tongue.
'What is his name?'

'His name is December,' said the woman. Did he
hear her correctly? It was the first time she had spoken
to him. 'That is the name on his card. Tomorrow
maybe he has a different name. A different card, a
different name, for the police, so that they mix him up.'
She bent down and took his penis in her mouth. He
wanted to push her off but his fingers recoiled from
the stiff dead hair of the wig. So he relaxed, allowing
himself to be lost in the spinning inside his head and in
the faraway wet warmth.

After a time in which he might even have slept, he

did not know, she lay down next to him on the driftsand, still holding his sex in her hand. She was younger than the silver wig made her seem. Her lips were still wet.

'So is he really your brother?' he mumbled, thinking of the man waiting outside.

She smiled. Leaning on an elbow she kissed him full on the mouth, her tongue cleaving his lips. Vigorously she pulled on his penis.

When it was over he felt that for the sake of both of them he ought to say something; but now all words had begun to escape him. The peace the brandy had brought seemed to be departing. He took a drink from the bottle and passed it to the girl.

There were shapes looming over him. He opened his eyes and saw the girl, wearing her shoes now. Beside her stood the man, her brother. 'Get some sleep, my friend,' said the man in a voice that came from a great distance. 'Tonight I will come back and fetch you for the party I promised, where there will be plenty to eat and where you will see how Sea Point lives.'

K thought they had finally gone; but the man returned and bent over him to whisper last words in his ear. 'It is difficult to be kind,' he said, 'to a person who wants nothing. You must not be afraid to say what you want, then you will get it. That is my advice to you, my thin friend.' He gave K a pat on the shoulder.

Alone at last, shivering with cold, his throat parched, the shame of the episode with the girl waiting like a shadow at the edge of his thoughts, K buttoned himself and emerged from the toilet on to a beach where the sun was going down and the girls in the bikinis were packing up to leave. Wading through the sand was harder than before; once he even lost his balance and toppled sideways. He heard the tinkle of the ice-cream man and tried to hurry after him before he remembered he had no money. For a moment his head cleared enough for him to realize that he was sick. He seemed to have no control over the temperature of his body. He was cold and hot at the same time, if that was possible. Then a haze fell over him again. At the foot of the steps, as he stood holding the rail, the two girls passed him, averting their gaze and, he suspected, holding their breath. He watched their backsides ascend the steps and surprised in himself an urge to dig his fingers into that soft flesh.

He drank from the tap behind the Côte d'Azur, closing his eyes as he drank, thinking of the cool water running down from the mountain to the reservoir above De Waal Park and then through miles of piping in the dark earth beneath the streets to pour forth here and quench his thirst. He voided himself, unable to help it, and drank again. So light now that he could not even be sure his feet were touching the ground, he passed from the last daylight into the shade of the passageway and without hesitating turned the handle of the door.

In the room where his mother had lived there was

a dense clutter of furniture. As his eyes accustomed themselves to the dimness he made out scores of tubular steel chairs stacked from floor to ceiling, huge furled beach umbrellas, white vinyl tables with holes in their centres, and nearest the door three painted plaster statues: a deer with chocolate-brown eyes, a gnome in a buff jerkin, knee-breeches and green tasselled cap, and, larger than the other two, a creature with a peg nose whom he recognized as Pinocchio. Over everything lay a film of white dust.

Led by the smell, K explored the dark corner behind the door. He groped and found a crumpled blanket on a bed of flattened cartons on the bare floor. He knocked over an empty bottle which rolled away. From the blanket came the mixed odours of sweet wine, cigarette ash, old sweat. He wrapped the blanket around himself and lay down. As soon as he had settled the ringing began to mount in his ears, and behind it the thud of the old headache.

Now I am back, he thought.

The first siren went off announcing the curfew. Its wail was taken up by sirens and hooters across the city. The cacophony rose, then died away.

He could not sleep. Against his will the memory returned of the casque of silver hair bent over his sex, and the grunting of the girl as she laboured on him. I have become an object of charity, he thought. Everywhere I go there are people waiting to exercise their forms of charity on me. All these years, and still I carry the look of an orphan. They treat me like the children of Jakkalsdrif, whom they were prepared to feed because they were still too young to be guilty of anything. From the children they expected only a stammer of thanks in return. From me they want more, because I have been in the world longer. They want me to open my heart and tell them the story of a life lived in cages. They want to hear about all the cages I have lived in, as if I were a budgie or a white mouse or a monkey. And if I had learned storytelling at Huis Norenius instead of potato-peeling and sums, if they had made me practise the story of my life every day, standing over me with a cane till I could perform without stumbling, I might have known how to please them. I would have told the story of a life passed in prisons where I stood day after day, year after year with my forehead pressed to the wire, gazing into the distance, dreaming of experiences I would never have, and where the guards called me names and kicked my backside and sent me off to scrub the floor. When my story was finished, people would have shaken their heads and been sorry and angry and plied me with food and drink; women would have taken me into their beds and mothered me in the dark. Whereas the truth is that I have been a gardener, first for the Council, later for myself, and gardeners spend their time with their noses to the ground.

K tossed restlessly on the cardboard bed. It excited him, he found, to say, recklessly, *the truth, the truth about me. I am a gardener*, he said again, aloud. On the other hand, was it not strange for a gardener to be sleeping in a closet within sound of the beating of the waves of the sea?

I am more like an earthworm, he thought. Which is also a kind of gardener. Or a mole, also a gardener, that does not tell stories because it lives in silence. But a mole or an earthworm on a cement floor?

He tried to relax his body inch by inch, as he had once known how to do.

At least, he thought, at least I have not been clever, and come back to Sea Point full of stories of how they beat me in the camps till I was thin as a rake and simple in the head. I was mute and stupid in the beginning, I will be mute and stupid at the end. There is nothing to be ashamed of in being simple. They were locking up simpletons before they locked up anyone else. Now they have camps for children whose parents run away, camps for people who kick and foam at the mouth, camps for people with big heads and people with little heads, camps for people with no visible means of support, camps for people chased off the land, camps for people they find living in storm-water drains, camps for street girls, camps for people who can't add two and two, camps for people who forget their papers at home, camps for people who live in the mountains and blow up bridges in the night. Perhaps the truth is that it is enough to be out of the camps, out of all the camps at the same time. Perhaps that is enough of an achievement, for the time being. How many people are there left who are neither locked up nor standing guard at the gate? I have escaped the camps; perhaps, if I lie low, I will escape the charity too.

The mistake I made, he thought, going back in time, was not to have had plenty of seeds, a different packet of seeds for each pocket: pumpkin seeds, marrow seeds, beans, carrot seeds, beetroot seeds, onion seeds, tomato seeds, spinach seeds. Seeds in my shoes too, and in the lining of my coat, in case of robbers along the way. Then my mistake was to plant all my seeds together in one patch. I should have planted them one at a time spread out over miles of veld in patches of soil no larger than my hand, and drawn a map and kept it with me at all times so that every night I could make a tour of the sites to water them. Because if there was one thing I discovered out in the country, it was that there is time for everything.

(Is that the moral of it all, he thought, the moral of the whole story: that there is time enough for everything? Is that how morals come, unbidden, in the course of events, when you least expect them?)

He thought of the farm, the grey thornbushes, the rocky soil, the ring of hills, the mountains purple and pink in the distance, the great still blue empty sky, the earth grey and brown beneath the sun save here and there, where if you looked carefully you suddenly saw a tip of vivid green, pumpkin-leaf or carrot-brush.

It did not seem impossible that whoever it was who

249

disregarded the curfew and came when it suited him to sleep in this smelly corner (K imagined him as a little old man with a stoop and a bottle in his side pocket who muttered all the time into his beard, the kind of old man the police ignored) might be tired of life at the seaside and want to take a holiday in the country if he could find a guide who knew the roads. They could share a bed tonight, it had been done before; in the morning, at first light, they could go out searching the back streets for an abandoned barrow; and if they were lucky the two of them could be spinning along the high road by ten o'clock, remembering to stop on the way to buy seeds and one or two other things, avoiding Stellenbosch perhaps, which seemed to be a place of ill luck.

And if the old man climbed out of the cart and stretched himself (things were gathering pace now) and looked at where the pump had been that the soldiers had blown up so that nothing should be left standing, and complained, saying 'What are we going to do about water?', he, Michael K, would produce a teaspoon from his pocket, a teaspoon and a long roll of string. He would clear the rubble from the mouth of the shaft, he would bend the handle of the teaspoon in a loop and tie the string to it, he would lower it down the shaft deep into the earth, and when he brought it up there would be water in the bowl of the spoon; and in that way, he would say, one can live.